THE RANCH

B. E. BAKER

Created with Vellum

For my mom
For showing me the right way to parent,
right from the start.

PROLOGUE

Dear Amanda:

I'm a creature of habit. I've been eating two fried eggs and two pieces of bacon for breakfast every single morning now for more than seven decades.

I've been writing these letters for almost sixty years, too, and I've come to the conclusion that I must also be a coward. Only a terrible chicken would love the same woman his entire life and not tell her how he feels. I have a huge stack of letters that I've never sent, and the person I'm writing them to lives right down the road. I don't even really think about sending them, anymore. I write all this while secure in the knowledge that you'll never read my innermost thoughts.

It just hurt so badly when I told you how I felt that first time and you picked my brother over me. I'm not afraid of nothing. It was something that caused me actual pain. Believe it or not, it took me a long time to realize how hurt I was.

For years, I thought I was just angry.

I loved you and I hated you at the same time. Some days I wished I could burn your house down. Others I wanted to burn down my own. Young people flash hot and cold, you see, and anger felt better than despair. Every time I saw you, I wanted to punch someone in the face.

No, not someone, my brother.

But he's dead, now. He died last week.

His death was harder on me than I thought it would be, considering how rarely we spoke. When we were kids, we were really close. But after everything that happened, I avoided him, even at holidays. I don't think it hit me how much of an idiot I'd been until I was standing in a black suit at his funeral. So many people got up and spoke about what a great man he was, and I thought they were all liars. Until it finally clicked. He wasn't the terrible person I thought he was.

I've hated him all this time for no real reason.

His only crime was winning the heart of the only girl I thought was worth loving, and then almost as quickly, casting her away. I think it made me more angry that he let you go than it made me when he stole you from me in the first place.

I hated him all that time on your behalf, you see. Losing him clearly wounded you so deeply that you never dated again. And I vowed that if I couldn't date you, I would never date. Where did that stupid promise leave me?

Alone for more than sixty years, that's where.

After all this time, I should be brave enough to walk to the mailbox and drop this letter inside. Or maybe I should throw these letters away and march down the road to your house with a fistful of flowers. But even the thought of that makes my old heart race and my fingers tingle, and I know I can't do it.

No matter how impossible it seems to pursue you, I've never been able to bring myself to ask another woman on a date, or even to think of another woman either. My one consolation has been that losing my brother has kept you just as lonely.

I don't think I could bear the thought of you with someone else.

Instead of doing something brave that might destroy me if it went badly, I sit here, my hand cramping, my heart racing, and write my thoughts on yet another piece of paper that will probably burn to cinder when I have a heart attack while frying my eggs next week, next month, or next year.

Seconds slip away into nothingness.

My entire life has been wasted alone.

Another part of my heart shrivels and dies, thinking that I'll never have my one desire.

This morning, as I ate the same breakfast I always eat, and as I thought the same things I always think, I thought of something both old and new. Old because I heard it first long ago, but new, because I'd forgotten all about it.

Growing up on a ranch, I'm not naive about the way the world works. I know where my breakfast comes from. The same two animals have contributed to my meal every day for the past seventy years.

A chicken gave two eggs, or two chickens gave me one egg each.

While a pig gave its life.

The chicken isn't nearly as committed as the pig, you see. The chicken squats and squawks and moves on, but the pig gave its all. A little part of me feels like, even though I lost you years ago, I'm the pig and my brother is the chicken. He may have taken you to prom, but I gave you my entire life.

Ah, Amanda. I saw you in the market last week, and I knew it was you from across the store. Your hair's almost all white now. Your shoulders aren't quite as straight, but your eyes flash just the same as they ever did. Your hands are just as graceful. Your voice is just as beautifully sharp.

I'm proud to have given my life for you.

Even if you're unaware I did it.

-Jed

1

AMANDA

Growing up, we never had nice things.

That was my mom's excuse for why we never took good care of anything. We lived in a trailer, after all, so what was the point? She was constantly expecting everything in our life to dramatically improve. She just didn't *do anything* to make it happen. Some days, it felt like I was the only person in our family who lived on planet Earth.

I was certainly the only one who ever bothered cleaning.

I did laundry at the laundromat around the corner when my friends laughed at me for smelling. I scrubbed the kitchen floor with a rag when it got so sticky my shoes would make funny noises after walking on it. And I even tried to clean the toilet a few times before I realized that the brown stains around the side of the bowl were pretty much permanent.

Unfortunately, I never really learned to clean very effectively, even after I moved out. I muddled my way through my few years of college, never getting my deposit back on any of the apartments I stayed in.

Once I was married, Paul quickly discovered cleaning wasn't my strength. He was a lousy husband, but he took care of me financially, and he made sure we had a cleaning lady to take care of things like mopping floors and bathrooms. After he died, well, there were a few rough months, but I always managed to scrounge up enough money to pay for her services, even if we missed a few weeks here and there.

Now that I'm living on a ranch in the middle of nowhere, you'd think I'd have to do some mopping or toilet scrubbing, but I swear, Abigail *wants* her kids to work for some reason, so they scrub all the toilets and clean the tubs and mop the floors every single Saturday morning like they're in the military. Maybe there's a little more complaining than you'd normally hear from soldiers, but they do just as good a job.

I never thought that cleaning might be something I'd think of as *fun*. Abby's kids don't seem to be having a great time every Saturday, either. But tonight, with Eddy wielding a mop while I scrub the Double or Nothing bathroom toilet with a bristled wand?

I can't seem to stop laughing.

"You're saying that cleaning your shop together *isn't* the worst date you've ever had?" Eddy asks. "You must be lying."

"I'm not," I insist. "I'm actually having a good time."

He chucks a Swiffer at me. "You should be working harder, then."

I stand up, my back aching a bit from the angle at which I was folded in half to clean the bowl and the porcelain around it. "I dunno. It sure feels like I'm working hard." I immediately wash my hands, even though I know I still need to clean the sink and the bathroom floors. "And at the same time, it doesn't feel that bad."

Because he's here with me.

I've never liked someone enough that I didn't care what we were doing, as long as we were together. I thought that was a Hollywood construct, to be honest.

Eddy finishes mopping the last bit of the kitchen behind me. "You can't walk across this until it's dry. You're stuck in there, or you'll leave footprints."

"You're pretty confident with that mop in your hands," I say.

"It's more that I now have you trapped." When he grins, it's like a 100-watt bulb graduates to two thousand watts. Sometimes, like right now, it slaps me in the face. I have no idea why someone who looks like him seems giddy to date someone like me.

But I'm not about to be the one who tells him he has bad taste.

"I wish we could go somewhere more fun," I say. "If *cleaning* isn't bad, imagine how great ice skating would be."

His face falls, and I wish I'd kept my mouth shut.

Maybe I can cheer him up with my tales of woe. "How about I share the details of one of the many, many dates that was much worse than this one?"

He hops up on the counter, his feet barely dangling thanks to his extraordinary height. "Alright. Sure. Let's hear how I don't measure up to them, seeing as it's my fault we can't do anything fun."

"How is it your fault?" I ask. "It's my dumb job that puts us at risk. My lack of marketable skills that means I have to peddle my lifestyle to people online."

He blinks. "If I hadn't been such an idiot as a teenager, and if I wasn't an alcoholic—"

"Eddy, you aren't the problem, okay?" I smile. I can't bear to hear him tell me he's a murderer again. Any way I look at it, it's not true. He happened to be driving when a pedestrian darted out of a building and into the street.

Even a sober person might have hit someone in the dark like that, and that's a fact.

He sighs. "Alright, how about those funny stories I was promised?"

I start scrubbing the sink. It'll be easier to change the subject if I'm not looking right at him. "Alright, so my first date after Paul died. Let's start there."

"Ugh," he says. "Really? You want to depress me?"

"I didn't go out for more than a year after he passed, and at the risk of sounding like a jerk, I was *sad* when he died, but not, like, devastated. You know how Abby liked her husband?" I sigh dramatically. "I didn't. We were in the process of splitting up when he died."

"You were? Really?"

Not exactly something I lead with. Actually, I don't really talk about Paul that often, especially around other men. "Let's not dwell on that. It really is kind of depressing. So for this first date—"

Eddy's making some kind of noise behind me that I can't quite interpret. I turn around, dripping sudsy water on the floor, and realize that he's literally scooching across the counters and reaching out as far as he can. . .to get a cowboy cookie.

"Hey, those are inventory."

"This is a date," he says. "We're supposed to have snacks when we're on a date. Plus, I just provided hard and skilled labor. I need compensation."

I roll my eyes, but I'm secretly pleased he likes my cookies. "Speaking of snacks, on that first date, the whole thing started with a cinnamon roll."

"A cinnamon roll?" Eddy's eyebrows rise. "I love cinnamon rolls."

"So did my first date."

Now he's frowning. Ha.

"A friend of mine in New York runs a bakery. It's a

pretty high-end bakery. Most people wouldn't spend what she charges for cinnamon rolls on a full meal. But that was kind of her gambit. She attracted a lot of wealthy clientele. In any case, one of the men who bought a dozen of these gold leaf cinnamon rolls asked her on a date."

"I thought you said it was your first date." In spite of his protest, Eddy's looking much less annoyed.

"I'm getting there." I can't help smiling, and I turn back to scrubbing so he won't see it. "She was happily married, Esther I mean, so she told him no. But she told him that her friend was just as pretty as she was, and she was a widow, and finally ready to date again."

"Ah." Eddy's voice is flat. "Now I get it."

"That's how she set me up with Vincent St. Croix, Manhattan business mogul."

"He bought a dozen cinnamon rolls?" Eddy sounds hopeful. "Then was he fat? Short and fat? Did he have a double chin?"

I laugh. "He was tall and ruggedly handsome. Actually, at the time, Esther described him to me as looking like a younger version of Michael Douglas in *Wall Street*. She wasn't wrong."

Eddy chokes on his cookie. "Hurry up and get to the stuff about the lousy date already."

"He picked me up right on time, and from the very first minute, everything was perfect." I suppress my smile, but I'm worried he can sense it in my tone. "He brought me a corsage, for heaven's sake. It felt like I was going to prom with the king of the school, only as an adult. He drove me in his Porsche 911 to a very *in* restaurant, where they knew him by name, and we sat at a table by a huge picture window overlooking the night silhouette of the skyline. He even asked me some nice questions about what I did and my girls."

"I thought you said this date was worse than scrubbing

a toilet." Eddy brushes his hands off, pointedly scattering crumbs on the floor he'd just mopped.

Instead of being annoyed, I'm delighted. "Be patient."

"Did I lie and tell you I was patient at some point?" He sighs.

"Eddy."

He rolls his eyes skyward. "Fine. Fine."

I finish up with the sink and tiptoe around the corner to grab the mop.

"Hey, the floor's not dry yet. Be careful."

"I'm going to mop here and by the time I'm done, it'll be dry enough for me to navigate to the counter." Or even if it's not, I don't care. My shop isn't exactly Saks Fifth Avenue.

"Just finish the story already." Eddy's sulking. He's actually sulking. Which means he's almost ready for the next part.

"I hadn't kissed a guy in a while, at that point. Paul and I had been fighting constantly near the end, and even my lousy husband had been dead for more than a year. I was pretty nervous, especially considering how well things were going."

I could look at his dreamy storm cloud face all day long.

"After dinner, we walked along the paths at Central Park. He even bought me a pretzel from a street vendor, so I knew he wasn't *too* snobby."

Eddy's hands are gripping the countertop. "I'm surprised you ever went on another date. I bet your second date was picking out a china pattern."

"He was kind of perfect." I sigh dreamily. "Right up until he kissed me softly while standing in the moonlight. I still remember the little thrill that ran up my spine."

"Alright." Eddy hops off the counter and stomps across the floor. "You said—"

I press my hand against his chest, slinging water on his

t-shirt. "And right after that magical kiss, Mr. Vincent St. Croix cocked his head sideways, exhaled with disappointment and said, 'Eh.'"

"Huh?" Eddy blinks. Which means he *gets* just how I felt.

"Yeah. In spite of him saying 'eh,' I was still all kinds of excited, and I thought, 'wow, this is what dating is like in New York City.' Only, I found out what it was really like about ten seconds later when he said, 'Well, thanks for a nice night.'"

"What?" Eddy's mouth is dangling open. "He kissed you and then just walked away? Was he mentally deficient?"

"I ran after him, of course. I grabbed his arm and said, 'You kissed me. It was nice, right? Or am I crazy?'"

"You really are amazing," Eddy says.

I laugh. "You know what he told me?"

He shakes his head. "Not a clue."

"He said, 'I mean, I had a nice time, just not a *nice enough* time.'"

"What does that mean?" Eddy asks.

"I asked the same thing. He finally confessed that he was married and that he took me out to see whether it would be worth the three million dollars he'd have to pay under his prenup to get divorced."

"Are you kidding me right now?"

"Nope." I say. "I think it's funny now, but I was pretty mad then."

"I bet."

"Mad enough that I punched him."

Eddy laughs out loud. "You did what?"

"I punched him on the nose. My hand hurt for days."

"Alright, you've redeemed yourself."

"Oh, it gets worse," I say. "About two weeks later, I got served with a lawsuit. For assault."

"What?"

"Yeah, and his wife filed an affidavit saying that it caused a terrible black eye. There were photos."

"His *wife*?"

"Apparently his disinterest in me saved their marriage, blah blah blah. That date cost me twenty-two thousand, four hundred and eleven dollars in legal fees. So, yeah. I'd say it was pretty awful." I pause and meet his eyes. "Much worse than scrubbing a toilet." I shake my head and sigh. "But."

"But what?"

"It did teach me a valuable lesson about the kind of men out there in the dating world." I drop the mop and wrap my arms around Eddy's neck. I lean up on my tiptoes and press my lips to his.

A second later, his hands circle my waist and he kisses me in earnest. Ten seconds later, I'm pressed against the wall, my hands entwined in Eddy's shiny hair. Luckily, a minute later my phone starts ringing, or I'm not sure what might have happened.

Kissing Eddy is like that.

Explosive.

Brain-shorting.

Dangerous.

Emery sounds like she's in tears when I answer. After several minutes of talking, I'm still getting nowhere. She's convinced that her life is over—some kid at school said something mean about her fingers? And Maren told her it was true.

Sometimes I want to throttle my older daughter.

"I'm going to have to head home before Emery steps in front of a stampeding bull or something," I say. "Parenting is the worst."

Eddy whimpers.

The side of my mouth turns upward. "If it helps, I don't want to leave either."

"It does help a little bit. Don't forget your promise."

This time, I smile broadly. "What promise are you talking about? To brush my teeth every single day, morning and night? My dentist is pretty serious about making me swear to that one."

"Ha."

"Oh!" I slap my forehead. "You mean when I told Abigail that I'd try praying in the morning to improve my attitude."

Eddy rolls his eyes again. He does that surprisingly often for a masculine guy.

"Or did you mean—"

He kisses me again, and just like the last time, every single thought flees my brain. He finally relinquishes my lips, so that he can whisper against them. "I meant the promise you made me. You can flirt. You can smile and wink and even hold hands with that guy tomorrow, but under no circumstances are you to press your lips to his."

"How about this as an alternative?" I ask. "If I do, I promise to punch him afterward."

His left hand grabs my waist and he brushes my cheek with the fingers of his right, his fingertips barely making contact with my jaw. "I might fly out there and punch him myself."

His jealousy is like a long, smooth stroke down a cat's back. I want to rub against him and purr. "Fine. No kissing."

"Except with me." He kisses me again, but this time he lets me go too soon. "Now, go save your precious daughter from the depths of preteen despair."

I laugh. "I'm not sure that's really possible, but I'll give it my very best effort."

"You always do," he says.

Eddy doesn't know it yet, but my best is never quite good enough.

2

ABIGAIL

Sometimes it's hard to enjoy motherhood thanks to all the drudgery it entails.

Once, a long time ago, when I was in the thick of raising babies, I had a thought. Wouldn't it be nice if I were mega rich? If I could pay someone to do all the things I didn't want to do, then my life would be so much better, wouldn't it?

I could pay someone to stay up all night with fussy little ones.

I could pay someone to change all the diapers.

I could pay someone to make the dinners that always seem to sneak up on me.

I could pay someone to do the laundry and bathe the kids.

I could pay someone to clean my home and care for my yard. Weeding, especially, I'd love to outsource.

I could pay someone to babysit the kids for a few hours each day so I could get a little break.

This was a recurring, not-infrequent, dream.

Then, during a small break in my exhausting daily routine, I watched a show about an upper crust family in

England in the 1800s or sometime around there. They essentially *did* pay someone to do all those things. . .and the kids didn't really have much of a connection to their parents at all.

The next day, after bathing my younger children and getting them put down, my oldest, Ethan, came to me. He told me about how a kid at school was picking on him, and he asked for my help with the situation. He was embarrassed about the things the kid was saying—he was worried they might be true. But he trusted me enough to bring this problem to me, and he believed I would have answers.

That's when I realized that life is nothing more than a sequence of small, interconnected moments. If we aren't there for the little things, we won't be the one they turn to when big things happen.

If I've learned one important thing as a parent, that's it. Be there for the little things so that you're their go-to for the big things, because it all happens in the blink of an eye.

When I met Steve, I essentially needed a U-Haul to house all of my figurative baggage: widow, four kids, a will with weird stipulations, a part-time-turned-full-time job. I also had, as a bonus, an old friend who wanted more, and a sister-in-law who had two kids of her own.

Steve took it all in stride.

When I panicked, he held up his hands and calmed me down while staying steady himself. We've now weathered a stomach bug and a winter storm. He's been there in the scary moments when Izzy was hurt. He's been there for the small moments and the fun things, too.

So now that his ex is here, turning his life upside down, I'm not about to bolt. It turns out that the lessons I learned as a parent might just help me to be a better person, or even a better girlfriend.

"I'm sure you're freaking out right now," Steve whispers.

"I'm so sorry I just blurted out that you're my lawyer without even asking you first."

"It's fine." It's messy, and it's weird, and I'm not sure I want to insert myself into what may devolve into a hair-pulling dog-pile of drama. But I'm also flattered that he felt he could trust me in that moment. I'm happy that he's turning *toward* me and not away.

I'm also glad he relied on me when someone picked on him. It says something good about *us*. Something promising.

"Is it really fine? Or is it 'fine' in the way that you say you're fine as your kid pukes in your hair?"

I laugh. "Are you trying to remind me that you were there in the thick of it for our latest stomach bug?"

He shrugs. "I figured the reminder couldn't hurt."

"This is going to take a lot longer to resolve than that virus," I say.

His expression's sober, his eyes intent on my face. "I know."

"My life's a disaster right now," I say. "I don't even know whether we'll be able to keep the ranch."

"I know that too," he says. "And it's not a one-way street. I'll be your lawyer on that if you want." His deadpan look seals it for me. If he could be my lawyer, I know that he absolutely would.

"How about you keep helping my kiddos when someone gets sick, and I act as the lawyer for both?"

"That would probably be best," he says. "But I really will hire someone else if you don't want anything to do with this."

"I know," I say, because I do know. "If it gets too intense, I'll let you know."

"I'm sorry about all this."

His ex-wife and Olivia, who's probably his daughter, are

standing just behind us staring, but all of that falls away in that moment. He's sad, and that hurts me.

Simple.

I step toward him, and press one hand to his chest. The muscle there is shaped perfectly from many years of hard work. This man whom I once thought to be an alcoholic with not much going on is actually a physician who works hard saving lives. He's a horse trainer who saves broken horses. He's someone who cares for and cultivates others in every aspect of his life.

"You have nothing to be sorry for. Sometimes, in the process of living, in the process of loving others, things go wrong. Sometimes people let us down. But we can only control our own actions, so don't apologize about this again."

A smile tries to break through his concern.

"But now it's time for me to go home. You don't need a lawyer right now. You need some space to talk to them." I drop my hand reluctantly, toss my head, and step back. "Don't worry about coming over for dinner. I'll keep an eye on my phone in case you need me, but take your time."

I know what this means to him, if Olivia is his daughter. I can't even imagine how upset I'd be if someone had lied to me like his ex did. And if Stephanie's lying *now*, well. I'll roast her alive over a slow spinning spit.

Poor Steve.

It's a good thing he's a tough guy.

"I'm heading out." I glance toward his ex and bob my head, because it seems rude not to acknowledge her at all, but I can't bring myself to do anything more polite. I smile at the little girl, even though she's glaring at me like I'm a home-wrecker.

Before I go more than two steps toward my car, Steve's hand wraps around my wrist, and he pulls me backward, catching me in his arms. "You were going to leave without saying goodbye?" His eyes are all for me. His arms hold me tightly, and his mouth descends slowly over mine, claiming me. It's quick, but it's a possessive kiss.

And I love it.

"You have got to be kidding me," his ex says.

"I'm not," Steve says. "You're the one who barged in here. Please be respectful to me and to Abigail, or I'll point the way you drive to go back home."

"You wouldn't dare," Stephanie says. "You're too happy to see Olivia again." She purses her lips like she thinks he's also happy to see her.

It's very hard for me to walk away.

I'm not the kind of person who walks away from fights very often. Usually I'm the one who rushes toward them, briefcase in hand. That way I can either argue them to death, or swing it to clock them in the jaw—either scenario will do.

But sometimes you only win by standing down, and this is one of those times.

I just really hate standing down.

Turning the key over in my minivan and putting it into reverse is tough. I grit my teeth as I drive my beat-up, old, gray minivan past Stephanie's shiny red BMW coupe. That's the beauty of having one child, I suppose. You can fit your kid into something sleek and fashionable. You don't have to completely transform your life, because one kid is portable. One kid is manageable.

I wouldn't trade my babies for a fleet of sports cars, and I trust that's one of the things Steve likes best about me. So I keep on moving, driving past the flashy red car, and I turn left down the country road toward the home I'm making here in the middle of nowhere.

I make the mistake of glancing back over my shoulder as I drive away. Stephanie's sauntering toward Steve as if they're the only two people in the world. She throws her arms around his neck when she gets close enough, and I almost swerve into the ditch, but I right my course and put my eyes back on the road.

I trust Steve to handle his life.

If he wanted someone like her, he'd already have found that.

She's not a threat to me.

I repeat those things the entire way home, and I text him the second I'm not driving. He doesn't reply while I'm making dinner. He doesn't reply while we're eating dinner.

"Mom?" Gabe asks.

"Yeah?" I look up.

"Did you forget the rule?"

I blink.

"No phones at the table." He tilts his head to the side.

I laugh. "I suppose I did." I lean my chair back and slide my phone up onto the kitchen counter, well away from the table. Amanda's not home yet, but that's okay. With her new business, she's often late. "Alright, sorry for being distracted. What did I miss?"

Emery launches into a story about a drawing she made that three other kids copied, and then proceeds to detail how, when she called them on it, they insisted she was the copycat. I think I do an admirable job of feigning outrage.

But Emery is nothing if not thorough, and she's not quite done when Whitney starts explaining how many kids now crowd around the monkey bars, wanting a turn to hang upside down. "Which is super annoying, because no one even went over there before we moved here, or that's what Ursula says."

That's how big families work. You squeeze your story in when you can, or you'll never get a chance to talk.

"Wait, there's a kid named Ursula?" Ethan asks. "Really? Like the sea witch?"

I'm a little bit proud that I've taught my kids so well.

Even my teenage boy is suitably conversant in Disney princess.

"Oh my gosh," Maren says. "No one cares about *The Little Mermaid* anymore." She rolls her eyes.

"Oh my gosh," Ethan mocks. "No one cares what you think, either." He rolls his eyes.

I should be annoyed. They're bickering and talking over each other. While I'm having those thoughts, Gabe and Whitney start arguing over the last roll.

And I just smile.

This is the home I wanted, and it's the home I have. I survived another miserable moment and made it through the other side, to one of the many small moments that make up the life I chose. It's these moments I've come to appreciate more than the flashy ones, even when the kids are snappy and irritable.

"Gabe, you've already had two." Izzy jumps in. "That means Whitney should get the roll, because she's only had one."

Izzy has always been my little mother, ready to do my job for me if I'm even a hair late to react. "That's true," I say. "Unless Whitney wants to split it with you."

Whitney groans, but she tears the roll in half and hands part to Gabe.

That earns her a smile from me, and I watch as most of her annoyance subsides. "I had a long day," I say, "and I'm happy to be home."

"A long day? I thought you went for a ride," Ethan says. "Steve told me he had a present for you."

Did that all happen today? Sometimes the important moments do that—they bunch other things up until you forget about the good stuff. I inhale slowly. "He did. He gave me a bridle and a saddle."

Izzy looks around. "Where are they? Did you leave them in the car?"

I smile. "I left them at Steve's."

"Why?" Whitney asks. "How often will you really use them over there? You should bring them here."

"I thought I'd better leave them," I say. "Since I'm going to leave the horse he gave me there as well."

We have twelve horses here on the ranch. You'd think no one would care about one more—but my girls start to squeal immediately, including Emery. Only Maren plays it cool.

But even she's interested. "What horse did he give you?" She's had a handful of lessons over there, now. She knows most of his lesson horses.

"He gave me my favorite one," I say.

Whitney and Izzy jump to their feet. "Leo!?" They're both screaming at the same time.

Gabe covers his ears.

"Women." Ethan shakes his head, but he's smiling.

Families require a lot of work and even more patience, but they're worth every bit of it. By the time dinner's done and the dishes are rinsed and put in the dishwasher, I'm not stressed and anxious anymore. I feel like myself again. Being around my family's like sinking into a familiar, fluffy bed and wrapping up in a down comforter.

"Mom!" Gabe shouts. "Moooom! Whitney popped my balloon! She did it on purpose."

"He was whamming it against the wall," Whitney says. "It was so annoying."

If the comforter is covered in prickly pine shavings, maybe.

Once I finally get the kids down, it's time to pay attention to the work stuff I delayed for the ride earlier. Thanks to a problem with a filing that's (luckily) not my fault, a small motion turns into a big nightmare.

I can't get it resolved until the next day, and then I dive right into working on the affidavit from Donna, which I need to prep ASAP so I have a decent position when we go to mediation with the alien foundation. Between my own personal stuff and work problems, I barely have time to answer the texts Steve finally sends the next afternoon.

Not that there are very many.

The following day, after barely any communication for a day and a half, I'm turning into a bit of a basket case. I decide a check-in is fine.

HANGING IN THERE? I hit send and wait.

Giving people space is hard.

CAN YOU COME OVER? I CAN'T SEEM TO GET THE PATERNITY TEST SET UP.

I'm not sure why he needs me to come to his house for that. I could probably get it set up in five minutes online, but I don't need to be invited over twice. I've been dying to see him since I walked away a few days back.

Plus, he's told me almost nothing about what's going on, and the girlfriend and drama queen living inside of me both want to know.

Girlfriend? Can I call myself that? I'm not sure quite where we are. I feel like I'm more than a friend. We've kissed and he gave me a horse... plus we've cleaned up puke as a team. But he's only called me that one time, and it was in front of the crazy ex, when he was defending me from her snooty attack. Did he really mean it?

All this dating stuff makes me feel like I'm fifteen again, sometimes. It's a very strange place to be as a woman who's almost forty and has four kids.

"Hey, I'm going to step out for a minute." I grab my purse.

"Going to see Steve?" Ethan wiggles his eyebrows.

Okay, I hate that.

"Ooh, can I come?" Gabe asks.

"Pipsqueak, there's no way Mom wants you to tag along when she's going to see her boyfriend," Ethan says.

"Boyfriend?" Gabe's eyebrows both shoot up. "What's that?"

Ethan shakes his head. "Kids, I swear."

Seeing a big child like Ethan call Gabe a kid makes me smile, but he's wrong. I would totally take Gabe along, if I'd told them about Steve's situation. Which I haven't yet. I figured it would be easier to keep it on the down low until we're a hundred percent sure how Olivia fits into his life.

Because the second I drove off, my confidence that she was his that was based on nothing more than facial expressions, started to erode, mostly because of my desperate hope that she wasn't. Even if Stephanie's husband is named Antonio. . .that's not conclusive proof he couldn't have blue eyes like Olivia has. Even though Stephanie's aren't blue either. And she has his nose. None of that is a paternity test.

It's possible that little girl really isn't his, right?

Great. Now I'm bargaining with myself. I crouch down and pull Gabe against me for a hug. "I'm sorry. I know I've been working a lot lately, too." I brush his hair into place. "I won't be there very long tonight. Steve needs some help with a legal issue. That's why I'm going, and if you came along, it would be really boring and take even longer. I wish I was going to ride and you could come see Cromey. That would be more fun for all of us."

"Okay." Gabe looks glum, but he doesn't whine or argue. The kids give him a hard time for being a whiny mess, but he's still so small. He's actually really good for a seven-year-old.

"I could go," Izzy says. "I've already fed our horses, but if Steve needs help with any of his, even mucking stalls—"

"I'm going to go alone today," I snap.

The hurt look in Izzy's eyes stings, and I immediately regret my tone.

"I'm sorry," I say. "I really won't be gone long, I swear."

"Everyone always needs your help with stuff." Emery stands up and crosses the room to hug me. "You're a really good person."

And now I feel like crap for not telling them all about Olivia, but it's not my secret. I can't forget that. "Thank you, sweetheart. I really will be back soon, and I imagine your mom will be back any minute too. She's got her first bachelor thing tomorrow, right?"

"She's just cleaning up the shop," Maren says from the chair near the front door. "She said she'll be here soon."

"There's still lasagna in the fridge," I say. Which reminds me that I'm empty-handed. I probably shouldn't go to Steve's empty-handed. I turn back and rummage around in the freezer for a bag of cookies. But which kind?

I still don't know his favorite cookies.

I think that answers the question of whether he's my boyfriend. A girlfriend would certainly know her boyfriend's favorite cookie. Right? I sigh and grab a bag of peanut butter ones, with little chocolate kisses on top. Hopefully those are alright.

They were Nate's favorite.

A pang of guilt eats at me. I'm ditching my kids during prime time—everyone is home from school and done with animal husbandry—to go see my *boyfriend*, or my wannabe boyfriend, at least. And I'm taking him Nate's favorite cookies. I turn back toward the fridge to pick a different bag.

"Mom," Ethan says.

I look up.

"It's okay."

"What is?" My eyes are too wide, but I can't seem to help it.

He tilts his head. "You can take Dad's favorite to Steve. They're really good cookies."

I burst into tears.

Ethan hugs me, setting the cookies on the counter in the process.

"Am I that transparent?" I whisper.

"You're pretty transparent," he says, "but only because I've known you since birth."

"Since *your* birth." I laugh. "I'm almost forty."

"But since I was the most epic thing that ever happened to you, I feel like my birth is the most defining milestone." Ethan's smiling. "But for reals, Dad would be happy to see you smile. He'd only be sad if you got all weird and weepy like you're doing right now."

I still step toward the fridge.

"Take these." Ethan picks up the frozen peanut butter cookies he took away before. "Seriously."

Whitney's hugging me next, and then Gabe grabs my waist and hugs me too. Izzy glares at them all, but the second Whitney lets go of me, Izzy steps into her place and hugs me, too.

This is why you have four kids. Moments like this right here.

I'm still wiping a tear away when I march out the front door with a bag of peanut butter cookies in hand.

ARE YOU COMING?

Steve's text surprises me until I remember I never responded. ON MY WAY NOW.

GREAT! PARK AT THE BARN.

The barn? He spends most of his time there, but I can't recall him ever telling me to park there. I wonder why.

When I pull up and the shiny red BMW's parked in front of the house, a chill runs up my spine. Steve's truck's parked in front of the barn, so I circle past the Beamer and pull around to the space in front of the barn. Why is that awful woman here at seven o'clock at night?

Is she hoping to get back together with Steve? He told

her he wanted nothing to do with her, but hate isn't the opposite of love. That's apathy.

He's definitely not apathetic about her.

I shove my concern away and climb out. He told me to park at the barn. He's parked at the barn. It feels strange to walk straight into the barn, but I'm not sure what else to do.

I do have a horse here. I shouldn't feel awkward. I have a right to be here. I walk to the tack room and grab a carrot for Leo, who whinnies when he sees me.

Then I remember that when we were sick, Steve offered to come sleep in the barn. There must be some kind of habitable space for humans out here. Maybe he's got stuff stored in this area and he's moving it around to make room for some of Stephanie's junk. I poke around a bit and find a door in the back that looks promising. I knock.

Steve whips the door open and glances back and forth down the main corridor of the barn. After finding it empty, he grabs my wrist and pulls me inside, shutting the door behind us.

He pulls me into a tight hug. "Thank goodness you made it."

I'm shocked for a moment by all of this, but mostly I'm delighted. At least he's happy to see me. He clings tighter even than Gabe did. Eventually, though, I push him away. "Easy there, boy. What's going on?"

He sighs and steps back, grabbing my wrist again and pulling me toward the sofa in the modest-sized family room.

"What are you doing out here?"

He pulls me down next to him on the sofa a little too exuberantly, and I flop against his chest. He wraps one arm around my shoulders and pulls me against him with a satisfied sigh. "I needed to see you. Really badly."

Almost as badly as I needed the warm welcome. It's a

little embarrassing that I'm so unsure as a grown woman, but this is all so new, and then with his ex. . .

"But if you're asking about why I'm here in the barn, my home has been invaded."

"Invaded?" I think about the red car, parked right out front. Irritation floods me. "You're saying that she's living in your house right now?" I can't even bring myself to say her name.

"Hey." He jostles my arm with his hand, and I realize that I've stiffened like a board.

I make a concerted effort to loosen up, but it's hard. "Your ex-wife is living here with your daughter?" I want to be cool and laid back, but that's just not who I am. He may as well figure that out now if he hasn't already. "Are you serious?"

"It's not like I want her there," he says. "And she's gone most days."

"Wait, she's gone most days?"

"She doesn't have a job, so I have no idea where she's been going, but yes. So far, she's left every day around ten or eleven, leaving me to watch Livy."

Olivia. His daughter, probably.

But if she's not his daughter, spending time with her, bonding with her again, it's going to hurt him all over again. "You said you haven't been able to set up the paternity test." I thought he meant he hadn't been able to find a place to do it, but now I'm wondering if it's not more complicated than that. "Did you mean you can't get Stephanie to agree to doing one?"

"She hasn't told Livy who I am, yet." He sighs. "She's pretty upset about her parents getting a divorce."

I'm confused. "Then who does she think you are, exactly?"

He scratches his head. "Her mom's ex-husband."

"And what reason did Stephanie give for the two of them living here?"

"She's not on good terms with her parents."

Shocker.

"And that meant that she didn't have anywhere else to go. They don't have anywhere else to go."

She's a Damsel in Distress. Looks like that's Steve's kryptonite. Ugh. If I start getting upset about the setup, then I'm the wild-eyed girlfriend, overreacting to his good intentions. "What did you imagine that I would do in this situation?" I arch one eyebrow.

"Other than hug me?"

I laugh and lean against him again, sliding one arm across his beautifully ridged middle section. I really love Nate—loved—love? What's the right thing to think? But he never had a six-pack. I'd written off that dream.

Until now. It's a really nice dream. A hard, firm, nicely shaped dream. Or, it would be if it wasn't being ruined by all this drama.

"What are you doing?" Steve's voice is bemused.

I realize that I'm literally rubbing his stomach like it's a washboard and his shirt is very, very dirty. I freeze and turn toward him slowly.

"I've never seen such a guilty look on your face," he says. "And suddenly I wish I was a judge and you were about to be sentenced." His smile widens. "I take it you like my belly."

I swallow slowly.

He laughs.

"The thing is—"

He doesn't care about the thing, apparently, because his abs contract beautifully as he tugs me upward, his face lowering at the same time, and suddenly he's kissing me. His mouth covers mine, his lips insistent but somehow still soft. I melt against him, my body too soft, and his hard in all the right places.

I realize my hand has gone back to rubbing his abs and I snatch it back against my own belly.

He laughs against my mouth, finally releasing me. "I needed to see you today, more than you could possibly know." He sighs, leans back further and pulls my face against his chest. "I needed to see my girlfriend. I really didn't see a blessing like you coming, but oh man. It feels really good to hear that out loud." He pauses, his eyes focusing on mine. "I needed time with my girlfriend."

"Oh, good."

"Good?" He shifts me around so I can see him, and his eyebrows lift. "What's good?"

"Today, I was thinking about what I'm supposed to call you."

"Anything you want," he says, his voice low and possessive. "But not Daddy or Papa or any version of that. That's always creeped me out."

I laugh. "I meant, oh good, you called me your girlfriend."

He smiles. "You think I'd give Leo to just anyone?"

"That's what I was thinking," I say. "But we hadn't really talked about it."

"I called you my girlfriend to Stephanie the second she showed up. I said you were my lawyer and my girlfriend, remember?"

"But you could have just been saying that to make sure she didn't—"

"I don't just say things." His words are soft, his eyes intent. "I may not be a lawyer, but I'm still careful with my words." He brushes my hair back from my face. "I couldn't be more serious, or more delighted, to be in a relationship with you."

"Oh."

"This is where you tell me you're glad, too."

"I would be a little more glad if I could see you every day," I say. "I feel like we took this huge step forward and then. . ." I can't quite explain it.

"And then plunged off a cliff?"

I shrug. "That might be a little dramatic, but something like that."

"I want to see you every day too. There's no reason—"

"I haven't told the kids anything yet," I say. "I wasn't sure what to tell them."

He freezes. "I hadn't even thought about that."

"You've been a little preoccupied," I say. "It's understandable."

"I'm not sure what to tell them either," he says. "One moment I'm sure she must be my daughter, and I'm filled with delight that I *have* a daughter, and the next I'm filled with rage that Stephanie lied to me. Then she'll say or do something that feels totally foreign, and I'm positive I can't be related to her and it must be yet another lie in a nonstop stream of deception. Then I wonder what in the world I'm doing, and how I could possibly co-parent a child with *that* woman. I swear, I vacillate between feeling lucky and feeling cursed in the same five-minute period sometimes."

"You really need to get that paternity test done," I say. "It's the only way you'll be able to proceed without winding up in a loony bin."

He inhales slowly, and I realize he's afraid. Or he doesn't even want to get it done, because he wants her to be his.

"Is that actually why you asked me to come over?"

"I wasn't sure whether you were upset," he confesses. "And I wasn't sure how to ask."

"So you don't need my help?"

"Actually." He cringes. "I've been trying to avoid seeing Stephanie, and it feels a little like she's stalking me. So I hide out here until I see that she's leaving, and then I sneak over."

I really like him. "You're cute. Alright, so you need to set one up, but you're afraid to coordinate it with Stephanie."

"Have you ever used sticky traps to catch mice?" he asks.

"Not that I can remember."

"They're stronger than glue, or tape, or anything else, really. The adhesive on them is possibly the stickiest substance out there. Stephanie's worse than a sticky mouse trap. So, yeah, I need to set up a test, but I don't want to see her or interact with her in any way or I'll be tortured incessantly."

"She didn't take over your house," I realize. "You ran away."

He doesn't argue.

"Or maybe a little of both."

"That's not very manly, is it?" He sighs. "The divorce nearly killed me. I've been slowly recovering ever since. The thought of being around her makes me want to break something. Or sob pitifully."

He's definitely not apathetic. Ugh. "Did you want me to go with you, so I can snatch you back when she gets all snatchy and grabby?"

I was totally kidding, but he nods vigorously, just like a little boy. "Yes, please."

It's impossible to keep from laughing. "Oh, fine. I'll go protect you from the big, bad, shiny woman."

"She's not shiny," he says. "She's the devil in high heels."

I stand up and brush off my jeans. "If I'd known I'd be facing off against your supermodel ex, I'd have come wearing something other than jeans and a t-shirt that says 'Yes, I smell like a horse. No, I don't think that's a problem.'"

Steve stands up and steps back, looking me over head to toe. "I've never seen a woman look half as hot as you do right now." He steps closer and drops his voice. "But if you ever call her a supermodel again, we'll have a problem. I've never seen a less attractive woman than my ex-wife. I'm still so embarrassed I didn't realize that right away."

He couldn't be more wrong about her appearance, but it still helps to hear how he feels. Especially as we approach the front door and it swings open and she steps out in spike heels and another tight sheath dress—this one white.

"Did you realize you were coming here when you packed?" Steve asks.

Stephanie ignores him. "Oh. You're here." She glares at me, and then as if she's just realizing it, she forces a smile. "How lovely for you to come visit us."

"She's not visiting you," Steve says. "She's here to see me, but my house is infested."

"Infested?" A smaller voice behind Stephanie pipes up.

"He's kidding," I say. "He got the ant problem taken care of last month." I squeeze his hand. "Remember?"

"Who are you?" Olivia pops her head out from behind her mother. "Steve's girlfriend?"

"She is," Steve says.

"It's weird he's living in the barn, isn't it?" Stephanie asks.

She's baiting us in front of Olivia. I know it, and it's still hard to clamp down on a response. "I think Steve's been looking for an excuse to live in that barn for a long time." I smile. "The only woman in the entire world who I worry I might lose him to is Farrah, you know."

"The horse named Farrah?" Olivia asks.

I bump Steve with my hip. "The beautiful bald-faced sorrel mare with the blonde mane and the bright blue eyes, yes."

Steve chuckles. "I offered to give her to you."

"I knew you didn't mean it."

"You offered to give her Farrah?" Olivia asks. "Really?"

"He did give me Leo," I say.

"That's so cool," Olivia says. "My mom won't even let me ride, much less own a horse of my own."

Only a twitch in Steve's jaw shows his agitation, but I can imagine how he feels about that. *His* daughter hasn't ever been on a horse—no, she *can't* be on a horse.

"On that note, I think it's probably time for Olivia to know what we've set up for tomorrow morning." I'm bluffing, but I'm relatively confident I can find a place for them to go on that kind of notice.

Stephanie frowns, but I plow forward, taking a calculated risk.

"You know your parents are getting a divorce," I say, "but your mom probably hasn't told you that you have to go to a clinic and get a blood test tomorrow. It's part of the usual proceedings, and it won't take long at all." I force a smile. "How's ten a.m.?"

I thought about telling Olivia what's going on point blank. It would probably be a relief to her—kids are smart. I imagine she's already guessed some part of what's going on. But she's not my child, so I'm giving Stephanie a way to mitigate the risk to Olivia if this is a lie.

Stephanie's mouth dangles open.

"I'm happy to take her," Steve says.

"That won't be necessary," Stephanie says. "In fact, I haven't heard a word from the court about—"

"I'm a lawyer," I say, my tone sharp. "And also a parent. There's an easy way to do this, or there are hard ways. Which would you prefer?" I shrug. "As a lawyer, I'm fine with either. As a parental courtesy, I'm starting by offering the easy way."

"I'm not an easy person," Stephanie says.

Steve snorts.

Olivia frowns. Yeah, she's definitely picking up some things.

"We'll be by to pick you up around nine," I say to Olivia. "Make sure your teeth and hair are brushed and you're ready to go." I turn toward Stephanie. "Steve's a lot nicer than me—and with my background, nothing about the court or its orders scares me."

Some people just don't make progress until you threaten them. I turn on my heel and start back toward the barn.

"My goodness, you're magnificent," Steve says.

I may not drive a red BMW or wear stilettos and white dresses, but it seems like Steve likes my horse t-shirts well enough. "We'd better hurry back and try and book an appointment for tomorrow, or all my bluffing will be wasted effort."

3
DONNA

This one time, in eighth grade, our math teacher told us about a math competition team she was forming. The team was called the Mathletes. I've never been very athletic. I'm the kind of person that trips over her own feet on her way to kick the soccer ball.

But the Mathletes? That I thought I might be able to do.

I stayed after school to take the selection exam, expecting a handful of other people to stick around too. Unfortunately, it wasn't just a few, maybe because Mrs. White said we'd get to go to San Francisco if we made the team.

There were more than twenty kids who wanted to get on that team of three. I figured I would be a lock, but as I looked around the room, I realized I might not be.

Jimmy Chang was the smartest kid in our class. I knew without any doubt that he would answer every single question right. The other slot would go to Hannah Landon. She wasn't quite as smart as Jimmy, but she was awfully close.

I was hoping I'd manage the third place. I'm smart, but not like Hannah or Jimmy. When Mrs. White passed out the screening test, I zoomed my way through the first nine problems.

That tenth was a real doozy.

I had no idea how to work it. Like, none at all. I even turned my paper upside down at one point, but nothing helped. I was stumped. I looked out the window, ready to accept that I was not going to San Francisco, but that's when I noticed that Jimmy Chang was still working on the very first problem.

Something about it confused him. I have no idea why. He had finished all the others, and the answers were written out in his clear, concise, easy-to-read handwriting.

I had made up an answer to number ten, on the outside chance I might luck into the answer, but now I could see the actual answer, right next to me.

It wasn't like I'd gone out there *looking* for the right answer, but once I'd seen it. . .I glanced down at my paper, wondering if I could figure out how to work backward to the solution he wrote.

I still had no idea how to do it.

But it's not like we were expected to know all the math things already. I mean, that was the point of this whole thing. We joined the club to *learn*, and practicing weekly would be how we got better.

I scribbled the correct answer down just before Mrs. White collected our papers. I felt a little bad, but not awful. I mean, I'd have been stupid not to accept the tiny miracle that had fallen into my lap.

But the next day, when Mrs. White announced that only *one* student had answered all ten problems correctly. . .I felt a little ill. Jimmy had lost only one point, for having the decimal in the wrong place on answer one. But me, Donna Ellingson, had gotten a perfect score. Not a day passed afterward when Mrs. White didn't mention that we had a math genius in class.

Sadly, that math genius didn't improve much, even with all the extra practice.

And when the big event came, we *lost*, because I still stunk at quadratic equations. Mrs. White kept saying, "Don't worry. It's different when there's so much pressure. We all know you're brilliant."

That only made me feel worse.

But if I had to do it over again, I'd probably still write down Jimmy's answer. After all, I got a trip to San Francisco out of it, and our team was unlikely to beat all those other teams from big fancy schools anyway. Ultimately, I'm the kind of person who always takes advantage of any situations that drop into my lap.

I learned to do that from my brother, Patrick. So he really shouldn't be so surprised that I used our relationship with his lawyer to get a copy of his land deal with the alien people. Or that I used *that* document to oust him from taking Dad's place on the panel of the three persons who will decide what happens with Jed's Birch Creek Ranch.

"You little sneak." He shoves past me and stomps into the kitchen. He slams a paper down on the counter. "What exactly are you getting out of this? That's what I can't figure out. Are they paying you?"

"Who?"

He swears loudly. "The women, Donna. Those gold-digging, desperate whores who showed up here wanting a handout."

"Gold-digging?" I arch one eyebrow. "As far as I know, they're actually working hard to try and get something that should rightfully have been a simple inheritance from the start."

"Is she gay, that blonde one?" He sneers. "Is that why you're divorcing Charles? I always suspected you might be like that."

"I'm aware—ever since I cut my hair short in high

school." I roll my eyes. "Stop being so idiotic. You want to buy the ranch. It stands to reason that you can't also be the person deciding whether it's for sale."

"But it would have been fine. No one knew, at least not until you went and told them." He steps closer. "Why would you do that? Why would you side with them instead of your own brother?"

"I'm not siding with anyone. Abigail even said—"

He crumples the paper up in his hand. "I don't want to hear what she said. I don't want you talking to her at all. I can't believe you let her manipulate you. You're many things, Donna, but until today I didn't realize you were so stupid."

"I've let you push me around for too long," I say.

"Push you around?" Patrick splutters. "Is that what you call giving you a free place to stay? Is that what you call giving you free beef for your table—"

"You stole that beef from the neighbors and slaughtered it the second you got those cows back home so no one would see the brand wasn't yours. You only gave some to me because it wouldn't all fit in your freezers."

His eyes widen. "You've lost your mind."

I can't handle his nonsense right now. "And you only gave me this house to stay in so that I'd take care of Dad for you. Let's cut the crap for once and tell things like they are."

"You think you're so smart. You always have—smarter than anyone else."

I'm tired, and being around him makes me so terribly sad. "The good news for you is that Abigail doesn't want me to just give them the ranch. She wants me to make a decision in accordance with the law."

"The other two people on that panel are basically sleeping with those women, so—"

"Get out," I say. "I'm embarrassed you're related to me."

"The fact that you would say that—the woman whose husband is on his way to prison—the college dropout who's a secretary at the high school." He shakes his head again. "*You're* embarrassed of *me*? That's rich."

"Rich is something I most definitely am not," I say. "But I can sleep at night without taking sleeping pills or drinking a lot of wine. That's not something I could say a month ago. I doubt you can say it now."

"You had exactly one person in this world who was on your side, Donna, and now?" He drops the paper on the ground and walks toward the door. "Now you'll see what it's like to be all alone."

The sad part is that he's wrong again. Patrick was never on my side. He's not even someone who understands what that means.

But luckily for me, he's also wrong about my being alone. For the first time in over a decade, I actually know some people who are good. People who wouldn't lie on a math test to get on the team. Patrick came running over to try to hurt me, but either he's lost his touch, or I'm not as afraid of vipers as I used to be.

He did remind me of something, though. Charles' trial is ending today. After Patrick finally leaves, I call the prosecutor, but he doesn't pick up. Maybe that's good. Maybe they just announced the verdict and he's celebrating.

I wonder whether sentencing happens on the same day, or if that will take more time. I hope he goes away for more than just a few years. With all the television reports about overcrowding in prisons, I'm worried his sentence will be commuted or something awful. I call again on my way back to work, but there's still no answer.

This time I leave a voicemail.

"Hey, it's me. Donna. Just calling to see if sentencing happens today. Call me back."

My lunch break is a full hour, which is pretty generous

for a secretary, honestly, but it never feels quite long enough. When I drive home, it feels especially short, but Dad needed to take his medicine and the nurse was having trouble. He's convinced that she's trying to poison him. Again.

The rest of the school day breezes by, and I'm about to head across the street to pick up Aiden when my phone rings.

It's the prosecutor.

"Hello?"

"It's Andrew Soco, the prosecutor on Charles Windsor's case." He always introduces himself, like I haven't spoken to him a dozen times this month alone. But speaking to him that often, I'm fairly familiar with how he sounds, the cadence of his voice, the timbre, and the words he uses. Which means I know right away that his voice sounds strange today. My stomach twists a bit as I wonder *why*. "Donna Ellingson, right?"

"Yep. It's me, Andrew."

He sighs. "I'm sorry it took me so long to call you back."

My phone beeps, indicating a call on the other line. "Hey, can you hold on for just one second?" As a parent, I don't have the luxury of ignoring that kind of thing unless my kid's physically with me.

"Sure."

"Thanks." I click over, realizing as I'm in the process of swapping calls that the other caller is Charles' mom. Fabulous. I'm sure she's been dying to bawl me out for hours now. "Hello?"

"Donna!" Julia Windsor doesn't sound weird. She sounds downright jubilant. And the twisting in my stomach turns into full-on knots.

"Are you calling to discuss details for this weekend?" I hate doing it, but as awful as my soon-to-be-ex-in-laws are to me, they're pretty decent grandparents. I promised them months ago that they could take Aiden this weekend.

"Yes and no," she says. "We can't wait to see Aiden, but it seems like you haven't heard the good news yet."

"Good news?" Anything good for them is probably bad for me. My stomach is roiling now. Did he get a commuted sentence? Is he only going to be in prison for a year? Please, please don't let him get time served.

"I know you've been busy out there in the middle of nowhere, and I'm sure with Aiden and your little part-time job, you've been distracted, but earlier this week, Charlie's lawyer did his job, and well." She laughs. It sounds like she's spent no less than a hundred hours perfecting the perfect little debutante laugh. It probably sounded great when she was a teenager. Now it makes my skin crawl. "Charlie was found innocent and released. I wanted to let you know he'll be calling soon to work out the details of picking up his son this afternoon. Be sure to pick up right away."

Oh, no. No, no, no. That can't be right. "But the records that I—"

"You should really call that bumbling attorney," she says. "I'm sure he can explain the boring details." She laughs again. "I can't tell you how well this all worked out for us. We don't owe you a dime, *and* our son will be out, free and clear, even after his horrid wife tried to send him to jail so she could get custody. We can't wait to get Aiden back into decent schools near us again."

I can barely breathe, much less speak coherently. This can't be right. She must be delusional. I don't bother saying anything to her. I simply click over to the call with Andrew. "I'm back." My voice doesn't wobble. It doesn't even crack. I sound like someone else. "That was my mother-in-law."

He sighs.

Nothing else. Just a sigh.

"Andrew, tell me something good."

"I'm so sorry," he says. "You have no idea how upset we are."

"How upset *you* are?" I ask. "Are you kidding me right now? My mother-in-law just told me he's coming after me—he thinks he can take my son from me!"

"I'd recommend you hire the best lawyer you can possibly manage for your divorce," Andrew says. "Because his law firm is really, really good."

When I hang up, my hands are both trembling. I drag in a ragged breath so that I don't pass out, and then I watch, dazed, as my phone rings again.

It's a number I'd hoped never to see again.

His parents must have been paying to maintain his phone. Were they actually hoping he'd get off? Did they realize it was possible all along?

Why am I thinking about stupid stuff like phone plans or their hopes and dreams?

Because my phone screen says that DEVIL is calling.

I don't answer it. I can't bring myself to do it. He calls three more times. On the fourth attempt, I finally swipe to answer. "Charles."

"Donna." He sounds just like his mother. Gleeful. Delighted.

"You must be happy right now."

"Happy?" Any light or eager part of his tone disappears. I forgot how he can do that. How he can turn and strike with no warning, like a summer rainstorm, or like a door slammed on your hand. "No part of me is *happy*, Donna. My *wife* testified against me. She wanted to put me in prison. Can you even imagine that kind of embarrassment? That kind of disloyalty?"

I swallow.

"I'm relieved she failed. I'm relieved to finally be back out, a free man, the way I should have been all along."

The sad thing is that he actually believes that, I think.

He's always believed his own lies. "You deserve to rot in prison."

"The court didn't agree with you," he says. "But I didn't call to talk to you about my release. I'm just calling to let you know that I'm about two hours away. I expect that Aiden will have his bags packed and that he'll be ready to go when I arrive."

Panic sets in. "You can't take him." His parents didn't really have a right, but to my horror, I realize that Charles does. One of the reasons I picked this weekend is that it was supposed to be Charles', if he wasn't in jail.

And now he's not.

"I thought you might try something like this. I've already called the sheriff's office in town," he says. "It's not my first time being stabbed in the back by you. But, as I'm sure you know, the temporary order for our pending divorce is quite clear. I have every other weekend and every other Wednesday if I want them, and I most certainly do."

"But today's a Thursday."

"You previously arranged for my parents to come get him one day early."

I could be spiteful and insist he wait until tomorrow. "He has school."

"Nice try. I may have been in jail, but even I know there's no school in that podunk town on Fridays."

I swear under my breath.

"That's just another reason why he needs to move back to California."

"You can't enroll him in school there. He's already enrolled here."

He scoffs. "Of course I know that. What would make you think I'd even consider violating a judge's order?"

My panic recedes just a bit at that. He's not the kind of person who would be quite that stupid. Maybe if he broke out of jail, he might run for the border, but that's not how it happened. He used the system to free himself, and now he's going to use the system to try and steal our son.

"Your mom said—"

"Mother gets carried away by her emotions sometimes," he says. "We will set things right, but we will, of course, do it through all the proper channels."

The proper channels?

I may have been a little opportunistic in my life, but my version of 'doing things the right way' is still worlds apart from his. "Why would you even want custody?" I ask. "You never spent any real time with him before."

"Save your story for the hearing," he says. "You'll need it."

"We were married more than ten years," I say. "I think you owe me an explanation about that, at least. Why do you want custody? Why not leave Aiden with me? It's better for him, and even as twisted as you are, you do love him, I think."

"Twisted?" He sighs. "That's why, right there. I can't leave him with someone who will feed him a nonstop stream of negative propaganda."

Not 'I love him.' Not 'being apart from him would hurt me.' Not even 'I don't want to pay child support.' No, the reason Charles can't let me keep Aiden is that he has to control the narrative, always. At least for once in our marriage, he didn't lie. "That may be the most honest thing you've ever said to me."

"Come now," he says. "You need to save some of that for court. It's good stuff." He hangs up.

After hyperventilating into a tiny paper bag from one of Dad's prescriptions that I find at the bottom of my purse for a few moments, I pull it together and pick up Aiden. He's actually delighted at the prospect of seeing his father, which makes me really sad. One day he'll realize just what a loser his dad is, and I will feel even worse on that day.

We pack his clothes when we get home, and then we wait. We wait for much longer than two hours. Almost four hours later, it's nearly seven p.m. when Charles finally pulls into the driveway. If my brother was at all supportive, I could have asked him for help. I tried calling Abby, but she didn't answer, and she hasn't called me back yet.

So I'm all alone when my ex-husband, the bane of my life, drives up my old gravel driveway and stops in front of the old farmhouse we're living in. It feels like time slows down as he opens his door, steps out of the car, and looks the property over with a half-sneer. Finally, he turns toward me and smirks.

Because before he can do or say anything else, he must gloat. It's who he is.

Once he gets all of that out of the way, he can finally glance down at his son and nod. "Aiden."

"Dad!" Aiden drops his bag and races, arms outstretched.

Charles picks him up and swings him round and round. At least my son's excited. I hope he has a wonderful weekend.

With as little as I want to do with Charles, I'm pleased that at least he feels the same about me. He doesn't prolong the misery of either of us, and simply goes right to buckling Aiden into the car. I walk over and hand off his bag. He looks behind me and says, "I feel much less angry, now that I've seen this place."

I don't justify that with a response.

"I mean, obviously I can't leave Aiden here to rot, but this almost looks worse than prison." He snorts. "You're caring for your dad in there, too?"

"Have him back Sunday night early. He needs to get a good night's rest that night before school Monday."

"Yes, I'm sure the kindergarten courses here are quite rigorous."

"It's first grade," I say.

"I'll be back by six."

"So, eight?" I can't help myself.

The side of his lip curls. He's slimy, but he still *looks* pretty handsome. I hate that. I'm sure he'll slide right out of our marriage and convince some poor, unsuspecting girl that I wronged him horribly. Then his life will simply reset. I wish that, once we got divorced, the court could label him. A tattooed stamp across his forehead that reads: Danger. Or maybe: Damaged. Or perhaps: Run Away. Maybe with a warning like that, girls might think twice. He's the Devil, so he'd cover it up with concealer or something. But a little water on his face, and they could discover the truth.

The next time I date someone, if I ever do that again, I'm putting them through the wringer before making anything even semi-permanent.

"See you Sunday." Charles salutes, like he's a Lieutenant Colonel or something.

Then he's gone as quickly as he arrived.

I don't expect the bottomless black hole that opens up inside of me after Aiden leaves, but I can only think of one way to deal with it. I offer the nurse overtime pay, and I get in my car.

I need a drink, stat. Or maybe five.

4

ABIGAIL

Donna doesn't pick up, even though we call her three times. Even though she called *me* earlier. "Should we go by her place?"

"Yes, I think stalking her is a good plan." Amanda rolls her eyes.

"It's been a long day," I say. "But the best thing that happened today was the court approving our request that she become the new representative for her father. That wouldn't have happened if she wasn't willing to defy her brother, who also happens to be her neighbor. I'm worried about her—why she called."

"She's also got a six-year-old at home," Amanda says, "and a father she's taking care of. What are the odds she can drop it all and come with us to Amanda Saddler's to drink wine with no notice?"

I'd feel better if I knew she was alright, but Amanda's probably right. I'm probably making it about me. She didn't text, and she didn't leave a voicemail. I text her one more time. GIRLS' NIGHT AT THE SADDLER PLACE. PLEASE COME! STEVE OFFERED TO BE OUR DESIGNATED DRIVER IF WE NEED ONE.

"Alright, *Mom*, you've texted her and she doesn't want to come, so let's go already." Amanda's a real brat sometimes.

"Hey, Mom?" Whitney asks.

"Nope," Amanda says. "You're not allowed to talk to her right now." She raises her voice to impressively yell. "Ethan!"

It takes a few seconds, but he opens his door. "Whitney has some kind of issue. Help her with it?"

"I just wanted a hug," Whitney mutters.

I laugh and open my arms. She rushes toward me and hugs me like there's no tomorrow. "I love you, princess."

"Love you, Mom."

I drop a kiss on her head.

"Can I get one too?" Emery asks.

"Of course." My sweet little niece clings on so tightly she feels like a barnacle. She's so skinny it's a little like hugging a needy skeleton.

Amanda's opening the front door, a look of irritation on her face. "Alright, June Cleaver. Let's go."

Whitney frowns. "Who's June—"

"Nope," Amanda cuts Whitney off. "No more questions, Cindy Lou Who. It's girls' night."

"I'm a girl." Whitney frowns.

I laugh. "A beautiful girl. Now go sleep."

Izzy and Gabe both rush over for hugs before I can get away.

"I should have known my own daughter would insist on hugging *you* before we could leave." Amanda's tapping the window on my minivan. "Ridiculous."

"She's such a sweet little girl." I can't help my smirk. "She probably thought if she asked you, you'd bite her head clean off."

"She has texted me 'good night' eleven times in the last fifteen minutes," Amanda says. "You shouldn't encourage it."

I can't help my laugh. "She has the tenderest heart I've ever seen."

"You say tender, I say needy. Tomato, tomahto."

As I start the car, my phone bings. It's a text message from Emery, with no less than twenty lines of little red hearts. I try to slide the phone back into my purse, but Amanda notices it.

"It's Emery, isn't it?"

I sigh and flip the screen toward her. Once she's glanced at it, I drop it into my purse and back out toward the road.

"Now you've done it. It's like petting Roscoe. The second you do, he becomes a black hole of desperate need. No amount of petting is ever enough to fill it up."

Actually, comparing Roscoe and Emery isn't too far off.

"No more thinking or talking about kids," Amanda says. "It's a girls' night."

"You can't talk about kids?"

"Not at Amanda Saddler's," she says. "It'll make her sad."

"She has family," I say. "You said she had a niece. The one she thought sent her all the Lolo clothes." Amanda Saddler lives so close that we're almost there.

Amanda shakes her head. "Try again. She finally confessed last week—she made up the niece the day I showed up. She knew they weren't her clothes, but she liked them so much, she put them on anyway."

"She didn't."

"Sure did."

She's hilarious. And canny. I love her. But the thought of Amanda Saddler, all alone in the world, makes me sad. And so wasteful. If only she and Jed had talked to each other, how different would their lives have been?

We'd never have come to live here, that's for sure.

But maybe we'd have come to visit—our kids playing with their grandkids.

That thought, as I park outside Amanda Saddler's house, makes me sad. There are a lot of things I wish had gone differently in my life, but I'm happy where I am right now. It's probably the first time I've felt this way since losing Nate. It's a scary feeling, but also an exciting one.

I'm happy.

I like where I am—even if the path to this place was bumpy and paved with devastating loss. I hope Ethan's right, and that Nate would be pleased. I hope he's happy, wherever he is now. Heaven, probably. At least, I really hope there's a heaven. I'm positive that if there is one, that's where he is.

"You coming?" Amanda's looking at me like I'm crazy.

"Right, yeah. I am." I hop out and close the door behind me. A cardinal dive bombs at my head.

"Arizona," Amanda shouts. "Knock it off. We're friends, remember?"

Amanda Saddler opens the front door then, a huge grin on her face. "Welcome!"

As always, there's a huge pile of sunflower seeds heaped in a bowl. But as if that's not quite enough for the three of us, she hustles into the kitchen and grabs two different types. I can tell they're different because one of them has a reddish powder—nacho cheese, maybe? And one has a sprinkling of whitish grey dust. I'm guessing ranch.

"I'll grab the spit bowls," Amanda says.

Amanda Saddler cackles. "Good girl. You're learning."

"Even city girls can learn things, eventually," I say.

The second we sit down, she pounces. "I hear you've got a big date tomorrow." She turns toward me. "And I heard that you've got an ex-wife to battle."

How in the world does she always know everything? "Who told you—"

"That one's easy." She tosses her head at Amanda. "She's

a terrible blabbermouth." Her eyes sparkle. "But guess how I know about her big date?"

I blink. Sometimes I struggle to keep up with her.

"Guess, I said!" She claps.

"Uh, you heard at the market?" I ask.

She rolls her eyes. "Terrible guess." She looks at Amanda. "You?"

Amanda shakes her head. "I didn't tell you."

"Of course you didn't, you ninny." She pulls her phone out of her pocket. "I signed up for Instagram."

I can hardly believe it. I barely have an Instagram account. The idea of Amanda Saddler on there—it's simultaneously horrifying and exciting. What is happening to the world?

"Now, who can explain hashtags?"

Half an hour later, after scrolling through Amanda's many, many photos of Jed the potbelly pig, she circles back to my ex-wife problem.

"It's true," I say. "Stephanie is—"

"A complete sow," Amanda Saddler says. "And I knew that the second I met her."

A sow. What a perfect word. "She's beautiful," I say, compelled to admit the truth.

"Oh, pigs can be quite pretty," she says, "but they all roll in filth, and they track it everywhere they go if you let them." She leans closer. "Don't you let her root around in Steve's life."

"That's what I said." Amanda tips back the end of another beer.

"What time did you say you had to be up tomorrow?"

She waves me off. "Plane leaves at three."

"A nighttime date," Amanda Saddler says.

Of course it is. "But don't you need to get up early and make cookies?"

She flops back against the sofa. "We're not all robots, Abby."

"I'll take that as a no."

"I already decided to close on Bachelor days, even before I knew what time the flight would be."

"But you won't be back the next day until—"

"Oh my word, I'm an adult," Amanda says. "If I close for two days for another project I'm being paid to do, it's fine."

I'm annoying sometimes. I can't help it. The more she acts like my kids, the more my parenting instincts spur me on.

"I see where Izzy gets it from." Amanda snickers.

"Tell me all about tomorrow's bachelor," Amanda Saddler says.

Amanda slams the beer she had picked up back down on the coffee table. "Does it really matter?" She shrugs. "I've been on a zillion dates, and they're all disasters."

"Why aren't you more excited about meeting rich, eligible guys who are keen to date you?" I ask.

Amanda Saddler straightens. "Yeah, why ain't you?"

I narrow my gaze at her. She's acting as weird as Amanda. I swear it felt like she wasn't really curious, but she's pretending she is.

"I'm trying not to get my hopes up," Amanda says. "I've been let down a lot."

"You're not still pining over Eddy, are you?" I ask.

"No way, definitely not pining." She shakes her head a little too much and has to rub her forehead to clear the daze away. She's definitely going to be hungover tomorrow.

"Then tell us about Bachelor Number One," I insist.

"He's an investment banker," Amanda says. "Which is strike one. But he does have a nice, square jaw. And he looks amazing in a swimsuit. His Instagram account has a lot of followers, which is good for me. But it makes him look a little narcissistic, to be honest. That's probably why I'm not more excited. It's essentially a steady stream of posts of him with a knowing smile, displaying his very decent abs."

"Maybe that's just his internet persona," I say. "Maybe he's a sweetheart underneath."

She curls her lip, and even I have to admit it's unlikely.

"Then why did you agree to it?"

"His following is almost all women from age twenty to fifty—my target demographic. Some of them will hate me for going out with him, but if our date bombs, that actually plays in my favor, as long as he doesn't despise me."

"You've really thought this through," Amanda Saddler says. "I'm impressed."

"It's my job," Amanda says.

"You two women." Amanda Saddler beams. "You're brilliant, talented, and gorgeous, but you need to stop moping around so much."

That was definitely not what I expected her to say.

"This whole night has been one long whine." She turns toward me. "You need to kick that vixen out on her pig's ear."

"But her daughter—"

"Tomorrow you'll find out how you have to handle that when that test result comes back, but letting her muck around in Steve's life is unacceptable. Set boundaries and hold them." She turns to Amanda next, and I breathe a tiny sigh of relief that she's done with me. "And you." She smiles, but it's more diabolical than friendly, like a shark about to go chomp. "Even if he's a shameless, awful disaster, take some beautiful photos and let him buy you something *delicious*."

Neither of us is quite sure what to say to that.

"You know that phrase?" Amanda Saddler asks. "A moment on the lips, forever on the hips?"

We both nod.

"Utter rubbish. I can still remember all the delicious things I've eaten, and at this age, no one cares what my hips look like. Eat all the delicious things and don't worry about your hips."

I think I may have found my new life mantra.

5

DONNA

For most women, the worst day of their life would have been the day their husband was arrested. Not me. That incident actually makes it into the top ten best days I've had. I wish Aiden hadn't been there to see it, but I was happy when it happened.

Delighted, really.

For months, I've been having nightmares that he would walk. At first, I'd wake up feeling guilty, because his freedom was all my fault for not testifying. I consoled myself with the knowledge that I was doing what was best for Aiden. I was keeping his dad from becoming a convict, and I was laying something aside for our future.

When I decided to testify, I slept much better. Most nights, I dreamt of years and years of time without Charles in the picture at all. Aiden and I were both safe, and we didn't have to deal with him. No lying, no broken promises, no manipulations. Nothing of the kind.

Sure, we'd be poor, but we'd be emotionally and physically safe.

Now that's all out the window.

I keep seeing Charles saluting me. "See you Sunday."

His words ring in my ears over and over. Each time, it's like a barehanded slap to my face. Not only do I have nothing at all to show for my decision to testify against him, but Charles is now out, free and clear and furious with me.

I'm still struggling to understand *how* he walked. How could there be such a miscarriage of justice?

The only thing that helps is when I don't think. I just drive.

And then, once I finally reach the bar in Green River, I drink. One shot, and then, as a wave of liquid relief washes through me, I order another. With each order, I resolve that it will be my last. I'll pay my tab and get in my car, and I'll go home. But then, I order *just one more* again.

At some point, the mantra in my head shifts. Instead of getting in my car to go home, I'll call a cab. And then things start to get blurry. That's when part of me starts to worry. Drinking has, largely, not been a good thing in my life.

I drank a *lot* on my wedding day.

I also drank a lot after pulling out my tuition for my last year at Stanford and handing it over to Charles for his seed money to get his business started.

The last time I got drunk was the night Aiden was conceived.

I don't regret Aiden, but I certainly wasn't planning to have a baby, not with Charles. By then, I knew what he was and I was starting to want out. One drunken night ruined the beginning of those plans. Everyone knows that a child needs a father, and his business was going well, or so I thought.

I usually avoid alcohol because I hate the lack of control. I hate the feeling that I could and should do anything at all. I hate the thought of feeling stupid. I hate the idea that someone might hear me say or see me do something that I could be mocked for.

I suppose that's my type-A showing.

But none of that matters tonight. For the first time in years, I'm not in charge of Aiden. I won't see him tomorrow, or Saturday, or even most of Sunday. Sure, I'll have to get up and take care of Dad, but if I'm a little hungover, oh well. He'll survive and so will I.

And so I keep drinking. Chasing oblivion. Chasing a place where I won't think about the fact that Aiden will be with *him* tomorrow. A time when I haven't wrecked my own life. A story where I'm not about to battle the world's worst person for custody of my own child.

Eventually, the bartender cuts me off.

I don't take it especially well. But I can't remember my address, and he says that's enough. He calls me a cab. A cab! Like a cab would take me to Manila. There aren't even any cabs there. I laugh.

"Ma'am. Your Uber is here."

I vaguely realize that a cab from Green River to Manila is going to cost me something close to what my rent used to be. "No," I slur. "Noway."

"You can't drive," the man says.

I squint. Who is that man?

"You have to get in," he says. "It's almost closing time."

"I'm not going anywhere." I cross my arms. But then the world tilts and I stumble into the horrible blue car.

"I'll take her," a deep voice behind me says.

"Who are you?" the pushy man asks. "I already called her an Uber, and she'll take her to the address on her license. I certainly can't let her go home with you."

"I've known her since we were four years old," the deep voice says.

I try to turn and look at him, but my feet get in a fight and I fall.

Strong arms catch me.

And I puke.

The strong arms are surprised I think, because they stiffen.

"Sorry," I mutter.

The man takes off his vomit-covered sweatshirt, and when he does, his t-shirt's tugged up into the air, too. It shows his stomach.

His beautiful, tan, flat stomach.

I reach for it.

"Whoa, there," the guy from the bar says. "Do you know him?"

I drag my eyes upward and squint. Do I know him? I blink, but it doesn't help much. Then he smiles, and I realize who it is. "Will Earl!" I beam, proud of getting the right answer.

"Do you want to let him take you home?"

Take me home? "Yes, please." I reach for his stomach again, but the bar man slaps my hands away.

I take a swing at the bar man—I'm really tired of him pushing me around. Unfortunately, he can duck and weave like a boxer. Strong Arms—no, wait, he has a name, and I know it! Will Earl! He has to catch me again.

And then he's dragging me toward his car. Does he have a car? I peer at it, and realize it's not a car. "It's a truck," I say.

He chuckles and chucks something into the truck bed.

"What was that?" I ask. "Trash? Because you shouldn't throw it back there. It might blow away and there's fines for that. Litterer. Litter bug."

He laughs again. "That was my puke-covered sweatshirt. Did you want me to keep it in the main cab?"

Cab? I look around. "There aren't cabs here." I lean closer. "We live in Manila. It would cost me a fortune to use a cab."

He rolls his eyes. "Truck cab, Dee. I'm talking about the

cab of my truck. You're awfully cute drunk, but your puke still stinks."

Stinks? I wipe at my mouth.

Then the rest of what he said registers. He said I'm cute. Awfully cute, in fact. I can't help my grin. My idiotic, enormous, unhinged grin. "Cute?"

He sighs. "It's not like you're going to remember any of this tomorrow," he mutters. "Sure, Dee. I've always thought you were stunning, but I've never seen you drunk. You're pretty cute."

No one has called me cute in twenty years. Maybe more.

"Like a kitten?"

"Huh?" He opens the passenger door and gestures.

As if I could climb up into that. I sit on the ground instead.

"Am I cute, like a kitten?" I ask. "Or, like the hot girl next door?" I blush. I can't believe I'm even asking him this.

"I hear you're still married," Will says.

"To the biggest loser on earth," I say. "Not to brag, but really, he is. There's not a single bigger loser anywhere."

The muscles in Will's jaw work and the muscles on his arm bunch up. "Here, let's get you in the truck and back home."

"I don't want to go home." I'm not sure why, but I know it's true. That's why I'm out drinking. Home is bad.

"It's late, Dee. You have to go home."

I like when he says Dee. It makes me feel all warm and fuzzy, like another shot. "Are you saying my name over and over because you think I'll obey if you do?" That thought makes me angry, and I glare at him. "I'm not your servant."

He snorts. "I doubt anyone could ever mistake you for a servant."

"If you'd seen me for the last ten years, you'd think I

was." That thought depresses me. "He's the world's biggest loser. Did I say that?"

"Yes, you said." Will's smile is soft. "Here. Let me help." He tucks his hands underneath my armpits and lifts me up, up, up, like I weigh nothing, like I'm a sack of flour.

My feet pinwheel around, looking for something to push against. They finally find a step—he has an actual step between the ground and the truck cab. A cab! Just like he said. There *are* cabs in Manila. Or, well. In Green River. His hands—his huge, warm hands—shift around and encircle my upper arms and push me all the way inside. But that puts my face right next to his, and I take a nice, long look. He might even think I'm staring.

I wonder if he'll stop me, but he doesn't. He just looks back at me. I study his eyes. A light, bright grey. I study his nose. Long, smooth, but crooked right on the bridge. Will used to get in a lot of fights. I remember one of them. The guy who hit him first was bigger—way bigger. And Will took him out in three punches.

He got suspended for almost a week that time.

"You're really good looking," I say.

He swallows and my eyes drop to his throat. He still doesn't move. His arms are holding me in place, my feet resting on the step leading to his truck. He's so tall that we're face to face.

"And you have really nice muscles. I liked your stomach, too." I giggle.

"Donna." His whisper is ragged.

I don't think about it. Thinking makes my head hurt. Everything feels too fuzzy for that. I just move toward him, my lips pressing against his. They're so warm, just like his hands, that I collapse against him.

And he kisses me back.

For one brief moment, Will's arms shift from holding

me up, to pulling me close. He kisses me intently, eagerly, insistently.

And then he stiffens and he breaks it off, shoving me into the truck and slamming the door.

I definitely need to ask him why he stopped kissing me. Definitely. But the side door of the truck is really cold against my face, and I'm kind of too warm, all over. I lean against the window for a moment, and then I close my eyes, and then I feel something—a click? No, you can't feel a click. You hear a click.

Everything goes dark.

6

AMANDA

In my business, I've met people who are absolute geniuses with filters, with cropping photos, and with finding the perfect angle to make things look just so. I've watched people use a toilet seat to make it look like they were sitting on an airplane, for instance. They tagged the post #Bali, and people believed it, hook, line, and sinker.

I've learned that the real world is rarely represented on Instagram. That's why I'm prepared for *anything at all* when I finally fly out to meet my first bachelor. For all I know, he could have a flabby gut and dainty woman hands.

Eddy calls me the second the plane lands. "You're safe?"

"A-okay," I say. "I'm full of dread, but otherwise intact."

My phone buzzes in my hand, and I realize it's text messages coming through.

"Hang on. I've got some messages."

"I know," Eddy says.

"Huh?"

"They're from me."

I check them, and it's a sequence of photos. The first is one of Eddy and me. He's drawn a big red heart around us.

The second is Eddy covering his mouth. He's typed the words, "No kissing" across the bottom.

I laugh.

The last photo is also Eddy, but he's shirtless and glistening.

"Let me clarify," I say. "Your plan is to turn me on and then send me to go on a date with someone else?"

My phone bings again. *The sender would like to unsend this message.*

Ha! "Fat chance, mister. I'm keeping that one for the favorites folder."

He groans. "Be good, missy. Don't forget what's waiting for you at home."

"Oh, man," I say. "I better go."

"Why?" he asks. "Is everything okay?"

"Um, yes. It's just that the photo you sent me? I'm staring at someone even hotter, and he's wearing even less clothing."

"Excuse me?"

"Perry's here to pick me up, and other than a pair of very small swim trunks and a little white sign, he's not wearing anything at all. And wow, can you say abs?"

"What?"

"Calm down, pretty man," I say. "I'm kidding. I'm still sitting on the plane. I promise to be good."

The woman next to me is looking at me like I'm a porn star.

I drop my voice. "I better get off the phone before someone reports me to a stewardess and they kick me off the plane."

"Aren't you deplaning already?"

The row ahead of me starts to grab their bags. "I am, in fact."

"You're a very strange woman."

"The lady next to me agrees with you," I whisper.

He snorts. "Miss you."

"Same." I hang up.

"The entire world isn't a joke." The woman next to me clutches her pearls.

Okay, fine, she doesn't clutch her pearls. But she does pull her sweater set tighter. "You might enjoy it a bit more if you made a few jokes yourself."

The next few minutes are a little tense, and I breathe a big sigh of relief when I'm able to wheel away from the woman as quickly as possible. Thank goodness I'm here for such a short time that I didn't have to check anything.

I'm expecting someone from Lolo to pick me up, so I scan the people waiting just past baggage claim absently, paying attention to the names written on signs.

"Amanda?" A man's voice rises above the general chatter.

I look up, and right into the surfer-guy smile of a man in his late thirties. Thanks to my familiarity with how adept influencers are at snapping photos, I wasn't expecting much, but to my surprise, Perry Giles is even hotter in person than he is in his photos.

His smile's relaxed and absolutely brimming with confidence.

Look at that, Abigail's rubbing off on me. Brimming? Get your head in the game, Amanda. Normal people don't use words like that. And now he's waving at me.

I wave back, only a little annoyed that he's here to pick me up himself. I thought it would be a car service and I'd get more downtime. I agreed to spend five hours with these guys, not—I glance at my watch. Six. Alright, maybe I'm overreacting.

"Amanda Brooks!" He beams.

"I wasn't expecting you to pick me up," I say.

He waves me off breezily. "It was the least I could do."

My brow furrows. What does that mean?

“After insisting you come to me.” He shrugs. “I know the agreement said we’d travel to you, and your boss told me you didn’t want to have to fly and drive and whatever, but honestly, what in the world would we have done for our date in the middle of nowhere? I googled it, and it doesn’t even have a grocery store. There are exactly two restaurants.”

I think of Manila as the middle of nowhere regularly. Abigail and I joke about it a lot. The school’s tiny. The hardware store is also the grocery store. There are barely 400 people who live within the town limits. . .

And yet, his comment pisses me off for some reason.

Does that mean that I consider Manila to be my home?

“I’m sure there’s more to do here,” I admit. “And I’ve always wanted to come to San Francisco.”

“Oh, you’ll love it,” he says. “It’s not as disgustingly perfect and boring as San Diego, and it’s not as congested or as hot as Los Angeles.”

“San Diego’s boring?” I lift my eyebrows. “I feel like that’s a controversial position.”

He laughs, and his laugh isn’t nearly as obnoxious as I expect it to be. “For the first month or two, sure, people love it.” He shrugs. “But after that, it’s like perfect people. They start to really wear on you, and so does San Diego.”

“You sound like you lived there.”

“I did, but I’m sure you know what I mean. Think about the most perfect person you know, and tell me they don’t bug you.”

I think about Abigail. I love her to the moon and back, but he’s not totally wrong. “Alright, I’ll give you that one. Perfection can get tiring.”

“Exactly.” He picks up my bag and starts walking. I have to trot to keep up with his long stride. “You need some overcast, rainy days, or you don’t appreciate the glorious days like this." As if he timed it that way on purpose, we walk outside and into the beautiful sunshine.

It's not really very cold to me in Manila right now—after living in New York for years, I can safely say that highs around mid-fifties aren't *that* cold. But days in the seventies are pretty far back in the rearview mirror. I'm not so loyal to Manila that I can't appreciate the warmth of the sun on my face and the breeze ruffling my hair.

I peel my Lololime jacket off and stuff it into my Lololime backpack. When I look up, Perry's snapping a photo. He shrugs. "It's in the contract terms. I figured it would be a good time to take a few photos, since you were putting away their jacket by tucking it inside of their bag."

"I'm pretty sure my boss would start planning our wedding this minute if she were here."

Perry waves at someone and when a guy jogs over, he hands him a ticket.

"What are you doing?" I ask.

He shugs. "Nothing. Valet."

At the airport? I guess I shouldn't be surprised. We're in California. The land of sunshine, smog, silicon, too much money, and lots of cars.

"But really, I'm pretty happy with how things turned out." Perry smiles. "At first, when Victoria called to tell me that there was a change of plans, it bummed me out."

What is with this guy? Is he really telling me he's upset that he's on a date with me? I don't even bother to hide my irritation. I let my eyebrows climb upward unchecked.

"Boy, was I wrong." He whistles. "You may be a few years older than me, but who cares? Call me Ashton, because you look even better in person. Besides, they say that forty is the new thirty."

"Tell that to my knees," I say.

His laughter is surprisingly loud. And long. He's still chuckling when they pull a yellow Lamborghini around.

"You're funny, too. I looked at this as like, I don't know, something to do. A few decent photo ops or whatever. Honestly, I wasn't too interested until my mom pressured me. She loves Lololime."

"Are you really still telling me how much you didn't want to take me out?" I finally ask.

His mouth closes with a click. "It's rude, right?" He shakes his head. "Sorry, I'm always too honest."

That's the last thing I expected from someone who posts a bunch of airbrushed photos on Instagram.

"It's not that I mind honesty," I say. "But kids these days don't seem to understand that you can be honest and also be considerate. They're not mutually exclusive."

Perry looks like I slapped him.

"Sir?" The valet gestures at the open car door.

I glance at my Lololime duffel. If he'd told me what we were doing on the date, I wouldn't have needed to pack quite as much. Or if he'd mentioned that I had to keep things to a minimum because he drove a speedy golf cart without trunk space, same.

"Don't worry." He picks up my bag again and carries it around to the front of the car.

What's he doing up there?

He presses on something and the hood of the car lifts up. Shockingly, there's no engine. He manages to stuff my bag inside—though what shape my dress will be in is anyone's guess—and returns to help me into the car.

Once we're on the road, he finally starts talking again. "Honesty, but also consideration. I swear, no one has ever said that to me."

He peppers me with questions, and within five minutes, I feel as much like a professor as I ever have before. When I reach the point that I can't handle tutoring him in dating etiquette and just how to be a good person any longer, I use my go-to conversation changer. I ask him about his job.

"What does an investment banker do, exactly?"

"Is that code for, do you have a real job?"

Actually, thanks to Paul, I already know it's a real job, and I know just what they do. But there's no point in trying to impress him. "Maybe."

"I must seem like a real idiot," he says. "First I go on and on about how happy I am that you're hot. Then I talk about my mom, while paying no attention to the basic etiquette she taught me." He shakes his head. "Then I shove your bag into my stupidly small trunk of my impractical, too bright sports car."

"I've met plenty of guys who were far, far worse," I say.

"Ouch." He pounds his chest. "Plenty, huh?" There's a boyish glint in his eye that most girls would probably love. To me, it just highlights what a kid he is, even if he does have a real job.

I whip out my phone and snap a photo of him. When he realizes what I'm doing, he tilts his head and smiles. Perfectly accentuating his jawline and the color of his eyes.

Geez. Is that what I look like?

I hate it.

"Here," I say. "Insta's still strongly preferring reels, so I'll take a few short videos, too."

"Good thinking."

An investment banker who also knows about Instagram algorithms. What's this world coming to?

"We're about to pass the Golden Gate Bridge. I'm embarrassed I didn't think of it sooner."

I roll my window down and hold my phone far enough out that we're both visible. Then I hit record. "Hey guys! It's me, Amanda, and you'll never believe where I am right now." I shift the screen a bit so it shows the Golden Gate Bridge behind us. "I've got the most amazing view." Then I pan back. "I bet you thought I meant the bridge, but check *this out.*" I focus on Perry and squeal.

Now I hate myself even more.

I say a silent prayer that Eddy doesn't check Instagram, but I know he's probably checking it incessantly. This job sucks. I tuck my phone back into my purse and look at the Golden Gate Bridge.

"Wow, you did that in one take."

"I've been doing this job for a while. It's not exactly rocket science."

"I never answered your question." Perry turns and faces straight ahead. The boyish, frolicking façade drops. His voice is almost. . .boring. "It's rare that I work less than ten hours in a day. Investment bankers essentially find companies with potential and help them locate the funds they need to go public, in a nutshell."

"What just happened?" I ask.

He glances sideways at me. "I just saw a completely different Amanda Brooks when that video came alive, and I decided that you might get it. I like work, but part of me hates the horrible, focused, almost aggressive guy I become at work. So I started my Insta page to be someone. . .different."

The rest of the date is better. *Much* better. If I didn't have the most beautiful man I've ever met waiting at home—the man who saved my dog, and me, and frankly, the man who's just what I want. . .I'd be tempted.

But after a romantic boat tour, complete with an amazing dinner and great ambiance, I ask Perry to take me back to the airport. "Really?" He looks as surprised as he sounds. "You're opting for a redeye back home?"

"I have two kids," I say. "You may have seen two different Amandas, but the real one hasn't even shown her face."

"Two kids." He whistles. "Victoria definitely didn't mention that."

"A little intense for you, Daddy?"

His eyes widen.

"I'm kidding, Perry. I knew this would go exactly nowhere, but it was a fun day, and I think we got some decent reels." I toss him my jacket. "And you can give this to your mom."

He steps toward me slowly. "I have a kid too, you know. His name is Jonathan, and he's three. You're not the only person who wears more than one hat."

Touché.

He slides my jacket back around my shoulders. "And my mom is the last person on earth who needs more clothes. You should keep it. It suits you."

"It was nice meeting you, Perry."

"But you like someone else," he whispers.

I glance around, a little bit panicked.

"Don't worry. I won't tell."

"No, it's not that. There's not—"

He puts one hand on my arm. "I know that look, trust me. If I hadn't recognized it early on, I'd have been a little more persistent. You don't owe me any kind of explanation, and I don't expect one. But as it is, I'll just say that if things go south, you should shoot me a message." Before I can stop him, he presses a kiss against my forehead. "Take care, Amanda."

He hands me my bag.

I'm a little dazed as I walk toward the ticketing counter, but I still recognize when someone says my name. "Amanda."

I turn.

Perry's grinning his surfer-boy-California-laid-back grin. "It wasn't a complete waste, you know."

"What wasn't?"

"This date." He smiles. "I try to learn something new every day, and. . .well. Kindness and honesty can coexist. That's my lesson for today."

He really was somewhat cute. Maybe I'll muddle my way through these just fine after all.

I have to run, but I manage to *just* make the last flight of the day. I call Eddy as I'm getting on the plane. "It wasn't so bad," I say. "I mean, it wasn't a love connection, but he wasn't a total creep either."

"I'm not sure I love that," Eddy says. "It sounds like you're compiling a fallback list."

I laugh. "Maybe I should."

"You won't need one," he says. "I've made my mistakes. That's the benefit of age—I know what not to do already. That kid's too late."

"Don't wait up for me." I won't get in until early morning, by the time this lands and I drive back to Manila. "I'll be completely fine, and you have patients tomorrow."

"I do have a lot of teeth to float," he says.

"Float?"

"I'll explain it later. Baby steps," he says.

I'm smiling when I hang up. I manage to get a nap on the flight, so I'm even in a reasonably good mood when I finally get home. Roscoe's sleeping in front of the door on the porch when I get there—and I shake my head. "Who let you stay out here all night? It's too cold for you, so someone's in big trouble."

I didn't think about how hard my leaving might be on my poor sweet boy. Maybe I should insist that the others come to me every time. There may not be much to do, but I can't have my little guy getting all stressed out.

He sticks to my side like a burr when I breeze through the door. It's four-thirty in the morning, so the last person I expect to see awake is Maren.

"What in the world are you doing?"

She presses a button on the oven and the light clicks off. "Your job." She crosses her arms. "I don't even like to bake."

"Excuse me?"

"A big order came in online last night," she says.

"The shop was closed," I say. "You should have simply declined it."

"You can't decline orders," Maren says. "The website isn't set up like that. They placed the order at full retail, for a hundred and eighty cookies, for pickup tomorrow."

"Tomorrow?"

Maren glances at the clock. "Well, now it's today."

"Oh, no. I'm so sorry," I say. "Well, I'll call them."

"We made them already." Maren yawns. "Me and Emery and Whitney and Izzy and Abby."

But Maren's the only one still awake.

"Why are you—"

"I was supposed to package them," she mutters. "I promised I would, but then I fell asleep, and Roscoe ate some of them."

Oh, no. "Is he—"

"That's why he was outside. He got an upset stomach and he's been going to the bathroom every five minutes."

"Maren."

"And I had to remake them." A single tear streaks down her cheek. "Luckily, no one could hear me, but they aren't very good."

I glance behind her at the sheets of misshapen cookies. "It's fine. Listen—"

"No, you listen." Her lip curls, and her eyes harden. "You aren't a baker. That's Aunt Abigail. You're not a hands-on mom, either. That's her, too. You're good at taking photos—that's it. So quit doing this stupid cookie thing."

"Maren, I know that with me gone—"

"No, you don't know. Everyone else sees it, but not you."

"Sees what?" I'm trying not to get too upset. We're both

tired, and she's a teenager. She has no perspective on life. That's why she's being so rude.

"You're a joke," Maren says. "And you're turning us into jokes, too. I wish you'd just give it up already." She shakes her head, spins on her back foot, and ducks into her room.

I'm too upset to sleep, so I bake two more batches of cookies to replace the ones that she tried to make. Mine are better, but not by much. Or maybe the problem was all the crying I did while making them.

Because teenager or not, I'm afraid she's right.

I am a joke.

And I was the only one who didn't know it.

7

ABIGAIL

My brain is a strange place. For years, I've woken up before my alarm goes off. It's not that I always wake up at the same time, either. But if I set my alarm for six a.m., something inside my brain just knows around what time it is. I'll wake up at five fifty-one. Or five forty-six.

I can't explain it.

It's strange.

When I set my alarm last night for five forty-five this morning, it was so that I could get a head start on a brief that Stephen asked for last week. I've been putting it off, but I need to get it done. When I wake up three minutes before my alarm was set to sound, it doesn't even occur to me that it might be due to a strange sound. I figured it was just more of the bizarre workings inside my head.

But I smell something odd—cookies baking. That's my first sign. And then I hear the clicking of toenails on tile.

That's Roscoe.

I remember that Maren insisted on being the one who stayed up to finish packing up the cookies. She so rarely offers to do things for others that I didn't argue with her. I figured her mom would be touched. And in general, I try never to shut down kind impulses, either my own or those of others.

But if she's still working right now. . .I made a mistake. There's no school today, but she still needs to function. No business thing, however new, justifies endangering her health. As I slide into my slippers, I consider what I'll say to Amanda. She left me to manage things during her trip, and I let her down. I'll owe her an apology. I should have sent Maren to bed and finished the cookies myself.

When I open the door, it's not Maren in the kitchen.

It's Amanda.

And she's bawling.

I don't think—I just move, jogging across the space separating us. I hug her and say, "Hey, it's okay."

"No," she sobs. "It's not."

I pat her back. "What's so wrong?"

"Do you think I'm a joke?" she asks. "Does everyone think I'm pathetic?"

I literally have no idea what's going on. "Pathetic?"

"Yes," she practically shouts. "Pathetic." She stumbles backward until she bumps up against the back counter. "Are you all just laughing at me?"

I can't keep up. "Why would anyone be laughing at you, Amanda?" I swallow. "Did the date go really badly? Did that jerk post something on his Instagram account?" I should have checked social media last night, clearly. We all got a little caught up in making the cookies for that huge order.

I actually thought she'd be thanking us, not having a breakdown.

"No, not the date." She clenches her hands and exhales. She looks absolutely exhausted. Usually she looks perfectly put together, but dark circles under her eyes and mascara flakes make her look a bit like a frustrated raccoon.

That thought makes me smile.

Which was a big mistake. "So you do think it's funny, that I'm out parading around town, flirting like a twenty-something in my forties." She drops her head in her hands. "Pretending to be you by making cookies, but failing utterly."

What in the world? Pretending to be me?

"I know what you were all thinking while you stayed up late, picking up my slack. Again."

It's taking up my slack, but I don't point that out. I cross the space between us and take her by her shoulders. "You're exhausted, and I think you might have lost a bit of perspective. You need to sleep, and we can talk afterward."

"Do you even care what people think about you?" Her eyes are wide—crazy, almost. She really is hopping around this morning.

"Do I care what people think?" She seems deadly earnest, so I think about the question. "I do, of course. I think everyone does. But mostly, I know who I am and what I want, so if people are unhappy with my decisions, that's their problem. Is that what you're asking?"

"That's as close to a no as I could imagine anyone giving," she says. "Of course it is."

"What's going on?" I hate being confused like this, but seeing her so upset is even worse. I have no idea how to help, because I have no idea what caused her distress.

"Maren was up when I got home."

"I'm so sorry about that," I say quickly. "I didn't realize how late she'd be up when she offered—"

"Don't apologize!" Now she's shouting.

Ethan shoots out of the door to the room he shares with Gabe, pulling one sock on his foot. "Is everything okay? Sorry I slept in."

"It's fine," I say. "Nothing's wrong." I glare pointedly at Amanda. The last thing I intend to do is drag my kids into her hysteria. "Amanda and I were just going to look over some color choices we have to make, but we can go do it in my room."

Ethan compresses his lips, clearly not buying it, but thankfully, he's also unwilling to contradict me. "Okay."

"Go ahead and grab something to eat before you go feed the animals." I march toward my door and glance over my shoulder at Amanda. She snaps for Roscoe to follow—presumably so he doesn't eat any more of the cookies we all worked so hard to make.

"Wake Izzy," I say before closing the door. "Tell her to go ahead and wrap up the rest of the cookies once they're cool."

Ethan mock-salutes. He's hilarious, but I can't just start laughing. Part of our game is that I play the straight person, the annoyed mother, so I roll my eyes at him and close the door.

"What in the world are you upset about?" I ask. "I've about lost my patience with the histrionics."

Amanda sits on the edge of my bed and looks at her hands. "Maren was awake when I came home, and she told me everyone thinks I'm pathetic and I should just quit the cookie thing entirely."

I sit next to her. "You can't listen to a thing a teenager says, especially at three in the morning or whatever ungodly hour you got back."

"What?" Amanda's tear streaked face turns toward me.

"Teenagers are slaves to their emotions. When they're angry, they shout or punch something. When they're sad, they actually think they're dying. When they're happy, they dance. Their filters haven't grown in yet—and we haven't had enough time to teach them how to responsibly react." I pause for her to assimilate what I'm saying. "But think about it, Amanda. She volunteered to stay up and help because she's proud of you. So what do you think she might be masking by yelling at you?"

"Masking?" Amanda's shoulders slump. "You think it wasn't about me at all?'

I shrug. "It might be about you. She could be upset about something else." I think about the piles of overcooked and misshapen cookies I saw on the corner of the counter. "She could be embarrassed that she tried to do something nice for you and messed it up. Or maybe it's something else. Maybe something's wrong at school and she's feeling pathetic herself, but I really think it's less about you and more about her."

"Are you secretly Dr. Phil?" Amanda glares at me.

"Are you a teenager?" I joke. "Now you're putting your irritation off on me. But you haven't slept, so I'll give you a pass." I pat her knee. "Look, parenting is rough on all of us. Being a teenager is rough on all of them. Losing parents and moving, all of that adds stress. We need to give a little more grace than we are. All of us do."

"You're so annoying sometimes." But she leans her head against my shoulder and closes her eyes.

"I love you, too."

She starts to cry then. "The difference is that I really *am* pathetic, whereas you're always put together."

"I am most certainly not," I confess. "I cry alone, most of the time, but I still cry. I'm not doing very well right now."

Amanda sits up and turns to face me squarely. "Really?"

I sigh. "This is me, falling apart."

"I hate you."

I laugh. "I may look about the same externally, but I'm a wreck inside, trust me. Steve's got his wife living with him. In a few hours, the results of the paternity test Steve and Olivia took yesterday should be available." I shake my head. "This afternoon we have the mediation with the alien foundation. If we can't agree on something, we'll have to wait and see what a judge has to say about things, and I'm afraid that the terms of the will don't support us."

"And it's all on you—the will and the ranch stuff, anyway." Amanda sighs. "I'd be eating my hair."

I laugh. "I'm glad you're here. I don't think you're pathetic. I think you're a little less armored than I am, and I admire that."

"Armored?"

"I never let people see when I'm struggling, and that means no one offers help. It's not a very healthy way to live, honestly."

Amanda blinks. "Huh. I'd never thought of it that way." She straightens. "But look, I don't look like it right now, but I am capable, I swear. If you need help, please tell me." Then her mouth opens a bit. "Actually, maybe that was your way of saying you did need help. Was it?"

I can't help laughing again. "Amanda." I shake my head. "No. There's nothing you can do about Steve's ex, and I doubt you could take over for the mediation. But if I think of something, I'll let you know."

She nods slowly.

"For now, I think you should get some sleep. When you wake up, see if you can figure out what Maren's really upset about. My guess is that very little of it has to do with your cookie shop."

"I'm supposed to be at this mediation, right?" Amanda gulps. "I have no idea what to wear, and even less idea what to say."

"Honestly, I'd love it if you came. If you can't, I understand. But I don't see what we will possibly accomplish. They're going to want a cash payment, and I'm not going to offer one. For me, we either get the ranch free and clear per Jed's will, or we don't get it at all, because the court pries it away and gives it to them."

She frowns. "Do you think that's likely?"

"We left for a long time," I say. "I think it's a coin toss. Jed wasn't one hundred percent clear—which I think works in our favor? But he did outline a week when he mentions leaving the ranch, and that's not promising."

"Mediation is. . .what is it exactly?"

"We basically go sit in a room with a paid lawyer, and he or she tries to convince each of us to take less than we want. It works a lot on divorces where people are being unreasonable or with custody arrangements. It even works pretty often with contract disputes, but in cases like this? I think it's just a waste of time."

"That's depressing," Amanda says. "I can't imagine Uncle Jed really wanted things to go like this."

"Probably not," I say. "But he's the one who drew up that will, and for better or worse, it's essentially a contract that we're all obligated to follow."

"I should have one of those, I guess." Amanda groans. "Not that I have much to give Maren or Emery." She freezes then, and turns to face me slowly. "This is going to sound a little crazy, but if I do die. . ."

"I'd be happy to draw up a will for you," I say. "I don't think that's crazy at all."

"No," Amanda says. "I mean, yes, that would be great. But what I wanted to ask was. . ." She licks her lips, and then slowly looks right at me. "Would you be their guardian? I can't think of anyone who would do better than you."

I'm not even related to them. I don't say that, of course, but I wonder whether she's really thought this through. "You have siblings," I say, "and parents who are still alive."

Amanda nods. "I know, I really do. But my parents—they're a mess. It's a miracle I'm as high functioning as I am, I swear. And my brothers." She sighs. "They can barely take care of themselves."

"I don't think it's going to be an issue. I'm sure you're

going to wind up marrying again before too long. Then you won't need me as a fallback anymore."

"Let's hope I pick better this time around."

"Was Paul really that bad?" I've been afraid to ask, but I've always wondered whether he could really be that different than Nate.

Amanda flops backward on the bed. "I suppose it depends on what you consider 'bad.' He and I weren't in love, and I'm not sure he *could* love another person. He was much more enamored with his own importance and with making a fortune. I always felt like. . .a necessary accessory to the lifestyle he wanted."

"Did he ever cheat on you?" If I'm crossing a line, I may as well really cross it.

"I'm not sure." Amanda shrugs. "As bad as this sounds, I don't think I'd even have been upset. But he was too careful for me to have ever found out if he had. He was meticulous and affairs are messy. He'd have been more likely to have financial accounts I didn't know about or something like that."

"Sounds hot."

She rolls her eyes. "Yeah, we were not hot and heavy alright. In fact, when Eddy and I almost—" Her eyes widen and she clamps her lips closed tightly.

What did she just almost say? "When you and Eddy. . .what?"

She shakes her head. "Nothing." Her entire face flushes bright red.

"Are you and Eddy. . .still talking?" I arch one eyebrow.

"No, of course not."

"You don't bump into him sometimes? Isn't the bakery right in front of his house?"

"I mean, I see him sometimes, and it's not like I ignore him, but we aren't talking in the way you mean it."

"Is it only Lololime that's keeping you away from him?"

"Not just that," she says. "My entire Instagram account would struggle if it came out I was dating someone like him."

"Someone like him?" I lift both eyebrows this time. "Was his past really that bad? I'd think that people could kind of understand if not entirely forgive someone for something they did as a teenager."

"You'd think that, but you'd be surprised what people aren't willing to accept."

I can't help my frown. I've known Eddy for a while—he's rushed over any time we had an emergency, kind of like Steve. He loves animals, including Roscoe, and I know he rescues animals he comes in contact with regularly. Steve has talked about it several times. "Steve thinks he's a great guy."

"He really is," Amanda says. "If there was something I could do to change the past, believe me. I would."

"But what if no one could ever find out—"

"Abby." Amanda's as serious as I've ever seen her. "This isn't something I need you to fix for me, okay?"

I nod, reluctantly.

"It's not even our business. It's Eddy's past, not mine."

It's kind of her business, if she's not dating the guy she likes because of it, but I don't bother arguing.

"Did you bring that up so that you didn't have to answer?" The vulnerability in her eyes is raw.

"Not at all," I say. "If you're sure that you want a will naming me as the guardian of Maren and Emery, I'll draw one up. But you should tell your family what you're doing so that there's no confusion or anger if something happens to you."

Amanda frowns. "Really?"

I nod. "These are the types of things that cause the most fights afterward, trust me. And I know it's awkward, but I would definitely inform them beforehand."

"Isn't that kind of like picking a fight for something that may never happen?"

"I'm not sure," I say. "Maybe we should ask Jed." I can't help my smirk.

"Touché," she says. "Alright. If you're willing to watch them, I suppose the least I can do is prepare the path."

"Go sleep."

She does. I manage to draft my brief, then I get some horse time in, going for a ride with the girls, and then I shower and change for the mediation. Amanda's still not awake when I prepare to leave, but I don't blame her. It's been a rough few days on all of us.

I know how adamant she was about Eddy's past being none of my business, but I can't quite help myself. I pull up my contacts and shoot off a quick email to two old friends —one detective I know from undergrad, and one friend of mine who's a circuit court judge in Sacramento. It may all amount to nothing, but every time I think about Eddy, I see the look on Amanda's face.

Naked longing.

I check the online portal one more time before sticking my paperwork in my bag, but there's no information yet. I text Steve. STILL NO WORD.

He texts back right away. OF COURSE NOT. THEY SAID 1–3 BUSINESS DAYS.

Duh. Why didn't I think of that? It's a Saturday. Gah. That means we may not hear back until early next week. How is he so relaxed about it?

I'm climbing in my van when Ethan comes jogging outside. In a suit.

"Whoa," I say. "You look sharp."

"I'm coming," he says.

I should have known he would. He's more interested in this outcome than anyone else. "Great."

He buckles.

"But make sure to keep calm. You can't be emotional at a mediation. It won't do us any good."

He nods. "Of course. I grew up with you and Dad, after all."

When I drive past Steve's farm on the way to the mediation, I notice the red car is noticeably absent, but Steve's still parked in front of the barn.

"I haven't seen him much lately," Ethan says. "Everything okay?"

"Fine." I want to tell him what's going on, but I also want to maintain Steve's privacy. However things turn out, I don't have much to share until I know the truth in any case. "I'm sure you'll see more of him soon. He's had a lot going on."

"Plus this whole ranch thing," Ethan says. "Does it stress you out that he's one of the three people on the panel?"

I'm surprised to hear him ask that. "Not at all. You?"

He shakes his head. "I don't think he's someone who would unfairly choose—"

I chuckle. "Oh, he 100 percent is. He doesn't care about the legality. He cares about justice and equity. He'll vote for us no matter what."

"What about Eddy?"

"Same," I say. "I think. Assuming he's not fighting with Amanda, that is."

Ethan grunts.

"But poor Donna."

"Oh, please." Ethan beams. "Beth says she's really cool. Plus you've done so much for her that of course she'll vote for us."

"It's not that simple," I say. "Donna's more like me."

He guffaws. "Like you? You're kidding, right? She's nothing like you. She's a secretary whose husband is going to prison."

"Neither of those things defines who a person is, and I mean that she'll do what the *law* says, and not simply pick what her friend might want. You should be glad she's like me." I glance at him. "Her brother wants us to lose the ranch."

He frowns. "Why is life so complicated?"

"I hate to say this, but it only gets tougher, kiddo."

The mediation is as big a mess as I expect. Leonard Nemoy knew Jed, and he's practically salivating over the proceeds they'll get from selling the ranch.

"It doesn't matter if you have a new person named," he says. "The law is clear. If you think a judge is going to look at all the evidence, which you aren't even arguing about, and choose to give you the ranch because your kids are cute—"

"My children's great-uncle left the ranch to them first," I say. "He stipulated that they would receive it if they came out and worked it for a year, and he established a panel that would determine whether they had achieved that goal."

"The sky is blue," Mr. Nemoy says. "And birds fly." He sighs exaggeratedly. "If we're done stating obvious facts, then let's get to the last one. You left for a month. The will states you may take week-long vacations."

We circle round and round a few times before I acknowledge we're not getting anywhere helpful. After three hours of the same thing, even the mediator throws his hands up in the air. "It appears unlikely that either of you will agree to an accommodation."

I fold my arms. "We're not going to offer a lump sum payment, no."

"We wouldn't take it even if you did," Mr. Nemoy practically spits. "We want the proceeds from the entire ranch."

"It helps that you were notified of the entire thing from an interested buyer," I say. "I hope that unfair dealing doesn't come back to bite you."

"You concealed our interest," he shouts. "How is that any better?"

"The estate lawyer, Mr. Swift, was the one with the duty to notify you, and that duty wouldn't have arisen until the bequest to us was deemed to have failed, a decision only that panel of three fact-finders could make." I shrug. "Don't worry. The complicated legal things you can't comprehend will be easy for a judge to decipher."

Ethan's fired up when we leave. "Wow, Mom. I've always known you were awesome, but that was just." He air punches a few times. "I mean, I'm not worried at all anymore."

I slide into my seat and click my seatbelt. "You should be."

"Why?" Ethan looks shocked.

"Because most of that was posturing. The judge will understand very clearly just how weak our position is."

Ethan doesn't speak the rest of the way home. Like him, I could use a pick-me-up. As we pass Steve's, I notice that the red car is still absent and I swing into the driveway. Before I can put the car in park, I notice that there are riders in the arena. Steve's holding a lunge line, and the palomino he's guiding is one I'd know anywhere.

His possible daughter, Olivia, who wasn't allowed to touch a horse last I heard, is riding Leo.

My horse.

Supposedly.

And it's probably his daughter.

Steve probably just won a big argument and is delighted to have his daughter up on horseback.

Even so, it stings that I had no idea what was going on —and that she's riding my horse. It's juvenile of me, but it's there nonetheless. I inhale deeply and bend over my phone to hide that my eyes are welling with tears. I swipe them away while my face is turned down so that Ethan won't notice.

"Looks like Steve's busy teaching a lesson." Ethan puts his hand on the door handle. "We should go see if he's almost done."

"Oh, no." I force a sigh. "I just found out that a brief I thought was due next Friday is due Monday."

"I'm grateful they let you work remotely," Ethan says, "but man, sometimes I hate your company."

Honest and open communication is key. I should probably tell Ethan what's going on. Maybe he'll have good insight. Or maybe he'll just be a shoulder to cry on. But that's not fair to him. He's a teenager and life is hard enough for him already. He can't be expected to deal with my stuff, too.

Sometimes, you just need a decent lie to get through the day in one piece.

"Totally," I say. "This job is the worst."

8
DONNA

Hangovers are the worst.

"Donna!" My dad's bellows are increasing in volume.

Maybe hangovers are the second worst. Dealing with aging parents who suffer from dementia is the actual worst.

"I'm coming, Dad."

And of course, as if he knows I was out late and he wants to punish me, I have a disgusting diaper to change. Not that there are lovely diapers to change when you're dealing with an adult. I stupidly thought, when I potty trained Aiden, that I was done with diapers. Compared to horse manure and even cow manure, I always thought baby's diapers smelled terrible. I really had no clue.

The smell, oh, the smell.

We're clearly not paying the nurses who help out nearly enough.

I'm washing my hands when my phone starts to buzz in my pocket. I miss the call, but I'm not too worried since I wasn't expecting any calls. When I check it, it's not a number I know. I'm in the middle of feeding Dad dinner—

and I can't help thinking that I'm just reloading—when a voicemail notification chimes.

Before I can check my voicemail, Dad's yelling again. I keep my focus on him until his entire meal is consumed. "See? That wasn't so bad."

Dad frowns. "Wonder if you'd say that if you were being fed like a child."

"Your hands shake too much," I say. "We feed you for your own good." I don't add that I don't want to feed him even more than he doesn't want to be fed. It hardly seems helpful.

"Why are you even here?" He blinks and looks around the room. "Why am I here? Where are we in this run-down old house?"

Not this, again.

The next step is always aggressive behavior, so I brace myself. He's about to start yelling and throwing things, which is even worse than the diapers. I'm glad it's not the nurse dealing with this—I don't want to lose another one—but I hate days like this. He's lucid enough to get angry, but not aware enough to really understand any logic or reasoning I try to apply.

"Donna Windsor." He stares at me intently, his brow furrowed.

That's new. Sometimes he remembers my name, usually not, but he almost never calls me Windsor. My marriage happened only a few years before his mental acuity started to slip, and if he knows me, it's usually as his young and incompetent daughter, Donna Ellingson.

"Yes, Dad. It's me."

"You're taking care of me?" He looks confused. "Why are we out here, in the old farmhouse?"

"Patrick's living in the big house now, Dad."

"Where's Charles?" He looks around like my husband

might leap out from behind a lamp or crawl out from underneath the bed.

"He's in California, Dad." I almost say that he's with Aiden, but I've learned never to mention any people he hasn't brought up himself. Dad was never a very reserved or cautious person, and he always covered his ignorance or fear with anger. It hasn't made for a very peaceful descent into memory loss, not for any of us.

These are the only days when I'm happy that Mom died first. This would have been horrible for her.

"California's the worst state in the entire country." That, at least, is a familiar sentiment for him.

"It sure is," I say. "The absolute worst."

"You went there for school." He frowns. "Your judgment has always been bad. That's why you married that horrible man."

I can't argue with him there, either. In a bizarre twist, I actually find myself agreeing with my dad. "Yeah. It was a big mistake."

"You should divorce him," he says.

"I probably should, yes."

"But you won't do it. You've always been the only thing worse than Charles. Useless. A complete waste of talent and intelligence."

"You think I'm talented and intelligent?" You have to learn to take your wins with my dad.

He laughs, but it's not delightful. It's ugly. "Is that what you heard, wax ears?" He leans toward me. "You're not talented or smart. You just inherited my talent. My intelligence. It was all wasted with you."

That's more along the lines of what I've come to expect.

"That expensive school was the biggest waste of money and time. You got our hopes up, you know. Then you did what you do best, and let us down."

That actually stings.

"Now you're a terrible wife and mother, and you can't even get rid of that lousy excuse for a husband."

"Actually, our final divorce hearing is next week."

"So you failed at your marriage, too." He starts coughing and it takes a good five minutes to get him calmed down. Once he finally settles down, I pull a blanket up to his chest. "Who are you?" He's scowling heartily. "Turn on *Wheel of Fortune*."

It's a good thing Netflix has some seasons that can be streamed, or I'd never get a break at all. Once I get Dad occupied and settled down, I sneak out with great relief.

But his words aren't as easy to ignore.

Failed marriage.

Failed education.

He doesn't know this one, but I couldn't even get my crook of a husband locked up.

And now I'm about to have to fight just to keep custody of our son.

What if I can't win that fight either? Is Dad right? Am I the failure he thinks I am? I wipe away the tears rolling down my cheeks. What good will sitting around bawling do me?

I remember the voicemail. Part of me wants to ignore it, but in my experience, ignoring something almost never makes it go away. I snatch my phone off the end table and open up the voicemail, and then I press play on the message. The voice that blares out of my tinny cellphone speaker is not one I expected to hear. "Donna." It's deep. It's resonant. It's rich. "It's Will Earl. I just wanted to make sure you're alright today. Also, somehow I have one of your shoes. Call me."

He has one of my shoes? Why on earth would he have one of my shoes?

I think about last night. I went out for a drink or two and then came home. Since I rarely drink, the two or so drinks that I had were too many and things are a little fuzzy. I guess I'm lucky I made it home safely.

Actually, now that I think about it. . .how did I get home? I don't even remember driving back. That's horrifying. I rush to the front door and look outside.

My car isn't in the driveway.

He said he has my shoe. Does he also have my *car*? And why on earth does Will Earl have either of those things? I want to crawl under a comforter and watch Wheel of Fortune and forget about everything.

How much did I drink, that I don't even remember seeing Will? How am I supposed to call him up, act nonchalant, and ask where my *car is*? Why in the world did I think drinking would improve my life?

Because Charles took Aiden.

And he's trying to take him away from me. And then I'll have nothing at all. I'll be exactly who my dad says that I am.

A failure.

At everything.

But doing nothing solves nothing. I need to call Will back. My finger hovers over the keys. My hand's shaking almost as much as my dad's has been. I need to hit talk, but I can't bring myself to do it.

Maybe if I see a photo of Will, that will help me remember that he's just an old friend. He's someone I can call easily. We go way back. It's fine. I'm seized by a desperate desire to see his face—a yearbook. That would have a photo of him. It's not current, but it's something.

I race to my closet and start digging through boxes. Most of them are mine—things I hauled back here when I left California. But some of them are things that Mom left behind when she passed. I keep meaning to sort through it, but even harder than dealing with Dad is processing Mom's death. She was fine one moment, and then she was gone.

It happened in a moment.

A blink of an eye.

Then I see it—a stack of yearbooks in the very back, at the bottom of a pile of shoeboxes. Luckily, the years are etched on the spines. I pick the one from our Senior year and grab it with my fingernails. It takes some patient tugging, but finally, I get a good grip on it and I pull.

It slides out, but unfortunately, the entire pile of junk precariously perched on top also tumbles to the ground. It takes me nearly ten minutes to pick up all the stuff I dislodged and stuff it back in boxes. When I restack them, I try to do it more neatly so that this won't happen again.

The last stack of papers I grab isn't like the others. They aren't business papers. They aren't old school assignments. They aren't tax returns.

They're letters from my mom.

For a second, my heart skips a beat. Since the moment she died, I've longed for a letter from beyond the grave. Did my mom write me letters she never mailed?

But like everything in my life, my hopes are quickly squashed. They aren't to me. Of course they aren't. They were letters she sent to my Aunt Catrina. She died two years before Mom, so I'm guessing her kids must have sent the letters to Dad in hopes of consoling him or something.

I'm shoving them into the last box when a word catches my eye.

My own name.

Donna.

What did Mom write about me?

D*ear Catrina,*

. . .

Patrick is after me to sign up for email again. That boy will never understand the solace I find in putting ink on paper. Besides. Email only works if my ancient sister also decides to sign up, and you and I both know that's never going to happen.

I hope your reflux has improved. It sounds awful.

I start skimming here. I don't need to know about Aunt Catrina's miseries related to aging. But then I see it—my name.

Thanks for asking after Donna. I feel like, now that she's moved out and had a child of her own, she's so often overlooked.

I tear up, then, and have to stop reading for a moment. My mom knew. No one else may have noticed, but my mother knew just how I felt.

Overlooked.

Irrelevant.

I wonder if she ever felt the same way.

To me, the hardest part of being a woman is that you're jammed into a category. Are you a career woman? Or a mother? Are you nurturing, or are you ambitious? Why isn't there room for both?

My darling Donna has always been the most beautiful balance. She's nurturing and kind, placing the future of her precious son on top of everything else. But underneath all that fierce motherly energy, I still see flashes of her brilliance and her ambition. Once

Aiden's older, once she has more time, I know she'll find it again, her own brilliance.

I feel, sometimes, though it may not be my place to say it, that her husband masks her talent to make sure he gets all the attention. Does that sound insane? He's like a toddler who runs around the room, insisting everyone look only at him. I know Donna loves him, and I know she chose him, but I can't help wishing that she had chosen someone who helped her shine instead of dulling her beauty so he can be the focus.

But when I start to fret, I always come back to the same thing. More than everything else, Donna is resilient. When Vern would hurt us, when Patrick taunted her, when kids at school mocked her, Donna would brush it off. When things went wrong for other people, they surrendered, but she never surrenders. She always keeps fighting.

Donna brushes off the bad things that happen in her life and soldiers on.

That's the reason I don't worry about her future. If I could have picked just one trait to make sure she lives a good life, it would be that. Resilience. And she has it—more so than anyone else I've met. I only hope that she won't need it quite as much as I fear she might.

I can't read any more. I'm bawling too hard.

Ah, Mom. How I miss you. How I needed to read your words. I wonder, sometimes, if we aren't more honest with other people than we are with our loved ones. Why didn't my mom ever say any of that to me?

I pick up the phone, and this time, my hands don't tremble at all when I dial. "Hello?"

"Donna?" Abby sounds surprised to hear from me.

"Is this a bad time?"

Abby's laugh is almost bitter. "There's no good time for me lately, it seems. What can I do?"

"I need help." I break down and start to cry again. "I'm so sorry to make things worse, but I really need help."

"I'll be right over," Abby says.

And she shows up not long after. She convinces Beth to sit with my dad, and we drive over to fetch my car. She talks about my options with custody and the divorce the entire time, and by the end I feel a lot better.

I may have a war looming ahead, but my mom was right. I'm not perfect, but I'm resilient.

And I'm not alone, not anymore. I may soldier on, but I've befriended a General whom I trust to lead the attack.

9

AMANDA

When Abby's around, it feels like everything will be fine.

But she's not my personal assistant or my bouncer, sadly. She has her own life to live, which means I have to do all the things she suggests. . . on my own. The one thing I can always be relied upon to do is botch things up, as it turns out.

First, I sleep so long that I miss the mediation. Apparently it does not go well. Then, by the time I find Maren, she's not interested in talking.

"How's school?" I ask.

"Fine, for a podunk school in the middle of nowhere."

"Are you making some friends?"

"I coordinated the pickup for the order we filled yesterday," Maren says. "They paid in full—and they seemed happy with the cookies."

"That's great," I say, "but right now I'm worried about you."

"You're worried about me?" She tilts her head. "That's rich."

"You're a teenager in a new place," I say. "I thought maybe you—"

"I was made cheer captain eleven minutes after arriving here." She's picking at her nails. "Even here, even without manicures, without hair salons around, without any decent shopping within five hundred miles of where we live, I'm still the uncontested queen of the school. Why would you worry about me?" She looks up and meets my eyes. "I think you should stop worrying about me and start worrying about yourself."

Either Abby was wrong and she really does think I'm pathetic, or she's not an easy nut to crack. Whichever option is correct, I'm not sure how much more of a beating I can take from my poor, delicate, suffering daughter today. "Great. Well, glad we could have this chat."

"And Mom?"

"Yes, Maren?"

"Please just give up on the cookie thing. It really isn't your style."

"I appreciate you looking out for me." That's a lie if ever I told one. She must know that, but she doesn't say anything else.

And that's how I end up slinking away from Maren without having solved anything at all. I wonder if that's how the conversation would have gone if Abigail had been directing it. I'm sure with her horrifying powers of interrogation, Maren would have squirmed, argued, postured, and then cracked, ending with a bunch of crying and some kind of hug and apology from Maren.

I stop outside her door and rest my hand against the doorframe. "I'm sorry," I whisper. "You deserve a better mom than you got."

"That's not true." Emery's the scrawniest twelve-year-old I've ever seen, but she gives the world's best hugs.

When her bony arms wrap around me, it's exactly what I need.

I cry silently for a moment.

Emery beams up at me. "I love you, Mom. I love Aunt Abby too, but I'm glad God gave me you."

I'm such a mess.

"I get sad sometimes too, but a hug usually helps."

It does. She's right. "Can you not tell Maren—"

"Duh." Emery finally lets go. "I'm twelve, not stupid."

Izzy and Whitney are rubbing off on her. It's probably good. The old Emery would never have been so sassy. "Thank you," I say. "For being the sweetest little girl in the world."

She reaches into her pocket and pulls something out. It turns out to be a rock. "I found this today, and I was going to add it to my rock collection, but I think you should have it instead. You can call it the love rock. Whenever I'm not around and you're sad, you can just look at this. It has a red streak in it, like the color of a heart."

"Oh, that's okay," I say. "You should keep it."

"I don't want to keep it, not anymore. I want you to have it." She's beaming up at me so sweetly, that I can't bring myself to tell her I don't really want a rock.

"Uh, thanks."

There aren't many people in the world like Emery. I'm not sure whether it's because the world crushes them, or whether they just aren't made that way very often. Forget being like Abigail. I wish I could be more like Emery.

Which makes me wonder—why can't I be happy with who I already am?

I think sometimes, as women, we're hardwired never to appreciate the person we are.

"I love you, Mom."

"I love you too, princess." One more hug, and it's time for me to start making dough. Having the cookie shop closed for two days is bad enough. Even though I'm usually closed Sundays, I should open up tomorrow. An awful lot of people in Manila go to church—maybe I'll catch some of them afterward. Church leaves you hungry, right?

Turns out, not so much. Sales Sunday are even worse than they were last week. And Monday's not much better.

It's a good thing I had the one huge order while I was gone—those have been the majority of my sales this week. Even my restaurant orders for the two local eateries in town have been halved for some reason. "People just aren't eating as many," was Venetia's explanation when I asked.

But why?

Cookie shops don't make a ton of money on each item, so we really need to move a lot of volume to survive.

And I do *not* have it.

So when Victoria calls and wants to know if we can move up one of the bachelor dates, I agree. Something I hadn't contemplated when I agreed to these was that I get extra money for doing them, money I can set aside and save to float me if it takes me a while to get the cookie thing off the ground.

Money that will give me the bravery I may need to break with Lololime and actually date Eddy in the open.

"One little detail," Victoria says.

"Please don't tell me I have to travel to this guy, too," I say.

"No, no, like I said, he offered to move his date forward. He'll definitely come to you."

"Great, then what is it?" It can't be that bad, as long as I won't have to give up nearly three days again.

"The bachelor you were supposed to be seeing this week had to drop out."

Now I'm confused. "I thought you said he wanted to move it up—"

"We found a replacement! Someone eligible, and incidentally, someone you already know."

Huh? "Who?"

"Derek Bills." Victoria sounds like she's holding her breath. And she should be. Of all the filthy, underhanded. . .

"We broke up," I say.

"That's not how he explained things to me."

"When did he explain anything to you?" I ask. "No, wait, *why* was he explaining to you?"

"My husband had him over for tri-tip a few days ago." Victoria sighs. "Is this going to be a problem?"

"You sent me a list of the bachelors, and Derek wasn't on it."

"I told you. Mr. Rouse cancelled."

"But—"

"I asked him whether he was upset about the bachelor thing, and to my surprise, he didn't even know about it. He said his trip had run longer than expected, and you'd left things in a weird place. Not 'dating,' but not 'not-dating' either."

That's fair, I suppose. It's not like I told him I didn't want to see him when he came back.

"He was sitting next to me when Mr. Rouse canceled and he offered to fill in. When you think about it, it makes perfect sense. He's handsome, rich, and not at all camera shy. When I told him that some television stations were wanting longer clips, he said he'd even be fine with camera crews—"

"Absolutely not," I say. "That's out of the question."

"Fine," Victoria says. "But even you have to admit that the engagement on the posts you and Mr. Giles posted was phenomenal. We sold double the backpacks *and* jackets that day that we usually do." She lowers her voice. "Dropping the links under the post and in the stories was perfect."

"It helped that they were on sale," I say.

"Which our products so rarely are." She's almost unbearably smug.

"You're saying that tomorrow, I have to pretend not to know him?"

"Not at all." I can practically hear her smile through the phone. "We're playing this as 'the guy who's been pursuing you wanted a chance to derail the whole bachelor thing.'"

"Which he won't be allowed to do," I say.

"Of course not," she says. "Even if you two rekindle the flame—"

I cringe inside.

"—we'd still need you to proceed with your other dates. Derek knows that. He's a big boy."

Derek may be a big boy, but Eddy's not going to like this. Not in the slightest.

10

AMANDA

"You can't hide in the bushes." I cross my arms.

"Why not?" Eddy sticks out his lower lip. "It worked fine last time. Derek's a city boy. He won't even notice me."

"Just because he didn't last time doesn't mean he won't this time."

"That guy's clueless," he mutters.

"I agree," I say.

"Then why are you doing this?" The muscles in Eddy's jaw work, and he looks even hotter than usual. He paces back and forth behind my cookie shop, and even wearing his normal work clothes—cargo pants, a somewhat worn green polo shirt with the words 'Dutton DVM' embroidered on the chest, and a flannel-lined canvas jacket—he's almost unbearably handsome.

"You're not being fair," I say.

He stops pacing and stares at me. "Not fair?" His green eyes flash. "None of this is fair, and yes, I know it's all my fault."

I think about how it must feel to him. Unfair is only the

beginning of it. I step toward him and catch his hands. "Eddy."

His expression looks more agitated than I've ever seen it.

I press one hand to his sharply carved cheek, completely smooth shaven. "It doesn't matter who my date is with." I feel a half-smile tugging at my mouth. "Because I already like someone else."

"I hate that I made such stupid decisions as a kid." With his lips compressed like that, unwilling to meet my eye, he looks like a teenager. He must have been absolutely breathtaking back then. I've only seen old photos, which probably don't really do him justice.

"It's because of those decisions you didn't marry some other woman a long time ago, and you're single so you can date me," I say. "Our past brought us here, and I wouldn't change it."

"That makes one of us," he says.

I push up on my tiptoes and press my lips against his.

Eddy doesn't miss a beat—he never does. I've never met someone who likes to kiss more than Eddy. His arms wrap around me immediately, gathering me even closer. Sometimes it feels like he wants me to crawl inside him—it's a disconcerting and dizzying feeling, and I love it.

His mouth on mine makes every other thing evacuate my brain, as always. He's warm and steady and intoxicating and I never want to pull away. But my phone alarm starts going off, and it's obnoxious, and persistent, and it makes me want to smash my very expensive cell phone.

"What is that?" he asks against my mouth.

"Phone alarm," I say.

"What did you set an alarm for?" His words, more than the alarm, bring me back to myself.

"Derek will be here in half an hour, and I can't risk him

catching us together. Not after last time. He'd figure it out for sure."

"Half an hour is a long time." Eddy's eyes are devilish.

"What if he's early?" I shake my head. "We can't risk it."

"Oh, he is early," Derek says.

I leap away from Eddy, nearly falling backward on my butt. My arms pinwheel wildly until Eddy catches me, steadies me, and wraps a possessive arm around me. "So you caught us." He doesn't even sound upset. He sounds smug.

"I suppose I did," Derek says. "How long has this been going on?" He glances from Eddy to me, pausing to examine my face. "Aren't you just the consummate actress?"

I shake my head and ease out from under Eddy's arm. "After the cougar attacked me, things shifted a little."

I expect him to glower and yell and threaten. Or maybe just turn on his heel and leave. With one call to Victoria Davis, he could ruin me. Actually, no matter what happens now, I'm pretty much done with the bachelorette thing and with Lololime. I've done the one thing Victoria was very clear she won't allow.

But he doesn't do any of the things I fear.

"He saved your life and your dog." He nods slowly. "Plus it's forbidden. I get it. That all sounds pretty hot."

Eddy's the one scowling.

Derek actually looks pleased. He's wearing a black, two-button suit with a deep blue shirt that makes his grey eyes look stormy. He crosses his arms. "But Amanda, it's not real life."

I swallow. "Look, I know that now you know, you won't want to go out—"

Derek spreads his hands wide. "Now that I know what?" He shrugs. "I saw someone helping you take the trash out." He glances sideways at Eddy. "Someone you would never go out with *in public*." His smile is pure evil.

"Someone your kids and your friends and your work colleagues probably don't even know about."

Eddy growls. Honest to goodness, he sounds feral.

"I am not a back-alley, hide-me-from-your-friends date. I'm a take-me-home-to-meet-your-mama, I'm-a-great-catch guy. Which means we have no reason not to go ahead with my dinner plans."

It's like he's transformed into a totally different guy than the stomping, angry, jealous guy from before. "You're saying you still want to go out tonight?"

"I'm assuming the reason no one knows about you and this guy—" He jabs his thumb toward Eddy. "Is so that you don't lose your job. If that's the case, I imagine you'll want to continue on with the date we have planned."

I swallow.

"Great. I made us reservations at Eve's, and while it's not the finest dining in America, it is the nicest place I could find within easy driving distance of here."

"Eve's in Rock Springs?" Eddy asks.

"Oh." Derek's eyes widen. "You've been there?"

Eddy nods.

"But I'm guessing you haven't taken Amanda?"

Eddy shakes his head, his lips compressed tightly.

"Excellent. I'm sure she'll let you know what she thinks." Derek offers me his arm.

I'm not quite sure what to do here. Clearly Eddy's not okay, but Derek's right. If he's not about to out us, I need to go on this date and pretend that everything is fine.

Ultimately, I decide that Eddy may be shaking with suppressed rage, and I may be nervous he'll head for the nearest bar, but I need to have more faith in him than that. He certainly wouldn't love it if I asked him about how he's doing in front of Derek. I don't take Derek's arm, but I do walk past him and duck into the shop to grab my purse.

Eddy follows pretty closely. "I'll close up for you."

"Thanks," I say.

"If you need me," Eddy says, "text. Call. Take out a banner ad. I won't be far away."

"That's so cute. You're going to follow us out there?" Derek chuckles. "Are you worried that I can't keep her safe?"

"You're the danger that bothers me most."

"Are you sure you're not driving out there to be closer to a bar?" Derek watches Eddy as he asks, like a cat playing with a mouse.

My jaw drops.

"Don't look so shocked that I dug into the past of the guy who clearly liked the woman I was dating," Derek says. "I just didn't know quite how much of a threat he was back then."

"Enjoy your night," Eddy says, finally seeming to pull it together.

Derek's still beaming when I climb into his shiny Lexus sports car.

"I can't understand why you're not upset."

He laughs, and it's a pleasant sound. I remember from when we actually were dating. He sounds just the same as he did then—not angry, not upset, nothing. "The business world is full of people who got lucky." Derek puts the car in reverse and backs out. "You almost can't read an article in *Forbes* magazine that isn't highlighting some moron who got lucky and is now completely loaded."

I'm lost.

He pauses, his car idling in the middle of the empty main street in Manila. "I'm not one of those guys." His smile this time is confident—no, arrogant. "I do my homework, always. I puzzle things out until I know what's going on. I never make guesses. Every single move I make is calculated, and I weigh and evaluate all the risks. I couldn't quite figure out what happened with us. . .until now."

"You must not like me much," I say. "Or you'd be a lot angrier." Hopefully once he realizes that, he'll let things go.

"Oh, on the contrary. I like you a great deal more than I've liked anyone, probably ever. You're sophisticated without being boring. You're a capable mother without letting it consume you, and without being a hovering, helicoptery mess. You're clever, but not at all conceited." He puts the car into gear, finally. "And you're absolutely stunning to look at."

I'm not even sure what to say to that.

"We had a great time, and you liked me well enough, but you definitely weren't *excited* to see me. It felt like I was playing a game, but no one had taught me the rules. Finally, today, I realized there's an opponent I didn't see. I feel a little stupid for not figuring it out before, but I'm not upset. On the contrary, it's game on."

Now I'm annoyed. "I'm not a game." I glare at him. "And worse, I'm not a prize that goes to the winner."

"That's where you're wrong. The whole world is a game board. I'll admit that you're certainly not a prize, however. That would be objectification, and I'm always opposed to that." He glances my way. "Have you ever played chess?"

"Chess?"

"I'll take that as a no. In chess, the king must be protected at all costs, but the most powerful player is the queen." He pauses. "You're the queen, here. Very much a player yourself. Let's just say that I finally understand the stakes and I plan to eagerly pursue a very friendly alliance."

Oh my word, he is not understanding. "I'm dating Eddy," I say. "I *like* him."

"Do your girls know?"

"Excuse me?"

"Your daughters—Maren and Emery, right? Do they know you're dating Eddy?"

It's a simple question, but it's one I don't want to

answer. He's going to misconstrue it and think it means something it doesn't. "We decided that no one should know," I say. "It was too much of a risk."

He whistles. "So even your ball-cracking sister-in-law?" His eyebrows rise. "Abigail doesn't know either?"

I turn pointedly and look out the window.

"If he can't be a part of your life, then you aren't really dating."

"Get to the point," I say.

"I just need more time," he says. "Eventually, if you spend enough time with me, time where I'm integrated as part of your actual life, you'll see that I'm the better option."

"I have a boyfriend," I say. "I think you're the one who's not understanding."

"Someone no one knows about that you have to see in secret isn't a boyfriend," he insists. "I see this clearly, believe me."

I cross my arms. "If you keep badgering me, I'll make you take me home."

He bobs his head. "Fair enough." He runs a finger across his lips. "Not another word from me about it."

And he keeps his promise. Eve's is delicious, and he dutifully takes a dozen videos, cracking jokes, sharing food with me, smiling, and touching my hand.

"Now, I'll admit to being a bit stumped, given the location and time of year, with what to do after dinner," Derek says after the waitress brings the check.

"Oh, it's fine," I say. "You can just—"

"Ah, ah," he says. "I followed your date with Perry. You spent all day with him."

I frown.

"Most of the things to do around here are best over the summer, and during the fall, they're much better during the day. The epic Rock Springs Museum, for instance, closes at five p.m." He mock frowns. "But don't worry. I found a fun brewery where we can go have a few drinks, and I hear they have live music tonight."

"It's really not necessary—"

He leans closer and whispers. "You should take me up on it. Your boyfriend can't drink, so if things go well, this may be the last time you go out for drinks in a very long time."

I roll my eyes.

"Come on, Amanda. I'm the driver—I won't drink. But go have a few beers, and then I'll take you home."

"You won't be drinking?" I quirk one eyebrow.

He shakes his head. "I solemnly swear."

At least he won't be having fun. "And you'll make sure I don't have more than two or three?" I lift both eyebrows. "I have to work tomorrow."

"Of course." His smile is warm.

"Oh, fine." I doubt Victoria would be satisfied if I just made him drive me right back home. She's the one shelling out all the money on this campaign. "But we have to take a walk first and get some images of the bag and jacket."

"Absolutely."

With the sun setting, the images and video Derek shoots are perfect. Eddy's not going to love the ones of the two of us holding hands, but it's not nearly as bad as I thought it would be. "I still can't believe you're not going to rat me out."

"Is that really the kind of person you think I am?" Derek actually looks hurt.

"I guess not." The more I think about it, the more he reminds me of Paul. My husband was also very focused on winning, and very adept at reading the situation and turning it to his advantage. "You do remind me of my girls' dad."

Derek takes that as a compliment when he really shouldn't.

True to his word, we listen to some music, we take some videos, and I drink a few beers. He stands up right on time and walks me back to his car. That's when I realize what's missing.

He's pleasant. He's good looking. Just like with Paul, I realize that on paper I couldn't do better than Derek Bills. He would provide for me and Maren and Emery. He would take care of all our physical needs, and our photos would be enviable. Everything about him looks perfect to the entire world, but he's not what I want. It's not the secretive part of Eddy and me that makes him fun. It's not hiding our time together that makes it different.

It's just Eddy.

With him, I can't control myself. No matter how much time we have together, it's never enough. Just thinking about him makes my heart race. I *hate* that the world can't know about us. I hate that I can't hold his hand and post a photo on my Instagram account. I want to tell Emery and Maren and Abigail. I want to tell people I knew in grade school and everyone I meet in the street. I worry about other girls, even in a town where he's known everyone for years. Decades, really.

Derek's wrong when he says that he now knows the game.

Or maybe he's not *wrong*, per se. For people like Paul and Derek, love is a game.

But with me and Eddy? It's not a game. It's the air I breathe. It's what I think about when I wake up and when I go to sleep and every moment in between. Sitting in his fancy car, right next to Derek, I realize that I love Eddy Dutton.

When Derek finally pulls up in front of Double or

Nothing, my cookie shop, I immediately grab the door handle on the car.

"Thank you for letting me take you out," Derek says. "I had a great night."

"It wasn't nearly as bad as I thought it might be," I say.

"Oh, come on. It wasn't bad at all."

"You're right. It wasn't bad," I say. "But what does it say that I'd rather spend the night with Eddy doing absolutely nothing at all—or even mopping my shop—than going to an excellent dinner with you?"

Derek's cheeks flush.

"I'm not saying that to hurt your feelings," I say. "I swear that I'm not. I wasn't totally honest before, and I'm so sorry about that. Now that you know, I want to make sure I'm transparent." I soften my tone. "I think you're a great guy, Derek. You're just not the right guy *for me.*"

"It's a credit to you that you're unwilling to even consider me," he says. "It only makes me like you more."

I sigh. They really should teach a class in high school, *No Means No.* He's not the first guy I've encountered who just doesn't get it. "Derek."

He leans back in the driver's seat. "I didn't want to do this."

"Do what?" I'm immediately nervous. Is he changing his mind? "You're going to tell Victoria?"

He shakes his head. "Please. I'm not that pathetic." He sighs. "But I will exercise my termination right on the cattle contract. . .unless you agree to another date." He squares his shoulders. "Actually, I need one a week, for the next month."

"You must be kidding me."

"A measly four dates—four evenings of your life. That's all." He shakes his head. "I can tell from the look on your face that you're appalled, but I'm a businessman. We always use any leverage we have. It's kind of our thing, and I firmly believe that all I need is more time with you to convince you that I'm a good option."

I close my fists so tightly that my nails dig into my palms. "You're wrong. I love Eddy."

The atmosphere in the car turns frosty. "You don't know what you think."

"I do," I say.

"My position stands. If you don't text me by three p.m. tomorrow, I'll assume you're refusing, and I'll have my office drop a termination letter."

"You're going to torch a business deal if I don't go out with you? That really doesn't seem gross to you?"

"All you have to do to keep things in place, an advantageous contract I agreed to because I liked you, is agree to go on a few dates with me."

I open the door and practically leap out. Another decent night, ruined entirely. I hate that I realized how I feel about Eddy on the same night I had to go on a date with *this* guy. It feels like dropping a piece of perfect cheesecake in the dirt. "Good night, Derek." I slam the door closed.

Eddy's waiting in my cookie shop, and when he drops his hands on my shoulders, it feels like coming home.

But when he asks how it went, I lie. "It was fine," I say.

"Really?" His beautiful grass-green eyes search my face.

"Of course." I roll my eyes. "As if I can't handle someone like Derek. Please."

"You're sure?"

I nod.

Eddy hugs me then. "Thank goodness—and now it's done, you won't have to see him again, right?"

"Mhm," I say.

"That guy gives me the creeps," he says. "I don't even think it's just because he likes you so much."

"He's not that bad," I lie. "Really."

"Do you think he was right about us?" Eddy's voice is the most unsure I've ever heard it. "Do you only like me because it's exciting to keep things hidden?" He sounds like a little boy, worried about whether he'll get ice cream after dinner if he doesn't eat all his peas.

I pull back far enough to see his gorgeous face, and I realize it's not even his absurd beauty and drool-worthy body that make me like him. In fact, they might be a little too much. If we went public, I'm sure the general consensus would be that he's too hot for me. Unlike most people, those comments aren't made behind my back where I won't have to hear. No, they'll be posted front and center on my account where I'm forced to see that no one thinks I'm good looking enough to be with him.

So it's not his outlandish good looks that draw me to him. Or at least, not entirely.

The reason I adore Eddy so much is his boyish eagerness. He's liked me from day one with the total abandon of a kid experiencing first love.

Which makes me wonder.

"I know you joke around a lot," I say, "but have you ever loved anyone, Eddy?"

He goes entirely still. "Loved?"

"I'm not asking if you love me," I say. "I'm asking, seriously, if you've ever loved a past girlfriend."

He swallows slowly, and then shakes his head. "I know that makes me sound pretty bad."

"It's a little odd, given our age," I say.

"I suppose, living out here, it's been easy to hide from the world, but hiding didn't give me a lot of chances to fall in love." He frowns. "But I can. I know I can. Don't give up on me, okay? Not yet, anyway."

He *can*, which means he *hasn't* yet. That's good information for me to have.

It's as easy as breathing to reassure him that I'm

nowhere near giving up on us. Not yet, anyway. When he walks me to my car, he's smiling.

"What's that smirk for?"

"I thought, when I first saw him, that Derek was a viper," he says.

"What?" Sometimes Eddy still surprises me. "Really?"

"Turns out, he's a toothless one. I can't believe he really didn't try anything else."

"Yep, total relief, right?" I suppress my groan and climb into my car.

But the second I get home, Abby's waiting. "How'd it go?" She looks stupidly hopeful.

"Not great," I say.

"What?" Her shoulders slump and her elbows drop to the counter. "Really? I liked Derek. I thought you did, too. I figured it might be like an encore—a lot of clapping and smiling all around." She wiggles her eyebrows.

I open my mouth to tell her about Eddy—but I can't bring myself to do it. Not yet. "Actually, when I told him that I wasn't interested in dating him anymore, he threatened me."

Her jaw drops and hangs there, dangling open, stupidly. I've never seen Abby look stupid in the entire time I've known her, until right now.

"Abby?"

"He *threatened you*?" Her mouth clicks shut and fierce anger replaces shock. "How? Because I will end him."

"Not physical danger," I say. "He said that he'll exercise the voluntary termination clause in the agreement if I don't agree to date him—four more dates. One a week for the next thirty days or something like that."

"You're kidding me." She blinks. "That's sexual harassment. That's—"

"Is there a voluntary termination clause in the contract?"

She blinks. "A reciprocal one, though it has a penalty. But if he's telling you that if you don't date him that he'll terminate, that's not voluntary. That's purposeful, and it's definitely bad faith."

And if we claim that, he'll out Eddy. I'm positive of it. There's no way someone like Derek would make a threat like that without the leverage to protect himself. Or maybe leverage isn't the right word to use. I am sick of this. It's *so* not my forté.

I sigh. "I don't want to have to testify, Abby. How bad would it be if he did terminate?"

She sinks onto a kitchen chair. "Bad. I mean, not like epic. We could take the cows to auction and get close to what he offered, I guess. Not quite that high, but something."

"It's where we'd have been without him signing that agreement with us earlier, right?"

"How's he going to find cows that meet with his stupid requirements if he cancels on us?" She stands up and starts pacing.

Why do all the important people in my life pace?

"I mean, this will hurt him as much as it hurts us."

"Oh, I'm sure he has a fallback plan and then another, second fallback." If he really is like Paul, canceling might even help him in some way. Maybe he already found someone to provide them with cows at a lower price.

"I think we should push back hard," Abigail says. "I can prepare an affidavit tonight, and even before he dares send a termination, we should email that to him." She crosses her arms.

I can't tell her why I can't fight it. I love Abby, but sometimes her incessant need to win everything is tiring. "Can't you ever let anything go?" I ask. "Does every single part of your life have to be a fight?"

Abby blinks. "You want to just. . .let him terminate it?"

I sit down and drop my head on my hands. "I'm tired, Abby."

"I know the shop and the dates and stuff have been a lot, but as women, we can't just let men—"

"Abby." I sit up and glare at her. "Please let it go."

"Aren't you worried about your daughters?" She sits next to me, her expression earnest, eager even. "We can't let men treat us this way. We have to show them that we have teeth."

I slam my hand down on the table. "Maybe your daughters need to see that. Mine are fine—Maren's doing better than I am, in fact. She's queen bee here, just like she was at home, and she uses her teeth plenty often. Maybe too often."

"But—"

"No buts," I say. "Spend all that manic energy trying to help your girls and leave my family alone for once."

Abby flinches.

"Maren's fine?" Izzy exits the bathroom and flips the light off. "Really?"

Both of us startle. Clearly we had no idea she was awake.

"I think you might want to check your facts there, Aunt Mandy." She arches her eyebrow just like her mom does and puts one hand on her hip.

What is she talking about?

"Your daughter's the most hated person at our school." She tilts her head. "Still sure my mom doesn't need to teach her anything?" She turns on her heel and ducks into her room.

This time, it's me who flinches.

11
ABIGAIL

Unlike Amanda, I'm not completely shocked by Izzy's statement. Judging by how early Amanda's out the door the next morning, I'm guessing she's not quite sure what to do about it.

I am surprised when Maren wakes up minutes after her mother leaves and sits down across from me at the kitchen table.

"Are you hungry?" I ask. "I've got—"

"Can I ask you something?"

I don't point out that she just did, even though it's kind of a pet peeve of mine. "Of course." It doesn't feel like the right time.

Maren looks down at her fingernails, picking at them dutifully.

"Maren?"

She freezes, but doesn't look up.

"Ethan's already left, as has your mother. The other kids won't be up for another ten or twenty minutes. You can ask me anything." Even if I think this conversation should probably be happening with her mother. Why did Amanda run away? Sometimes I want to shake her.

"Do you care whether people like you?"

Izzy's words replay in my brain on repeat. *Your daughter is the most hated person at our school.* I need to proceed with extreme caution. What is she actually asking? She cares a great deal, clearly, but she probably wishes she didn't. That means she's hurting.

I sigh. "I do, and I don't."

"What does that mean?" She glances up and then drops her eyes right back down to her fingers.

"I care a great deal what some people think," I say. "For instance, I care what my boss thinks. That determines the prospects I'll have at my job and the safety of my family. I also care what my children think. If they don't have faith in me, they'll be scared or nervous about their future. If they don't respect me, they won't feel comfortable asking me for advice."

"What about everyone else? People who aren't your kids or your boss?"

I lean a little closer. "I think everyone on earth is hard-wired to care what people think of them, at least to some degree. We're human, and humans are social. But I try not to let their opinion be a guiding light with regard to my actions. At the end of the day, what they think doesn't impact my life nearly as much as other things. When I have to choose whose good opinion to seek, I put theirs last. Does that help?"

Her nostrils flare. "Sort of."

"Maren, if you have something else to ask—"

My fierce little niece, the confident, self-assured cheerleading debutante of New York City, bursts into tears. Her lean, athletic body shakes.

"Oh, no." I stand immediately and circle around behind her. If it were my kid, I'd already have pulled her in for a hug, but I'm not sure what to do with her. She's not the most affectionate child—actually she's close to the least affectionate child I know.

Before I can worry any more, she spins in her chair and wraps her arms around my waist, bawling against the waistband of my jeans.

Parenting should come with a manual.

You'd think after *thousands* of years, humanity would have some answers to basic things, like when to let someone cry, and when to encourage them to get it together. Unfortunately, the one universal answer we've been able to come up with is, "Don't shake a baby."

It's a start, I guess, but it's not very inspirational. And it's utterly useless once they're almost grown.

I think if I had to write a handbook, my first and foremost instruction would be, let children feel their feelings. Anger, grief, delight, fear, anxiety. We're so quick to tamp down all those things—stop being *so happy*. It makes people uncomfortable. They'll think you're bonkers. Similarly, expressing sadness makes everyone rush to cheer you up.

But there's value sometimes in just being sad.

So I pat her back and stroke her hair, and I let her cry.

Eventually she stops, and the sobs downgrade to simple bawling. And finally, bawling leads to hiccups, and then even those stop. That's when I pull a chair close and sit down right next to her. When I place a hand on hers, she doesn't pull away.

"I've ruined my mom's business," she whispers. "It's my fault no one's buying her cookies."

"I don't understand," I say. "How could it possibly be—"

"There aren't many families who live here, and they've been here a long time," she says.

"Okay."

"The coach immediately named me as cheer captain," she says. "I know more than she does, and she realized it right away. They've never done well at any competitions, and she saw a chance."

"That's great," I say, "but I do understand how jealousy—"

Maren shakes her head, and I realize it's not time for me to talk. It's time for me to shut up.

"Go on."

"The captain before I arrived was named Ellie."

I pat her hand.

"She was upset." Maren's hand trembles. "She was rude, and I did something I shouldn't have done."

Uh-oh.

"I made fun of her—I made her look stupid." She frowns.

"I'm sure that—"

Maren's fingers dig into her knees, and I realize I've done it again. Sometimes I think I need a muzzle. For myself.

"I'm sorry. Keep talking."

"That was on the first day." She hiccups again, and it looks like she's going to start bawling again.

"Oh."

"That was pretty basic behavior back in New York," she says. "Kill or get killed, right? It didn't take long before everyone on the cheerleading squad, and then everyone at school, was afraid of me."

That's. . .dramatic. But it's probably also true.

"But this girl, Ellie, she kept sniping at me. She wouldn't let it go."

Uneasy rests the crown, I suppose.

"So I took it a little further."

Amanda mentioned she'd been a bully, but like a dope, I only really made sure she wasn't being mean to my kids. I should have paid more attention to her interactions with others.

"I stole her boyfriend, just to show that I could."

"Her boyfriend?" For some reason, that hadn't even occurred to me as a possibility.

"He's not bad looking, for a farmer."

Oof. I hope that's not something she actually said to anyone.

"But he thought that since I'm from the city, I'd. . ."

Oh, no. He didn't. I suddenly want to punch that little farmer.

"He got kind of angry when—" She cuts off and gulps. "Anyhow, when he gave me a hard time, when he said that he and Ellie—" Her nostrils flare again. "I made fun of him, too. I dumped him in front of the whole school, and I told him that it was stupid of me to even consider dating an inbred, backwoods hick from somewhere like Manila."

Oh, dear.

"Everyone told their parents, and that's why no one's buying Mom's cookies anymore."

I doubt their parents needed a lot of provocation. It's not a place that has a lot of outsiders. I was shocked their welcome was as warm as it has been. "Maren."

She shakes her head again, but this time, I'm not going to stay quiet.

"Maren." She looks up toward me slowly, and the second her eyes meet mine, she yanks her hands back and looks down at them again.

"You're a teenager," I say. "First and foremost, remember that. Teenagers are in training. That means that you'll make mistakes. You've been getting that training from a bad place for a while now. It seems like you can see that already—Manila isn't perfect, and neither is New York City. Our job as humans is to learn what we can, and cast away the things that aren't suitable."

I'm being way too cerebral.

"The city sentiment of acting better than everyone else is bad. Putting others down isn't a good way to stay safe.

It's a great way to wind up alone. Similarly, the country sentiment that since there's nothing else to do, sex is a good way to pass the time is also wrong."

Maren's eyes widen and she swallows.

"You need to take the good things from each place you've been and ignore the bad. Does that make sense?"

"But Mom—"

"You yelled at your mom the other day. You told her she was pathetic for starting a business."

Her face falls.

"You did that because you're scared. You hurt her, but instead of telling her what you'd done, you got angry. It's almost always a masking emotion."

"Why are you so smart?"

I laugh. "I'm really old, Maren. I've done most everything wrong that can be done, but I try to learn every time I make a mistake."

"My mom's not that smart, and she's older than you," she mutters.

"Don't say things like that," I snap. "Ever."

Maren straightens up with a jolt. "Why not?'

"It's not at all true." I cast about for a good analogy. "What's Roscoe good at doing?"

"Sleeping?" She looks around for him.

"He left with your mother." I arch one eyebrow. "He's a guardian. He loves fiercely, and he will do most anything for a piece of cheese."

"Okay."

"But if I needed something to take me up into the mountains to check on the cows, could I ride him?"

Maren rolls her eyes. "Of course not."

"He'd make a terrible horse."

She nods.

"Your mother isn't a horse either."

"Huh?"

"I'm a great horse. I barge in and toss my head and give people rides. Your mother is fiercely loyal and she is really good at a lot of things I can't do at all."

"I think you might be more of a protector than—"

I snap my fingers. "Maren, focus. It's an analogy."

"Sorry."

"You've made some big mistakes. It's not going to be easy to smooth things over at school."

"I know."

"But I'm more worried about you setting things right at home."

She frowns.

"You need to have an honest conversation with your mother."

She shakes her head vehemently. "No, I can't. She already hates me."

That breaks my heart. "That's not true. Your mother would never—"

"Trust me. I think I know her better than you do."

"But you're not a mother," I say. "In this one instance, in spite of your special qualifications and close connection, I'm going to disagree with you. There's no way you're correct about that. You need to talk to her."

Of course that's when the door from Izzy and Whitney's room opens. Whitney's rubbing her eyes and yawning as she shuffles out. "Izzy snores."

"She doesn't snore," I say. "Not usually. Only when she has a cold."

Maren's eyes light up. "I think I have a cold, too. I'd better stay home from school."

I snatch a bowl off the counter and plonk it down in front of her. "Not a chance. Eat breakfast and go change."

"But—"

I spear her with a stare. "You will go to school today,

and I'll stop by before cheer to talk to your coach. I have some ideas."

She tries to stare me down, and I admire her effort, but she's a baby. I could eat her for breakfast. Finally, she drops her eyes and grabs a spoon and a box of cereal.

"Do you trust me?" I whisper.

She gulps, but then she nods.

I smile. "There's a reason you came to talk to me."

"Came to talk to you?" Izzy bounces through the door into the kitchen. "About what?"

"She's having trouble choosing between two different songs," I say.

"Um, why would she ask you? Is it, like, a super retro routine?" Izzy asks. "Like, really old? Maybe early nineties?"

I throw a kitchen towel at her. "I have clothes from the early nineties, punk."

Izzy grins.

"Clothes I can still wear," I say. "I'm proud of those clothes."

"It's not retro," Maren says. "But your mom has good taste in music."

"Not nearly as good as yours," Izzy says.

"But I liked both. I needed a wise person to help me choose." She hides it well, but now that I know the truth, I can see the sad shadow behind Maren's bluff. She feels bad that her mom's working so hard, and she's damaging her chances at success with the shop.

After I get the kids off to school, I debate what to tell Amanda. I'd want to know everything immediately, but I'd also have been hovering outside Maren's door this morning, eager to question her the second she awoke. I'd never have bolted to my store early enough to be sure I'd miss seeing her.

If I didn't already know, the last few days have made it crystal clear that Amanda and I aren't very much alike.

But we're still mothers. I should tell her, right? Ideally, I'd call Steve about something like this to ask for guidance. If Nate were alive, he'd be the first person I'd ask. But Steve's already in a bind. Something at the testing center was delayed and they *still* haven't gotten his results back. I suspect I know what it will say, but suspecting isn't knowing. Calling him about Maren feels. . .mean. Plus, I know just what he'll say. He'd tell me that absolute honesty is always the best call with all parenting matters.

The problem is that I agree with him, mostly.

Only, Maren and Amanda have a different relationship than I have with my kids, and I learned just this morning that my method of barging in and pushing my thoughts on other people isn't always the right way. Every time I tried, Maren clammed up. I'm worried I'll do more harm than good if I march into Double or Nothing and tell Amanda everything that Maren confessed to me.

Or am I just worried she'll be upset with me like she was last night?

No matter what way I twist the puzzle, I can't figure out why she got so upset when I was ready to come to her defense. She should be as outraged as I am that Derek is trying to bludgeon her into dating him by threatening to terminate our contract. Instead, it felt like she wanted me to simply agree to ratify his actions.

It's like she wanted me to say, "Sure, Derek. Let's cancel the contract because my sister-in-law doesn't want to date your disgusting self."

Ugh.

The whole thing makes me sick.

And confused.

I'm not someone who often jumps to conclusions, but I don't need to. I'm almost always in possession of the relevant facts. When I'm not, I serve an interrogatory, or I demand a deposition. I keep digging until I know what I need to know in order to make an informed decision.

But right now, it feels like I'm staring at a puzzle and half the pieces are missing.

What could they be?

While I'm wrestling with frustrating personal life nonsense, my phone rings. It's my realtor. My stomach sinks.

Never in my life have I had as many people I want to avoid as I do right now.

"Hey Adam," I say.

"Abigail!"

He sounds almost painfully cheery.

"I have great news."

Of course he does.

"A couple from California walked through your house today. Their company is being transferred, and thanks to the California housing market, they're cash shoppers."

"Brilliant." I force excitement I don't feel. The thought of selling my house makes me feel a bit sick. If our future is here, at Birch Creek Ranch, that's fine. I'd come to terms with it, even if it's nothing like the life I imagined in the months before Nate fell ill.

But what if we don't even get the ranch? What then?

"Aren't you pleased?" he asks. "I wanted to talk to you about preliminary dates. Your stuff isn't moved out yet."

I groan.

"Abby? Are you having second thoughts?"

"No," I force myself to say. "No, that's good news." But that might be a lie. A cash offer would move fast. I'd need to fly out immediately to clean things out and ship them this direction.

And if things fall apart here, we'd suddenly be homeless. That possibility makes me want to hurl up the toast I just ate. I inhale and exhale slowly. "Well, keep me apprised. Let's hope for a good offer."

Houses come and go, I try to tell myself. Even if we sell that one and things don't work out here, we can buy another.

But it won't have our memories with Nate.

It won't have the marks on the wall in Gabe's room, a new set every six months for every child. It won't have the breakfast room where Nate and I would relax and sip coffee while the kids played and squealed and fought. It won't be *my* house.

Would I be this upset if things were settled here? If the ranch might not be yanked away at any moment? If Steve's ex-wife wasn't living in his house while he taught lessons to his new daughter on my horse?

I hate feeling this way.

I'm supposed to be in the middle of the excitement of new love. Ah, if only real life got the memo that it shouldn't mess up the bright spots that bring me joy. Why can't things work that way?

But I'm too young to obsess about that stuff for very long. My relationship is new enough that I do still gravitate toward thoughts of Steve when things get dark. I suppose that's how I find myself sitting in my car, keys in hand, ready to drive over to my boyfriend's house. He worked yesterday, but he's off today. I've given him nonstop space since Stephanie showed up. Surely I'm entitled to a few moments of his time.

Right?

He's smart enough to be able to suss out the differences between his situation and Amanda's and give me decent advice about what to tell her, surely. Minutes later, I'm driving past that stupid red sports car to park next to Steve's truck in front of his barn.

I feel guilty about this, but I'm relieved he's not out

riding with Olivia again. It's stupid and it's irrational, but I'm jealous of her—his, well, probably his daughter. As a mother, I'm delighted for him, and as his friend, too. I know how important it was to him to have children.

But as his girlfriend, I resent that, right now, at the beginning of *us*, he's focused entirely on this.

I don't blame Olivia, of course.

No, I've saved all my anger and irritation for Stephanie. If I had a paintball gun, I might blast her. Repeatedly. I feel like she'd look a lot better with some bright blue paint drying in her hair.

Not that I'd ever admit to any of that.

"Abby!" Steve must have seen me pull up, because he's running toward me.

My heart soars. He's so happy to see me that he's *running* toward me? Maybe all our zing hasn't been smothered after all. I beam at him.

"You heard!" He lifts me in the air and swings me around in a circle. "Isn't it great news?"

News? What news?

"I mean, you knew all along. You never wavered."

I swallow, suppressing the sinking suspicion in my heart that his running and his joy have nothing to do with me. "Olivia?"

"You didn't know?" He looks puzzled. "Then why'd you come over?"

So she is his. Of course she is. I knew it. I forcibly resurrect my smile. "Can't I come over for no reason at all?" Because there's no way, now, that I can possibly dump on him about Maren.

Once again, my issues have been rendered less important. I know I'm lucky to be dating an ER doctor, but sometimes the triage of life really sucks.

"Of course you can." He's still beaming, but I can't tell how much is for me and how much is just a generally good mood. "Come in!" He tugs on my hand the entire way to his barn apartment.

"Now that it's been confirmed, how long do we expect that Stephanie will be living in your house?" I try to keep my tone light, but I'm not sure I entirely succeed.

He slows, his smile slipping a bit. "You're sick of it?"

I want to scream, but I don't. I shake my head. "It doesn't really affect me," I lie. "But I'm sure you're eager to get back to—"

"Oh good. As long as you're fine with it, I don't mind. I love having Olivia close, and of course she wants her mom around."

Now I'm really regretting eating so much for breakfast.

Steve sits, and he gestures for me to sit, too. "How lucky am I?" he asks.

"What?"

"Well, I've just found out I have a daughter, a beautiful, talented daughter. And before I'm stuck working out custody and whatnot, I manage to land a girlfriend who's a lawyer." He beams. "And on top of that, she's a parent herself." He inches his chair a bit closer and takes my hand. "I'm sure I'm going to have a lot of questions about what to do and how to do it, and I'm so glad that you already know all the answers."

Suddenly it hits me like a bat to the face.

Maren needs help with school and her mom.

Amanda needs help with her business and her dating life. On top of that, she hurls wrenches at the ranch and expects me to fix them.

Donna needs me for the criminal case. The divorce and custody hearing. Her dad.

Ethan's freaking out about the upcoming hearing over the ranch.

And now even my boyfriend, the doctor, needs me to hold his hand.

"I can't," I say. "I can't help anyone else." I stand up abruptly, pulling away from his hand.

Steve's eyes widen.

"I'm not a perfect parent. That doesn't even exist. I'm a terrible aunt. I'm a moderate lawyer, but I'm not even licensed here." I realize that I sound a little frantic, and I moderate my tone. "Between the ranch case, and the cattle contract falling apart, and Amanda's new company and all her traveling, I just *cannot* do anything else." My hands are shaking like Maren's were earlier.

"Whoa, Abby, did you come here just to see me, or is something else going on?" He stands up and steps toward me. "You look pretty upset."

I back up, unwilling to touch him right now. It feels like everyone and everything in my life is clawing, begging, demanding, insisting on a piece of me. Instead of a safe place, Steve's barn feels like another danger zone, another place I have to be *on* and ready to go.

I'm so tired of being *on*. Some days, with Nate gone, I just want to huddle into a little ball and cry.

"I need to go," I say.

"Wait, Abby." Steve steps toward me again.

I spin on my heel and race for the door. "I can't. I really can't. Not right now."

He chases me out the door, but I turn and block him with my hand against his chest. "No. I need to drive back home, and I need you to leave me alone for a little while. I have enough of my own stuff going on that I just can't handle yours right now. Can you understand that?"

Steve looks concerned, borderline panicked, but he nods. "Yes."

And unlike Derek, at least Steve knows that no means no.

Perversely, in that moment, I wish he'd push. I wish he would chase me and demand to know what's going on. But he doesn't. He respects my boundaries, and later on, once I've calmed back down and put my shields all back in place, he listens while I tell him that it was just a long day at work, and that everything is fine.

What's worse, I think he believes it.

12

DONNA

My dad is a bully.

Since I was a very small child, I remember learning that you give in to bullies right away. If you don't, their behavior only gets worse and worse. If I was looking to excuse my brother, I'd say he didn't have much choice.

We were both taught how to bully people from a very young age.

"Why is it so hard to promise me that you'll fix this mess you created?" Patrick drops a stack of paper on the table. "Are you unable to read?"

"I can read just fine." Never taunt a bully. It only makes things worse.

"Then do you think I'm lying? Look at the papers, Donna. It's there in plain English."

"I know you're in charge of both houses, and I know that when Dad passes, you'll inherit both."

"Then what is it that I don't understand?" He drops into a chair as if I'm making him so tired he can barely stand. "When you came to me, broken and pathetic, and you needed somewhere to stay urgently, did I turn you away?"

I shake my head.

"Did I charge you rent?"

I shake it again.

"No! I offered you the very house we grew up in, for free. I even pay the utilities. So tell me, Donna, what exactly did I do that was so monstrous that you're betraying me for these women you don't even know?"

I could tell him that he wanted me to let Dad die. I could argue that my stay isn't rent free, since I literally care for Dad all but the thirty-five hours of nursing care a week that Medicare covers. I could remind him that I'm changing diapers, and making and cleaning up meals. I'm bathing and cleaning sheets. I could walk through the fact that his plain black and white paperwork simply makes him the power-of-attorney, and doesn't say a word about who has the right to live where.

But none of that will help. He'll still do what he'll do, and I'll still do what I'll do.

"I am going to go and listen to the evidence presented by Abigail and Amanda, who are my *friends*, and who are good people beside, and whose children are the great nephews and nieces of Jedediah Brooks who wrote that will, and I'm going to vote according to the dictates of my own conscience."

Patrick swears under his breath. "Dad never should've let you go to Stanford. I swear, you've been an uppity nightmare ever since."

"Knowing that I won't kowtow to your demands, what's your next move?" I've been waiting for him to get on with it for almost twenty minutes. "Make good on all your threats."

Bullies aren't great at follow through, luckily. I'm guessing he'll just storm off again.

"Get out," he says. "Gather your pathetic belongings and your whiny son, and get off the property."

Apparently my older brother can still surprise me. "You can't be serious."

"I am." He folds his arms. "You have until tonight at six. Good thing you have pathetically little in the way of possessions."

I wonder if he's thought this through. "It's three o'clock." I wouldn't normally state the obvious, but he's a rancher whose cattle are already sold for the year. He's not a slave to the day nearly as much as he is most of the year. He might not realize he's giving me three hours to pack and vacate.

"I'm aware."

"Fine," I say. "Get out so that I can."

I'm lucky Aiden's not actually whiny like he accused him of being. My sweet little guy actually helps me pack.

Looking at our belongings, I realize there's some truth to what Patrick said. We have pathetically little that really belongs to us. We look like impoverished nomads. Everything we have will easily fit into my beat-up old car.

I'm leaving all the food, with the exception of some things I could make in a microwave and keep in a mini-fridge, of course. It's not like Manila has a lot of options for someone who's needing immediate accommodations.

Before loading up to go, I pack Dad's stuff. "What are you doing?"

Luckily, he's having a pretty lucid day.

"Patrick wants to take care of you for a while," I say, "which means you get to go back to the big house. That's exciting, right?"

Dad frowns.

"I think you'll be much more comfortable there."

"I don't want to go."

That's not what I expected. "Dad, the bathrooms are

nicer. The floors are nicer. The televisions are twice the size of the ones here."

"But I like your food better." Dad folds his arms and sighs. "And Patrick wouldn't take me to the hospital when I was sick."

I'm absolutely flabbergasted he remembers that. "Well, he just didn't know how sick you were," I lie. "Or he'd have taken you himself."

Dad frowns, but in the shock of the moment, he doesn't argue with me about it. He's batting my hands away from his arms on our way to the car when he finally stops. "Is this because you're getting back together with Charlie?"

Most days he either doesn't know who Charles is, or he doesn't realize we've split. "Uh, no."

"Good." He nods. "I never liked him."

That's no shock. Dad never likes anyone. But it is the first time he's told me that he disliked him. "Why didn't you tell me you hated him before now?"

"Would you have listened to me?" He shrugs. "It would have just made it more likely you'd marry him. Your mother and I decided to keep quiet about it."

Mom didn't like him either?

"Let's go. My legs are shaking."

"Right. Sorry." I help him into my car. It's a little sad that he needs to be in a car to go two hundred yards, but it's still true. I pull up as close to Patrick's front door as I can get, nearly driving onto the sidewalk. I heft Dad's bag with one hand and brace his arm with the other.

When I knock on the door, Amelia answers. Her mouth drops open in a very satisfying way. "Is there some kind of problem?"

Am I evil for being pleased that Patrick's car is gone, and he won't be able to stop me? I don't even have to force my smile. "No, not at all." I release Dad's arm and he slumps. "I told the nurse to gather up all his information and his medical things and bring them by. Her shift just ended, of course. She'll be over in the next few minutes, and she'll fill you in on anything you don't already know."

Amelia presses her hand to her throat, opening and closing her mouth like she's gasping for air instead of just completely unsure what to say.

"Did Patrick not tell you?"

"Tell me what?" She glances behind her like her husband might appear and save them.

"He kicked me out," I say. "He said I wasn't paying rent, and it was only fair that I should get out, seeing as I'm not serving his interests in lying to the court to get him the Brooks land for cheap."

My sister-in-law is usually the most self-assured person I've ever met, other than perhaps Abigail Brooks. She wears the latest fashion and is constantly buying new and trendy accessories. She hosts brunches regularly. Her hair is always perfectly done, and her makeup just so. I swear, she thinks she lives on the Upper East Side, not in the middle of a secluded mountain range surrounded by bovines.

I wish I wasn't being kicked out of my home, but if it has to happen, this almost makes it worth it.

"You'll want to grab his arm before he collapses," I say. "Broken limbs for people his age are really, really bad."

Amelia is absolutely speechless.

Just then, as if some kind of karmic debt owed to me is finally being repaid, Dad's face turns red. "I really need help to the bathroom," he says.

Amelia couldn't look more horrified if she were being paid.

"You should probably hurry," I say.

"I couldn't possibly—"

Judging by the sound and the smell, she missed her window.

"What—"

"I'm so sorry, but it's a school night and Aiden's waiting in the car. Your husband only gave me six more minutes to get out of here, and I better go." I wave and head back to my car.

If my dad were a better person, I might feel bad for leaving him here. As it is, they kind of deserve each other.

I should have thought of bailing much, much earlier.

The second I leave my brother's driveway, all our pathetic belongings stacked high on the passenger side, the trunk, and over half of the back seat of my dilapidated old car, I breathe a little easier. I call Mrs. Earl the second I'm on the main road.

"R-Hideout, how may we brighten your day today?"

She still sounds exactly the same as she did in high school. "Hey Mrs. Earl. It's Donna Ellingson."

"Donna! It's wonderful to hear your voice. I heard you were back in town."

"I'm working down at the school," I say.

"Sadly, I *still* have no grandkids. Will isn't even *dating* anyone right now. Can you believe it?"

Are all mothers the same? "I was hoping you might have a spare room. I'll need it for at least a week." Hopefully by then I'll know whether Patrick's just bluffing, or whether I need to look for a longer-term rental.

"Of course we have space. Do you have that sweet little boy with you? What's his name again?"

"It's Aiden, and yes, we'll both be there."

"You'll want the King Cabin, then. It has a king bed, and a sofa bed in the family room."

"Actually, funds are a little tight for me right now, so the cheapest room you've got—"

"It's off season, missy, and you're family, even if we haven't seen you in a long time. If you're willing to help me clean up a few rooms, you can stay for twelve and a half bucks a day."

She must be kidding. "I couldn't possibly—"

"That's the state fee," she says, "or I wouldn't even charge you that. I won't hear of you arguing with me about it."

When I hang up, I'm crying. Sometimes in the ugliness of the world around me, it's easy to forget that there's a lot of beauty out there, too. Most of it takes the form of kind people.

"Mom? Are you sad?"

I shake my head. "No, sweetie. Sometimes people cry when they're happy."

"Really?" Aiden's brow furrows. "I've never cried when I was happy."

"One day it'll make sense, I promise."

"Maybe."

And then we're there, and I'm wiping my eyes.

"Mom? I'm really hungry."

"I'm sorry, baby. Once we get this stuff unloaded, I'll heat up a cup of noodles for you."

"I don't want noodles," Aiden says.

Even the constant dinnertime battle doesn't feel quite as dire today, not knowing that someone in the world out there cares about us. "We'll come up with something." I climb out and wait for Aiden to catch up to me.

Mrs. Earl is waiting on us with keys and a smile. "There are only two other occupied rooms right now, so we don't have much to do. If we get many more, I'll let you know and—"

"We're totally fine to move to another room if you need us to," I say.

Mrs. Earl shakes her head. "Don't be silly. I meant that I can clean those two quickly, but if we get more, I won't evict you. I just thought you might be able to help me turn the rooms over in the morning or on your lunch break."

"Oh," I say. "Of course."

"Normally Fiona would lend a hand," Mrs. Earl says. "It's been harder with her gone."

"Where is she?" The name Fiona conjures up an image of a tiny little girl with pigtails.

"She's in college," Mrs. Earl says with pride. "UCLA."

"Oh," I say. "That's wonderful."

"We miss her, though." Mrs. Earl sighs. "Especially with Mr. Earl—" She cuts off abruptly and swallows. "Alright. You're right here." She points at the third cabin on the left. "There's no one in the cabin next door, so don't worry how much noise you make." Mrs. Earl ruffles Aiden's hair.

"Thank you so much."

"Please, don't think of it. Happy to help, and glad to see more of you."

I get Aiden settled in front of the television—luckily *The Ultimate Beastmaster* is playing. He won't move an inch while it's on. "I'll bring our stuff, okay?"

Aiden barely nods.

I trot back to the car and open the passenger side, grabbing the biggest box, and the most annoying to carry, first. I've always been the kind of person who wants to get the worst over with right away, but I've barely hefted it out of the seat when strong arms take it away from me.

"Who—"

Will Earl smiles. "Mom said you might need a hand."

I remember our last awkward call. I've dodged three more calls since. "Oh."

"She said you'll be staying here for a while?"

"Uh-huh," I say.

"I imagine Aiden's already inside?" He tosses his head toward the open cabin door."

I nod.

"Great, well, I can get this stuff if you open the trunk. Why don't you keep an eye on him while I—"

"He's watching television," I say. "I couldn't possibly let you—"

"Donna." I forgot how wide Will's grin is. "Let me do this, please."

I wait until he starts walking and then duck inside to grab a duffel bag and sling it over my shoulder. Then I snag an overfull shoebox and follow him.

"You've never been good at accepting help."

"Charity," I say.

"Mom said you were arguing with her about the price she set. Trust her to run her business," he says. "She's always done really well."

She didn't tell him she's not charging me anything? That makes me like her even more. "Alright."

I follow Will back and forth a few more times, only stopping once when a shoebox full of Mom's letters to Aunt Catrina spills. I gather them up before they can blow away and shove them into a pile on the bathroom counter. Will's carrying the last thing over—a suitcase—when Aiden's show ends.

He looks around as if he's just noticing that we're here and all the stuff is inside. He looks up at Will and says, "Who are you?"

"I'm Will Earl." He holds out an enormous hand. He's exactly what people expect when someone says 'rancher.' He's tall. He's broad. He's well-muscled in all the right places.

He's basically as opposite as he could possibly be from Charles Windsor IV, Aiden's dad.

"I'm a friend of your mom's from high school."

"Why are you here?" Aiden doesn't sound accusatory, thankfully, just curious.

"My mom owns this hotel," he says. "She texted me to tell me that someone might need a hand moving their things in."

Aiden looks at Will for another moment, and then he turns to me. "I'm starving, Mom. I really don't want noodles again."

Embarrassment flares up. Who wants people to know that they eat cup of noodles regularly? Or that their kid eats it so often that he's sick of it? I understand why—I'm starving too, and I'm sick of ramen. But the idea of loading him back into a car this late and driving to the Grill to try and get burgers while he gets more and more impatient feels overwhelming.

I desperately want to change into my pajamas and get into bed.

"Aiden, it's been a long day, buddy. I know you're not a fan of noodles," I say.

"I just want something good!" Instead of yelling more, Aiden starts to cry. He must be more exhausted than I thought, or he's overly stressed, what with another bizarre move to another strange place.

My poor little man.

"Don't cry," Will says. "It's going to be fun to stay here, I promise."

"Crying isn't bad," Aiden wails. "Mom just said. She cries when she's happy."

"Your mom was crying?" Will looks concerned.

"No," I say.

Aiden stands up, incensed. "Yes you were."

"Okay." I walk toward the door. "Thank you so much for your help, Will, but I fear things are about to devolve quickly here."

"Right." Will glances from me to Aiden and back again. "Okay. But if you need something—"

"You and your mom have already done too much. Thank you."

"I'll bring your shoe—"

"Okay." I usher him through the door and close it

behind him with a relieved sigh. Something about Will makes me feel... strange. Embarrassed. I still can't remember why or how he came to have my shoe. When I think about that night, I feel nothing but apprehension.

I make a cup of noodles for Aiden and promptly have to scoop it up and throw it in the trash when he refuses to eat a single bite and knocks it on the floor. Luckily it hits the tile, so I don't have to add 'ruining their carpet' to the list of horrible things the Earls will have endured, thanks to me.

"I'll see if I can make instant mac," I say. "How's that?"

Aiden's still so upset that nothing I say is helping. "I want a burger."

"I don't have a burger," I say. What he really needs is to eat *anything*, so that he can take a bath and go to bed, but the bathroom's still stacked up with stuff. "Give me a minute. I need to clean up the bathroom, okay?"

"No, I want a burger." Aiden drops to the ground, and I realize that I'm standing on the brink of a full-on meltdown. I couldn't be more grateful that Mrs. Earl told me the cabin next door is empty.

"One more episode," I say. "You can watch one more episode of *The Ultimate Beastmaster,*" I offer.

"It's not on right now," he says.

"On my phone," I say. "Streaming."

"Fine."

Just long enough for me to clear out the bathroom. Once I have him plugged in, I start shifting things around. The last thing I have to clean up is the wad of Mom's letters. I finally get them all stacked when I notice my name again. I really need to get Aiden dunked and in bed, but he's calm for the moment. . .

. . .

You were asking about the kids' inheritances, and I know we promised Patrick, and we did pay for Donna's tuition like we agreed, but frankly they just aren't the same level. Even Vern agrees that the value of the ranch is much greater than the value of her education. I think in another month or two, I may convince him to fix it. It just doesn't sit right with me, and I think if Vern didn't favor boys so much he'd have changed it long ago.

Changed what? Could she be talking about the life insurance policy? Would Dad have changed the beneficiary to me? Or is that just wishful thinking? What would Patrick have done if he found out? Would he have told me? Or would he have offered to let me have the life insurance proceeds in exchange for a ranch, never telling me the truth: that they were mine all along?

No, that's too horrible, even for my brother.

Right?

"Mom!" Aiden's clearly at the end of his very limited patience.

I turn on the water for the tub. "I'm coming," I say. "I'll look for the macaroni cups and get that cooking while you're in the bath. Okay, buddy?"

Just then, there's a knock on the door.

It's probably freaking Will with my stupid shoe.

I want to ignore it. I mean, could this day get any more depressing? Only someone without kids would come *back* after seeing how close Aiden was to an utter disaster.

But what if I ignore it and it *is* Will? He has master keys. He could just barge in. Right? Would he? I really hope not. I finally answer the door, opening it just an inch.

Only, there's no one there. Did I imagine the knock?

Then I look down and notice the bag. It's a to-go bag from The Gorge. The smell reaches me, then, and my mouth floods with an embarrassing amount of saliva. I crouch to grab it and notice there's a note.

Donna:

I know you're his mom, and I don't want to interfere, but you looked tired. I wasn't sure what you'd like so I got a few things. Hopefully one of them makes his transition to a hotel a little more bearable.

-Will

When I carry the food inside—a burger with fries, a chicken sandwich with seasoned potato wedges, and a grilled chicken salad—I start crying again.

"Are you happy or sad this time?" Aiden asks.

"Happy again," I say. "And you should be too."

"Why?" Aiden frowns.

"Because I've got a burger."

13
AMANDA

I'm a criminal, basically. I have to hide what I'm doing and who I like. I have to steal moments from my day just to see my boyfriend. And I'm lying to everyone just to cover up for that stolen time.

But when Eddy smiles, it's all worth it.

Only, he's not smiling right now. "Hear me out."

"I did listen," I say, "but I'm not ready yet."

"What's the one thing that would be worse than simply admitting that we're dating?"

"Breaking up?"

He sighs and rolls his eyes simultaneously. "I mean, yes. That would be worse. But the thing that might happen that would be worse—" He throws his hands up in the air. "If *someone* ratted us out, you'd wish you'd just confessed first. That's my point." He scowls. "Silly me. I was assuming that breaking up wasn't on the list of options."

I don't remind him that it's always on the list of options, for every couple. "Look, I wasn't saying we should break up."

"Derek knows about us, and he may not have told anyone yet, but his knowledge is like a gun to your head,"

Eddy says. "He's still hopeful, so he hasn't pulled the trigger. But once his hope is gone. . .boom."

Is he right? He doesn't realize that Derek has another way to harm me, and it's one he's going to follow through on, if I don't agree to go out with him again. And again.

"Don't you have cows to check on or something?" I ask. "Because I have cookies to bake." That no one will eat.

Maybe I'll eat them all and gain 200 pounds and then Eddy will dump me *and* Lololime will fire me and none of this will matter anymore and I won't care because I'll be too busy eating mediocre cookies with both hands.

"Amanda." Eddy takes my hands in his. "It's not my career that's on the line, and it's not my family that you're lying to. It's yours. I'm not trying to dictate what you do, and I understand that it's my fault we're here, and that my past caused this. I'm merely saying that if you decide you want to brave the storm, or face the music, or whatever, I'll face it with you. I'll help pay your rent on this store. I'll work in the cookie shop for free." His dimpled smile is shining at the full 1000 watts. "And if you lose the ranch, you and your girls can come live with me."

I shove his shoulder. "Stop."

"I'm not kidding," he says. "I would be willing to endure the misery of having the woman I'm crazy about around me all the time, if that's what it comes down to."

I roll my eyes.

"I may not have the best past, but I earn a great living now, and my house is paid off, and I have a flexible schedule." His eyes search mine. "I'm in this, okay?"

From the guy who hasn't had a relationship with anything but his comb, to a guy who's offering up his house to my family? "I'm not sure what to say."

"I don't want you to feel like you're alone," he says. "There are two of us."

"Thanks."

"Now, I'm going to go see a guy about a horse." He winks.

I swoon for a moment, but get it together quickly. "Bye."

"Try to breathe. Everything will be alright." He ducks out the door.

I'm just putting a sheet of cookies in the oven when the door jingles. "I'm so sorry," I shout. "I'm back here—we don't have many cookies ready yet."

The cackle warns me that it's not a normal customer just before Amanda Saddler rounds the corner. "And how many cookies do you think I could eat before I'd gain enough weight to fill out these wrinkles?" She gestures at her neck. "A dozen? Two?"

"You look amazing. Don't try and fill out anything."

"That's why I give you free rent, that right there. You lie to me."

I know she's kidding, but it feels like I'm lying to everyone right now. Amanda's the only one who knows the truth. That's probably why I start to cry.

"Oh no," she says. "I was making a joke. I know it was just a compliment."

I double over the counter and keep right on sobbing.

After a moment, Amanda realizes it's not about her and circles around to pat my back. A few minutes later, her patting gets a little harder. I think that's the warning that my time for self-pity is nearly up.

"What in the world is going on?"

"What *isn't*?" I fill her in, as I work to get myself back together, on how I've ruined our cattle agreement, and how Maren's a pariah at school and she's lying to me, and how I'm stuck lying to everyone about Eddy and me, and how Derek might out us at any time.

"Oh yeah, and as if all that's not enough, we might lose

the ranch, and my cookie business is totally failing." I sigh. "You bet on the wrong horse."

"Amanda," she says. "I might not be good at choosing horses, but I'm never wrong when I bet on a person."

I grab a paper towel and blow my nose. Then I wash my hands, because it smells like the cookies are done. "Hang on," I say. "Lemme check these."

Sure enough, they're perfectly golden. I snag a mitt and pull them out.

"Look at you," Amanda says. "I didn't hear a timer ding. You told me that's a thing that Abigail does—smelling when they're done. And now you're doing it, too."

"Which would be great," I say, "if anyone wanted to buy my cookies."

"Who cares?" she asks.

"Excuse me?"

"If the people in this hick town are too stupid to realize what they've got, if they aren't supporting a new local business, then screw them." She arches one eyebrow. "Do you think that none of my businesses have ever not worked out?"

"You've had businesses?"

"I buy buildings, dear. Did you think I run a charity? Other than you, I've never given anyone free rent."

Duh.

"I've had plenty of buildings I bought not turn out to be a smart purchase. Once you've made repairs and paid taxes on something that only costs you money for a few years, you'll learn to be a little more cautious when you select a place to buy."

"I'm sorry," I say. "It's only been a few weeks, though."

"Do you love cookies?" she asks.

"You mean, eating them?'

"Do you love making them?" she asks. "Do you dream

of new types? Are you always thinking of who might want them, or of how to market them?"

I blink.

"That's your answer. If it's not your passion and it's not your expertise, it was doomed to fail from the start. You only started this shop in a misguided attempt to be like your sister-in-law."

"Misguided?"

"I told you—you need to be *you*. You need to play to *your* strengths, not someone else's. So who cares if this fails? You spent, what? Twenty grand on it? I've wasted more money on an ATV."

I try to think of Amanda Saddler tearing it up on a four-wheeler and I can't. She's too. . .I don't know. Fragile?

"I wasn't always ancient, dear. I used to do crazy things like rev the engine as I was crawling down the side of a mountain. Unlike you, I've never had any kids to come home to."

Can she read my mind?

"You're so transparent, there may as well be a thought bubble floating over your head, like a cartoon."

"No one has figured out that I'm dating Eddy," I say.

"I'd have figured it out. Your family's a bunch of idiots."

"But I don't see—"

"That's always the problem. You young people never *see*. You're always too busy talking and working and fretting to see what's right in front of your face."

"Okay."

"What part of your story is the most distressing? What's the most urgent?"

"Derek has ruined my cattle contract and Abby's mad at me."

"And with regard to him, what else?"

"At any point he could tell Victoria and get me fired."

"Or leak the information to another social media

influencer who hates you, and that would be even worse. You'd lose any sponsors you have, including Lololime, right?"

"That's what Eddy's worried about, yeah." Although, perhaps as a parent I should be most worried about Maren's trouble. "Also, my daughter is—"

"Nope. I said the one thing that distresses you the most. You're feeling guilty for not picking the small issue with your daughter, and I applaud the mother in you. But if you can't provide for your family, Maren will be a lot more upset and worried than she is right now. You picked the right thing. Stop second guessing everything and learn to trust your gut."

How can she do that so easily?

"Besides. It's not as if I said you'd *only* fix the one problem. But you have to take things one at a time. No one can slay six dragons with one sword, my dear."

Six dragons? Sometimes Amanda's hard to follow.

"It's an analogy." She smirks. "Try to keep up, young'un."

"But how can I fix—"

"You started the cookie shop because you wanted a career that didn't force you to rely on the whims of Instagram. Right?"

I nod.

"But let's circle back to your problem. In life, I've found that my problem usually contains the key to my solution."

I have no idea what she's talking about. "How could Derek—"

She pats my hand. "I'm leading you to it. Be patient."

I'd be annoyed, except I need her. My life feels like a ball of tangled yarn. If the one person who knows how big the mess really is thinks she can find the end and pull a thread free, who am I to argue?

"Okay, Derek's here to do what?"

"He's starting a processing plant for cattle," I say. "He

works for a leather company and partners with some high-end beef company."

"Great, and he said that will create *how* many jobs?"

I dredge that conversation from the recesses of my foggy brain. "A few hundred, I think?"

"And that's happening when?"

I shrug. "In the near future. The plant is pretty easy to set up, in the grand scheme of things. It's already underway."

Amanda smiles. "I've seen the site. It's six months out, but they'll be phasing operations in slowly over the next year and a half."

"Okay."

"What does that mean? Two hundred new jobs in a town of four hundred, give or take?"

I shrug. "Sure."

"Where are all these people going to live?" she whispers.

My eyes widen. "I have no idea."

"Two hundred jobs, conservatively, means about five hundred new people. Why?"

"Families?"

"And support personnel. Think about it. Two hundred new people means more restaurants, maybe another convenience store? Expansions to what we have? Extra hours?"

"Okay."

"A hair salon?"

"If they bring more tourists and visitors, maybe another hotel?"

"Could be," Amanda says. "Those people can't all stay in the hotels here, and they can't all live in the housing that's already in place." She taps her lip. "If *only* you knew the person in town who owned most of the land and buildings."

My eyes widen.

"If it were, say, an older lady with limited energy who owned it all, she might need someone to help her. Someone with an eye for design and color schemes. Someone who knows what's fashionable and has connections to people who make and sell decor."

"You mean me?"

"Bingo," she says. "I trust you, and you have great taste. You did a lovely job on your own remodel, which is nearly done, right?"

"But that's not a job," I say. "I'm happy to help you with any free time I have."

"Shut down this cookie thing," Amanda says. "Or have your daughter run it herself, if that plays into your plans to deal with her teen angst. You have five more rent-free months, after all. Maybe it'll become viable during that time. But stop wasting your day on it. Start working for *me*, and we can split the profits from the buildings we remodel and flip over the next eighteen months."

"You're serious."

"Dear, I'm too old to make jokes. I don't have that kind of time or energy."

"But I've never flipped a house."

"I already told you—I've flipped plenty of properties, but if the buyers are sophisticated people from big cities, I'll need your eye and your youthful energy. Are you in?"

"We split the profits 50/50 but you front the costs and own the buildings?"

"Any profit above our expenses and my investment in the building? Yes. We split them."

"That hardly seems fair," I say. "All I'm doing—"

"Amanda, without you, I wouldn't even have known about the new plant." She winks. "I believe in compensating people who bring me truckloads of money."

Truckloads of money? I like the sound of that. "Okay." I can barely believe that in one short conversation, she essentially killed my cookie shop and hired me for a new job, a job I'm already more excited about. "I'm in."

14
ABIGAIL

Derek's office emails over a notice of termination of our contract, just like Amanda said they would. I immediately call him, of course.

"Abigail Brooks. I had a feeling I'd be hearing from you."

"Have you lost your mind?" I wanted to talk to Amanda about this first, but she's been AWOL all day.

"Not that I know of." He chuckles. "Nope, I just checked and it's intact."

"You're terminating the agreement because Amanda won't *date* you? That's sexual harassment."

"Whoa," Derek says. "Is that what she told you? That's not at all the reason we gave. We simply found a better deal on the cattle we need, and we're executing our right to cancel without cause. As it stipulates, we'll pay you the lump sum damages in Article Nine."

"Don't make me sue you, Derek. It won't make you look good."

"With those lump sum damages, and with what you'll surely get for those cows at auction, I doubt you'll have much in the way of lost profits. Would it really be worth a lawsuit for that small amount?"

"Is twenty thousand dollars small to you?" I ask.

"It is, yes," he says.

I sigh. As far as lawsuits go, it is small. "We're a small ranch," I say. "Please rethink this."

"I'll tell you what. Amanda knows why I'm cancelling and it's not what you think. You go have a chat with her and ask her what I'm really upset about. If she tells you, and if you call me back and explain it, then fine. I'll honor the agreement. Okay?"

I mash 'end call' so hard that it leaves a thumbprint on my screen.

"What did he say?" Kevin asks.

"It didn't go well," I say.

"The thing is, we're running low on hay," Kevin says. "We had just enough to keep the cows for the time stipulated without running out before spring, but we can't wait much longer."

"Translation," Ethan says. "We need to sell them at auction this weekend, or we'll lose our shirt buying more hay."

I groan. "Fine."

"It's not a big deal," Kevin says. "Not really. We always sell them at auction. It's normal."

But I hate when things go wrong.

"Don't count your chickens before they hatch," Kevin says. "I think that's why they came up with that phrase."

"Who doesn't count their eggs before they hatch?" I ask. "It's a stupid saying. That's the whole point of contract law, to prepare and get things set up in advance. The saying should be, 'Don't trust sleaze bags. They always suck.'"

"That's not as catchy," Ethan says.

"Did you say this weekend?" I ask.

"I mean this Saturday," Kevin says.

"Like in two days?" I ask. "How are we going to get them all there in time?"

"I'll call Chris Billington at the auction yard," Kevin says. "They have some trucks, and we can use the one we've got. I bet we can take more than a third of them down tomorrow. If we're lucky, maybe even half."

Some days I forget how fortunate I am to have Jeff and Kevin with us this year. Without them to guide us, we never would have had a chance at working this ranch for a year. "Thank you," I say. "For everything, really."

"It's just my job," Kevin says. "And Jed helped us when no one else would."

"Did he really want us to get the ranch?" Ethan asks.

"Yes," Kevin says. "He talked about your dad a lot."

"He did?" Ethan looks like Roscoe does when he's watching bacon in someone's hand, his eyes latched on Kevin with pathetic desperation.

"I never met your dad, but I know that he came out every summer for years. I know that he only liked boiled eggs—not scrambled, and not fried. I know he hated being cold. Jed was sure that's why he moved down to Texas, to get away from the snow."

"Yes," Ethan says. "Wow. I wish I knew Uncle Jed better."

"He was a jerk," Kevin says. "You'd have thought he hated you. But the things he *did* were always much nicer than the stuff he said. I think that's why he got along with Roscoe so much. Dogs will always forgive what you say—it's all noise to them—as long as you're nice."

It's humans who get caught up on words.

I realize that I should probably cut Steve a little more slack. It's not as if I've been very clear with him, word-wise, on how stressed I've been. And he's probably pretty confused since I didn't tell him about the lousy mediation, the issues with Amanda and Derek, or the struggles with Maren.

Ethan keeps begging for more scraps from Kevin, but I excuse myself and head for my room. Work comes first, so I call the auction yard to see whether they can accommodate us—they can—and then once that's set up and firm, I text Steve.

OUR CATTLE DEAL FELL APART. LONG STORY. ANY CHANCE YOU'RE OFF SATURDAY TO HELP ME AT THE AUCTION YARD? FIRST TIMER, HERE.

His reply is immediate. I'M WORKING THAT NIGHT, BUT I CAN STAY MOST OF THE DAY. JUST NEED A QUICK NAP THAT AFTERNOON.

Even with Jeff and Kevin on board, I'm relieved that Steve will be available. Since all the final decisions fall to me, it's great to have someone who's used to making them around, even if he's not a big cattle rancher.

I spend the rest of the morning on work stuff—always a new emergency to deal with. That afternoon, when I still haven't been able to find Amanda anywhere, I text her. GOING TO SEE MAREN'S CHEER COACH. SHE'S STRUGGLING. CARE TO COME?

She doesn't reply. Not for more than twenty minutes. In the world of texting, that's practically a lifetime. If I thought she was super busy at the shop, I'd cut her more slack, but. . .especially knowing what I know about her sales from Maren and Izzy, I doubt that's the case.

Regardless, I told Maren I'd come by. I flaked on doing that yesterday—after school she confessed she was relieved—but I can't ignore her issues forever. Not as an aunt, not as a mother, and not as someone who cares for her. People who think that high school drama is just that aren't paying attention. Some of that stuff can scar a kid forever, and most of it shapes who they'll become for their entire life.

I'm just pulling into the school parking lot when my

phone rings. It's my real estate agent again, and his name on the caller ID makes my whole body tense. "Hello?"

"It's Adam Bradford," he says. As if I don't already know that.

"Hey Adam."

"I've got amazing news. The couple I called you about before have put in a cash offer, and it's ten thousand dollars over asking price. Given your circumstances, being out of town, and with your husband, they're not even asking for an options period or an inspection. The one thing is, they want to close in the next three weeks. Can you get out here and get things wrapped up that fast?"

Three weeks.

I'm sure I could make it work, but do I want to? Now that I'm actually staring the prospect of selling our home in the face, I'm not sure I can do it. It's not just the memories with Nate.

It's the safety net.

If Ethan knew, he'd tell me to sell. He'd say that I need to have faith in our future, in the ranch, and in him. But I'm a lawyer, and I know that's not realistic. You can't rely on something that rests on the whims of a court or a jury or a panel. No matter how well you prepare, if it's out of your hands, which makes it unsteady.

Heck, even some things I thought were totally within my control turned out to be unpredictable. Like cancer. Like college. Like where I'd be living in five years. Like Steve putting me first.

"I need to talk to the kids and look at the schedule, Adam. But I'll be honest. Things are a bit up in the air out here right now. I'm increasingly worried about the prospect of selling it at all."

"Oh." Adam sounds shocked. "Wow. Okay, well, the agent wants to know by the weekend. Can you do that?'

I want to ask for a few more days, or even a week, but

that's not the real world, and will my answer really change? Our hearing with the judge isn't until the end of next week. "That's fine. I'll call you tomorrow."

"Thanks. And Abby?"

"Yeah?"

"As your agent, I say jump on this deal. But as a friend, do what's best for you guys, even if that means pulling the listing for a few months."

I didn't really consider us friends, but now I actually do. Friends are the people who act in your best interest, even when it goes against theirs. Being a lawyer has taught me that. "Thanks."

I steel my resolve and march into the high school. Since I called and let them know I'd be coming about half an hour before practice starts, during the cheer coach's off period, she greets me immediately.

"Mrs. Brooks. I'm Rachel Hanna, and it's so nice to finally meet you. You already know this, I'm sure, but your daughter is so talented. We're happy to have her leading our team."

"Actually, Maren's my niece. Her mother just started a business and she's been really swamped."

Maren snorts from the seat behind the coach. I hadn't even realized she was present until she made that sound.

"Maybe we can go into the conference room?" Coach Hanna says.

"Of course." I follow her in, glaring at Maren. If she can't even behave in this meeting, we have more things to deal with than a little rivalry on the team.

"I know you have practice," I say. "So I'll get right to the point. Maren comes from New York City, as you know—"

"We are all so delighted for her wealth of knowledge. With her help, we're increasing the difficulty of our cheers and we hope to be real competitors—"

I shake my head. "No, you're not understanding why I'm here. I couldn't care less about her success as a cheerleader, or your team's chances at winning."

Coach Hanna's jaw dangles open.

"I'm here because Maren's not enjoying the relationships on the team, and she knows it's her fault they are the way they are. I wanted to talk to you about strategies for fixing those."

"You're talking about Ellie?"

"I sure am." So she's not totally clueless.

Maren's staring at the table, not making a peep.

"Ellie was always a bit of a brat," Coach Hanna says. "So I hope you're not blaming Maren for their discord."

I'm surprised *she's* not blaming Maren. She's the newcomer, after all. "I'm not actually here to blame anyone," I say. "I'm here to help fix the problem. That's always my focus. It seems like you understand what it is, but haven't done anything to change it."

She blinks. "What would you suggest we do? It's a squabble between teenage girls. It'll blow over."

Apparently she doesn't know about the boyfriend and how it has escalated. "I don't think it's going to blow over," I say. "I'd like to propose a possible solution."

"I'm all ears."

"I think we should Parent-Trap them."

"Excuse me?"

Maren sits up straight, her eyes full of horror. Clearly she's seen the movie.

"When you put people together—forced proximity—they either work things out, or they hate each other more. You took an existing power dynamic and dramatically modified it. I'm suggesting we restore some balance."

"Aunt Abby!" Maren stands up. "She can't come live with us. We'll claw each other's eyes out."

I chuckle. "I wish I had the power to stick you both in

the same room at home for a week or two. I doubt that would be possible. But I do think you could be co-captains of the cheer team."

"In my experience, co-captains rarely work," Coach Hanna says.

"Right now, they're taking their anger with one another out in school," I say. "I'd rather see them arguing on the team instead."

"I wouldn't," Coach Hanna says. "How will we get anything done?"

"To put it lightly, I don't care about that. If you never competed a single time, I would lose no sleep at night." I lean closer. "Do you know how many people cheer for their entire lives?"

She blinks.

"None." I sigh. "That's how many. This is a strictly high school problem. But being able to smooth over an argument, being able to make friends with someone you've wronged? Maren will need to learn how to do that for her entire life. The only way for her to figure out how to do it is for her to be forced to figure it out. Put them in as co-captains and force them to work together." I pause and turn to face my outraged niece. "And you'll apologize and listen to the suggestions she makes."

"I will not apologize," Maren says.

I stand up. "Great. If you won't apologize, then I'll bow out. I'm sure you'll handle things just fine on your own."

"Wait." Maren's eyes widen. "Don't go."

I sit, but I glare. "If you want my help, then *take it*. You told me yourself that you did some nasty things. You don't have to apologize for being a snooty brat who has had very expensive, very posh cheer training that no one here had access to. You don't have to apologize for thinking you're better than everyone else, or for convincing them it's true, when the difference amounts to being able to do a better leap or splits or something inconsequential. But you do have to apologize for stealing her boyfriend, for mocking her, and for generally being a little witch. Are we clear?"

Maren gulps.

"You will get nowhere in life if you doggedly cling to your own perfection. If you're unwilling to admit your mistakes and do better, if you won't do that when you're given a chance, when your coach is behind you, this problem will never be solved." I pause. "If you won't do that, I'm wasting my time, and I don't have time to waste right now. Am I clear?"

Maren nods.

"So you'll graciously accept a new co-captain and apologize to her?"

"Do I have to do it in front of everyone?"

"A public apology that feels sincere would be the best," I say. "But if you don't think you're a big enough person to manage it, you could do it privately. It would at least be a start."

Maren looks at her hands.

"I love you, you know. I think you have the capacity to do great things. But great things start with doing small things the right way. An awful lot of those small things aren't fun, and they aren't glamorous, either."

Coach Hanna looks a little shell-shocked.

"Were you expecting me to come in here and make sure you were supporting my niece?"

Her head turns slowly toward me, and she nods.

"And instead, I'm ripping my niece a new one." I chuckle. "Just think, Maren, how Ellie will feel. She's been abandoned and ridiculed and ousted by you, but now you're reinstating her, you're apologizing, and you're making a place for her. If you can withstand the tantrum she'll surely throw once she has the space and an audience, if you can hold to a sincere apology, you might actually be able to salvage this team and repair the damage you did to your mother's business." I smile. "It's up to you from here."

I stand up and grab my purse. "Call me when things go wrong," I say.

"It sounded like you expected everything to go really well," Coach Hanna says. "But now you're not sure?"

"The one thing I'm positive of is that nothing will go well. That's life—adjusting our plans when the world busts them to rubble." I drop my voice a little, looking directly at Maren. "I throw tantrums when that happens to me, too, by the way. I'm just better at apologizing afterward."

And I think I owe Steve a big one. I'll have to think about what to say when I pick him up for the auction Saturday.

15

ABIGAIL

For most of my life, I picked up a dozen eggs whenever I needed them from my local grocery store dairy and meat aisle. There were a lot of things about eggs that I didn't know. For instance, each egg laid is coated with something called a 'bloom,' which is an antimicrobial coating that keeps the egg fresh and clean. It's absolutely vital that eggs that are going to be incubated or left to sit under a hen for hatching have the bloom left intact, but even for unfertilized eggs someone wants to eat, they last longer and don't require refrigeration if the bloom remains intact.

The FDA makes commercial operations wash that bloom off, of course. It's necessary that commercial eggs be scrubbed, because most of those hens spend their entire life in a 2x2 box. The eggs are almost certainly covered in chicken poop.

No one wants to see (or eat) that.

Now that I'm living on a ranch, complete with free-ranging hens, we don't wash our eggs. I grabbed a little circular rack at the local hardware store to display them and to make sure we eat the oldest ones first, and I love looking at them on my counter, and I love the flavor of fresh eggs.

I've enjoyed learning more about the food we eat, and I also like the fact that a lot of our food literally goes from farm to table on the same day. But there are a few things about it that I don't love. Most of them revolve around poop. Ranch life involves a *lot* of poop.

Chicken poop.

Horse poop.

Cow poop.

So much cow poop.

I rake the hemp shavings inside the chicken coop once a week so the poop will break down. It's a deep compost system that saves time and resources, but it still smells. I suppose there's a life lesson I should share with my kids in this—life is full of poop, but it's also full of beauty.

Only thing is, you don't get the beauty without dealing with the poop.

I've been focused a little too much on the poop lately, so when I woke up this morning, I resolved to focus on the beauty instead. That's why I'm not getting annoyed by having to rake the chicken shavings—Emery's job—or by scooping the horse stalls Izzy didn't have time to finish. Or by having to drag the trash cans full of garbage to the curb—Gabe's job.

After all, we all fall behind sometimes.

It just feels like I'm the only one who cleans up when they do. Amanda, like the last few days, ducked out early. Today, she's leaving again for yet another bachelor date. They really seem to be cramming them in, which I suppose is kind of the point, but it's making for a wearying few weeks of disproportionate poop cleanup on my end. Figuratively, of course. Amanda has never been someone who did anything with the farm animals, and I think she'd die before scooping their poop.

I'm washing my hands when Kevin knocks at the door.

Roscoe isn't here to go nuts, so I guess technically Amanda's caring for one of the poop factories. Wherever she is, he's clearly with her.

"Hey, Kevin," I say. "Everything on track for getting the cows to the auction yard today?"

He bobs his head. "Yep. I'm actually here about the remodel."

I slap my forehead. "You need to do the final check, right?"

"I'm not too worried about my portion—I figure you're good for it. But the painter and the flooring guys are bugging me to get their final payment."

"I haven't had time to walk it with Amanda yet." I had big opinions on a lot of things, but she was a lot more concerned about the floors and paint colors than I was. "Um, I guess I can walk it now and let you know. I mean, if there's a problem, it should be obvious, right?"

Kevin shrugs. "I didn't see any problems, but Amanda communicated with Lenny and Jorge directly on a few parts, so I'm not sure."

"Let's take a look. They've been really patient."

We walk through the rooms the kids have been circling around like vultures for almost a week, now. The new bathroom looks perfect to me, and the bonus room feels bigger than I expected. The carpet's a little darker than I thought it would be, but I'm not sure what we can do about that. It's not as if we're going to have them redo all of it because it's a little dark. It should show less dirt than if it were lighter. "It all looks good to me."

"Great." Kevin smiles as I write him the final check.

"Thanks for your help," I say. "You did every bit of the job you said you would, and it was faster than we thought, too. You don't see that often."

"It was really fun," Kevin says. "You two were great to work for."

I arch one eyebrow. "Really?"

He laughs. "You didn't always get along, but trust me. Most of the couples I deal with are worse."

"Assuming we don't lose the ranch next week, we'll want to add a garage as soon as possible," I say.

"I'm so sorry you're dealing with that," Kevin says. "Please let us know if you need us to testify or anything."

"I will," I say.

At this point, I just want to know what's going to happen, even if it means we lose the ranch. I'm dreading having to call my realtor back. I still don't know what to tell him.

Most of the rest of the day flies by without event, but when he calls me at five p.m., I'm still not sure what to say. "I'm sorry," I confess. "I have been so busy—we had to move hundreds of cows from the ranch to an auction yard, and we're still loading and moving them."

"I wanted to tell you that the agent said the buyer loves your house and they're okay to give you one more day to decide."

I exhale. I'm not sure what one day will change, but I feel like I need it. "Thanks."

By the next morning, I'm just as torn, but Amanda's finally around. "Well hello, stranger."

"Did you see the carpet?"

I blink. I've barely seen her in three days and it feels like she's accosting me. "It looks a little darker than I thought it would—"

"It's entirely the wrong color." She fumes. "They wanted me to switch to that color, and I told them no. I should've guessed they'd try to pull something like that. If they think I'm going to pay for—"

Aww, geez. "Um, I kind of already paid."

Her eyes flash. "Why would you do that without talking to me first?"

"You haven't been here," I say. "You can't expect the entire world to wait on hold while you hide from your problems." I regret the words as soon as I say them, but now there's no way to take them back.

Amanda looks like I slapped her. "Excuse me?"

"I know you and Maren are struggling, and I know the cookie sales haven't been great, and I know—"

"That's exactly your problem," Amanda says. "You *think* you know everything. The great and perfect Abigail." She huffs. "In fact, you're so brilliant that you can approve the wrong work, and you can barge your way into my child's life and stick her into an awful position without even checking with me first."

"I must have called you twenty times in the last three days," I say. "You leave before I wake up, and you crawl in here after I'm asleep. I'm not sure how you've been managing that, given that you usually sleep about twice as long as I do. I even went by the cookie shop yesterday, and you weren't there, either. I honestly have no idea what you're doing, but don't put this all on me. I'm defending the ranch, I'm dealing with all the kids—dinner, schoolwork, refereeing their fights, cleaning—"

"The entire world won't fall apart if things aren't cleaned and wiped and mopped every day, Abby."

"Children need consistency and a routine," I say. "You aren't providing either. I'm sorry if you didn't like the way I—"

"That isn't an apology. That's an *I'm sorry but*, which is the opposite of an apology. It's a defense. Spare me the false apologies and let's get down to it. You paid for the wrong carpet, you forced the girl making Maren's life miserable into a position where they work together every day, and now you're rushing all the cows to auction without even telling me."

"Which is also *your* fault for whatever thing happened with Derek that you won't talk to me about! I tried calling you," I roar. "But you won't answer your stupid phone. And yes, I've done all those things alone, because you're a terrible mother and a lousy sister-in-law who hides anytime things get hard."

Amanda, finally, has no response. She simply stares at me.

And she's not the only one. By now, all the kids are awake, their heads poking through cracked doorways. Every single eye is wide. Every single mouth is dangling open.

And I'm Voldemort. Or Maleficent. Or someone even worse.

But I'm too angry to apologize in any way but the one Amanda just rightly accused me of using. The 'I'm sorry, but.' It's a crap apology that isn't really an apology.

So I do the one thing I can manage right now. "Come on, Ethan. Let's go sell some cows."

Five minutes later, either my own bad luck or karma, not sure which, bites me on the backside. When we knock on Kevin and Jeff's door, no one answers. I try calling next—no dice. Ethan finally circles the tiny house and peers into their bedroom window. They're both asleep. He bangs on the glass until Jeff finally rolls over. . .and pukes on the floor by the bed.

"We're both sick," he says when he sees us.

And boy, are they. I actually feel a little bit guilty when I leave them to go to the auction with my eighteen-year-old son. Alone. One of the worst things about being an adult is that no one takes care of you when you're sick anymore. You can't call in sick to most things in life.

For instance, we transported more than a third of our

cows to the sale yard—someone has to be present to sell them, even if that person has no idea what she's doing.

My sympathy for the two guys doesn't outweigh my panic. I'm going to have to handle the auction without the two farm hands I was counting on to help me. I've spent a lot of years of my life honing certain skills. Speaking clearly, negotiating, deciphering complicated and confusing language, and carefully crafting documents to ensure the exact result I want. I'm pretty competent with loads of child-rearing adjacent things as well, like diapers, bathing, potty training, feeding, and clothing. Unfortunately, none of that will help me today.

The only thing that keeps panic from clawing a hole in my chest is that Steve's coming.

When we pull up in his driveway at six-thirty a.m., the red car Stephanie drives is conspicuously absent. And more concerning, his truck is parked in front of the house. Ethan checks the barn apartment first, but there's no answer. It's irrational, but I'm nervous as I walk up to my own boyfriend's front door. I knock hard—rapping my knuckles heavily against the solid wood.

Unlike Kevin and Jeff, Steve answers and he seems to be in perfect health—but he doesn't look very chipper. "Abby." He grimaces. "The auction's today, isn't it?"

"We're on our way right now."

"Oh, man, I'm so sorry, but Stephanie had some kind of emergency and just left. I'm kind of stuck watching Olivia today."

"You don't want to watch me?" Olivia asks.

Steve shakes his head, "No, no," he says. "It's not that. It's just that I promised Abby I'd go with her to the cattle yard to help her sell some cows."

Olivia peers out at me around Steve. She looks unimpressed. "You can't sell cows by yourself?"

I'm not sure how to answer that. I'd never let my kid

talk to someone as rudely as she is right now, but generally speaking, I don't discipline other people's kids. "It's just that I've never done it before."

She turns toward her father. "Have you sold cows?"

Steve shrugs. "I've been to auction quite a few times, but not for cattle."

"See? He doesn't know anything about it either, and I don't want to go." Olivia crosses her arms, her slipper-clad foot tapping. "You said we could watch *The Great American Bake-Off*."

"I did promise her that," he says.

It feels like the words are being dragged painfully out of me—like you'd extract a particularly robust thistle, or maybe a wisdom tooth. "That's fine," I say. "I'll be fine without your help."

"Are you sure?" Steve asks.

"Of course," I say. "I'm a big girl."

Olivia rolls her eyes and shuffles off, probably to watch the baking show.

"I'm so sorry," he whispers. "This whole being a dad thing has really thrown me for a loop."

"It's hard on everyone, but I'm sure it's harder when you don't get to start at the very beginning."

Steve flinches, and I realize that we're both hurting each other without meaning to. "Yeah, it sure is."

"Alright, well, I'll see you later." I spin around and practically sprint to the minivan.

"Where's Steve?" Ethan asks. "And why did you go to the barn first?"

I sigh, and then on the way to the auction, alone, I confess the details about what's going on to him. I should really have told all the kids as soon as the paternity test came back, but it's been a rough week.

Ethan whistles. "And now he loves his little girl more than you?"

I laugh. "I'm sure he does, but that's not what bothers me." Or, to the extent it *is* what bothers me, I know I need to get over it.

"Did you tell him Kevin and Jeff bailed?"

I shake my head. "He would have felt worse if he knew, and he might have made Olivia come along. Believe me, that would have been really bad."

"She sounds like a brat," Ethan says.

I laugh. "She's an only child who didn't meet her real dad until last week, but that may be the worst thing she's guilty of." I think about how hard things must be for her right now. Having someone like Stephanie as a mother is probably hard enough, but losing her dad and getting a 'new one' she doesn't know, right away?

I can't even imagine.

In this circumstance, I'm clearly the one in the wrong. Even so, I can't help feeling like, lately, life has been all poop and very few eggs.

"I'm sorry, Mom." Ethan's voice is heavy.

"For what?" My silver lining in all this is that my kids have been borderline angelic.

"Just, you know, for all of it. You wouldn't be here at all if it weren't for me."

"We have a buyer on the house," I say. "Last month, I'd have agreed to the deal right away. But now?"

"Can they hold off until after the hearing?"

"It's a cash offer and they already want a quick move." I sigh. "I have to tell them something by tomorrow."

"I really am sorry," Ethan says.

"Normally, I'm pretty good at fixing things," I say. "But lately, it feels like nothing's going right, and no matter what I try, things only get worse."

Ethan's quiet for a while. "Is there anything I can do?"

"So many things are out of my hands right now." I

realize the last time I felt this way was the weeks before Nate died. That's when I break down sobbing.

Ethan tugs on my arm until I pull over on the side of the road.

That's why we're late to the auction yard, and it causes us to lose our spot in line, which means we're stuck selling our cows last. When they first go up, I realize we're making much less than everyone else. Like, a substantial amount per animal less. "What's going on?" I ask. "Why are ours selling for so much less?"

"It's the same price per pound." Ethan's brow's furrowed.

A man standing a few feet away spits something brown on the ground next to us. "Did you give 'em water?"

"They have waterers on the side of the fences," I say.

"But you gotta fill them up." He's looking at me like I'm a complete moron.

Because I am.

"They're dehydrated," I say.

But it's too late. We've already agreed to a price per pound and they're being weighed. It takes me a few minutes, but I calculate how much my oversight cost us—not to mention the misery of the poor animals who haven't had anything to drink since last night—and it's not insubstantial.

Instead of crying, instead of having a mental breakdown, I do the one thing that's within my power in this moment. I pick up my phone and I call my agent. "Hey, Adam," I say. "I hate to do this, but things are not going great here. I'm going to have to turn that offer down. And can you pull the house off the market?"

"Of course I can, Abby. I'll do it right away."

16
DONNA

Anxiety isn't exclusive to humans. I've seen dogs shake when they saw children with grabby hands. I've seen birds hop away nervously when someone offered a piece of bread or a pickle.

But I'm pretty sure humans have perfected it.

We worry so much about what's going to happen in the future that sometimes we let it utterly ruin our here-and-now. I've been the President, the Captain, and the Team Leader of the Anxiety Club for the last year or so, so I know just how much it can impact someone's life.

I think I'd forgotten how to have fun.

"No, you can't throw it." Will's smiling.

"You have to flick it, Mom." Aiden shows me how to flick with his fingers. "Like this, see?"

As if I don't know how to flick. "I just don't see the purpose of it."

"So you can get a touchdown," Aiden says. "Duh."

"I don't hear 'duh' enough these days," Will says. "It's an underused word." He's smirking, but Aiden doesn't pick up on his sarcasm.

"What's underused mean?" Aiden asks.

"It means that something isn't used enough," I say.

"Now stop trying to delay and take your turn," Will says.

"Yeah, Mom."

I pick up the paper napkin that Will turned into a tiny triangle and line it up, using my index finger on my left hand to hold it upright. "You guys are going down." I cluck. "Come on, though, you're the ones who aren't ready. Make my end zone."

"Mom, it's a goal post," Aiden says. "Sheesh."

"There's something called the end zone down there, too," I say.

Will's smirking. "That's the area right *before* the goal post."

"Whatever," I say.

Will lines up his fingers—thankfully it's Will doing it, because Aiden's hands are ridiculously small and hard to hit—and I take my shot. The paper 'football' sails up and over. . .and then it just keeps on going.

It plops in a lemonade glass at the table behind us.

Will cringes.

"What in the world?" Helen Wallace stands up and turns to glare at me.

It had to be the principal. My *boss.*

"I'm so sorry," I say.

Principal Wallace looks like she's about to snap me into several pieces. Or maybe just fire me.

Will snaps upright and turns around. "It's all my fault, Helen. I was showing Aiden how to play football."

Helen's entire face softens. "William Earl." She beams at him. "You were always so good with kids."

"But not so great at football." He sticks his hands in his pockets and I can just imagine the *aww shucks* face he's making.

"I don't know about that. You got our team farther than

they've ever gone before. It wasn't reasonable for Coach Bristol to expect you to carry them all the way. One amazing quarterback does not a competent team make."

"Whoa," Aiden says. "You were a quarterback?"

Our waitress ambles over then, and Principal Wallace taps her shoulder. "Marge, put their tab on my check, would you? Just thinking about the playoffs Will's senior year makes me smile."

"That's not necessary," Will says. "Really, I am more than capable of paying—"

"I insist." She winks at him. "Now you kids enjoy your meal."

"He's not a kid," Aiden says. "He's really old, like my mom."

Principal Wallace is laughing when she finally turns back to sit down next to her husband.

"Do you get free meals a lot?" I ask.

Aiden pipes up. "I never pay."

Will and I both laugh.

"Just in case your mom was asking me, I'll defend myself by saying that for many, many years now, I've paid for all my own meals. This is a strange anomaly that I can't explain." Will's sitting again, but he's still sporting a boyish grin that makes me want to lean across the table and ruffle his hair.

"Oh, maybe she was talking to you," Aiden says. "Yeah, she probably was."

"I should hope you never pay for your own food," I say. "You're only six."

"Seven next month," Aiden says.

"What day?" Will asks.

"Why do you want to know?" Aiden narrows his eyes, like Will's asking for nefarious reasons.

Will throws his hands up in the air. "Completely innocent curiosity, officer," he says, "I swear."

"It's November 27," I say. "Some years it falls on Thanksgiving."

"Oh, man," Will says. "That's probably annoying."

Aiden shrugs. "Not really. I usually don't have to go to school on my birthday."

"Fine," Will says. "I was going to invite you to join my club, but if you don't want to. . ."

Aiden's eyes light up. "What club?"

Our food arrives just then, another burger for Aiden, with tater tots instead of fries, and a salad with grilled chicken for me. It's not lost on me that we ordered almost exactly the same thing that Will brought us a few days ago.

"Thank you," Will says. "This chicken fried steak looks amazing."

Marge smiles and points at our drinks. "Need more?"

I cover my water glass. "Not for me. I always drink too much and spend the rest of the night hopping up to go pee."

Aiden snorts. Any mention of bodily functions is always worth a laugh when you're six.

"I'd love another lemonade," Will says.

"Oh, me too." Aiden grins his angelic little grin—the one he always makes when he desperately wants something. It's typically reserved for when he wants to watch TV, but apparently it extends to sugary drinks as well.

"Fine," I say.

The second Marge leaves, Aiden pounces. "But what about the club?"

"Well, I was born on a very strange day," Will says. "I thought you might want to join my Bummer Birthday Club. But if you love yours. . ."

"I do get just one present for Christmas and my birthday sometimes," Aiden says. "And I think people just say that it's a better gift, but really they forgot or they don't want to spend more money. It doesn't usually *seem* like it's nicer."

Will laughs. "That's our theme song."

"What's your birthday?" he asks.

"What day do you think it is?" Will asks.

Aiden sets his chin in his hand and taps his lip with his finger. "Hmm."

I don't answer—I know his birthday, but I'd forgotten. Inserting the right day wouldn't be fair for their little game. But for some reason, I want Will to know that I know. "Dashing through the snow," I sing.

"Donna!" Will's eyes are bright and happy—belying his chastisement. "No helping him."

"In a one-horse open sleigh," I continue. "O'er the hills we go...laughing all the way."

"Christmas Day?" Aiden shouts.

"Close," Will says. "Want to try again?"

Aiden frowns.

"Christmas Eve," I say.

"No fair," Aiden says. "She already knew."

"Having a birthday that falls on Thanksgiving qualifies you to join, I think," Will says. "If you want."

"What do you do?" my tiny son asks.

"Mostly we complain about how it stinks having a birthday that falls on a big holiday," Will says. "But it also means I'll get you two presents every single year. One on your birthday, and one on Christmas."

Aiden doesn't immediately agree. That surprises me. "But what about you?" he finally asks. "If you're doing that, and we're both in the club, do I have to get you two presents? And are there other members?"

"Yeah," I say. "How many people are we talking about?"

"You're a pretty smart little kid," Will says. "Would you mind getting me a present?"

"I don't have any money," Aiden says, "and my mom

doesn't have very much. But if you got me something and I didn't get you something, that wouldn't be fair."

"How about this?" Will asks. "What if you make me something?"

"Like, I could draw you a picture?" Aiden asks.

"I would love that," Will says. "I don't have a single bit of decoration up in my entire house. My mom's always making fun of me for it."

Aiden beams, and I cringe a little inside, imagining what pictures Will might get stuck with. I love Aiden, and he's very bright. Unfortunately, he inherited my artistic ability, which is to say, his is nonexistent.

After we finish dinner, we walk across the street to buy some cookies. I'm shocked to see the sign in the window of Amanda's shop.

TEMPORARILY CLOSED.

"I heard she's doing some kind of TV show," Will says. "Maybe that's why it's closed." He pauses. "Wait, you're friends with her, right? Someone told me that. Maybe it was Mom."

"I do like her," I say, "and we've hung out a few times. But I hadn't heard she was closing."

"Hopefully she'll be open again soon," Will says. "Though having a cookie shop in town's probably not great for my belly." He pats his midsection, which looks just fine to me.

"Hey, isn't that Uncle Patrick?" Aiden points.

It surely is my brother, practically speed-walking toward my cabin. One of the great things about small towns is that it's easy to walk across the street from the only diner to the only cookie shop. One of the bad things is that it's almost impossible to hide, even when you want to.

I glance sideways at Will. "We probably ought to call it a night."

"I ought to at least walk you two back," Will says. "Dangerous criminals could be hiding near your room."

"Daggett County has one of the lowest crime rates in Utah," Aiden says. "We just learned that in school."

I'm not entirely sure that's true, but I don't argue. "Believe me. You don't want to be anywhere near me when Patrick—"

As if he somehow heard his name from two hundred feet away, Patrick pivots and looks around like a greyhound scenting a squirrel. "Donna?" His eyes meet mine and he starts off again, only this time, he's dashing across the street.

With the teensy bit of automobile traffic we get, it's almost inconceivable that a car would be crossing the road just then. I almost regret it when it zooms right past him, leaving him unharmed.

I'm a terrible person.

"Hi, Pat."

"We need to talk," he says.

I sigh. "You kicked me out, and you're angry that I took your spot on the panel. I know both of those things already. What else do we have to talk about?"

Will frowns, but says nothing, thankfully.

"It's time you stop throwing a tantrum and come back home."

"Throwing a tantrum?" I actually actively wish that car had squashed him. He deserves a good smashing. "You kicked me out."

"And then, instead of taking Dad with you, you dumped him on Amelia, like expired milk."

"Wait, you're saying I could have been dumping expired milk on Amelia all this time?"

Patrick looks upward like he's praying for help. I happen to know he's never prayed in his entire life, so that also feels like a lie. "You can't act like an adult for even a moment, can you?"

"You kicked me out of the old farmhouse and promptly vacated the property, so I left Dad with your wife. I'm still not sure what part of this is tantrum-like or in any way wrong."

"Just come back," he says.

And that's about the closest I've been in my entire life to my brother apologizing. Unfortunately, Will chooses that moment to stand up for me. "Your sister's not an indentured servant. She was caring for your father because she's a good person, but she doesn't need to be abused on top of that."

"None of this is any of your business," Patrick says.

"When a citizen of Manila starts yelling at another citizen in front of me on the street, it becomes my business."

"She's sleeping with you, isn't she?"

Will punches Patrick.

I want to be upset about it, but I can't quite help being giddy. My brother's a huge guy—he's a rancher. He's tough, and I've never engaged in any kind of physical altercation with him because I knew I'd lose.

But Will is even bigger.

And apparently he's not afraid of my bully of a brother.

Patrick comes back up swinging, but Will catches his left hand and then his right. "Calm down. Watch your mouth. Your nephew is standing two feet away." Will's mouth twists. "And apologize to your sister or I'll give you a matching set of black eyes."

Patrick splutters.

"He doesn't have to apologize," I say. "It's fine."

"I disagree." Will doesn't even look at me. "Some people never learned how to treat a lady, but when that lady is staying at my mom's hotel, I'll make sure their education gets fixed."

"Let me go, or I'll sue you for assault."

He really will. "Let him go," I say, knowing it may already be too late.

"Nothing this guy says or does scares me," Will says. "That's the difference between your little sister and me." He inches closer to Patrick, twisting his hands until Patrick squirms. "Not a single jury in this county will convict me when I tell them the way I saw you treat your sister just now, or the things you said about her in front of her son. So go ahead. Keep threatening me, and we'll see if you win a dislocated shoulder before you learn to *apologize properly*."

"I'm sorry," Patrick practically spits.

"I'll come home," I say. "But I want the terms of my return in writing. I want a lease that details my right to be there, and that you can't kick me out on a whim." I touch Will's arm, a little in awe of the bulging muscle I feel there. "Let him go so I know he's not coerced into agreeing."

Will's lips tighten, but he does it. "Fine."

"Yes, that's fine," Patrick says. "But move back tomorrow."

"I'll have Abby draw up an agreement, and I'll make sure you sign. Only then will I move back in."

"My lawyer can—"

"No way. Abby."

Patrick looks like Will just force-fed him slugs, but he nods sharply. "Fine, if you want to spend your money on the agreement, go ahead."

"Let Amelia know, between now and then, that if Dad gets really upset, Hot Tamales calm him down."

Patrick rolls his eyes and stomps away.

"I don't wanna go back," Aiden says.

"Me either," I admit. "But doing things you don't want to do because they're the right thing is part of life."

Besides, the only way I'm ever going to get enough information to check whether Mom and Dad might have changed the life insurance beneficiary to me is to somehow pry it out of Patrick. And the only leverage I have is how badly Patrick wants me to take care of Dad again so he doesn't have to. I plan to make him share the details of that policy as part of my return.

Who said you can't make doing the right thing work for you at the same time?

17

AMANDA

In my mind, closing my cookie shop would involve fanfare and shame. I'd have to tell everyone that it was losing money, and that I didn't really love it, and maybe they'd argue with me.

The reality was that it took me thirty seconds to find a piece of paper and write TEMPORARILY CLOSED on it. Then I stuck it in the front window and locked the door.

Voila.

I wonder how many other things in my life have a much simpler solution than I ever realized. Certainly not the issues my daughter Maren created. When I finally got up the nerve to talk to her coach, I discovered that my sister-in-law had indeed already beaten me to the punch. The whole interaction with Coach Hanna left me feeling like a delinquent parent.

I didn't even agree with what Abby did, but it wasn't as if I had much grounds to argue about it.

But when I walked inside and saw that the carpet people had installed the wrong color—the color they tried to foist off on me that I refused? I was irate.

Hearing that Abby had approved it only made me more

angry. I still can't believe I yelled at her like I did, or that I criticized everything she did and said. The person I'm really angry at is myself.

She was right.

I've been relying on her shamelessly to do everything hard while I hide. My daughter Maren's issues. My cookie shop's failure. My duty to oversee the remodel as the one with the most flexible job. Cooking and cleaning around the house. Any responsibilities with the ranch. I still can't believe I slept through the mediation.

Abby called me more than twenty times, just like she said, and I never called her back. I was too ashamed. And if I was too ashamed then, how much worse do I feel now? I should just disappear.

The world would be a better place.

But I can't do any of that. I have two little girls to teach, to support, and to take care of. I can't keep wallowing and hiding and delaying, not for another moment. Except, I have to for today, at least. The only reason I finally force myself to face Abigail is that I have another date tonight. I actually slept in long enough that I had to come out to prepare for my flight, and there was no way to avoid seeing her for any longer.

I can feel Abby's kids' eyes on me.

Forget that—I feel *my* kids' eyes on me.

"Just a few more things to pack." I duck back inside my room.

I don't blame them for judging me. I'm judging myself. I did cause the issues with the cow sale contract, and then knowing that Maren was struggling, and that the remodel was wrapping up, I ignored it all.

Because that's what I do. I run away and hide when things are hard.

I did it as a child when my parents fought.

I did it as an adult when Paul got upset.

And I did it as a widow after Paul was gone.

In my experience, most every awful thing kind of shrinks the further in time you move away from it. Plus, my kids kind of learn to manage things on their own, which is good, right?

Even my lies to myself don't sound very good right now, and that's a crappy place to be.

Since I'll only be gone until tomorrow afternoon, I don't need to pack very much, but when I check my bag it contains three pairs of shoes and a toothbrush. I might need more than that. I stuff two outfits, some underwear and some deodorant, as well as my makeup tote into the small roller bag without giving it much thought, and then I finally poke my head out the door again.

The kids all freeze where they're standing outside in the family room and kitchen. Everyone but Ethan's present.

Maren won't meet my eyes. Izzy and Whitney glance my way and immediately return to what they were doing—unloading the dishwasher. Gabe's spoon is still dangling in the air above his cereal bowl, but when I look his way, he smiles encouragingly.

But it's Emery who rushes over and wraps her arms around my middle section. "I've missed you so much."

Her words claw at the ice that's formed around my heart.

"And I think the carpet looks really good, Mom. Maybe we'll like the darker color. The rest of the room is really bright, right?"

Which is exactly why it needed to be lighter, but I don't argue, not with sweet little Emery who's only trying to make me smile.

I pat her back awkwardly. "Thanks, honey."

"Besides, isn't it so exciting that the new part of the house is done?"

My grumpy attitude ruined something that should have

been beyond exciting. "Yes, it is. We can move stuff in tomorrow, once I'm home."

Emery beams up at me. "You did such a good job. I know we weren't supposed to go over there, but Izzy said her mom said it was okay—" She freezes, as if she too has now crossed a line.

"So you all looked, then?"

Emery swallows and nods.

"And what did you think?"

"I just *loved* it!" She beams at me. "The bathroom especially, and that one bright blue wall in the game room!"

Ah, the bright blue wall. The one I insisted was perfect when I spoke to Abby. The one that looks like crap. Of course Emery would like the one thing that's way too loud, way too bright, and way too obnoxious.

Oh, well. I may know it's a disaster, design-wise, but that doesn't mean my family can't appreciate it for just the reason I tried it in the first place: it brightens the room, and winter here is long. Maybe, sometimes, the mistakes we make can be what brings the most joy to our lives.

Or in this case, Emery's manufactured enthusiasm tells me just how much she loves me, even when I'm wrong.

I wrap my arms around her tightly, all my awkward embarrassment fading away. "Thank you," I whisper against her hair. "Thank you for loving without restraint. I needed it."

When I finally pull back, her smile is genuine, and when I look around the room this time, everyone else is smiling too, even Maren. As I load my stuff into my car, it occurs to me that maybe all they really wanted was to see me happy. Maybe all they wanted was to hear me tell them everything was okay. Perhaps the hardest part of my job can be accomplished just by showing up.

The one thing I haven't been doing much lately.

I'm in the driver seat, about to back down the driveway,

when a white SUV turns and veers down the drive. I immediately look toward the front door, but so far, no one has come outside. I fly out of my car and wave for Eddy to roll down the window.

"What are you doing here?" I hiss.

He grins the same grin that always makes my heart stop beating. The grin that, if he lived in a town with more than four hundred people, would have women lining up around the block.

I force myself not to lose focus. "Seriously, what in the world are you going to say if someone sees us?"

"I'll tell them I came by to check on Roscoe." He points to my black and white shadow. I hadn't even noticed he followed me out.

What if I had run over him? What's wrong with me right now?

I drop my head in my hands and start to bawl.

He flies out of the Tahoe, slamming the door behind him, and pulls me out of my car, too. He wraps me in his arms, murmuring against my ear, "Whoa, what's going on?"

I can't quite form sentences. I can barely drag in enough air to keep sobbing.

His strong arms just wrap more tightly around me, one of his hands stroking the back of my head. "Shh."

Finally, I calm down enough to formulate words. "I got in a fight with Abby."

"What did she do?" He scowls.

Something inside me snaps when he asks that.

I know I was wrong, not her. My kids know she was right and not me. Everyone in the world knows that, if the lawyer version of Mary Frigging Poppins, Abigail Brooks, fights with someone, it's not her fault. It's clearly all mine.

But I needed someone to be on my side.

"Bless you, Eddy Dutton." I kiss him then, and it shouldn't be hot. My face is wet from tears. I'm sure my eyes are puffy and bloodshot, but Eddy meets me where I am, kissing me back eagerly. And just like always, something flares to life inside of my chest. My fingers thread through his silky hair. My heart nearly beats out of my chest.

Which only makes it harder to spring apart so that no one in the house notices.

"I'll take you," he says. "Then we get a little time together."

"How will I explain my car sitting here?"

"Drop it at my place."

I like it—hiding my car so he can drive me. Maybe Derek wasn't totally wrong about it being hot to keep things a secret. Once we reach his house, I park behind his garage where no one will see. He opens the SUV door for me and deadlifts my bag into the truck like it's a purse. Roscoe, who hopped into his SUV the second the door opened, sits at my feet, licking my hand to get my attention whenever I stop petting him.

My bad mood lifts like fog melting away in the heat of the day.

In a normal place, a drive to the airport would be no big deal. But since we live in Manila, it's a three hour round trip. "Don't you have patients to treat today?"

He shrugs. "My patients tend to be flexible." He smiles. "No one was colicking, and there was nothing I couldn't move."

"But your practice—"

"You matter more," he says. "You matter more than everything."

His quiet words strengthen me once again. "Maybe I should just quit this dumb bachelorette thing," I say. "I mean, how bad could it be—"

"Aren't you starting something new with Amanda Saddler?"

I nod.

"Give it a month or two. Once you feel solid about it, pull that trigger."

He doesn't say *once I feel more solid about him*. He doesn't have to. For the first time in my life, I really *get* someone else, and he seems to get me. On the drive, I fill him in on just how awful and derelict I've been. . .and he remains on my side.

"But Amanda?"

The signs for the airport departures are all over now. "Yeah?"

"I say this from a good and supportive place."

My hands tremble, so I tighten my fist around the handle of my purse. "Okay."

"Call Abigail and apologize."

So he is disappointed in me after all.

"It's almost a miracle that two strong women like you are able to cohabitate, frankly. It's not all your fault or anything, but you're a big enough person to apologize and mean it. She might need that right now."

"Abigail's doing fine. She's like superwoman in stilettos."

"Maybe."

Abigail has been handling a lot—but she always does. That's kind of her thing. She did say that she was 'falling apart' before. I thought she was trying to make me feel better about being a mess myself, but did she really mean it? If so, I'm a truly lousy friend. "I'll think about it."

He smiles. "I know you will."

And I do. On the plane, I run through all the time I've spent with her in the past few weeks. It's an appallingly small amount, given that we live together. That tells me just how much I've been relying on her to handle things. I begin to worry that Eddy was being nicer than he should, more supportive than he should, and that Abigail might be 100% right.

I might actually be the villain.

I'm thinking about what that would mean when a hand reaches out and grabs my wrist. I shriek loudly—before my eyes meet the grabber.

It's David Park—my date.

And he's a *lot* hotter in real life than he was in his promotional photos. My scream cuts off abruptly. "Oh."

"Amanda?" His full lips twist upward on the right side into a half-grin. That gives me hope he might somehow see a forty-something woman screaming as more cute than horrifying.

I bite my lip. "Sorry. You startled me."

"You have an excellent set of pipes," he says. "Have you ever considered voice acting?"

I laugh. "Yeah, right." That reminds me—he's an artist. Maybe he wasn't kidding. "I'd be a terrible actress of any kind, I assure you."

"Why?" He releases my wrist.

My shoulders slump. "I lack that special insight into people that actors need to have."

"The fact that you recognize it already puts you above most Hollywood actors." He smirks.

"You're not too bad," I say. "I like you."

When he grins, he looks even more handsome. I don't usually think of Korean men as looking rugged, but it's the best word I can think to describe his sharp cheekbones and wide smile. "Right back at you." He inhales deeply. "Maybe it's the time you've been spending in that tiny town, but you're refreshing."

"Where to?" I ask.

"Baggage claim first, I assume," he says.

"Okay."

"And then, I was thinking, since you're in Chicago, we should get some deep dish pizza."

I scrunch my nose.

"Not a fan?"

"Too many toppings. I prefer the pizza you get in New York—or, like, Rome. You know, where pizza was invented?"

He cringes. "But that's basically crackers with a little cheese sprinkled on top."

"Crackers?" I laugh. "Maybe not quite."

"And saying it's the best because it's the closest to the initial idea is flawed logic. Then you'd be stuck with computers the size of a living room or cell phones as heavy as bricks."

"You're saying Chicago improved on pizza by making it both heavier and greasier?" I whistle. "Wow, we're off to a bad start." I cross my index fingers in an x. "If we aren't pizza compatible. . ."

"For the right woman, I might be able to overlook a few almost fatal flaws."

I pull out a fake notepad and pretend to jot down notes. "Magnanimous in his ignorance."

He chuckles.

He's no Eddy, but the date's not onerous. In fact, if I hadn't already met Eddy, I might even be interested. But when, after an excellent dinner at a delicious sushi place, he leads me around the corner. . .to a rack of rental bikes?

Game over.

"You must not follow my social media account," I say.

"What?" He unlocks his phone, presumably to open some kind of hippy account through which you can rent bikes to tool around the city.

"I am not an outdoorsy kind of person. I don't hike, or, like, mountain climb, or I don't know, fling myself at oncoming traffic when I bump into an uneven curb."

He chuckles. "I'd generally advise against that as well."

"I haven't been on a bike, other than a spin class, in at least twenty years." I take a tiny step backward. "The only thing I'm less likely to ride is a horse. If you don't believe that, ask my sister-in-law. She'd be happy to tell you all about it."

"Bikes don't bite, or poop, or buck," David says. "And you've probably heard that phrase, 'it's like riding a bike'? Yeah, there's a reason that's a phrase. I bet you can ride just fine."

I cross my arms and arch my eyebrow. "How old are you, David?"

"Forty-four," he says. "And if I'm fine to ride—"

I hold up my hand, palm out, to ward off more arguments and rah-rah type cheering. "You're not young. You should understand me when I say that in my twenties, I'd have gotten on. In my thirties, maybe. But I'm in my forties too, and I'm old enough not to do anything I don't want to do at this point. That includes making a fool of myself or breaking my ankle. Capice?"

David frowns, and I wonder if this date is going to be ending early. And then he starts laughing. "Well, I may be in my forties, but I'm clearly not wise enough to set up a backup plan yet. Now I have no idea what to do."

I point at the street ahead of us. "How about we walk and shop?"

"You don't want to ride a bike, but you'll walk?"

I gesture at my high heels. "No one should ride a bike in these, which you might have considered, Mr. Over Forty. But I can walk miles in these when shopping is on the schedule."

If there's a Lololime shop anywhere near, we'll definitely have to stop in. But if I buy something from another company that's not a direct competitor, perfume, for example, or a makeup company, I might get another endorsement out of it.

David sulks for a moment, but he pulls out of it quickly. By the time the date is through, he looks pleased. We found him a very handsome scarf at the Lolo store we finally reached, and a pair of sneakers they just released, too. I didn't tell him, but I'm sure they'll reverse the charges on them as a thank you for drawing even more attention to their new line.

When he drops me off at my hotel, he walks into the lobby with me, his hand brushing against mine. "In spite of our terrible incompatibility—" He ticks things off on his fingers. "Pizza, bikes, cross-country distance issues, etc., I had an awesome time. I'd love to see you again." His grin may not have two dimples like Eddy's, but that jawline and the way his jet-black hair falls over his eyes really works. "I'd be happy to bring you out here, or I'd even make the trek to. . .where is it you're living? Wyoming?"

I inch my way backward. "The thing is—"

"You're dating someone, aren't you?" he asks.

My jaw drops, and I splutter.

"I could tell—plus, it makes sense. Women like you aren't really single for long."

"No, I mean, I'm not—"

"Clearly there's some reason you're not making it public," he says. "And if that reason leads things to not work out, call me." And with that, the most promising first date I've ever had walks away.

I don't even regret it.

And the next day, when I finally get back to Utah, my non-public boyfriend is waiting for me, leaning against a column at baggage claim. His distressed jeans are slung low across his hips. His t-shirt clings to his flat stomach and tightens across his broad chest and arms.

And when he smiles?

I'd walk away from a hundred perfect Davids for this.

He waits for me to go to him, his eyes following me the entire way. Once I'm close enough, he takes my bag and brushes a kiss against my cheek. "I've decided not to follow your social media account anymore." His voice is low and rough. "Last night looked. . .way too fun."

I slide up on my tiptoes and press a kiss to his mouth. He drops my bag and wraps both arms around me, pulling me closer. I can't help a little whimper, and Eddy's arms tighten when he hears it.

"I hate this," he says.

"I love you," I say, and then I freeze. Sleeping babies aren't as still as I am. Ice sculptures. Marble statues.

I feel his smile against my mouth. "I love you, too, Amanda Brooks." He sighs then, and his breath, minty from the gum he's chewing, washes over my face, warm and comforting. "I needed to hear that."

As his words permeate my brain—he loves me too—I slowly unfurl. The doubts, the fears, the stress that's been swirling around and around inside of me for days dissipates a little, and I realize that I needed to hear it, too. Badly.

And for the first time in my life, I believe that his words are true. A man I care about deeply *loves me*. I wonder how long it will last—how long until he finds out something about me he can't live with and that love evaporates?

I plan to savor every last second.

18
DONNA

I love boiled eggs, but I'm picky about them. There's only one way I'll eat them. If the yolk is boiled so long it gets that grey coating? Blech. If it's not boiled long enough and the yolk is mushy because it's still raw? Hard pass.

The only way I've found to consistently get a perfect boil on my eggs is to place them in a pot when the water is room temperature and wait for it to reach the point of boiling. Then I immediately cut the heat and pull the eggs out and let them rest on a towel to cool out of the hot water. The yolk is soft and moist without being undercooked, and they make the perfect egg salad, for instance.

Because of my obsession with boiled eggs, I've watched plenty of pots.

Even with someone watching them, they always boil.

The reason people say a watched pot never boils is probably because it feels like nothing's happening for a really long time, and then there are a few bubbles, and then, BAM. Rolling boil.

It sneaks up on you, and humans get bored really easily.

That's how illusionists trick us so easily, of course. They

rely on our boredom, on our lack of focus, and on how distractible we are. It's not magic—it's exploitation of the foibles of human nature.

When I told Abby that I'd do anything I could to help them, I meant it. When I agreed to go up against my own brother, I thought I was prepared. I stuck to my guns, even when I got kicked out. I managed to use his desperation to get me back to care for Dad to negotiate my way to the information on Mom and Dad's joint life insurance policy —and then I called. They told me the policy is payable to the estate.

Which means Patrick didn't lie. I've seen the will—drawn up shortly after I started college. He gets everything, and my parents really did shaft me right up to the bitter end.

Patrick's inheriting the ranch, and he's getting the two million dollar life insurance policy, and I got a hundred and sixty thousand dollars over four years for tuition and housing. I try not to dwell on the fact that it feels monstrously unfair. After all, it doesn't help, and I agreed to it.

Teenagers shouldn't be able to make huge decisions.

But that's a rant for another day.

Because the water that sat quiet, still, and boring is finally boiling, rapidly. Today's the hearing where the court decides what happens to Birch Creek Ranch, and I'm so nervous that I can barely button up my shirt.

"Mom?" Aiden asks. "Are you okay? You look like a ghost."

"A ghost?" I ask.

"Your face and your white shirt are the same color," he says.

I'm pale, that's what he means. "I'm fine, honey. I've just been thinking a lot this morning."

"Did Dad make you sad again?"

I crouch and pull my sweet boy against my chest. "No, sweetie, this isn't anything to do with your dad." For once.

"Then it's Uncle Patrick." He scowls and his fists ball up against his sides. "I wish I was big enough to punch him like Mister Will did."

"Me too." I suppress a laugh.

"You should call Mister Will," he says. "I think he'd do it again."

That makes me laugh out loud. "But punching someone won't fix your problems. In fact, it usually only makes them worse."

Aiden frowns. "It made me really happy."

I can't argue with that. "Are you ready for school?"

"Grandpa's nurse just got here," he says. "And I put my lunch in my bag." He points at his blue backpack, bulging at the top. He probably shoved it in upside down again. I stand up and grab his bag and adjust the lunchbox as I walk out to the car.

"You just focus on school today, okay?"

"Is Gabe going to be okay?" He looks up at me with hope in his eyes. "He's the only person who's always nice to me."

That makes my heart lurch. "I thought you said that—"

"I don't want him to move back to Texas." Aiden's lip trembles.

After the past few months of misery and constant change, Aiden needs a friend. He deserves one. It doesn't surprise me at all that Abigail's son is a sweet kid and treats my son well. I'd be lying if I didn't admit, at least to myself, that Aiden's little proclamation redoubles my resolve to set things right for Abby, and Amanda too, of course.

With Steve and Eddy on the panel with me, I have high hopes it will be an easy repair. But as with all things in my life, it appears that my high hopes may be misplaced. The judge, a crabby old man on loan from

Vernal since Daggett County only holds civil court one day per month, snaps at Abigail the moment she tries to speak. I've never seen him before in my life, but based on the expression on his face, Judge Beckett isn't a very happy person.

"I've read the stack of motions and briefs from both sides," he says. "And I want to keep this hearing as short as we possibly can." He sucks air through his teeth. "It's my niece's baptism today, I'd like to get back in time to attend."

Is he kidding? He's telling us to just move things along because of his personal life?

"Of course, your honor," the tall, well-dressed lawyer representing the Institute of Research into Alien Life says. He picks an invisible piece of lint off his suit. "I can't imagine this will take very long. If you've read the documents, you know that the parole evidence—"

The judge practically shouts. "Sit down, Harris. I learned the parole evidence rule when you were still in diapers."

At least he's equally crabby with everyone.

Mr. Harris sits down next to his client and begins to whisper.

Unfortunately, we're stuck waiting for docket call, and then there are a handful of small cases that have to be dealt with before we can begin. I follow Abby and Amanda out into the hall while we wait, and Eddy and Steve trail behind. Patrick joins Mr. Harris and Mr. Nemoy to hatch whatever additional evil plots they've been incubating.

For the first time since I arrived, panting and out of breath thanks to being five minutes late, I notice that Amanda and Abigail aren't really talking. In fact, they aren't even looking at each other. Steve and Eddy are the only ones chatting.

"Are you two okay?" I ask.

"Don't ask me," Amanda says. "She's the one freezing me out."

Abigail blinks. "Freezing you out?"

"You barely said three words on the drive over this morning, and I still don't have any idea what to expect—"

"If you'd come to the mediation, or if you'd taken the time to read the briefs I forwarded you, you'd already know the main arguments come down to whether Jedediah wanted his relatives to receive the ranch as long as they complied with the spirit of his demands, or whether he meant for it to be strictly construed."

Amanda pretends to be sleeping, then opens her eyes again. "I'm sorry, were you speaking to me or boring everyone again?"

Abigail frowns. "I'm sorry you find the entire gist of our case boring, but someone had to prepare the arguments. Unless you'd prefer that we just hand the ranch over to Mr. Nemoy?"

She rolls her eyes. "Yes, that's what I meant. I wasn't saying that perhaps you could boil it down to something your *client* can understand. I was saying we should just give up."

"What happened?" I ask.

"Amanda hasn't been home enough for anything to happen," Abigail says. "But she's still upset that I approved the wrong shade of carpet and forgot to water the cows when I was selling them all alone, unexpectedly, thanks to some kind of fight she got into with the organic meat company."

"I'll fix things with Derek," Amanda says. "We can still sell the rest to his—"

"All of this will be moot," Steve says, "if you two are fighting so much that you can't go in there and explain what you want."

"I'm not sure she even wants the ranch," Abby mutters.

"And you do?" Amanda asks. "I was only gone for two and a half weeks. You and your kids were gone a month."

Jeff and Kevin sidle up next to the women then, effectively interrupting their bickering. "Everything okay?" Kevin asks.

"Perfect," Abigail says. "I'm so happy you made it."

The stenographer in the electric blue pantsuit cracks the door. "Judge is ready for you."

Abigail calls her witnesses first, starting with Jeff. She walks him through how long he's known Jed, and in what capacity he works at the ranch, and then she asks more pointed questions.

"Since our arrival, have my children and myself been involved in the running of the ranch?"

"Yeah, for sure," Jeff says.

"How exactly would you say we've been involved?"

"Well, your son Ethan's done downright near everything we've done." He scratches his head. "He's watered pasture, tended cows, and cut hay. He's dragged the pasture and met the vet, and he's moved the cows, too."

"Alright, and what about the rest of us?"

"You've been right there alongside him a lot of times. Izzy does a lot with the horses, which we use for the cattle and ranching stuff. She also helped a lot with the calves and went up a few times to check them when they's on the forestry land, taking salt and whatnot."

"Great. What about Whitney or Gabe?"

"Whitney's young, but she's pretty tough. She cleans water troughs and helps with feeding. We had her along to mend fence a few times, and she watches and learns. Gabe hasn't done much, but he's always helping out around the ranch with stuff as he can, like gathering eggs from the chickens and feeding the cats."

"So would you say that we've been 'running' the ranch, in the way that Jed intended?"

"Objection, Your Honor," Mr. Harris says. "She's—"

"Overruled. Please answer the question," Judge Beckett says.

"I would," Jeff says. "For sure. I think old Jed woulda been real happy with your work."

"Did Jed ever talk to you about the will, or the things he intended for you and Kevin to do after his passing?" Abigail asks.

Judge Beckett holds up his hand. "Wait."

Abigail turns.

"What about her?" He points at Amanda. "You didn't ask what she's done."

Jeff's eyes move from Amanda to Abigail, questioningly.

Abby shifts from foot to foot nervously, but pursues the line of questioning the judge requested. "What about Mrs. Amanda Brooks and her two daughters? How involved in the day-to-day management of the ranch have they been?"

Jeff glances at Amanda apologetically. "Well, the older Miss Brooks is always at cheerleading stuff, and the little one, she takes some riding lessons. She also helps Izzy and Whitney sometimes."

"What about Mrs. Amanda Brooks?" Abigail cringes as she asks.

Jeff inhales and exhales slowly. "Well, I can't rightly say she's done anything." He pauses. Then he shrugs. "For the ranch, I mean, at least, not that I've seen."

"Nothing at all?" The judge asks.

"She did help remodel the farmhouse," Jeff says.

"But with the cows and livestock?" The judge asks.

Jeff shakes his head.

Unfortunately, Kevin's report is the same, and when Mr. Harris questions them, he specifically targets the issue of what Amanda does. He really hammers home that of the two families, one of them has done nothing at all.

Judge Beckett shuffles some papers, and looks over

some things, but eventually he calls up the panel of three. "Steve Archer, Edward Dutton, and—" he squints. "Mrs. Donna Windsor."

I cringe.

"I prefer Donna Ellingson."

He squints again. "But it says here—"

"My divorce is being finalized," I say, "but for now—"

Judge Beckett sighs. "Just come up here. The will stipulates that you three will determine whether the one-year commitment has been made. As such, I'd like to know your opinions both on what Jed wanted, and on whether these women and their kids are on track to comply with the will requirements."

"They are," Steve says. "And Jed would have wanted his nieces and nephews to have that ranch. He only included the other people as a fallback, because he didn't want it to go to the government."

"Objection," Mr. Harris says. "That's not—"

Judge Beckett waves his hand. "Overruled. I asked the question."

Mr. Harris is scowling when he sits.

"Go on."

"Jed hated the government more than anything else, but he loved his family a great deal. He spoke of his two nephews all the time. He would have wanted their children to inherit before anyone else. He certainly wouldn't have minded that they left for more than a week. It was a huge change of life for them to commit to move out here, especially since his nephews had passed away, and their two widows who had never experienced ranch life were caring for the children."

"And what do you think about the division of the ranch between the children, if they are found to qualify?" The judge cocks his head. "Do you think both women have been meeting the requirements?"

Steve frowns. "I think that if the women themselves can't agree, we can deal with that issue once the year is up. I don't think it has much to do with the question today."

"I think it has a great deal to do with it," Judge Beckett says. "Only one of these families needs to meet the terms of the will. If the other isn't complying, they're already out."

This doesn't look promising.

"What about you?" Judge Beckett turns to Eddy.

"I think Amanda has done plenty to comply," Eddy says. "Does the homemaker not support the ranch because she's not out roping cows?"

"Are you saying that Abigail Brooks has been running the ranch and that Amanda Brooks has been tending to the house and children?" the judge asks.

Eddy scratches his head. "Well, not exactly, but—"

"The affidavit mentions that you've been to their house quite often, Mrs. *Windsor*." The judge tilts his head when he stares at me. "What's your opinion on whether Mrs. Amanda Brooks, who was gone for less time, has been meeting the will requirements by running the ranch?"

As far as I can tell, Amanda has done absolutely nothing, other than live in the house with her girls. "The thing is, I think her kids weren't quite as familiar with riding horses or—"

"And have they been anxiously engaged in learning how to ride so they can help in the future?" he asks.

I'm no lawyer, but it's beginning to feel quite clear. Our little panel might be able to save the ranch for Abigail, but only if we don't fall on an Amanda-shaped sword. I doubt Steve or Eddy will be able to say what needs to be said, and if they dither about this, Abigail may lose her chance, too.

I don't like being the bad guy, but if Charles' acquittal taught me anything, it's that sometimes the law gets confused if you're not absolutely one hundred percent clear. After everything Abby's done for me, I'm not about to let

Amanda drag Abigail down. And Aiden needs Gabe. I can't let him move away, not if speaking the truth can possibly prevent it.

"As far as I know, Amanda and her children haven't done anything at all to help with the ranch. Abigail and her children have done everything."

The trial moves along after that, but I don't pay as much attention, because the look Amanda keeps leveling at me is similar to the one I imagine was leveled at Judas when he accepted those silver coins. I've betrayed her, and she didn't see it coming.

When the interminable hearing is finally over, it's almost five o'clock. I hope Beth got Aiden alright, and that he's safely eating macaroni and cheese right now.

Judge Beckett stands, and I steel myself to hear his ruling. I wonder how Amanda's going to react when she loses the ranch. Will Abigail kick her out? Surely not. But she might head back to New York anyway, if her children don't stand to inherit. How will Abby feel about that? Based on their interactions earlier, she might be relieved.

"As you all know, I've listened to a lot of testimony today. I've read affidavits, too." He grunts. "However, after careful consideration of all the testimony and after looking at the relevant case law, I do think that the four corners of the document are clear. I think that more than the week stipulated as a break from the ranch was too long, and that Jedediah Brooks' will requires a very simple solution." He pauses and makes eye contact slowly. "I therefore order that the terms laid out by the will have not been met, and that Abigail and Amanda Brooks and their children have thirty days to vacate the premises so that the ranch may be sold or possession of said ranch assumed by the Institute of Research into Alien Life."

Patrick whoops in the background.

"However," the Judge says, "I further order that no sale

shall be allowed of said ranch to Mr. Patrick Ellingson." He narrows his eyes. "The evidence of an agreement between the Institute and Mr. Ellingson was what gave me the most pause during these proceedings."

"That's beyond the scope of your jurisdiction," Mr. Harris says.

Judge Beckett stands up. "Is it?"

Mr. Harris blanches.

"Mr. Nemoy, will you agree to put the property up for sale by auction and sell to the highest bidder, in the event that you decide to sell?"

The agent for the Institute stands up so fast that his hand catches a stack of papers and knocks them flying to the ground. "I do, Your Honor. Most certainly."

Judge Beckett bangs his gavel. "I'll get the official order distributed shortly. Court is dismissed."

19

ABIGAIL

The cowardly part of me is relieved.

I never wanted to work a ranch. I never wanted to leave Houston at all. Maybe now life can go back to normal. I won't have to navigate the awkward situation with Steve, his ex, and his daughter. I won't have to suffer through more remodeling and fighting and drama with Amanda and her undisciplined children.

I can go back to living peacefully in my beautiful, comfortable home, where we have a pool, no animals to care for, and I have my own bathroom. We can have movie nights on Fridays, and I can work during the day and have my evenings free to attend the kids' many school and church activities. And. . .then I can sink back into the quiet despair that a move and working outside and being surrounded by new people temporarily freed me from.

I have no idea how I'm going to tell Ethan that I failed him. I still can't quite believe that we lost. Apparently Donna and Amanda are having the same issue. They both look dazed.

Steve and Eddy, not so much.

Steve's complaining so loudly that I'm legitimately

concerned he might be held in contempt. Eddy's standing next to him, his fists tightly clenched, a vein in his neck popping. Who knew he'd be this upset? It's not like he and Amanda have seen each other lately, but clearly he was still harboring hope for their future—hope that this judgment has now squashed

And now Steve's actually swearing.

I grab his arm. "Hey."

He cuts off and spins around.

"I'm so sorry, Your Honor," I say. "I think we're all a little shocked."

The judge doesn't look mollified, but instead of calling the deputies, he simply turns and walks out. That's a win, frankly.

"I'm sorry," Steve says. "I didn't mean to make a scene, but I can't believe—are you alright? You must be even more upset than I am." He sinks onto the chair next to me and wraps his arm around me. "We can appeal it or something, right?"

"We could, yes, but I don't think I want to." I sigh. "I'm tired of fighting for something I didn't even want in the first place."

Steve looks like I punched him. "Something you didn't even want?"

"Last year at this time, no, even six months ago, I wouldn't have considered running a cattle ranch. I mean, yes, this is where we've come, and it felt like the right thing for my family each step of the way, but one thing I've learned in the past two years is that some things in life are inevitable. Fighting against them is like hurling ourselves against sharp rocks."

"You're just giving up?"

"Sometimes in life, you lose," I say. "And this is one of those times."

"It's November 9th," Amanda says softly. "That means we have to be out two weeks before Christmas."

It's not ideal timing, that's for sure. "Obviously the kids will need to finish out this semester before I move them back home."

Amanda blinks. "So you're going back, just like that?"

Why is she, of all people, asking me that? "Aren't you?"

"Aren't I what?" she asks. "Moving back to New York? Pretending that this past six months never happened?"

I'm missing something important, but I can't for the life of me think what. Maren hates it here. Amanda's never home, and meeting bachelors all over the country is practically impossible from out here in the boondocks. "Does Lololime want you to stay, even if the ranch is sold?"

"Obviously they had no idea it might be sold out from under us." She sighs. "No one expected that you'd lose."

No one expected. . .that *I'd* lose? As if this is all my fault? I inhale through my nose and exhale through my mouth. "I've always said we had fifty-fifty odds," I say. "I never acted like this was a slam dunk."

"But you're Abigail," Amanda says. "Perfect Abigail never loses. None of us thought you *could* lose."

I'm flabbergasted. Is she kidding right now? "We both left because we didn't want the ranch," I say. "The will gave us a week for trips during our trial year, and we left for a month. We only had an argument to justify keeping it because the will didn't explicitly state that we *couldn't* take a month off and then make it up. That was our angle. That, and the fact that people would probably assume that Jed would prefer his land go to his family and not a foundation."

"I'm still shocked," Donna says. "Who'd have thought the judge would rule for the crazy alien people?"

As if she didn't even hear Donna's attempt to lighten the mood, Amanda plows on. "The reason we never expected you to lose is that you're such a control freak that you handle every single thing yourself. You dig and push and prod and pry until you get exactly what you think is best."

"Are we still talking about the ranch?" I ask.

Amanda seems to be ignoring me, too, she's so caught up in ranting. "*Only* Abigail knows what to do and how to do it, and everyone else who disagrees is wrong."

"I don't insist that everyone do things my way," I say.

"Perfect Abigail would never insist on such a thing," Amanda says. "She always knows the right way, and it just takes a while for us stupid mortals to see it."

"You need to calm down," Donna says. "I'm sure Abigail doesn't think that she knows more—"

"And you," Amanda says. "Do you really think that I do nothing to help with the ranch or to help out with the kids?" Amanda crosses her arms. "Is that what Abby says?"

I'm quick to defend on that count. "I never said you don't do a single thing—"

"You have no idea what I do," Amanda says. "Neither of you do. You had no right—"

"The judge asked her point blank," I say. "She had to give an answer, but it doesn't matter now, anyway."

"You didn't defend me," Amanda says. "When she said I'm useless."

I hear the hurt in her voice that she's masking with anger. I know she's upset and sad and scared, because I feel all those same things, but as an adult, as a friend, and as a sister-in-law, I'm not lashing out. That's not what grown up people do. We think and ponder and reflect.

But right now, I don't have it in me to do those things, either, even though I know I should. I'm so exhausted that I only have room for my fury. Am I masking for something else? Probably, but I'm done letting her just attack me.

"Are you really mad that we were *honest* on the stand?" I

ask. "Did you want us to perjure ourselves and say that you actually *did* ranch stuff?"

Amanda's eyes flash. "Perjure yourself? Defending me is lying?"

"I don't even know why you're mad," I say. "Honestly, I don't. You won't ride a horse. You don't like the cows, and you certainly don't help with other animal chores or even household chores. You don't make your kids help either. I can't figure out why you're here in Utah at all, other than your competitive streak, forcing you to prevent my kids from inheriting something yours could have had."

The second the words leave my mouth, I know I've gone too far. Ever since I was a child, I've been able to carefully sharpen verbal razors and plunge them into other people's hearts. Once I hurt my sister badly, and ever since then, I've made it my life's work not to harm the people I love with carefully crafted barbs.

But now I've done it to Amanda.

Like a boat whose sails have been cut, she deflates right before my eyes.

"That's not what I meant," I say, but I can tell that it's too late.

"I don't think anyone could accuse you of being imprecise," Amanda says. "Actually, I'd be afraid of accusing you of anything at all." She spins on her heel and marches off.

Eddy trots after her. Hopefully he can give her a ride. I doubt she'd get back into the car with me for a million dollars right now.

"That was awkward," Steve says. "And I'm a little scared of you right now."

"Me too," Donna says.

"But I'm also a little turned on," Steve says.

"And now you lost me," Donna says.

"Thank goodness for that." Steve reaches for my hand.

"Let's go get some dinner and we can talk about how to deal with all this in the best way possible."

Deal with this? Is he kidding? "There's not much to deal with," I say. "I just need to locate a place for us to stay until school finishes out, and start coordinating the details of our trip back home."

Steve drops my hand. "Are you serious? You're just going to decide, right here, right now, to move back to Houston?"

"Ethan wanted to work a ranch," I say, "but now we don't have one. You may not have looked at the same numbers as me, but a cattle ranch only really works in this day and age if there's not a big mortgage on it. If you have a bank note to repay, you're lucky to break even—you have no profit to live on."

"But there are other things you could do here," Steve says.

"There may be other things most people could do here, but not me. My legal career's coasting on fumes already," I say. "I turned down an offer of partnership to support my son in pursuing this dream I never understood, but I'm not going to keep watching my career evaporate for no reason at all."

"Actually, you know what? You two keep talking. I think I can find another ride," Donna says.

"No," I say. "It's fine. Steve drove here—he can drive himself home."

Donna looks like she wants to run very far and very fast and hide. But I need her around to keep things civil and calm, so that I can get out of Dodge myself. I don't have the bandwidth to have some kind of knock-down-drag-out fight in the middle of the courthouse with the boyfriend of five minutes I'm dumping in order to go back to Houston.

"I've been busy lately, and I'm sorry," Steve says. "But this isn't the kind of decision you make on the steps of the courthouse."

I'm not going to get away from any of this easily. I'm not sure why I thought I might. Optimistic exhaustion, maybe? "Of course not," I say. "Let me take Donna home, and then I'll call you."

"Your kids will need dinner," Steve says, "but once that's done, we need to talk."

I nod, and then, blessedly, Donna and I make a beeline for my car.

"That was awful," Donna says. "And I'm pretty sure that Amanda hates me."

"You're not alone. We should start a club," I say. "I'll be the President, and you can be the secretary."

"How about the treasurer?" she asks. "I hear they don't do anything when you embezzle money."

I wince. "I still can't believe he walked."

"Please don't feel bad," Donna says. "You weren't even part of the prosecution. And that money you found that was in Aiden's name is paying for the lawyer you found me for my divorce."

"Is the hearing soon?"

"Next week," she says. "But after the criminal trial and today's hearing, I'm even more nervous." Clearly, legal stuff can go sideways fast.

"Most people fail to realize that there are two sides to everything. To the Institute of Alien Studies or whatever, justice was just served. They built a case just like we did, but ours rested on equity, and theirs rested on the plain and simple text of the law." I shrug. "I always knew we might lose. I thought everyone knew."

"Even so, you must be more shaken than you seem." Donna clicks her seatbelt into place.

"Do I seem fine?"

Donna frowns. "You seem completely unflappable."

The last time I heard that word, it came from my mother, also referring to me on the day after Nate died. I'm not sure why, but it hits me strangely, and suddenly I'm huddled over the steering wheel, bawling.

"Oh," Donna says. "Wow, I was wrong. I thought that nothing could be odder than seeing you completely composed after losing your family ranch, but this is worse. I'm so sorry I made you cry."

Why do humans work so hard to eliminate all suffering and all misery? It's a part of life. A valuable and critical part of life. Mourning. Changing expectations. All of it.

But for Donna's sake, I choke back my misery, bit by bit, and soon my sobs become hiccups, and then they disappear entirely. My voice sounds smaller than I've ever heard it before when I say, "It feels like my life has been in a nosedive for weeks."

"A nosedive? Why?"

"First, I got warning that this might happen."

Donna looks guilty.

"I don't blame you, you know, or your brother Patrick, though I know he kind of forced this whole situation. But if we hadn't left for so long, none of it could have happened. We were the ones who made a mistake."

"But surely—"

"Blaming people is rarely helpful," I say. "It's why I never should have said what I did to Amanda. She's not been much help with the ranch, but she's been the best friend I've had in a very long time. She's been there for me in a way I haven't had since Nate died. I was out of line."

Donna's facial expression is strange. I can't tell quite what she's feeling.

"I always know just the right thing to say to ruin everything."

"You should be making a game plan for the future with Amanda, not Steve." Her facial expression is odd. Her eyes are tight, and her mouth is twisted.

She's jealous, I realize. She's jealous that Amanda and I are close. "Is Patrick your only sibling?"

Donna nods.

"I'm so sorry," I say. "I can relate, though. My big sister's not an easy person to get along with, and I don't think she'd ever take advantage of me, but she's usually not my biggest fan, either."

"Why'd you ask about Patrick?"

"You probably always wanted a sister," I guess.

Donna's eyes widen. "That kind of thing is why people didn't think you could lose. How in the world could you know I was thinking that?"

"You looked. . .like you wished you had an Amanda to apologize to."

Donna sighs. "I'm like an open book. I'm doomed next week. Charles will take all the money and get custody of Aiden, I just know it."

"Sufficient unto the day is the evil thereof," I say.

"What?"

"It's from the Sermon on the Mount," I say. "Jesus told people that they should worry about the problems they have now, and try not to fret about things that haven't happened."

"I guess enough bad things have already happened today," Donna says. "I should save some terrible stuff for next week."

I finally put the car into drive and head out toward Donna's place—which is also Patrick's place. I can't believe he got his way, and his alien people will be selling him our ranch soon. "Why does he want more ranch land?" I ask. "I mean, doesn't your brother already have a huge ranch?"

"Patrick's the kind of person who's never happy with what he has. He's always wanted more, ever since we were kids."

"But can he even manage—" My phone rings. I answer

it without looking with the flick of my thumb and put it on speaker, since I'm driving. "Hello?"

"Abby," a warm voice says. "You asked me to look into Edward Dutton, and I have good news."

You have to dig and push and prod and pry until you get exactly what you think is best. Amanda's words accuse me, even without her here.

"Abbott," I say. "Here's the thing. I asked you to look into Eddy Dutton back before—" I sigh. "You know what? It doesn't matter. Nevermind about the whole thing. It was none of my business in the first place, and the woman I was digging for doesn't want my help."

"Really? Because I found something pretty strange, and I thought it might help."

Dig and push and prod and pry.

Amanda's right. I really do all those things. I'm the worst. "I'm sure. Thanks for calling me back, but just chuck whatever you found in the trashcan. Even if it's amazing, it won't do us any good. We're all about to go back to our regularly scheduled lives."

"Uh, okay then. If you're sure."

And I've reached Donna's place. "I really have to run, but can I call you in a few days? We should catch up, and I definitely owe you a thank you for digging around for me, even if I don't need it."

"Sure, any time. After that spider thing, I feel like I still owe you."

I laugh. "Yes. I did slay that tiny black spider while we were studying for the bar, and you should be forever grateful."

"That tiny spider was a black widow," he says. "I *am* grateful. Did I mention that one bit my uncle on the *face*? He still has these two gnarly holes on his cheek."

"Then maybe you do owe me," I say. "But I don't need to collect today."

By the time I finally get off the phone, Donna's already headed for her door.

"Wait." I unbuckle and trot after her. "I wanted to thank you. I know it wasn't easy, but I appreciated your support today. Truly."

"I'm sorry it didn't help at all."

"I only wish I'd known we were doomed," I say. "Now Amanda's hurt for no reason at all."

Donna places a hand on my elbow. "I know you're in retreat mode, and I get it, believe me. But you should talk to Steve and Amanda and really listen to them. Amanda's hurting, and Steve's a really good guy. He might even be worth changing your plans for."

After the day I've had, I'm not sure anyone really wants me to stick around.

20

AMANDA

"She didn't mean any of that," Eddy says. "It was a rough day for all of you." He sighs. "I'm actually still having trouble believing that happened."

"You and me both." I sink a little lower on his bouncy, squeaky seat. "You might need a new truck."

He laughs. "You know this isn't my normal truck. I'm borrowing Dad's farm truck because I dropped mine off to get the brakes done."

And now I have no idea what else to say.

What can I say to the guy I'm crazy about, maybe the first guy I've ever really loved, when I know I'm about to be homeless?

"You could live with me," he says.

Elation. Panic. Hope. Fear. I have so many emotions about his probably offhand comment that I don't even know where to begin.

"Or not," he says. "We could find you another place, I'm sure." His eyes widen. "Or what about Amanda Saddler?"

"I'm sure she'd love to have me invade the home she's had all to herself for decades with my two little brats."

"Your girls aren't brats," he says.

"I'm pretty sure the official court record specifically reflects that people think we're lazy, useless, and spoiled."

Eddy glances my direction. "It wasn't that bad."

"Basically it was," I mutter.

"All they said was that you don't ride horses and rope cattle, and that's true."

The plastic coating on the armrest of the side door is peeling in one spot, and I pick at it. "If the court had ruled in our favor, would you say, as an official member of the panel, that my girls and I should get half the ranch?"

Eddy frowns.

My heart breaks. "You agree with them."

"Believing that the will required you to actually work the ranch to inherit it and thinking you're useless aren't the same." He reaches for my hand.

I snatch it away.

He pulls onto the muddy shoulder just as it starts to rain. "Amanda."

I shake my head. "Just take me home, please." As I say the words, I realize it's not really home any more. I mean, sure, we won't be kicked out for thirty days, but something has shifted. Yesterday I was imagining how we'd decorate for Christmas. Emery and I were looking at hand towels for the new bathroom on Amazon. We have six months of the happiest memories Emery and Maren and I have had in that house, and they're all about to disappear. After I put all that effort into the remodel, the alien people are going to sell it to the highest bidder.

It's not my home. Not anymore.

My future is, once again, completely up in the air. I have no reason to stay here. I have no direction. I feel like a kite—or actually, a grocery store sack, rolling and spinning and crumpling in the wind, is probably a better comparison.

I'm trash-bag-rolling through my life once again.

One little court order and everything is wrecked. A tear slides down my cheek and I swipe at it.

"Amanda Brooks, look at your boyfriend, please."

I drag in a ragged breath. I can't start sobbing. I just can't. He must already think I'm a pathetic sponge. "Why would you even want me to live with you?" I steal a glance in his direction.

He's looking at me the exact same way he looks at puppies, at baby ducks, and at newborns.

"Don't do that," I say. "Don't pity me, or patronize me, or like, pat me on the head and coo."

He laughs. "Why on earth would I do that?"

"You have a look in your eye like you can fix me, or like you can pep talk me or, I don't know."

This time, when he takes my hand, I don't pull away, because his entire expression has shifted. "Amanda, I wasn't thinking about how I could fix you. I was thinking about how ridiculously lucky I would be if you moved in with me and I had you close all the time."

His smile is crooked and I've never wanted to brush my fingers against his lips more.

"You bring me joy. You brought light to my life again—actually, *again* is the wrong word. I can't think of a time I've ever been as happy as I've been the past few weeks."

"But—"

"No, I'm talking right now. Your job is to listen. And I mean, really listen. You, Amanda, are funny. You're caring. You're energetic, and you give your all to things when you commit to them. Don't let your insecurities steal your future, and don't let them steal your faith in your new family and friends. Not in me, not in Amanda Saddler, and hear me when I say this. Not in Abby. She loves you almost as much as I do."

I turn to look at the dead trees and think about what he's saying. Am I projecting things I fear about myself onto

Abby and Donna? Did they really just say I hadn't been helping around the ranch because I don't like ranch stuff?

I'm sick of always being the one who's wrong.

"Amanda?"

I turn.

"You may be thinking that you have no reason to stay now, but you're wrong. Actually, as I sat there listening to that testimony, it struck me clearly."

"What did?"

His grin isn't crooked this time. He's beaming from ear to ear. "You were never here for the ranch, right? You don't love cows or horses or chickens or farming or any of that."

"I think that was pretty clearly established."

"Then that was never why you came back, and so losing it shouldn't matter."

My heart swells. "You want me to stay, even with absolutely nothing to keep me here."

"You have me," he says. "I like to think that I matter."

"But no one knows we're dating," I say. "What would we tell them as my reason to stay?"

He looks around us frantically. "Who are these people? Why do we have to tell them anything?"

I whap his shoulder. "You know what I mean."

"You have a dear friend who's giddy to go into business with you. She wants your help to remodel properties for sale."

"But she doesn't really need me," I say.

"If you think about it, her belief that property values are about to rise and that modern, remodeled properties will sell like hotcakes soon is all thanks to you."

"What?"

"Derek picked this site for you—don't argue with me. I heard him say that myself."

"While hiding in the bushes." That image of him popping out of the shrubbery still makes me laugh.

"I'm not ashamed of that," he says. "Okay, maybe I'm a little ashamed. I'm a grown man who hides in bushes. But I'm not ashamed enough not to do it again, and I'm planning to use the information I managed to gain from it any chance I get."

I am excited to remodel properties with Amanda. We're supposed to go over a list of her properties tomorrow and prioritize them, and then visit our top sites and make a game plan.

"Do your girls want to leave?"

I'm too ashamed to admit that I don't know. "It's not like I was giving them an option before."

"They knew there was a hearing today," he says, "surely. Were they nervous? Or did they say anything about it?"

How's he a better parent than I am? He doesn't even have any kids.

"Amanda, you need to stop stressing over everything. It's fine if you don't know—I just thought they might have said something."

"No, Abby's right about that. I've been a terrible mother lately."

He chuckles. He *chuckles* about me being a bad mom.

"You're not a terrible mother. You're a busy one who knows that they were with cousins, in a safe place. And you're not a helicopter parent, which helps your kids learn to manage things, but they know they can come to you. And they're both doing well. Stop worrying that every single comment anyone makes means you're a failure. Abby never said you're a terrible mother."

"Not today, but she said exactly that a few days ago."

Eddy frowns. "How's Abby doing?"

"You're not even mad at her?" I'm a little pissed at him, now.

"I work with animals a lot. Have you ever seen an animal that's hurt? Or scared? That's when they lash out. I don't know Abby very well, but I'd say that her attacking you might tell us more about her than it tells us about you. I already know you're not terrible. I bet she knows that too. I think the only person who might not know is you."

Could Abby be hurting?

"She's still dating Steve, right?"

I nod.

"And his crazy ex and his kid are still hanging around?"

"Yeah."

"What about Donna? Isn't Abby helping her out?"

I swallow. Why is Eddy so calm about all of this?

"Plus, she's working remotely, and that can't be easy."

"I freaked out on her about the remodel, and Derek canceled our cattle contract, and the guys got sick and she had to go to auction alone."

Eddy whistles.

I may not really be a horrible mother, but I'm beginning to think I'm an epically bad sister. "You're really smart."

"Have you ever tried to look at a painting from an inch away?" Eddy scrunches his nose. "You just see dots and smears. I'm not actually that smart—I'm just further from things than you are."

"Thank you," I say. "Really, I mean it. I felt like. . ." I hunt for the right words. "When the judge announced that we were losing the ranch?" I sigh. "It felt like the sky was falling."

He squeezes my hand. "The sky is fine. The world is fine. And if you cut her a little slack, I bet you and Abby will be fine, too. It's just been a lot of stress in a very short time."

I release his hand and then capture it. My index finger traces the lines of his bones. "Thank you."

He taps his free hand to his temple, like he's tipping an invisible hat. "Well, shucks, ma'am. I'm a simple country boy, but I do what I can."

"I've never had a place," I whisper. "I've never belonged anywhere. I guess when Abby said that I don't do anything, well. It felt really true."

"When you're drowning, you grasp at anything at all," Eddy says. "I think Abby might need a little patience and a little support, but she loves you. Because you're awesome."

My eyes well with tears.

"Oh, no. What stupid thing did I say now?"

I shake my head, smiling as I cry. "You said all the right things."

"So you're not planning to immediately pack up and go back to New York?" His tone is carefully playful, but I can hear it. He's scared, or at least nervous.

"Abby may be planning to retreat," I say. "But not me. I have a little fight in me yet."

Eddy kisses me then, without warning. He simply dives across the car, his lips pressing against mine hungrily. I forget all about the ranch I never helped with. I forget about being a terrible mother.

I even forget about the guilt I feel for not paying attention to Abby.

There's only Eddy's lips, Eddy's mouth on mine. And then his hand on my hip. And his other hand cupping my jaw. When my phone starts ringing, it's as jarring as that court ruling from earlier.

It's *Happier*, by Marshmallow. That's Emery's ringtone. I pull away from Eddy reluctantly and answer. "Hey." I wish I didn't sound like I'd tried to run home.

"Mom?"

"Yeah, baby?"

"Abby just got home. She said. . ."

Crap.

"Do we have to move back to New York?" She sounds like she's about to cry.

"No, sweetheart, we do not. Don't panic. I'll be home soon."

"Are you sure?"

"I'm sure."

"What about Izzy and Whitney? Are they going to move away?"

"We'll all talk about it, I promise."

"Okay." She doesn't sound very sure, but I have to believe things will be alright. If Eddy could talk me down, I can talk Abby down. Right?

Will she even talk to me?

"I better get you home," Eddy says.

I nod.

"There's never enough time," he says. "I'll be honest. The second the judge said what he did, my first thought was, 'ooh, maybe she'll need to live with me!'" He sighs. "Pathetic, right?"

"It makes me happy." It's never a bad feeling to be wanted.

"Happy enough to consider it?"

I roll my eyes. "We might need to go public with our relationship first. Baby steps."

"I like big, bounding steps."

I slap his arm. "Just drive, smarty."

We haven't gone far when I notice we're almost to Steve's place. "I wonder how he and Abby are doing with the whole ranch thing."

"Didn't look like they were doing so great," Eddy says. "But Steve's pretty determined when he sets his mind to something. I wouldn't bet against him yet."

"I think he's good for her," I say.

"Oh, I agree. Posh and polished big-city girls need a laid back country doc to balance them out." He's grinning that lopsided grin again and it almost distracts me enough that I don't notice what's right in front of my eyes.

But not quite.

Ethan's walking out of Steve's barn carrying a rake scooper thing. I grab Eddy's arm. "Stop the car."

"What? Why?" But he listens.

We screech to a halt a dozen paces past Steve's house. I don't explain or argue—I wrench the door open and call out loudly. "Ethan!"

When his head whips around and he sees me, his eyes widen and he swallows, his Adam's apple bobbing.

"What are you doing here? Did you see your mom already?"

He frowns. "My mom? What do you mean?"

"The hearing was today," I say.

His mouth drops open. "What do you mean, did I see my mom?" All the color drains from his face.

Oh, no. What am I doing? Why am I the one telling him? But it's too late to get out of it. "The judge—" My throat constricts.

"The judge gave the ranch to the alien people," Eddy says from behind me. "You have thirty days to pack up and clear out."

Ethan's jaw drops. "You're kidding."

Eddy sighs. "Wish we were."

My big, brawny, sweet, loud-mouthed nephew stumbles and lurches his way to the side of the barn. He leans against it, ducking his head so that he's staring at the ground.

"I'm so sorry," I say. "It was rough on everyone."

"I thought that if I went, I'd be bad luck," he whispers.

I take a few steps closer. "What?"

He looks up at me then, and his eyes are wrecked. "I was playing ball when Dad collapsed." He closes his eyes. "I was with him when we went to the ER, the day we found out he was sick. And then." He chokes up. "The day I made him soup and took it to the hospital." His whole face scrunches up. "That's the day he died."

I take two more steps and put a hand on his shoulder. "Ethan, honey, none of that had anything to do with—"

He jerks backward. "I'm bad luck," he says. "That's why I didn't go today. I figured maybe if I didn't go, then things would be fine."

"Things are fine," I say.

"No." His voice is so emotionless that it scares me. "This was the only good thing in my life."

"That's not true," I say. "Not at all."

"And now it's gone. Mom will make us move back to Houston for sure."

I can't even argue with him about that. She already said as much.

"Did she try?" he asks. "Did she really try?"

I hug him then. "She did everything she could do," I say. "And I think she was genuinely upset when the judge ruled like he did."

He nods.

But he doesn't pull away.

Sometimes, when everything goes wrong, having someone else hug you really helps. After a moment or two longer than I expected, he finally pulls away.

"At least we know." He compresses his lips and nods, as if saying that will make it true. He really is his mom's son. He's already soldiering on?

"What are you doing over here, anyway?" Eddy looks around. "And how did you even get here?"

As if he'd asked whether Ethan had committed a murder, my nephew shuts down like an old school Apple IIE computer. Black screen, game over.

"Why are you here?" Abby drove this morning, so how *did* he get here? That's why I hopped out at first—curiosity. Then it hit me that Ethan probably didn't know, and he's been the most vested in the ranch from the start.

He kicks at a tuft of dead, brown grass. "I'm doing some work for Steve."

"Work for him?" I ask. "Like, what kind of work?"

"Nothing much," he says.

"Steve has you scooping stalls?" Eddy asks. "Why?"

Ethan shrugs.

"Does your mom know you're here?" I ask.

Ethan's desperate panic tells me that I'm onto something.

"Why doesn't Abby know you're here? What's going on?"

"Nothing," he says, clearly trying one more time to evade. But since he's a teenager, he's not very good at it.

"Nothing?" I shrug. "No problem. I'll just call Abby and ask."

He brings his hands together and clasps them, interlocking his fingers. "Please don't call her. Please." His eyes look even more desperate than they did a moment before, when we told him the news about the ranch. "Ethan, you'd better tell me right now, or I will call her so fast your head will spin."

"I owe him," Ethan says. "I'm helping Steve to pay him back for something."

That doesn't sit right with me. What could he possibly owe Steve? I like him, but what if he's a pervert? Is something strange going on? Abby would grill him in this situation. I try to channel my inner Abby. "You'd better tell me right now, because right now, I've never wanted to call your mom more."

"He caught me doing something I shouldn't," Ethan says. "And he agreed not to tell my mom, but he thought I needed some kind of punishment so I remembered that what I did wasn't smart."

"What did you do?" I ask.

He shakes his head. "Just call my mom. I may as well just tell her myself."

I press my lips together. He looks scared, but not guilty or shameful. I don't get that kind of vibe. If I push too hard, I may be channeling a little bit too much of Abby. After all, he's eighteen and technically an adult. "Fine."

"Fine? Does that mean you won't tell Mom?"

"Ethan Brooks." I step closer, and I eye him with my best mom look. "You promise me that nothing strange is going on with you and Steve, and I'll keep it quiet."

"Strange?" His lip curls. "Ew. What are you asking?"

"He really is the good person I think he is?"

Ethan grimaces. "What? Yes. Steve's helping me, okay? He's a good person."

"Fine," I say. "But I think you should tell her yourself."

"Duly noted," he says.

He is *so* Abby's son. "And go home soon. Your mom needs you."

I can tell from his face that he needs her, too.

So do I. I just hope I can fix the damage I've caused and convince Abby to stay.

Ethan's still putting something away in the barn when we head for the house, but he says he's right behind us. When we pull into the driveway, Abby's minivan is already there, parked right where it always is. My heart leaps into my throat.

"I changed my mind," I say. "Just take me to your place. You can come back and get my stuff, right?"

Eddy laughs. "By *your stuff*, do you mean your kids?"

"My kids," I say. "My dog."

He gets out and circles around to open my door.

"I'm not ready," I say. "I still have no idea what to say."

"Tell her you love her," Eddy says. "That always works for me."

I slap his chest. "You're a mess today."

"I'm trying to distract you," he says.

My fingers brush against the soft fabric of his t-shirt. Sometimes, with a jacket on, I forget how his chest feels. "You're really good at distracting me."

He carefully grabs my fingers and pries them away. "As much as I like this—all of this—it's time for you to go inside."

But before I can even leave the truck, my phone rings. It's my friend Zoey, from the GlamBamThankYouMan account.

"Hey," I say.

"Where are you?" she asks. "On the moon, or something?"

"What?"

"Your Insta is *blowing* up. What's going on? Is it true?"

"Is what true?" Could my followers somehow already know about the ranch? "I just found out myself not even an hour ago."

"You just found out you were dating him *an hour ago*?"

"Huh?" Dating who?

"What are you talking about?" I ask.

"What are you thinking, dating a *murderer*?" She exhales. "No one can believe it."

My heart leaps into my throat. "Are you talking about Eddy?"

"So it's true? Oh my gosh, girl. He's hot, but are you insane? What's Lololime going to say?"

I have a pretty good idea, but I'm about to find out for sure. Because my boss is calling in on the other line. "I've got to go, Zoe. Lolo's calling right now."

She swears under her breath. "I'll be praying for you."

I don't think that even prayers can help me right now. They were really clear about this, and I ignored them. As if losing our home wasn't bad enough, I'm pretty sure that I'm about to lose my job.

21

ABIGAIL

I broke up with Nate once.

After a lot of chats with my sister and my other girl friends, I decided that I'd started dating him as a rebound. Trying to find a good job and finishing up law school was hard enough without trying to make a relationship work. I decided to end things. I figured I could try and find someone later, once I'd established myself in some kind of career.

It's been years since I came to that conclusion, but I still remember exactly how it went. I told him that, while I liked him, I didn't think we were a good fit. I laid out my reasons calmly and rationally, and he let me speak.

After I was done, he said, "Could anything I might say or do change your mind?"

I shook my head.

"Alright." He stood up and walked off.

I was a little disappointed, to be honest. It's not that I wanted to defend myself or argue or any of that, but I thought he might at least seem disappointed.

He didn't, though.

When I found out I was pregnant a few weeks later, I

was nervous to tell him. I thought he'd be annoyed, or even worse, feel trapped. But as easily as he accepted my decision with regards to the breakup, Nate flung himself into the news of a baby. His eyes widened. His hands shook. And his face broke out into a huge smile. "*My* baby?"

I nodded.

He whooped and hollered and danced around. Thirty seconds later, as if the information had only just finished processing in his brain, he dropped down to one knee and asked me to marry him. He pulled a twist tie out of his pocket and wrapped it around my ring finger when I said yes.

Not the most romantic of proposals, perhaps, but Nate always—for more than twenty years—accepted every single thing I said immediately. He didn't dicker and argue and complain. He didn't harangue or wheedle or negotiate.

He and Steve could not be more different, apparently.

"I didn't say that losing the ranch doesn't matter," Steve says. "I said that the ranch isn't the only great thing here in Daggett County. I said there are more reasons for you to stay."

"Don't you think I'm a rational person?" I ask.

"Of course I do," he says. "One of the most rational I know, in fact. But my *job* is to isolate traumas, stabilize patients, and then help disposition them. It's what I do, and I know that when something huge happens, it's easy to make a snap decision. Your brain, like the human body sometimes does, goes into shock. But shock can be bad for humans, and similarly, you're not well-served by making big decisions so quickly, or all on your own."

"What are you wanting me to do, then?" I ask.

"Give it a few days."

"I don't have a few days," I say.

"You have thirty, to be precise," he says.

"I have four children to care for," I say. "I can't simply

dither while the time the court gave us to get out drains away."

He sighs. "Abigail Brooks, you are infuriating."

"Steve Archer, same back at you."

"You have options," he says, "that don't include packing up and moving home."

"But the only reason we came in the first place was so that Ethan could—"

"Have you asked the kids—"

The front door swings open. I leap to my feet. "That's Ethan now. I've got to go."

"Call me back," Steve says.

He's like taffy stuck in my hair. He just won't let go. "Fine," I hiss.

But when I rush out of my room, it's not Ethan.

It's Amanda.

And she looks *wrecked.*

I actually feel really bad about what I said to her, but I'm not sure she wants to hear it.

"Ethan's still not back, Mom," Izzy says from the kitchen. "I told you I'd let you know when he comes home."

Right. I should have known it was Amanda and not Ethan—none of my tiny human guard dogs were braying. Before I can even try to formulate an apology, I notice something odd.

Amanda's not alone.

She's distraught, and she's standing in the family room, and Eddy's right behind her. When Roscoe jumps up, Amanda stumbles back, and Eddy braces her. . .

By putting his hands on her hips.

"Um. Hello, Eddy," I say. "How ya doing?"

"I'm great, Abigail. How are you?" He releases Amanda and jams his hands into his pants pockets.

Speaking of which, Eddy in a suit is a marvelous thing.

If I thought he was pretty before, dressed up? He's off the charts.

"I rushed out here to tell you I'm sorry," I say, before I can lose my nerve. "And I really, really am. I was out of line, and I never should have said any of what I said—not a few days back, and not today." I pause. "But it looks like you may have something even more pressing to tell me."

When she doesn't say anything, I lift my eyebrows and look pointedly behind her. At Eddy.

"The secret appears to be out," Amanda whispers.

Huh? I'm not quite sure what she means until. . .if they've been dating—because this doesn't look new—and they were hiding it even from me. . . "Wait. Out? Who exactly already knows that you're dating?"

"Lololime certainly does," she says. "They just terminated their contract with me."

"Oh, no," I say. "I'm so sorry."

"What I can't figure out is *how* they know," Eddy says.

"It had to come from Derek," Amanda says.

"Derek?" I'm confused. "Is that why he terminated the contract? Please tell me that had nothing to do with it."

Amanda sighs. "My stupid boss used him to fill in for one of the Bachelors, and he came out here and saw Eddy and me. . ."

"Saw you?" Izzy frowns. "He just saw you and you think he told your boss?"

"He saw us kissing." Amanda scrunches her nose. "And then he still insisted on having our date. He said if I didn't agree to another date every week, so he'd have a chance to change my mind, he'd terminate our contract."

"You should sue him," I say. "For intentional—"

"We can't prove it was him," Amanda says. "Two years ago, I got into this flame war with an influencer named MadamePerignon." She sighs. "She got it into her head that ChampagneForLess was somehow infringing on her territory, because Dom Perginon wanted me to do a series of endorsements."

Now I'm lost.

"She's the one, according to my friend Zoe, who released the information, but any influencer in our area knows that we don't get along, and the only person who caught us was Derek. So whether he reached out and told her, or whether he told Lololime and *they* had her release the information, it came from him."

"Now I'm even more annoyed than the day I went to auction." At least Jeff and Kevin will now be handling the sale of the rest, per the terms of the Court. "If I ever see Derek again, I might just punch him in the nose."

Maren pokes her head out of her room. "Mom?"

Emery pushes past her. "You said you'd be home quick."

"Did I?" Amanda shuffles to the side and falls onto the sofa. Roscoe rests his head on her lap. She pets him absently, as if she's not even aware of what she's doing.

"Are we moving back to New York?" Maren asks.

"Do you want to move back?" Amanda asks.

Maren shakes her head slowly.

"You don't?" Amanda sounds surprised.

"Things are getting a little better," Maren says. "Now she's a captain too, Ellie hates me less."

"Great," Amanda says. "She hates you *less*."

"Why is he here?" Emery's brow's furrowed and her sweet little face is turned upward, toward Eddy.

"It's time I share some big news with you two," Amanda says. "I've been dating someone."

"Gosh, I hope it's Eddy," Maren says, "or this is about to get super awkward."

Amanda rolls her eyes.

"I thought that if you dated him, you could go to jail," Maren says.

"No, dummy," Izzy says. "It's that he went to jail, and if they date, your mom will lose her job."

"Wait, you will?" Maren asks.

"I already have," Amanda says. "It's a bad day all around, to be honest. This afternoon, we found out we were losing the ranch. Then when I pulled into the driveway, I found out that someone had leaked the information about me and Eddy dating, and I got fired."

Ethan walks in the door while Amanda's talking.

He freezes in the doorway. "Is that true?" My son is tall. He's strong. He's a hard worker. I hated the idea of him running a ranch instead of focusing on school. I wanted him to join a fraternity, or become a study nerd, or complain to his friends about his terrible part-time job. I didn't want him laboring with his hands and watching baby cows get fattened up for steakhouses all over America.

But here we are.

No matter how much we might like it to be the case, we don't get to choose how things turn out in the lives of others. I'd finally come around to understanding his dream, just in time to watch it get snatched away.

"It's true," I say.

"But who would tell stuff about you like that?" Emery asks. "Why is it any of their business?"

Two different conversations, almost like two divergent train tracks. Two families. Total chaos, and a lot of drama.

And it hits me in that moment just how much I'm going to miss this. Just as we finished changing the inside of this old farmhouse so that we have enough space, it's being taken by someone else. Just as I adjusted to a mixed family, and a new life, and a sister-in-law who's closer than my actual sister, it all evaporates.

"When do we have to leave?" Ethan asks. "Can we stay until after the new year?"

"What could we do to Derek?" Eddy asks.

“Do what to Derek?” I’m too distracted to keep up with the parallel conversations.

“We only have thirty days before we have to be gone,” Amanda says, answering my son’s question. Both of us have changed conversational paths. Maybe neither of us wants to deal with our own realities.

“This sucks.” Whitney plops down on the sofa next to Amanda and starts to pet Roscoe.

This is why people have pets. They really help in situations like this. Of course, if Amanda goes back to New York, we may get stuck taking little Roscoe back home to Texas. New York isn’t exactly large-dog friendly.

“Why is everyone so mad?” Gabe trots into the room, his eyes moving in a line from one person to the next. “Just because we can’t keep all the cows?”

“Actually,” I say, “the judge ordered we should get the profit from the sale of the cows this year, as compensation for our time.”

Gabe’s brow furrows. “And you can use that to buy more cows, can’t you?”

“Well, we could,” I say, “but without the land, we’d have nowhere to put them.”

“So you’re all really mad because of the land and house?” Gabe asks. “Someone else is taking them? Like when that kid, Drew, stole my Legos?”

“It’s a little more complicated,” I say.

“Why?” Gabe asks. “I was super mad when he took my Lego house.”

I cross the room and sit in one of the recliners, and then I pull Gabe onto my lap. “You’re right. It’s like that. We’re upset that someone else gets the house, because it felt like home.”

“And Aunt Amanda’s mad because someone was saying mean things about her boyfriend?” Gabe asks.

He's paying more attention than I realized. "Uh, yes. That's right."

"She should just say they aren't true."

"That's hard, because some of the mean things are correct, but they're taken out of context."

"What's context?" Gabe asks.

"Yeah, what is that?" Emery asks.

"It's like, remember last week, when Whitney asked Gabe to show her his ninja skills?"

The kids nod.

"Then Gabe kicked her and punched her?"

Amanda's suppressing a laugh.

"And then Whitney ran to me and complained that he hit and kicked her? I made him stand in the corner. But then later, when I finally listened to him, I found out she'd kind of *asked* him to do it. Do you remember that?"

The kids nod again.

"That's context." I sigh. "Sure, hitting and kicking your sister is wrong, but when you think she's *asking* you to do it, maybe you still should have air-kicked, but at least you *thought* you were doing something she wanted. For her to tattle on you for something she asked you to do was pretty rotten."

Whitney's eyes go wide.

Gabe smiles. "So can Aunt Amanda just explain?"

Everything's so easy when you're seven and the ramifications include not getting a cookie after dinner, or standing with your nose in the corner. But then it hits me. I was too angry to listen, but my friend *did* call with interesting news about Eddy.

And I didn't even hear him out.

"Actually."

"No," Amanda says. "I can't just explain. People online are more interested in hearing something outrageous and commenting about how upset they are than they are about finding out the context."

Gabe's shoulders slump. "So you're stuck in the corner, then?"

"Something like that," Amanda says. "It's been a really lousy day, between the Lego kicking and the lack of context bad-mouthing."

Eddy drops a hand on her shoulder.

"The one good thing," she says, "is that now all of you know my great news." She forces a smile. "I have a wonderful boyfriend who cares about me. So we'll have some hard decisions to make about where to live, and what to do, but I really do want to talk about them with all of you. Okay?"

"You've been lying to us this whole time?" Maren asks. "And lying to the world, kind of, by dating all those guys when you had a boyfriend?"

Amanda's eyes fly wide, and she stills on the sofa. "I guess so."

Eddy shakes his head. "The only person who she could be accused of wronging was me, and I told her to do it."

"That's awesome," Maren says. "I had no idea you were so cool."

Awesome?

Amanda looks as confused as I do.

"I wish I had a super hot, secret boyfriend," Maren says.

"Um, as a parent, let me just say that I don't want any of you to—"

Maren waves at me. "Yeah, yeah. We know."

But I do wonder. Could Maren be on to something? If my friend found out some kind of mitigating circumstances, or if there's new information, would the public listen?

Lololime firing her might not be the end of the world. She didn't get that contract until recently. If she could somehow come out of this, she might not lose all her income and her home on the same day.

I open my mouth to tell her that my judge friend called, but then I snap it shut again. After all, what am I going to tell her? That I pried into her life and into her boyfriend's history, before I even knew he was her boyfriend? And then, I'll explain that I didn't get any information, but I think there might be something of value?

I hate when I think about something all day long, like eating the last slice of chocolate cake, and then when I open the fridge, someone else has already eaten it. Telling her I have good news when I don't know whether I do or not would be like that, wouldn't it? I'll need to call my friend first, see what he found, and *then* tell her what I know.

"I'm starving," Ethan says. "Is there any dinner left?"

"Me too," Amanda says. "Ditto."

I stand up again, shifting Gabe to the chair. "Of course. Izzy made chicken pot pie." I cross to the fridge and pull out the leftovers. "All of you need to breathe just a bit. Steve told me we should all take a few days to think about this before making any decisions, and I think maybe he's right. Let's take a day or two, let's think about what this all means, and I want each of you to come talk to me about what *you* want. We have a whole month to make up our minds, and that's more time than it seems."

"I like it here," Gabe says.

"Me too," Whitney says.

"Do we have to leave Kronk?" Izzy asks. "And Maggie?"

"What about Snoopy?" Whitney asks. "He follows me around whenever we go out to feed them." Her eyes are welling up with tears.

I wish I could tell them we can keep the horses. I wish I could fix everything. But I can't. Even if I wanted to buy the ranch from the alien people, I don't have enough money to do it, and by the time we take out a mortgage, the numbers don't work.

Plus, my savings are my security net for the future. I can't blow it on a cattle ranch. It wouldn't be responsible. I wish I could punch Jed on the nose. Why did he bother dragging us out here, only to take the whole ranch away? We wouldn't have known we wanted this life if he hadn't shoved our faces in it.

Eventually, I'm able to extricate myself and duck back into my room. I want to call Steve back, but I try calling my judge friend in California first. It goes to voicemail, and I ask him to send me whatever he discovered on Edward Dutton. I also apologize for being so abrupt before. "Things have been a little bumpy since Nate passed, the last week especially. But I really do appreciate you looking into it, and I'm so sorry I cut you off earlier."

Hopefully that'll get him to call me back quickly.

Then I call Steve back, and I update him on Amanda's news. "They've been dating this whole time?" He chuckles. "That sly dog. I had no idea."

"None of us did," I say. "Except Derek."

"It must have been him," Steve says. "I never liked that guy at all. I'm sorry your contract with him got canceled, but maybe it was for the best. What kind of jerk would do something like that?" He snorts. "The same kind who would reach out to her online enemy and give them a loaded gun."

He's not wrong. "Or maybe someone saw them together. Who knows?"

"I guess." Steve sighs. "And listen, Ethan mentioned something to me today."

Ethan did?

"I bumped into him before the hearing this morning, and he told me that the day I didn't go with you for the sale, Jeff and Kevin were sick. He said no one told you guys to water the cows and you sold them for way less because they were dehydrated."

"It hardly matters now," I say. "We aren't even keeping the ranch." I'm shocked at how glum I feel about all of it. I really should be relieved. I made the right call, not selling our house. We won't even have to pack up all our stuff or find a place for it in an already overcrowded home.

"It matters to me. I let you down that day, and I had no idea how badly."

He had no idea? I came to his doorstep that morning after asking for his help.

"I guess I should've been paying more attention. But Abby, you have to tell me when things go wrong. I don't read minds."

"You'd have to be around in order to read them, anyway," I mutter.

"So you are mad."

"I'm not mad." A bone-wearying exhaustion sweeps over me. "Everything's fine."

"But you're out here all alone. Amanda's been gone with cookies, and then with her secret dating, and you're managing six kids alone. And the ranch. And then your ranch hands bail and you ask your boyfriend for help and he bows out too."

"It was fine. Ethan and I managed."

"Knowing you, it was more upsetting that you screwed up than it was that you lost some income on the tonnage of the cows."

"They must have been so terribly thirsty," I say. "I can't believe I didn't know we had to haul water for them."

"Abby, I know you're doing more than me—more than anyone—and one of the things I admire about you is how you just shrug and shift the entire planet onto your shoulders and make it work. But you're not really Atlas. You need to get some help."

I tried.

"This is my fault. I'm not trying to blame you. But you should scream at me when I don't realize you need me, not just walk away. You're my girlfriend—that means we're a team."

For another 29 days, anyway.

"Unless you've already checked out. Did I screw up that much?"

"It's not that big of a deal," I say.

There's some kind of commotion outside—Roscoe's barking like a mad dog.

"Hey, I need to call you back. Someone else is here—probably someone from the government, ready to shut us down for toxic mold or something."

Steve laughs. "That's fine. Call me later. And hey, try not to breathe that stuff in. It's really bad for you."

But when I open the door, the person standing on our front entry, petting a now-calm Roscoe, is Steve. He's changed into a khaki work jacket, navy polo shirt, jeans, and his normal boots with spurs, and he smiles when he sees me. "I live just down the road. Calling you felt. . ." He shrugs. "I wanted to see you."

I've been thinking about all this like I always do—rationally. Steve and I have been dating for a month. Organic milk lasts longer. He has a new daughter and a lot of drama to deal with. I just lost the ranch.

I should go home and stop working remotely. After all, we were kicked out. It's not our fault. Focusing on how Steve let me down, or on how he wasn't there when I needed him, helped me to feel better about leaving.

But looking at Steve right now is like inhaling the scent of wildflowers in a meadow. It's like lying on the beach and feeling the warmth of the sun sink into my bones. It can't be properly described and it can't be explained rationally. Something about my frayed edges calms when he's with me.

"I needed to see you," I say.

He smiles then, and practically races toward me. He picks me up and spins me around in a circle, like we're kids in a high school love story. "So did I," he says. "I needed to hold you."

And then I'm clutching his back, my face pressed against his neck, my mouth crushed against his shirt, breathing him in. He smells like his normal cologne, with just a faint hint of horse and outdoors. I can't get enough of it.

I haven't cried, not since the judge ripped our future away. Not when my kids bawled. Not when I broke Ethan's heart and let everyone down. But I cry now, at the thought of leaving Steve, at the thought of losing this—my chance at having someone who rushes over to hug me—at the thought of walking away from the first bright thing in my life, other than my children, since Nate passed.

"I don't want to leave Leo," I whisper. "He's such a wonderful horse."

Steve freezes. "He's yours. You could take him with you."

I pull back enough to see his face. "I'm not sure he's ready to leave his trainer," I say. "He still has some quirks."

He bites his lip. "Really?"

"It's complicated," I say. "Really complicated."

"But we have time to figure something out, right?" His eyes plead with mine.

I swallow, and then I take the plunge. "I think so," I say. "I hope so."

He kisses me, then, and I've never wanted to figure out some kind of solution more. His mouth on mine, his arms around me, his familiar smell, the knowledge that someone cares, that someone else is out there, pulling the same direction as me, it's exactly what I needed after a day like today.

All the hoots and hollers from the audience I didn't realize we had, and the feel of Roscoe licking my hand?

Yeah, that I didn't need.

But I wouldn't change a bit of it. Because this is my life, and they're my people, and I'm in it.

22
DONNA

"It's bad timing, and I know, and I'm so sorry," I say for the third time.

"You have got to stop apologizing," Abby says. "By definition, most everything I do as a lawyer happens at a bad time." She grins. "People don't call me when things are going great."

"But you passed this off to another lawyer," I say, "and with the ranch stuff." I cringe. "I know you're busy, but I just really wanted to have you here."

"Your soon-to-be-ex is a real piece of work. I don't blame you." Abby pauses. "You must not be superstitious at all, because the last two cases I was involved with didn't go so well."

The criminal case where Charles walked, and then the will contest for the ranch. She's not wrong—but neither of those was her fault, no matter what Amanda might think. Even though the case against Charles didn't go the way we wanted, I still sleep well at night again knowing I did the right thing. If it hadn't been for her, I might not have changed horses in time.

"The law really does get it right more often than not," she says. "I swear I really do believe that."

"It has to get it right today," I say. "I can't lose Aiden."

Abby's phone rings. "Hang on—this shouldn't be a long call."

I'm surprised she has reception out here. We're almost an hour from the hearing, still. And it's early enough I'm not sure who would be calling her.

"Hey Franklin—or should I be calling you Judge Abbott? I can't believe how fancy all my old friends have become."

I can't even imagine having the kind of life where judges call me regularly.

"Yeah," Abby says. "Things have been crazy here. Remember I told you we inherited a ranch? Well, easy come, easy go. We just lost the ranch to an Alien Institute."

She laughs.

"No, I'm afraid it's no joke. It's a long story, but we violated some of the terms by going home for a month and now, poof, gone."

She pauses briefly.

"I appreciate the offer, but it's really a done deal."

She laughs again.

"I actually felt sorry for that judge. Can you imagine rotating between a bunch of tiny counties, hearing all their cases one day a month?"

I wonder how Judge Abbott's voice sounds. I imagine him as a stern, deep-voiced guy, but there's no way to know for sure. He could sound high and squeaky.

Abby sighs. "It's a little embarrassing. First I call for a favor, and then you find something, and then I tell you to throw it out. But here I am, calling you back because I need the very thing I told you I didn't want. Let me just assure you that it has everything to do with the strange and extenuating upheaval in my life, and nothing to do with my regard for you."

Good grief. Does anyone compliment people as elegantly as Abby?

"I really appreciate that, Franklin. Truly. You've always been a good friend."

She pauses again, and this time her fingers tap a steady cadence on the armrest.

"That is strange. I'm not sure what it means, exactly, but it's definitely not the same story I was always told. Is there a way we can get more information about it? I'd love to get my fingers on the evidence, for instance."

She pauses.

"I get that. It was a long time ago, but sometimes they cache that stuff, don't they?"

She sighs.

"Yeah, I know it's a long shot. I mean, the statute of limitations—but on murder isn't it longer?"

Murder?

"Alright, well, I appreciate anything you can do. Speaking of, did you ever know Britt Clark? I asked her to look into this too, and she might have more in the way of evidence. I'll follow up with her, but you might get further, since you're official."

She pauses again.

"I can send you her information, of course. Yeah. Thanks again, Franklin. Really." She hangs up and leans her forehead against the window.

"That sounded intense."

Abby's words are a little muffled, probably because her face is mashed against the glass. "You heard about Amanda's illicit love affair?"

"What?" I never hear about anything interesting, obviously.

"She's been dating Eddy in secret."

"Eddy Dutton? The vet?"

"Who used to be a singer, and was high when he struck and killed a pedestrian? Yeah, that Eddy."

"I forgot about all that. It was like twenty years ago."

Abby sighs again. "Unfortunately, it's still a salacious headline, and now that it's out, it's bad news for Amanda. Her followers are not pleased to hear she's dating a murderer."

I can't even figure out how anyone would know to look for something like that. "People have too much time on their hands, to worry so much about other people's lives."

"People are quick to throw stones," Abby says. "Speaking of. I'm not sure you're going to get sole *legal* custody, but I can't imagine what the Windsors could possibly say that would convince a judge not to give you sole *physical* custody."

"Physical means he lives with me and just visits Charles, right?" I clarify.

She nods. "And legal is about parenting decisions. What sports should he do, can he leave the country, etc. They don't like to leave one parent out of that, at least, not unless the parent poses a threat to their physical well-being."

"Everything about Charles is a threat to Aiden's well-being," I say.

"I imagine his lawyer will argue that evidence of the court case and jail time are prejudicial, since the charges were dropped."

"But the judge will hear it all the same," I say. "Right?"

Abby smiles. "Exactly. It's not a jury trial, and in order to rule on whether the evidence is admissible, the judge will have to see the evidence in the first place. That's all we really need to undermine his credibility and image as a fine and upstanding father."

I try to relax my hands on the steering wheel. "Alright. We have a plan. It's a good plan. We can do this."

I really believe we can.

Right up until Charlie's lawyer introduces new evidence that they claim they *just* found. "I had no time, your honor, to make copies and distribute this in advance." He clears his throat and points at the display screen. Then he presses the button.

An enormous image of me, stumbling, slurring my words, and then puking on the shoes of some guy, on the side of a very dark road in front of a bar is broadcast in the middle of the courtroom.

"Something our would-be custodian has failed to disclose is that she has a drinking problem and can be found most nights stumbling out of a bar around two in the morning." He arches one eyebrow. "I'm not sure what the Court's opinion is on drinking while caring for a six-year-old child, but I wouldn't want that for my kids. I certainly think the judge should consider it when deciding what's in the 'best interest' of darling Aiden."

Abby and my new lawyer do a decent job of giving me a chance to dispute his claim that I drank regularly, or that it even happened more than once.

But that's not the only new attack.

"When I picked her up," Charles testifies, "I snapped some photos of the pathetic place she's calling home. And she confirmed that she's caring for her aged and demented father who is sometimes quite aggressive."

The problem with sharing your life with someone who's despicable is that they know all your most vulnerable spots, and they don't pull any punches. I'm practically shaking as I answer his lawyer's questions about my dad on cross examination. The worst part is that he's not entirely wrong. I hate that Aiden's around my dad. I hate that he hears him yelling and shouting profanities at me. I hate that I can't provide a better place for him to live.

But I believe, deep down in my gut, that Aiden is better off with me.

When we take a break for lunch, I'm less certain than I've ever been that I'll get granted sole physical custody.

"How bad is it?" I ask.

Abby and Mr. Perret exchange a glance.

"You can tell me." Depression spreads across me like a rolling pin, weighing me down, stealing all my hope.

"The judge said she's not a fan of granting sole physical custody to anyone who lives outside of the state," Abby says. "That's my biggest concern."

"The picture they've painted of the situation with the Windsors is quite rosy," Mr. Perret says. "A posh school, three stable adults on tap to help at all times, and a prodigal son who went astray but is back under his parents' wing, ready to do his duty as a father and model employee to their family-owned company."

I snort.

"But your picture isn't as bad as they tried to make it. You're caring for your aging parent, which is a very common situation, and you're working, and still caring for your child very well."

"Our last witness is the psychologist," Abby says. "And we know her opinion already. She's delighted with the progress Aiden's making, and she's happy with the stable and healthy environment Aiden has found at school and home."

"Are you ready to make a deal?" Charlie asks, his cultured voice invading my space like a snake slithering toward my foot.

I spin around on my heel, noticing the toe of my shoe is scuffed and showing white spots through the black of the leather. I hate how shabby I look compared to him. Charlie looks more expensive than a Rolls Royce driving down a gold-paved road, as usual. His three-piece suit, his shiny, bright tie, and his pristine haircut can't disguise his slimy smile, though. I hope the judge can see it.

Unfortunately, most people can't.

"What are you talking about?" Abby asks.

He smirks. "You're about to lose custody of Aiden. Unless."

I hate how my heart leaps to hear that word. I've been baffled in all of this—Charles never wanted to spend a lot of time with Aiden. I figured his parents were behind the grab, or perhaps his desperate rage to hurt me in any way possible. But if there's another option—I'll take it.

"Don't you want to know what I'm offering?" He inhales slowly, stretching casually, as if he doesn't really care one way or another. He's always been like this—excellent at negotiating because he always looks ready to walk away over the least bit of resistance.

The difference is that, while I know what he's doing, I can't ever walk away. Not from Aiden.

"What do you want?" I can't keep my lips from twisting in disgust.

"If you simply agree to give us custody, I'll agree to child support of only two hundred dollars a month." Charles looks me up and down slowly. "I figure it's better to set it at something I might get than to spend all my time chasing you down."

"You son of—"

Abby grabs my arm.

"That's not an offer. That's an insult."

"Or." He sniffs and glances down at his fingernails. "I suppose if it means *that* much to you, I'd be willing to let you keep primary *physical* custody, but you'd owe me a thousand a month in child support and regular visitation rights."

"You want me to pay *you* child support even though I have physical custody?"

"We could call it alimony." He shrugs. "Whatever you prefer."

I can't help spluttering. "You have the ivy league degree, all the money, and your parents backing you up. You think I should care for our child, and pay *you* for the privilege of doing it?" Even as disgusting as his offer is—I'd totally agree to it.

Except I flat out can't.

I don't have the money. As soon as my dad passes—and that could happen in one year or in ten, there's no way to know—I'll have to find a place to rent. There's no way I can feed us, house us, clothe us, and pay Charles a thousand a month on my salary, not even with the extra money Abby found.

Why would he even ask for something I can't possibly do? He's seen the numbers on my income. . .

Except, his main goal is to torture me.

He doesn't even want Aiden. He just wants to make me pay.

If I agree, I'll pay and then some. I'll go bankrupt. But if I refuse and he gets Aiden, I'll never sleep again. I'll feel too guilty, knowing that I *could* have kept Aiden with me if I'd found some way to make more money.

I didn't think I could hate Charles more, but here we are.

"I'll give you a few moments to talk it over with the smarter professionals you're paying with the money you stole from me."

"He really is awful," Abby says.

"You can say that again," Mr. Perret says. "His lawyer is the most hated family lawyer in the entire city."

"What do I do?" I want to curl into a fetal position and

bawl, except he'd *love* that. "Do I take it? I could sell a kidney, maybe."

"You could request a modification after a year," Mr. Perret says. "The court is reticent to change the child's situation, but at that point, he'd be in Utah. You could make the request there. Then your ex would be the out-of-state party, not you."

I'm literally shaking with anger. And fear. And confusion. And stress. "I hate him, and I hate this."

"Tell him to screw himself," Abby says.

"But what if we lose?" I ask.

She shakes her head. "We won't lose."

"How do you know?" I search her face.

Her face is calm. "I know that you've now watched me lose, twice, but I never felt safe, secure, or calm, not either of those two times. I do right now."

"The judge is a real wildcard," Mr. Perret says. "She's emotional, and she gets invested in things, and she often makes rulings no one expects."

Abby shrugs. "I think that might work for us. Anyone can see that he's a piece of crap, if they really look."

"She did look disgusted when she ruled that the evidence of his criminal charges would be too prejudicial," I say.

"I think you counter with a lesser amount," Mr. Perret says. "If they're offering a thousand, they'd probably take a few hundred."

"No." Abby shakes her head. "Paying any amount of money to him so that he will *let you* care for your child is disgusting. Tell him no, and see what she says."

I think about Charles having Aiden for a full year if I'm guessing wrong, and my hand trembles. "I don't think I can do it."

"If he wins, offer to honor the deal then," Abby says. "He doesn't really want Aiden. He just wants you to suffer, and you'll suffer just as much *after* the judge's order as before."

"What if he wants *more* money then?" I ask.

"I'll pay the difference," Abby says. "Out of my own pocket, for one full year, if you lose and he wants more."

A tear rolls down my face. But she's right. If I step away from this whole situation, I can easily see that this is the right decision. "We'll tell him no."

When court resumes, the child psychologist's testimony goes just as expected. Aiden's well adjusted, and he likes his school, and he's making new friends. He's doing well, and she doesn't recommend that he be moved.

"Now comes the moment of truth," Abby whispers.

The judge looks down at her papers and notes. Her nostrils flare. She taps her pencil against her lip. "Alright." She ruffles some things around. "In the petition of Donna Ellingson Windsor against Charles Windsor the third, I grant the divorce. That's the first thing. The marriage is hereby dissolved, and your assets are divided as follows."

She rattles off a rather generous distribution for me. She gives me pretty close to eighty percent of the assets we acquired during the marriage.

"But your honor," Charles' lawyer says. "Did you read the paperwork we submitted about the proposed division?"

Her eyes flash. "You would do well to keep your mouth shut, Ivan. I've had about as much of you as I can handle this week. Your client is a liar, a crook, and he's been playing fast and loose with the truth here in my courtroom. You must think I'm either senile or a total fool to believe I'd buy any of it."

My heart hammers in my chest. Did she—did she see through all of it?

"I'm well aware of what I'm doing. I'm not ordering a single penny of alimony, because I have zero faith that horrible human would ever pay it. I'm splitting assets accordingly. After analyzing the record, there's no way a single appellate court would doubt my position. I'm the trier of fact, and I've reviewed the facts as I saw them. Is that clear?"

A tear rolls down my cheek, and I let it slide.

The judge notices, and she smiles at me.

"And as for the custody of their child, Aiden Windsor, I grant the rather irregular petition that his name be changed to Ellingson. I've never liked it when the custodial parent and the child's name don't line up. It causes too many questions and too much confusion."

Abby gasps next to me. She reaches under the table and squeezes my hand.

"And for the record, I called the judge who tried his criminal case. He said he'd never seen a more disgusting miscarriage of justice on a white collar case. Even though I received that information, I assure you that none of that information in any way colored my decision here today. I'm doing as I do because that sweet, abused mother, the woman who's voluntarily caring for her aging father, who by all counts is also relatively abusive, is also caring for her son. She never put forth discriminatory or biased videos. She never shared texts and tried to besmirch the name of her now-ex-husband. She played a clean game, while he snuck around with private investigators trying to concoct some ridiculous smear campaign."

Now I'm bawling full out. I can't help it.

"I'm granting full legal and physical custody of Aiden Ellingson to Donna Ellingson, with full child support based on the earnings helpfully provided to this court by the Windsors to show how reliable he is. Visitation will be limited to once a month, monitored by the testifying child psychologist for a year—thereupon the issue may be revisited by a Utah judge upon a petition made by Dad. I'm going to suggest that this case be moved to a Utah court for easier attendance by Mom and eventually Aiden."

No part of me expected a slam dunk.

I can barely compose myself enough to thank the judge before she stands and leaves the courtroom, but her smile is enough. She understands. I've never been more delighted to have a wildcard judge in my life.

And I'm so glad I listened to Abby. It finally feels like I have my life back.

23

AMANDA

When I was a kid, Mom signed me up to compete in a lot of beauty pageants.

A lot.

I'm not great at singing. I don't have the patience for piano. At one point, in a fit of desperation, Mom thought maybe I could stack playing cards. The thing is, there's a time limit. So we came up with a comedy routine that could be recited as I stacked cards.

Only, every single time I reached a certain point—the fifth level of cards, to be precise—I'd inevitably bump a part of the bottom of that layer. . .and the whole thing would collapse.

When I actually performed that act, the one time I tried it, I made a joke to cover for it. When the cards on the rickety table fell, I said, "Oh, no. I guess I have only my shelf to blame."

Everyone laughed.

But now, my life is like that stack of playing cards. Every few moments, I get another notification on my phone. It's a new email every time, terminating my representation of a particular vendor.

Two minutes ago, a company that I've never even worked for canceled our agreement. That's a new low.

I shut off my phone and grab a rubber ball. "Let's go outside, Roscoe."

He leaps from the corner—moving almost the same as he always did—and races for the door. At least he doesn't look at me differently. I'm chucking the ball for him when the bus arrives to release all our little hooligans back to our care.

"Mom!" Emery races toward me, her mouth already full of all the many words she wants to share about her day. "Guess what? Today, Elana, who never wants to play with me, wanted to swing next to me. And then, when we got off, Yvette said she wanted to play four square with me."

"That's great," I say.

"Yvette's the one who pushed me last week." She frowns.

"Oh, then that's bad."

"It's good she asked," Emery says, "but I told her that I won't play unless she apologizes for shoving me and promises to stop making fun of my best friend, Matthew."

"Wait, your best friend, who?"

"Matthew." Emery sighs. "Mom. He's been my best friend for weeks."

I tune her out too often. "I'm sorry, sweetie. I know that, of course."

"Anyway, she wouldn't apologize, but then Elana was super impressed. She said I'm the kind of friend she wants to have. Which means it would have been a perfect day, because I really like Elana. She takes turns pushing you on the swings, which most kids don't do, but she doesn't like Matthew either. She makes fun of him a lot, so right now I have to take turns picking which of them to play with."

I love Emery. I really, really do. But I swear, she's a lot

to process some days. "Well, that still sounds like good progress."

"It is." She beams.

This time, when Roscoe drops the ball at my feet, covered in slobber, his eyes shifting from the ball to my hand and back again, showing me that he's ready and ready and ready to get it, Emery points. "Can I?"

"Oh, sure." I beam. "Knock yourself out."

She picks up the ball, grimaces a bit at the slobber and bits of debris stuck to it, and hurls it as far as she can.

Which is about fifteen feet. Roscoe twists in mid air and catches it right after the first bounce. He's back in a shot, and he drops it on my shoe, as if to say, "You do it this time."

I do throw it farther.

But Emery will only improve if she practices. I hand it to her again. Roscoe, true to his wonderful, loyal nature, simply stares with complete devotion at her hand. Until she throws it.

Now that the kids are home, it's easier not to think about the complete collapse of my own life. Because my life used to be nothing more than social media, but now I'm surrounded by kids playing, doing homework, dogs chasing balls, beautiful sunshine on a chilly day, and family.

Oh yeah, and the boyfriend who caused all this mess.

I should be upset with him. Or perhaps, regretting my decision. But instead, I still smile whenever I think about him. The media is so backward. They're harpooning me for dating the most healthy and wonderful man I've met in my entire life. It's never been more clear to me how toxic the internet can be.

Maren sneaks past me and ducks into the house.

I point at Roscoe. "Can you throw for him for a while?" I ask. "I need to check on the older one."

Emery giggles. "Of course. Just follow the trail of broken hearts and shattered dreams."

She's such a weird kid. I'm chuckling as I beeline toward Maren's room. Only, she's not there.

I check every room in the house, but other than a discarded book bag, I find nothing.

"Maren?" No response.

Where on earth could she be?

I finally find her—in the back yard, practicing one-handed cartwheels. "Whatcha doin'?"

She jolts and nearly stumbles. "Mom. Don't sneak up on me when I'm tumbling."

"I've been calling your name for at least five minutes," I say. "Maybe we should check your ears if you think I'm sneaking up on you."

She pulls air pods out. "I was listening to the music for the routine. Duh."

Oh. It's for cheer. "How's that going?"

"Fine." She puts her air pods back in.

I gesture for her to take them out. "I'm not done," I say.

She tugs them out and sighs in an exaggerated fashion. "What now?"

"Abby convinced the coach to make your enemy your co-captain, and you've still never talked to me about it, except to say it was going 'awful.'"

"It's fine," she says.

"What does that mean?" I hate that this is how she talks to me.

"It means just that—it's fine." She tries to put her air pods back in.

"So help me." I step toward her. "I'm going to crush those to dust. Tell me what's going on."

"I don't have anything to tell," she says.

"You talk to Abby," I say.

"She listens," Maren says.

I frown. "I'm listening right now."

"No, you're demanding that I tell you exactly one thing," Maren says. "But you never ask what I want to talk about."

I think about what she's saying. Is that what I do? "What do you want to talk about?"

"I got an A in math today," she says. "And I brought my grade in English up to passing."

She wasn't passing English before? My hands start to shake, but I still them with great effort. "Oh."

"I knew it."

"What?"

"That 'oh' basically said you're upset that I didn't tell you I was struggling in English. It's not like you could help me."

"I would be happy to—"

"It's fine, Mom. Aunt Abby already helped me with my last two essay revisions. She's the reason I'm passing."

I swallow.

"And if you'd just ask her, she could tell you that her plan worked. Ellie hated me because she wasn't important any more. Bringing her in as co-captain took a while to calm her down, but it did fix it. We're almost friends, now."

"Oh."

"She invited me to her sleepover next week."

"Are you going—"

"Don't worry. I told her Aunt Abby never allows sleep-overs. She's too worried to sleep when her kids aren't home."

"You're not her kid," I say.

"Don't I know it." Maren gestures at me with her air pods. "Can I put these in and practice now? I have to have this perfect to show everyone tomorrow."

I nod, and then I hide behind a bush for ten minutes

and watch my daughter do a very complicated routine. I've never been more impressed or more ashamed of myself. I had no idea how much Abby was doing for my kids. I've been just as bad as she said.

How does she do it all without getting mad or bored or irritated? Is she human? No one ever taught me how to talk to teenagers.

"What on earth are you doing?" Amanda Saddler cackles. "Did someone tell you to look for snipes?"

"What are snipes?" My back aches as I straighten. "And why would I be looking for them?"

"I hope you're not spying on your own daughter." Amanda arches one imperious eyebrow. "Although, I'm not sure what would be a better option."

"She won't talk to me," I say. "She only tells Abby stuff."

"You're not still angry with her, are you?" she asks.

I lean against the side of the house. "Not angry. I'm jealous, I guess."

"She's a good sister-in-law," she says. "Actually, she's a good sister. For a sister-in-law, you'd be hard pressed to find a better one anywhere."

"I know," I say. "That's what pisses me off."

Amanda cackles again. "I swear, you are a delight."

"Me?"

"But why didn't you come meet me today? I felt like the ugly girl at the spring formal."

Oh, no. "I was getting notifications on my phone nonstop," I say. "I shut it off, but that means it didn't remind me of appointments, either. I'm so sorry."

"That's okay," she says. "I was wondering if it was your way of telling me you're bailing."

"Bailing?"

"You have a lot of decisions to make," Amanda says. "You could move back to New York, you could stay here, you could move out by your actual family."

I laugh, but it sounds more bitter than I hoped. "That's not an option. My own family would never welcome me."

Amanda looks oddly thoughtful. "So New York, or here?"

I shrug. "I can't afford an apartment in New York right now. I think my options are, move in with my boyfriend way before either of us are ready for that, or find a hotel that will let us clean rooms to pay for our board."

"You could come live with me," she says. "I have a seven-bedroom farm house, you know."

I didn't realize it had that many bedrooms. The kitchen is pretty small, but then, so is Jed's. "Are you kidding?"

"Not at all," she says.

I don't even need to think it over. "I would love that."

"But I have a condition."

My heart sinks. Of course she does. "What?"

"You have to bring Abby along."

That is not at all what I was expecting. "But she's moving back home," I say. "Unlike me, she has family that loves her and a beautiful, paid-off home in Houston. She also has a job waiting for her."

Amanda shrugs. "Not my problem."

"But what would I even say to her? Hey, wanna come live with me at Amanda's?"

"Tell her you don't want her to leave," Amanda says. "Tell her you need her here. Thank her for what she's done for you." She lifts her eyebrows. "Just random ideas."

"I'm not sure she even wants to talk to me," I say.

"It's Abby. She'll talk to literally anyone and help most everyone."

"But—"

"Surely you have something you've done for her you could mention. Or a secret you could share. Or some kind of favor you can call in. I don't care—just convince her to stay, and then you've got a place to live too." She spins on her heel and barks at me as she marches away. "Let's meet same time tomorrow to go over our top properties and figure out which to start with. This time I'll pick you up so you don't nap through it."

"Hey!" I shout. "I wasn't napping!"

She's so busy laughing, I'm not sure whether she could even hear me.

It doesn't occur to me until she's already gone that I never argued with her about the terms. I never told her I don't want Abby to stay, because I do. Probably much more than Amanda Saddler does, I want Abigail Brooks to stay here. I want her kids around my kids. I want her in my life, showing me a better way to be. I want her here to laugh with, and to cry with, and to learn and grow alongside.

My family back home doesn't want me—but that's not home anymore. No, now home for me, and I'm pretty sure home for Emery and Maren, is wherever Abby and her family is. I wish I knew whether she would want to hear that, or whether it would make me sound truly pathetic.

It's Abby. She'll talk to literally anyone and help most everyone.

Amanda's right. She will help anyone. Why wouldn't she at least hear me out, even if she's upset with me?

It's late when Abby finally gets home, but she's beaming as she walks through the door.

"You look happy," I say. "I take it that Donna's hearing went well?"

"She would have to give you details on that," she says.

Oh my word, she's such a stickler. "Alright, I'll ask her myself."

"But I think she'd be happy to talk to you about it." Abby's smile dims a little, but not much.

I suppose if it was my case, I'd be happy to know that Abby wasn't sharing my business with anyone unless I told her she could. "You're a good person."

Abby freezes, and then turns toward me very slowly. "Is something wrong?"

Have I been that stingy with compliments? "No, nothing's wrong. I was just talking to Maren today, and she mentioned that things are going well with Ellie. Your intuition was right. I should have thanked you for helping with that, and instead I yelled at you. I'm sorry." It's hard to say, but it also feels like. . .like popping a zit, maybe. It's painful, but I'm happy to get it done.

I wonder what Abby would say if I told her that talking to her was like popping a zit. I can imagine how round her eyes would get.

"I'm glad she's doing better." Abby drops her purse on the counter and turns to duck into her room.

"Can we talk for a minute?"

She swallows, and then she sighs like I'm asking her to mop the floors. "Sure." She turns and faces me, very clearly not about to drop into a chair for a long conversation. I know it's been a long two days, driving to Salt Lake, and flying to California, only to fly back and drive home. But she looked so happy a moment ago.

Which means I'm the one dragging her down.

"If you're tired, we can talk tomorrow."

"I'd rather get it over with," she says.

Get it over with? Not an auspicious start. "Um, okay, well, the thing is. . ." I have no idea what to say. I'm not good at asking for favors, and this feels like a lot more than a favor.

I know she wants to go home to Houston. I know it's been hard on her to be here, to work here, to manage her family and mine, and now I want her to stay when she has no other reason to stick around.

Other than Steve, but things there don't seem so great.

"Amanda, just spit it out."

"Are you moving back to Houston?"

She nods. "Probably. I told Steve I'd think about it, and I have been, but all roads point back home."

I bite my lip.

"I assume you're going back to New York City?"

I clear my throat, but I have no idea what to do next. I mean, she says she's going home. This is hopeless. I'm the only loser with nowhere better to be.

"How much money do you need?"

Money? She thinks I need money? I suppose if I was going back to New York, I would need money.

"I don't need money," I say.

"But if you're dumping Eddy and heading home, you'll need a deposit on an apartment." She frowns. "You are dumping Eddy, aren't you?"

I shake my head slowly. "I love him."

Her expression shifts, but it's not what I expected. It looks like she pities me. "You're planning to stay here?"

I nod.

"Really?"

"Yeah. I was hoping you might stay, too." There. I did it. I said the words.

She laughs.

"Why is that funny?"

"Oh." She frowns again. "Were you serious?"

"I was," I say. "I know it may not feel like it, and I know I've been a little. . .erratic and kind of bratty lately, but I will really miss you if you leave."

She looks like I punched her. "Oh."

I've done an even worse job as a sister-in-law than I realized. Geez. "Abby, I'm really sorry about everything I said. I was just scared—without a place to live, without a reason to be here, I was a little lost."

I should tell her that I can't stay with Amanda Saddler unless she agrees to stay, too. I should be honest.

But I can't.

If I think there's no chance she'll stay now, she definitely won't if I try to guilt trip her. Plus, she'd never believe I asked her to stay for any reason but my own selfishness if I tell her about that.

Is that the only reason?

The thought of her leaving panics me, honestly.

"I need you," I say. "As pathetic as that sounds. Plus, I think it's good for your kids to be in a new place, and to be pursuing new things. Maybe you could just stay through the end of the school year?"

Abby circles and sits in the chair next to me, but it's not the coup I thought it would be. She looks resigned, exhausted, and frustrated. "We're about to be homeless," she says. "Not all of us have a boyfriend we can go stay with. And once you're there, it's not like we'll see each other that often." She snorts. "It's not like I see you that much now."

She's right. "I've been too busy. I've been worried about the wrong things, and I've taken you for granted. I'm sorry."

Abby shakes her head. "At the end of the day, I have to do what's best for my family."

I play my only remaining card. "Won't you miss Steve?"

Too many emotions to interpret flash across Abby's face. "It's complicated."

"How could it not be, with us?" My smile is twisted, that much I know. "But that doesn't mean it's not worth it. Have you asked your kids what they want?"

"It's a moot point." Abby shrugs.

And then it hits me. I don't have to tell her that Amanda's offer is contingent on her agreeing, but she needs to know the offer is there.

"Amanda Saddler said we can come live with her, at least until the school year is out."

"Is she going senile?" Abby asks. "Does she know how

many of us there are?" Now she looks bemused. "I imagine she'll change her mind about three seconds after we arrive."

"She has one more bedroom than we have here," I say. "And three bathrooms."

Abby rolls her eyes. "But instead of two families coming together, we'd have three, and we'd have to walk on eggshells around her."

"Have you met Amanda Saddler?" I chuckle. "She's capable of letting us know what she thinks."

"Why aren't you going back to New York?"

I think about her question for a moment. "There's nothing for me there anymore. My future is here."

Her brow furrows.

"Look, Abby, I've been a mess. I know I have. But I have loved having a sister. I know you have a real sister, but I don't. You're it. And you've done more for me and my kids than anyone ever has, even if you leave right now."

That penetrated—I can tell.

"Can you promise me one thing?"

She shrugs.

"Just think about it—the future you want, and whether you can find it back home, or whether you'd be happier here."

She frowns. "It's just that, Steve and I were doing so well, but lately, he's so busy I never even see him. He wanted a family, and now he has one. He doesn't need me for that anymore."

I think about Ethan—shoveling stalls at Steve's for some unknown reason. I think he may be more involved than Abby realizes. "I'll just say this one last thing, and then I swear I'll let you go to bed."

"Okay."

"You're amazing, Abby. You're organized, and you're hard working, and you're caring, and you're always doing the right thing. It's hard to compare to, sometimes, but it's really impressive."

She arches one eyebrow.

"You can sense the but, I know. Here it is. You're so great, that sometimes it's easy to forget that you're a real, fallible person. I know I took you for granted, and I let you do too much—things I should have done myself—and you were suffering because of me. I'm really sorry about that, and I'm not trying to make excuses, but it's possible that Steve didn't even know you needed his help. He might still want to be with you all the time, but not see a space for himself by your side."

"You're saying I shut people out."

"I'm saying you *shine* people out. You're so bright that sometimes it's hard to see what you need or even be able to tell when you're struggling."

Abby nods.

"And for what it's worth, you should talk to Ethan. He's the reason you came here, and he might have some insight into Steve and whether he really cares about you. Tell him how you feel, and ask him if you should go back to Houston."

Abby blinks, but after a moment, she nods.

Now all that's left is to wait and hope.

24
ABIGAIL

I've specifically been avoiding Ethan.

I know he wants to stay out here, but there's nothing left for him to do, not anymore. The ranch he wanted?

It's gone.

The life he imagined?

It's nonexistent.

When Nate died, our world shifted. I wanted to cling to things. I wanted to keep doing the same stuff we did before, but it wasn't healthy. My friends told me so. My family told me so.

A therapist told me so.

Life is change, and if we can't accept it, then we aren't living.

But it's really going to hurt to hear my sweet son tell me how much he wants to stay, and then to tell him that we just can't, because I failed him. If Amanda's telling me I need to talk to him, I really do. It might just be a convenient excuse, but I can't talk to him today. I've got to leave this morning for Houston. There's a case I have to be physically present to help with, and I've known it was coming. I hate that my trips are falling back to back, but I don't have any control over that.

My phone buzzes in my pocket, which is a big shock given the time. It's Robert—who must have calculated what time I'd need to wake up for this flight.

"Yeah," I whisper. "I'm up, and I'm about to leave for the flight. Why are you awake at this hour?"

"Oh, you know," Robert says. "Same old insomnia I've always had. I just remembered you saying it was a three-hour drive."

"I hate leaving them," I say, "but at least it's good weather in Houston right now."

"The hearing shouldn't take more than two days," Robert says. "You won't be gone long."

"Alright, I'd better get going. See you soon." I hang up.

"Mom?" Ethan's hair sticks up in thirteen different directions, and he rubs his eyes. He closes the door behind him carefully. "I thought that was you. You always have to leave so early."

Four a.m. "That's just part of living so far from anything," I say. "It'll be better once we get back home."

His face falls.

"I know it's not what you wanted."

He turns away.

"Honey."

He's still glaring at the wall.

I step closer. "I can't talk very long or I'll miss my plane, but I know this must be hard for you."

His head snaps back. "You didn't even talk to us about it."

"About what?"

"You didn't tell us we might lose. And now that the ranch is gone, you're not even giving us any options. You're just going to pack us up and slink back there."

I knew he'd be upset.

"Did you even consider staying?"

"For what?" I ask. "There's no ranch. There's nothing for you to do here, and there's certainly nothing for me."

"They don't have a lawyer," he says. "Not here, not in Flaming Gorge, and there are hardly any in Green River."

"Honey, they don't need one in any of those places. That's why there isn't one."

"But if you were here, you could find work to help people with."

"Suing someone over their lost cattle? Maybe they can pay me in chickens." I snort. "Great plan."

"I mean it," Ethan says. "Do you know how many people have asked me about you doing their wills? And Kevin and Jeff said that—"

"Ethan."

His eyes are absurdly full of hope. As a parent, it goes against every fiber of my being to squash it so mercilessly, but letting it drag out won't help him either.

"There's nothing for us here. Not anymore."

"What about Steve?" he asks.

"The guy who can't be bothered to come to auction when he says he will?" I'm not being fair, and I know it, but I need to give myself permission to walk away.

"He cares about you a lot," Ethan says. "More than you know."

"What's with people saying that?" I sigh. "I know he cares about me. But you know what? He might be better off without me. His gorgeous ex is available, and now he's got the family he really wanted."

Ethan shrinks, like one of those buttercup flowers after the sun goes down. "Do you really think that?"

"Ever since she came back, Steve has barely glanced my direction." Saying the words out loud acknowledges that I really feel that way. "Every second of his spare time, which used to be directed toward me, is now going to Olivia and her mother. I don't fault him for that, but I feel kind of stupid for diverting any of my time away from you guys for him."

"Mom," Ethan says.

"I really need to go," I say. "Can we talk when I get back?"

"Steve has been doing more than you think." He looks at his feet.

"What?" Why's he embarrassed? What's going on?

"He caught me," Ethan says. "I was with Beth Ellingson—Donna's niece."

"*What*?" Caught him doing what?

"She had beer," he says. "She picked me up a few weeks ago, and we were down by the creek, drinking. I guess his headlights hit us wrong, and Steve stopped and found us, and I begged him not to tell you."

"You're not twenty-one," I say.

"Oh please, Mom. No one follows that."

"He didn't even tell me." I was sad before, but now I'm livid. It's the excuse I've been looking for. "He thought I didn't deserve to know that my own son was breaking the law? That you were hiding out with a high school girl?"

"I begged him not to tell you," Ethan says. "He disciplined me. I've been going to his place and shoveling stalls ever since."

"He kept it from me, and he got free labor out of it?" My fury turns to pure rage. "How in the world does that show that he cares about me?"

"Sometimes I shovel stalls alone, but usually he's there. And when he is, he spends the entire time telling me stories about all the stupid things he's done because of alcohol."

"That's not his decision," I say. "He doesn't get to—"

"Mom, I'm an adult," Ethan says. "It's not your decision, either."

"You were still breaking the law," I say. "And you're still my son. He should have told me right away."

"He knew you were busy," Ethan says, "and he knew you'd overreact."

"Your uncle died, thanks to a drunk driver," I say. "Drinking can cause all kinds of—"

"Mom, I know. Steve's an ER doc, remember? He sees plenty of that, and he's lectured me on all of it."

I still can't believe—I don't know who I'm more angry with, Steve or Ethan. On my drive to Salt Lake, and then on the flight, I think about it. I mull it over, fuming. When I swipe airplane mode off and a flurry of texts from Ethan come through, I'm still annoyed.

And when I see the message from Steve, I seriously consider sending him a blistering response.

I MISS YOU ALREADY.

Miss me? How can he? He's too busy with his ex and lying to me about my son to miss me.

Ugh.

I'm not being fair, and I don't even care.

I almost don't see Robert—I didn't know he was coming. "I was going to get an Uber," I say. "You didn't have to come pick me up."

"We can talk about the case on the way to the office," he says. "It was efficient." I always took his looks for granted, but now that I haven't seen him for a while, they're like a slap to the face. He's so polished, so clear, and so bright. He looks. . .rich, and sharp, and just familiar in a comforting way.

"It's efficient for a partner who bills $800 an hour to pick me up?" I roll my eyes. "Just admit you missed me."

"Of course I did," Robert says. "Everyone at work wants to know when you're coming back. Beth, Deb, Barbara. They all noticed that I'm crabbier when you're gone."

I should tell him. This is my window. All I'd have to do

is say, 'We lost the ranch. I'm actually moving back—I need a while to go by the house on this trip to make sure it's ready for us.' He'd be delighted, clearly. We could talk about the terms of my return. Obviously I can't waltz back into being partner. I'm not sure how long it might be before they offer me that opportunity again, but I'm sure it'll eventually circle around. Being a widow has got to buy me a little latitude.

But the words just don't emerge. Somehow, they're lost on the way out.

"Are you hungry?" he asks.

"Only if Moonshine is open. I've been craving their green chile macaroni since the day I left."

Robert laughs. "I should've known."

He doesn't ask again—he makes straight for Moonshine's downtown location, tossing his keys to the valet without a second thought. By the time I order their peanut butter mousse pie, we're done hammering out our final trial strategy.

"The new associate seems organized," I say. "I liked the way she laid out the exhibits."

"She's the best we've had—since you, obviously."

"Ha," I say. "What are you trying to butter me up for?"

"Come back," Robert says. "Your work is still exceptional, even remotely, but it's not the same. We've all missed you, but me more than anyone else."

"Robert."

"I promise not to make any moves on you at all. I know that was a mistake, and I feel awful that I drove you away." He looks utterly sincere. "I've missed our friendship more than I can say."

I did pull away—more than just putting physical distance between us—after he tried to kiss me. I wasn't sure what else to do. How can things ever go back to how they were?

"I won't lie and say I don't have feelings for you. You're too astute for that to even work, but I've loved you from afar for twenty years. I can keep doing it forever. Just don't stay a million miles away."

"Robert, I don't know why I didn't tell you this before, but we lost the ranch."

His jaw drops.

"The kids want to stay—"

"There's nothing to keep you there," he says. "Come back."

"My kids—"

"They want a change, and that's understandable. Sell the house, buy a new house in a new school district. Or, I don't know. We can come up with some kind of plan."

We? "It really doesn't feel like you're going to be able to maintain—"

"I said 'we' before," he says. "All the time, after Nate passed away. I've always been on your side, and I still am. I meant what I said. Nothing weird from me. Just support."

Someone who will be there when he says he will? Someone whose entire attention is and always has been focused on me? It feels nice, I'm not going to lie. "I'll think about it, Robert."

"I can't ask for more than that."

I MISS YOU ALREADY.

I don't know why Steve's text keeps coming to mind. I mean, he's still my boyfriend, but only because my attempts to dump him haven't been accepted.

He's gum on my shoe.

Right?

It's the safe play to go back to what I know, to where I have a safety net. But. . .

I MISS YOU ALREADY.

I sigh, because I miss him, too. I shouldn't. He's distracted. He lives in the wrong place. He has too much going on. Robert has always been there for me, and he's willing to accept whatever I can give, nothing more. I know he'll be patient and true to his word.

But it's Steve I want.

Why?

What's wrong with me?

Robert drops me off at my house, but it feels different. It *looks* different, and it's not just the silk potted plants Adam left on the front porch as part of his staging.

"You alright?" Robert has always paid careful attention to the people and things around him.

"I'm fine," I say. "It's just weird being here."

"You don't see it as home anymore."

I don't realize it's true until he says it. I shake my head slowly.

"That's okay, you know," Robert says. "Maybe you needed that, to get through it."

"Maybe."

"But that doesn't mean that Houston isn't home. It doesn't mean you shouldn't come back, especially now that the ranch is gone."

"I have a boyfriend," I blurt out. There's no reason for me to tell him, per se, except that it feels weird that I've never said it. "You met him—Steve Archer—back in Utah."

Robert scrunches his nose. "The doctor horse guy?"

"The horse trainer who's also an ER doctor," I say. "Yes. He's one of the things that makes my decision hard."

He nods, but I can tell he doesn't like it.

When I walk into my own house, the feeling of wrongness just expands. It's probably because it's so pristine and empty and the kids aren't here, but for whatever reason, it reminds me of looking at Nate's body after he died.

It feels. . .familiar, and yet also *off* somehow. I still can't bring myself to reply to Steve's text, but Ethan must have gone over to see him, because he's got more to say.

I KNOW YOU KNOW, he texts around eight p.m.

I still don't reply.

He calls me, three times, but I don't answer, because I have no idea what to say.

WE NEED TO TALK.

He's right. We do. But I'm not ready.

ABBY. CALL ME.

Finally, I can't help myself. AREN'T YOU TOO BUSY TO TALK? GO SPEND TIME WITH OLIVIA AND LEAVE ME ALONE.

THAT'S NOT FAIR, ABBY.

I know it's not. I know. But I can't help feeling hurt. I can't help feeling like I always come in second place for him. Like I always will. When he came over that night after we lost the ranch, it was like he finally did the things that the old Steve did. But I know it can't last, because Stephanie is a flake and Olivia is always there. I can't expect him to put me before his own daughter. I won't put him before my kids. I can't. It's not who I am.

There's a knock at my front door.

Probably one of the neighbors saw me get out of Robert's car. Or, what if it's Robert? Ugh.

I could hide.

Whoever it is knocks again.

They probably saw me. If it is Robert, how embarrassing will it be if I delay? He'll probably think I'm pooping. That has me sprinting to the door and ripping it open.

"You are one hard woman to get ahold of," Steve says.

"What on earth are you doing here?"

"Ethan told me that he told you that I caught him drinking—with a girl."

I blink. "You're in Houston." Standing in front of the house I shared with Nate.

"It's weird, right?" he asks. "I wasn't invited, and my girlfriend—who keeps trying to dump me—won't answer my texts, but here I am anyway." His grin is self-effacing and still adorable. "I guess this means I'm Robin and you're Batman, right?"

I have no idea what to say.

"That kind of sucks. Robin's lame." When he chuckles, the skin around his eyes crinkles and his bag strap shifts and he has to rearrange it. The muscles in his forearms bunch. "Is it always this hot in Houston in November?" He mops his hand across his forehead. "Are you really going to leave me standing out here in the heat?"

I'm overcome with an overwhelming desire to hug him. I need his arms around me like kittens need to bat at string. Like woodpeckers need to hammer on trees. Like Roscoe needs to scratch his ear with every ounce of dedication he has.

The desire doesn't go away when I don't act on it. It only strengthens.

I finally give in, stepping into his personal space and wrapping my arms around his waist.

"Oh," he says.

I press the side of my face against his sculpted chest. "You're here."

"I'm here." His voice is deep and rumbly and it's surround sound, coming from his mouth and also from his chest.

"I'm glad."

He exhales then and his arms come around me. "Thank goodness."

I finally pull away, but his arms don't let me move far. "What about Olivia?"

"She's with her mom," he says. "Abby."

I look up into his dark blue eyes.

"I love you. Don't leave. Please, please don't move back here."

"I can't stay in Utah just because my boyfriend asks."

"Your kids want to stay, too," he says.

I know they do.

"You felt alone, and I'm so sorry. All I can say is that I'm someone who makes mistakes. I got too caught up in my stuff, and I got too nervous about screwing up things as a dad, and I didn't realize how well you'd cover things up when you were struggling."

That's almost painfully close to what Amanda said.

"I'll know now to watch more carefully. I won't let you down like that again." He ducks his head in that boyish way he does. "But I'm sure I'll screw up again, and I promise that when I do, I'll apologize again, and I won't make that same mistake again."

"You're in Houston," I say again. I still can't quite believe he's here.

"I'm in Houston," Steve says. "And if I'm being honest, I'm not that impressed. Even in November, it's muggy."

I laugh.

"And there's a lot of congestion, and the people say 'Howdy' too much."

"No they don't," I say.

"No, they don't," he agrees. "But I'm going to insist they do when I go back home."

"You're ridiculous."

"Say you'll come with me." He looks around the house. "This house is way, way nicer than anything we have back in Daggett County."

"It is," I say.

"But you won't love it, not anymore."

He's right about that, too. "Maybe Amanda Saddler will sell me a place out there, close to Birch Creek."

"Sell you a place?" Steve quirks one eyebrow. "Don't do that. It's too *permanent*. Maybe just rent something." He grins his cocky grin. "Keep your options open."

"I hate moving," I say. "I'd rather not do it any more than I have to."

"What if you didn't have to do it?" he asks. "What if there was a big, strong man who would be willing to hire people to do it for you?"

"A big, strong man who will. . .hire people?" I can't help my grin.

He shrugs. "I'm not afraid to throw my money around."

I roll my eyes. "I'll only agree to look for a place to rent if you agree to help me move in, shirtless."

"It's a deal." He flexes his pecs.

I press a hand flat against them. "Do that again."

"You've changed, Abigail Brooks."

"What if I have?"

"It's a good thing. Life's about rolling with the changes, and that means coming back with me, finding a new place to live, and kissing me. A lot."

"Kissing you?" I raise my eyebrows.

And then Steve dips his head and presses his lips to mine.

I expect it to feel *wrong*. We're standing in the home I shared with Nate, a home we designed together and lived in with our children.

But it doesn't feel wrong.

Can love ever really be wrong? That's when I realize it. His warm, strong lips press against mine. This man who flew last minute to Houston, just to tell me he loves me. A man who's willing to risk it all, who's willing to bare it all, who's willing to beg me to come back in the home I shared with someone else. He admits he's wrong. He promises to do better.

And it makes me happy.

It doesn't feel wrong, because I love him, too. So I kiss him back ferociously. And I don't stop.

25

DONNA

The last Thanksgiving we spent together as a family was a miserable disaster. Patrick mocked me for not graduating from college. Charles, who was the only one allowed to put me down in his mind, ripped into him. My dad waded into the melee, verbal assaults flying. After all, he himself had never been to college either. He ripped into me, into Charles, and then into my mother. Anyone who came near.

Mom wound up in the back room, crying.

It's safe to say that I was never overly grateful to spend Thanksgivings with my dad. Even so, I feel a little guilty ditching him with a nurse and going to Birch Creek Ranch.

Not guilty enough to deprive Aiden and myself of a happy gathering and delicious food.

But a little guilty.

"Mom?" Aiden asks.

"Yeah?"

"Will Gabe be there?"

"He will, sweetie, but I'm not sure whether his Legos will be unpacked or not. They're moving next week."

"I don't understand why they have to move. Gabe likes his house."

Ah, Aiden. None of us really get it. "Their Uncle Jed was an idiot," I say. "That's why they have to move."

"But they're not leaving to go back to Texas, right?" Apparently Gabe talks about Texas a lot.

"They aren't," I say. "Abby was really clear about that. They're moving in with Amanda Saddler, who lives down the road."

"The old lady? With the white hair?"

"I don't know how long they'll stay with her," I say. "But yes, that's who. It's not polite to call her old, though."

"What do I say, then?" Aiden asks. "She's not young."

Things are so black and white when you're that young. "I doubt anything you say will upset her," I say. "She's a pretty awesome old lady."

"How come she's really nice and funny, and grandpa is mean and yells all the time?"

I wish I had an answer for that one. "His heart was probably always a bit too small," I say.

"Like the grinch?" Aiden asks.

I shrug. "Maybe."

A miracle happens after that—he mulls the whole thing over, and the questions stop for the rest of the drive. When we finally reach Birch Creek, I pull the bag of soda out of the back seat.

"Is this all we're bringing?" Aiden eyes the four two-liters of soda sideways.

"That's what Abby said to bring," I say. "I asked a few times, but she insisted."

"She's a really nice lady."

I ruffle the hair on his head. "I agree."

"I'm glad I can go with you here instead of going to see Dad."

He doesn't talk about his dad much, but it makes me

happy when he says he's pleased with where he is. "I'm glad too."

"I hope Dad's not sad."

I doubt Charles has any real feelings at all, but I can't very well say that. "Me too."

"Really?" Aiden peers up at me. "Sometimes I think you hate him."

I squeeze my little boy tightly. "Sweetheart, I really do hope your dad isn't miserable today." I need to be more careful about what he hears. I can't have his feelings being skewed by mine.

Walking through the door of Abby's ranch is like walking into a Norman Rockwell painting. It's warm, it's bright, and it's welcoming. Abby's turkey comes out of the oven a moment after we arrive. The skin is crackly. The cranberry sauce and gravy are bubbling on the stovetop.

Knot rolls emerge from the lower oven a moment later, and Izzy brushes butter on the tops of them.

"I still can't believe you started a cookie company because you screwed up your first ever batch of cookies." Amanda Saddler slaps her knees. "And I'm the idiot who bankrolled you."

"Hey, if my daughter hadn't picked a fight with the local beauty queen, I might still be doing that," Amanda Brooks says.

"It's too confusing to call you both Amanda," Abby says. "One of you has to go by Mandy."

"I'm too old to go by such a silly nickname," Amanda Saddler says. "I call Amanda."

"Oh come on," Amanda Brooks says. "You'll die soon, and then I'll be stuck as Mandy forever. You should take one for the team and let people call you Mandy for the little bit of time you have left."

"I'm too old to answer to anything new," Amanda Saddler says.

"Plus we already call you Aunt Mandy," Whitney says.

"Traitor," Amanda Brooks hisses, but there's no real sentiment behind it.

Everyone's smiling.

No one's tearing anyone else down.

But when the soda bottles hit the table, the gloves come off.

"Get it, Steve," Abby says. "Not that crappy orange soda. The good stuff—Dr. Pepper."

"You realize you could buy some at the store yourself, and then you could drink soda all the time," he says. "Then you wouldn't need to argue over who got it first."

Abby rolls her eyes. "Soda's bad for you. It's only a special treat."

"Silly me," Steve says.

"Hurry!" Abby shouts.

But Eddy's already grabbed the Dr. Pepper. "What will you trade us for it?" He holds it up as high as he can, just outside of Steve's reach.

"I want the floral room," Amanda Brooks says. "You get stuck with the en suite bathroom this time."

"That's not fair," Maren says. "You have two daughters, so having us walk through is no big deal. Are you really going to make Aunt Abby have Gabe and Ethan trot through her room every time they need to go to the bathroom?"

Amanda groans. "Fine! Ugh. Just give her the Dr. Pepper. It's disgusting anyway."

"What do you like?" Steve asks.

"Sparkling water." Eddy grimaces. "Gross, right?"

"The kind without any sugar at all?" Olivia looks a little overwhelmed by all the noise and activity, but Whitney and Izzy and Emery sort of roll her into their little group, like an ocean wave descending over a dinghy. Eventually, she's laughing right along with them over ridiculous things, like lopsided napkin shapes and wonky placemats.

Stuff that only makes sense to the people who are bonding over it.

Thanksgiving descends after that into an all-out melee of conversation and jokes. Ethan badgers Maren mercilessly, which Emery enjoys a little too much. Gabe and Aiden eat exactly as many bites as we force them to eat and then disappear into Gabe's room, because it turns out the Legos haven't been packed up yet.

"Of course not," Abby says. "Those get packed the very last moment." She shrugs. "They're my sanity."

The food is the best I've ever had at Thanksgiving—all thanks to Abby, Izzy, Whitney, and Emery, apparently. Although, Steve made the mashed potatoes, and Eddy made the stuffed mushrooms.

But the jokes, the laughter, and the sense of belonging? That's even better.

Until we clean everything up and break up into groups to play games. Steve sits next to Abby and grabs her feet, propping them up on his lap. Eddy slings a casual arm around Amanda and drags her closer, breathing in the scent of her hair.

And for the first time all day, I feel out of place.

"It's a little disgusting, isn't it?" Amanda Saddler says. "And she wants *me* to go by Mandy."

They all start laughing then.

But when it's time to go, I'm ready to leave. As beautiful as it is to see that love is really possible, it kind of hurts to be one of the people who hasn't found it. I wonder how Amanda Saddler can withstand it so happily.

"The secret, dear," she whispers as I bustle Aiden out the door, "is to spend enough years alone. Longing and regret aren't as bad as utter loneliness. Seeing them happy doesn't upset me anymore. I'm just glad they're near."

I think about that as I drive home. I'd never considered it before, but I wonder whether my mother was happy living with my dad. And whether she'd have been happier alone, or if she was glad they were married, even though he was kind of a terrible person.

When I reach the house, I'm welcomed inside by the sound of howling. Sounds like things have not been going well for my nurse.

Rena throws her hands up in the air when I walk inside. "He's horrible today."

"I'm so sorry," I say.

"Not even worth the overtime." She shakes her head.

"I do appreciate it," I say.

Dad's already bellowing. "Hey, wax ears! Get in here!"

I wave Rena off. "Go and enjoy what you can salvage of your day."

"Good luck," she says as she ducks out.

"I'm coming, Dad," I say.

"Can I go watch television?" Aiden asks.

I nod, reluctantly. I don't like how much TV he's been watching, but nothing else drowns out the shouting when Dad's really mad. "Just don't turn it up *too* loud, okay?"

Aiden shrugs before he disappears.

I've barely entered Dad's room when a slipper hits the wall next to my head.

"Hey," I shout. "Don't do that. We've discussed this before. No matter how upset you are, you can't throw things."

Dad's eyes fix on me. "Donna."

"Yes, it's me."

"I was defending myself. That nurse is trying to kill me."

"Rena's not trying to kill you, Dad. She's trying to help you."

He narrows his eyes. "You don't know. You weren't here. You were out traipsing around like a slut."

"She's been your nurse for months, Dad. If she was trying to kill you, you'd be dead."

"You'll be relieved when I'm dead." He frowns.

I actually feel guilty when he says that, because it's a little too true. "Dad, what's wrong?"

"My stomach hurts," he says. "And so does my head."

"Let me call Rena and ask her if you can have Ibuprofen," I say.

"Don't call her," Dad begs. "Please. She'll confuse you. You'll give me poison by accident."

I walk toward him and sit on the edge of Dad's bed. The man who made my life a misery for years is now so frail. He's so unsure. "Dad, no one wants you to die."

He takes my hand in his gently, maybe more gently than he ever has in his life. "I was really mean to you," he says.

Unexpectedly, the words actually make me *feel*. "Why are you always so mean?" I can't tell if he means just now, or in life, generally.

"I didn't tell you when I was proud of you. I felt like, if I did, you might quit trying hard."

Is he serious?

"You were so smart, smarter than my whole family. And you were so beautiful. But if you knew it, you'd have stopped trying to be smart and working to be beautiful."

"Did you really think that?"

He clutches my hand against his chest. "I knew it. I was trying to help you."

In his own way, was he? If so, that may be the saddest thing he's ever said to me. "Dad, I forgive you."

"Do you really?"

"Today's Thanksgiving," I say. "That may not mean much to you, but it means something to me. It means that I should be grateful for what I have. You and Mom decided that my school tuition was all I was ever entitled to, and I agreed to it, so I don't fault you. But you're not what I'm grateful for today."

"That's not true," Dad says weakly. "We changed our mind."

I'm not dumb enough to believe anything he says right now. Him saying he changed his mind is tantamount to him telling me that Rena poisoned him. I pat his hand. "Alright, Dad. It's okay. Because I won custody of my son, and I have court ordered child support, and you know what? I actually like my job. And I have friends who have found love and they're happy, and that gives me hope. My parents may not have been in love, and my brother may be awful, but there are people out there who are happy. I aim to be one of them."

"I loved your mother a lot," Dad says. "And she loved me, too."

I pat his hand again. "I'm glad to hear it." But if that's love, kill me now.

"Your mom is an angel up in heaven."

She probably is. "Okay, Dad."

"I love you, too, Donna. I'm happy you're happy."

It may be the single kindest thing he's ever said to me. There's no biting backhanded comment, and no undercutting or sniping, either. In fact, if I thought he knew what he was saying, I'd probably write it in my journal so I never forgot it. As it is, I get him some Ibuprofen, and he takes it nicely, and I tuck him in and close the door.

And the next morning, when I go to check on him, he's a little too peaceful and a little too calm.

Before I even press my hand to his forehead, I know.

My dad's gone.

I thought I'd feel nothing but relief, but it turns out, that's wrong. Looking at him now, the broken shell that could no longer house his defiant, angry, mean-spirited soul, I'm terribly sad.

I'm sad he's gone.

That's a shock.

But I'm also sad that any chance I had of becoming close to my enigmatic, rude father is also gone. Right there at the end, was that who he really was? Was what he said true? Was he mean to me in some twisted attempt to motivate me? Was he actually proud of me? For my intelligence and my appearance? He never once told me that during my life, at least, not until last night.

I'm so conflicted that I don't expect to cry, but I do anyway. It takes me a full five minutes to calm down enough to call 911. They go through the motions when they arrive, but we all know what's happened. Finally, they call it.

And that's when I phone Patrick.

He may be as messed up as my dad, but he deserves to know that our father died. We're officially orphans, if you can be an orphan at our age.

Can you? I'm not sure, but if you can, I am. We are. No parents at all.

"He's finally gone?" Patrick's sneer perfectly reflects the way I thought I'd feel.

"You're not sad at all?"

He shrugs. "Should I be? I figured you'd be doing cartwheels."

Last week, I'd have said the same, but I'm still inexplicably sad. Maybe for Dad's wasted life, maybe for the loss of hope that he could improve, or maybe just because now that he's gone, it really hits me what a disappointing father we had. "I hope he's with Mom."

"For her sake, I hope he's not." Patrick looks deadly serious.

"She loved him, didn't she?"

"In the sick way that abused women love their abusers,

maybe," Patrick says. "I sincerely hope he's gone where he belongs, and that Mom's up in heaven."

I guess there's no way for us to know where either of them is, but after Dad's pathetic apology last night, I kind of hope he can be forgiven. I hope that his twisted, confused morality and attempts to motivate us will be unkinked, and he can be happy somewhere.

Maybe I'm a chump after all.

Patrick isn't nearly as conflicted. "Let's just cremate him and dump his ashes in the trash," he says. "Or maybe they'll just keep them wherever we send his corpse."

We can argue about that later.

He looks around the room. "Either way, it'll probably take a week or so to get this craphole all cleared out."

"At least," I say.

He rolls his eyes. "There's no reason to ham it up. You can stay through January first, either way. I'm not the devil. I'm not going to kick you out with no notice, even though he's dead."

"Wait," I say. "You're really kicking me out?"

"We can finally rent this place." Patrick walks toward the front door. "No offense, but I doubt you'll be able to afford it."

As his words permeate, I decide he couldn't pay me enough to stay. "Don't worry," I say. "I'll be out long before January first."

"Don't leave until you've cleaned all this stuff out." He glances around, scrunching his nose in distaste as he walks to the doorway. "That way I don't have to fight with Amelia about you again."

"You know," I say. "You should look into divorce. It freed me." I give him a little shove and slam the door in his astonished face.

26

AMANDA

I don't decorate for Valentine's Day, for Easter, or for the Fourth of July.

But I always decorate for Halloween, for Thanksgiving, and especially for Christmas.

I'm not one of those people who spends their entire annual expendable income on Christmas lights or anything, but since I lived for so long in New York City, I would go all out on a wreath for my front door, a festive mat, and then I'd spend quite a while making sure that my patio looked amazing.

Actually, I was lucky. It rarely cost me anything to decorate at all. Vendors sent me all kinds of things in the hopes that I'd feature their products in some of my holiday photos or stories.

I do miss that.

Not that I'd have time to do anything with them this year, anyway, because we're moving. I should just be happy that Abigail decided to stay and that Amanda Saddler is taking us in. I should be counting my blessings, really.

But I'm not that kind of person.

"Why oh why am I the only one who moved her stuff out here?" I ask. "I'm such an idiot."

"And it's *snowing* today," Maren says. "The day after Thanksgiving, I should be shopping. Instead, I'm packing while it snows like crazy outside, the day before we're supposed to move all our crap to yet another clapped out old barn house."

"It's not a barn house," Emery says. "It's a *farm* house. She has a barn, and that's where the animals go. If you keep complaining this much, I'll suggest they put your 'crap' out there too. A few days out there might fix your lousy attitude."

"Or it could make it worse." Ethan bumps Maren's precariously perched pile of shoeboxes and sends them flying all over the hall, shoes clattering against the old wooden floorboards. "Why are you stacking those up out here, idiot? Just take them all out of the boxes and chuck them into one pasteboard box like the rest of us."

"These are designer," Maren wails. "Like you could understand."

"Yes, I'm too stupid to get that they're more expensive than my New Balance sneakers," Ethan says.

"Stop," Abby says.

Ethan huffs, but he walks away.

I'm kind of proud of him for not picking them all up like he usually would. Abby, clearly, is less pleased. "Ethan! Get back here and stack those boxes."

"I have no idea which of those very posh shoes goes in each box." His excuse is decent, at least. "I'm sure an uncultured bumpkin like me would only mix them up."

"Nice try," Abby says. "The boxes have a name on them, and it matches the one on the inside of the shoes. Even a college dropout should be able to figure it out."

He grumbles, but he helps Maren.

I need some of that magic elixir that makes my kids

listen to me. "It's fine," I say. "He doesn't have to help. It's obnoxious of her to be using shared spaces to stack her stuff."

But Ethan listens to his mother, not to me, and keeps right on stacking. Magic elixir, going on my list. Surely Amazon has it, right?

Abby's already done with her room, and she's moved on to the kitchen. I need to buy something that gives me her energy, too, clearly. But when her phone rings, she stops packing to pick up the call. "Hello?"

I'm focusing on getting my clothing all packed in between my bedroom decor, so I'm definitely not eavesdropping.

"Are you kidding? Send it to me right away," Abby says. "Finally, something I can show her."

Show who? I sneak, quietly, to the doorway and peek around.

I'm not the only one. Maren and Emery are both peeping, as well as Izzy.

"Who was that?" Izzy asks.

Abby races to her room and emerges with her laptop. "So, I haven't mentioned this because there wasn't a lot to mention. Yet. But a while back, I reached out to two of my friends. One's a detective with the Los Angeles Police Department, and one is a judge."

What is she talking about?

"It never sat right with me—Eddy's story, I mean. What are the odds that the man he struck happened to be a murderer? Someone who had *just* been released? I figured he either made that up, or that it was unlikely to be a coincidence. Sure enough, my judge friend immediately found a strange discrepancy between the story and the case."

"What?" Every muscle in my body is taut, now. "What right did you have to go poking around in my life?"

Abby's eyes are round, and her mouth is slack. "You're

upset?" She winces. "Maybe I should've told you from the start."

"Or just left me alone," I say. "Not everyone needs you to save them, and this is a painful—"

But she waves at me. "Just listen, for now. Get mad at me later."

I splutter.

"My judge friend Franklin discovered that Eddy wasn't charged with murder. I mean, the news articles do say that he was—I found them myself. But the actual charges against him? Nope. He was charged with negligent homicide. It's not a charge that's still around, and the details, including the initial filings and evidence, had been purged, so we had to do some more digging."

I have no idea what she's saying.

"That's where my detective friend came in handy." Abby beams. "It took some time. I mean, that stuff was eliminated years ago, even though there's no statute on murder, because the case had been plea-bargained out."

"But what does—"

She waves again and turns the computer around. "We had a few false starts and a few missed leads, but look what she just found!"

My hands tremble as I approach her laptop screen. The video's grainy, and it looks like it was taken by some store's security camera, but it's a car driving down the road, going very, very slowly. And then, a man darts out into the street —and the car speeds up. Dramatically.

And strikes the man directly.

Does that mean? My heart flies into my throat. Did Eddy *mean* to kill the man?

"Okay, so I saw this video not long ago, and I was a little horrified," Abby says. "I won't lie. It sure looks like he *meant* to kill him, not that he was not in control, doesn't it?"

I can barely meet her eyes. Why is she showing me this with triumph? "Abby, if you—"

Again, she waves me off. "Okay, so here's the best part. Are you listening? My friend found the connection between the serial killer and the driver." She bounces on her toes, her eyes wide with excitement.

"I can't believe—"

"I'll cut to the chase. The driver's cousin was killed by the serial killer, so imagine how upset he'd be when the serial killer guy was released."

"Abby—"

"Man, you're a real story killer. Because here's the video I got *today.*" Abby bends over her laptop and opens a new file. This time, the video clip zooms in on the interior of the car. It's fuzzy, but you can see the driver's face.

And the passenger's face, too.

It's clear as day, and Eddy isn't driving.

"The prosecution charged Eddy with negligent homicide just for being in the car! It's outrageous, but they had to have a fall guy. They knew the jury would never convict the kid for homicide for killing the serial killer who killed his cousin, and it would get them all kinds of bad press. So instead of dealing with any of it, his rich parents made it all disappear."

"Except the media got wind of the band being involved and so the record label's manager threw them a bone. Poor, alcoholic kid." Abby sighs. "They framed Eddy. He was a victim, too, but he didn't remember because he was *non compos mentis*."

"You're kidding," I say. "You must be kidding."

Abby shakes her head. "I'm not kidding at all. I had to do this slowly, one little step at a time, so that I had absolute, unassailable proof. They've already disposed of it legally, but my detective friend is going to package it all up and send it to a reporter." She pauses. "Unless for some reason you don't want me to."

"I need to ask Eddy," I say. "He's the one who should decide."

"Of course," Abby says. "Let me know."

But Eddy's dealing with a colicking horse, so it takes me hours to hear back. I feel like I ought to show him the information in person, and that means another delay. But finally, I meet him at his place—with Abby's laptop in hand.

He's just out of the shower when I arrive, his hair still damp. "What's going on?"

"Clearly my timing was bad," I say. "I just missed the real show."

Eddy rolls his eyes. "I can arrange for an encore any time." His boyish grin still gets me. It's almost enough to make me forget why I came, but not quite.

"Maybe later," I say. "I actually have some news."

He sits down at the kitchen table. "Wanna set that down and tell me what's up?"

"Remember how you always said you wished you could change the past?"

His head tilts, his eyes alert and a little concerned. "I do wish I could, but I can't, though."

"What if things weren't what you thought?" I set the laptop in front of him, and I hit play on the first video. "Abby has some friends she's been calling in favors from, and they did a little digging."

Eddy's eyes are glued to the screen, his breathing shallow and sharp. "Why didn't they show this video before?" When the car hits the pedestrian, Eddy jolts, his entire body tensed.

I put one hand on his shoulder. "It's okay," I say.

His movements are jerky and unsteady. "How can you say that? It's so much worse than I remember." He turns toward me slowly. "It looks like. . .it looks like I hit him on purpose, but I swear I didn't."

"Eddy," I say. "You probably don't remember much about that night."

"It's really fuzzy," he admits, "but—"

"Which is why you didn't remember that you weren't even the one driving."

"No, I was," he insists. "It was me, Amanda."

I shake my head. "Take a look."

I open the other video, and he watches, subtly shifting closer and closer to the screen with every second that passes.

"It wasn't you," I say. "And in fact, your 'friend' had a reason to want him dead. Apparently that serial killer murdered your buddy's cousin and was going to walk thanks to some kind of mistake with the evidence."

"How could—why did—" Eddy jumps to his feet, shaking his head. "But that means the people who—my agent, our manager, my friend—no." He's blinking and shaking and he looks utterly ill.

"Eddy, the police messed up and they didn't want that showcased. Your friend only knew about it because his family was getting updates from the prosecutor. The prosecutors didn't want it getting out there either—the public would be livid. The families of the victims were upset enough. And you really were not in your right mind—that was why they thought maybe you could save your friend." I sigh. "But they never even asked."

"He kept on performing," Eddy says. "He went on like nothing happened."

"You could have too," I say. "It was your decision to leave everything and walk away."

"Because they told me that I killed someone!" He runs his hands through his hair, leaving it rucked up in the back.

"For more than twenty years, I've thought I was a murderer, and all I was guilty of was being in the wrong car at the wrong time."

"I know," I say. "It's awful. Horrible. According to Abby, what they did to you was 'unconscionable.'"

He swears under his breath. "My family, my reputation, it was all destroyed."

"It's still not really justice, but Abby's friend's prepared to deliver all of this to a reporter, who's ready to take it to the world."

"Do it," Eddy says. "If you're here to get my permission, my answer is yes. Do it right now."

So we do.

Since Eddy's a social media ghost, they link to *my* account, as his girlfriend. Over the week that we're moving, dozens of stories hit the press, and hundreds of huge accounts on social media break different versions. They all circle back around to me, posting my images of Eddy far and wide.

"You need to create your own account," I say. "I know you don't want to, but a story that's generating this much attention in the middle of the Christmas holidays? It would be so much simpler for me if you had your own platform on which to share."

"Would it help you?" Eddy's eyes are clearer, less haunted. "If it would help you, I'll do it."

"I don't know about helping me," I say. "But it would make things easier for me online." Now that Eddy's been cleared, Lololime has asked me to come back, the idiots. And I'm getting a dozen new requests a day for products to sponsor.

"Help me figure out how," he says, "and I'll do it today."

Within an hour, he has two thousand followers. By the next morning, he has a hundred thousand.

"Am I really trending as #smokinhotmurderer?" He picks up his guitar and starts to play a few chords. "What's wrong with the internet?" His chords turned into a melody.

"If it helps, it's a joke. They're poking fun at the media for getting it wrong."

"It doesn't help much." He plays the melody again, changing a few things, tightening it up.

"Is that a new song?" I ask. "I like it."

"You asked if it helps to know that they're only kidding when they call me that," he says.

"Yeah, I did."

"Music helps me not to be angry," he says. "It used to make me more upset. I saw it as the reason I got into all that mess, the thing that set me on that path. But now I don't get mad when I think about it anymore." He sets the guitar down. "But you help more than music." He reaches for me.

I let him pull me right up next to him. My shoulders fit perfectly underneath his arm. I curl up against him and sigh. "You help me, too."

"How's the move going?"

"There are three strong women living in the same house," I say.

"That bad?"

"It's fine, really," I say. "Amanda barks and snaps with a smile on her face. Roscoe looks lost unless he's lying on my feet." At the sound of his name, he stands up and trots over. He won't settle down until he can lick my hand.

"Which is why you bring him over every single time you come."

"He stresses Jed out, too," I say. "He's always trying to herd him to the corner. But poor Abby—she can't sleep until things are put away. Even though she has way less stuff than we do, since most of it's still in Houston, she went about two days on less than two hours of sleep until things were in their places. She looked a little rough there for a bit."

"But you have your people, so that's good," Eddy says.

I shrug. "It is, yeah. I love it, and I hate it."

"What do you hate?"

"I used to decorate for Christmas," I say. "I didn't have much this year to decorate with, but I've gotten so many offers now, I could decorate the White House."

"Isn't that good?" he asks. "People want you to push their stuff again."

"But I've got no place to put them."

"Put them here," he says. "Decorate my place. You can pretend it's yours." He presses a kiss to the tip of my nose. "I told you to move here instead of there, but no. You had to be stubborn."

"We're not ready for that," I say. "Not even close."

"Not even close?" He makes me regret saying that.

But then I go a little crazy answering all the offers for Christmas decor, and I have it all shipped here, to Eddy's house.

"Maybe I should play my new song," he says. "I could put it up on my shiny, new Instagram account, once you get the place decorated."

"You know nothing about this stuff," I say. "You can't just post things for free. You have to release a teaser and then tell them to buy the whole song."

Eddy laughs. "That's what I'd do if it was my business, but my business is helping sick animals, remember?"

"Oh, right," I say. "I forgot."

"Do you wish I was a rock star?" He kisses the side of my jaw. "Would you like me more if I had girls following me around and screaming?"

I shove him. "Stop."

"Would you?" He grins at me then, and pulls me next to him. "You can't escape that easily."

"From you? Or from the question?"

"Both," Eddy says.

But when I kiss him, he forgets about all of it.

And to be honest, so do I.

27

ABIGAIL

The Christmas tree goes up the day after Thanksgiving, and it comes down the day after Christmas. There's no deviation from this, and there's no room to negotiate. It's just what happens.

Except we don't even have a tree.

Or our decorations.

And the day after Thanksgiving, we were packing up to move. We moved with the help of a lot of neighbors, which was a big surprise to me. Apparently the Amandas knew that everyone would turn out to lend a hand.

People turned out to help in spite of the snow.

Steve came and shoveled the walkways and salted them early on the morning of the move. Then Steve, his Sheriff uncle, and a dozen friends I'd only met in passing all came to help, including Venetia from the True Value and all her family.

Eddy brought his own cadre of friends along as well.

And Amanda Saddler hired a few people who came over from Green River. All in all, given the rather limited quantity of belongings we shifted, it was a fairly simple task to accomplish, even with six inches of snow on the ground.

We only had one slip. Steve checked him out to be sure, but he was fine.

After we got things settled in, and after even Amanda and her kids finished unpacking, no one made any movement toward setting up a Christmas tree. I finally force myself to ask Amanda Saddler about it. "When do you get your Christmas tree out?"

She's making herself tea, and she pauses mid-pour. She almost makes a huge mess. I snatch the teapot out of her hand before the cup can overflow.

"Do you not have one?"

She glances at the window, as if that's the answer.

"If you don't, I can drive into Green River and—"

"Girl, why would you drive out there? There's dozens of trees within an easy walk of the farmhouse. You can take your pick, but these old knees won't let me lug it back anymore."

"Oh," I say. "You use a live tree."

"Well, I hate to be the one to break it to you, but when you cut it down, it ain't alive any more." She bobs her head. "But we can have a little service for it after Christmas if that would make your kids feel better."

I laugh—she's such a weird old lady. "I think we'll all bear up under the strain of that death just fine. It's just not very common in Texas to use a live tree, much less cut your own. I suppose I hadn't even considered it."

"The worst part about the tree is that Jed, and probably Roscoe too, will drink out of the base and dribble water all over the floor around it. But the best part about having a tree is how it makes the house smell." She shakes her head. "City folk."

It takes Ethan and me almost two hours to find and cut a tree, and another hour to cut it down to the right size, but we're proudly bringing it inside when Amanda stops us.

"What are you two doing?"

I figured this part was rather obvious. "Uh, you said—"

"Have you ever cut a live tree in your life?"

We both shake our heads. "Not a Christmas tree," I say.

"You gotta leave it in the barn overnight in a big bucket," she says.

"Oh," I say. "So the bugs crawl off?"

She cackles. "Bugs? This time of year?" She shakes her head. "I swear, you're a real delight. No." She points at the base of the tree. "See that slice there?"

"You mean where we cut it?" I ask.

She nods. "How long since you did that?"

"Ten minutes?" Ethan asks. "Maybe?"

"You'll have to do it again, then," she says, "just an inch or two up from the bottom, and then immediately dunk it in a full bucket of water. One of them orange five-gallon ones like what you use to haul horse water and whatnot."

We had auto-waterers back at Birch Creek, but I don't argue with her. I know what she means. "Okay, but why?"

"Those evergreen trees are full of sap," she says. "If you want it to stay fresh, you gotta make sure it can drink as much as it wants after you cut it. But within a few minutes of being cut, that sap seals off the trunk and it can't get no water. It needs gallons of water that first night. Leave it out there overnight, and then we'll refill the base every single morning and maybe every night while it's here and it'll stay soft and smell good for weeks."

I'd never have thought of that. "Thanks."

"She couldn't have mentioned that *before* I cut the base?" Ethan may be grumbling, but he's excited too, I can tell.

That gives me time to line up a proper tree-decorating party. Steve comes, along with Olivia and her awful mother Stephanie. Donna brings Aiden, since she said they aren't doing a full tree this year in light of their impending move. Eddy's there too, and we wait until all the kids are off school. Amanda Saddler may be acting like she doesn't care, but when I notice the scarf she put on Jed—Christmas wreaths and jingle bells—I know it's just an act.

"We don't have a lot of Christmas ornaments," I say. "Amanda's happy to contribute the few she has, but I thought we might make some as well."

"Make them?" Stephanie frowns at the bowls of popcorn on the table. "Like, what? Putting popcorn on strings?"

"No," I lie. "The popcorn's to eat." I hate her.

"Then what?" Olivia asks. "I hope we get to paint something."

I tell Alexa to play Christmas songs, and then I start showing people the different ornament crafts I've prepared. I was limited by what I could find on my one quick trip into town.

"We have sock snowmen," I say. "Izzy has agreed to supervise this one. She'll help everyone fold the socks into the snowman shape, paint on the face and glue on the eyes, and then once you're all done, she can move on to the next station herself."

"I'm running Walnut Rudolphs," Amanda Saddler says. "And you better believe we're going to get those eyeballs glued on in the right place."

I'm not proud of it, but I bought every single hot glue gun they had in the craft section of Walmart in Rock Springs. If anyone else has malfunctioning Christmas decor, they'll be out of luck.

"I'll be your guide for making wrapped yarn stars, hearts, and trees," Steve says.

"In the kitchen, we're making dried orange slices," I say. "Which should add a great smell as well as a classy and beautiful look."

"But let's hang those high on the tree," Amanda Saddler says, "or Jed will eat them."

It's so strange that we have both a dog *and* a pig living in the house with us.

"Abby already made ornaments for each kid with photos she took," Amanda says. "So once we're done, you can each hang your ornaments on the tree yourself, wherever you want."

"This is even more fun than our party usually is," Gabe says.

Something about those words eases the anxiety I was feeling. Christmas is mostly about how we feel, after all. It's not about the actual tree or the gifts.

It's good that's true, because shortly after he says that, Gabe knocks over the white paint, and Jed trots right through it. After we calm everyone down and clean everything up, Emery bumps the glitter tray for the confetti ornaments and scatters it all over, some of it billowing across the walnut Rudolph table.

"It's fine," I reassure a distraught Emery. "Rudolph always looks better with a little more bling."

"Now my Rudolph's sparkly," Ethan says. "Ugh."

"Beth will love it," Izzy jokes.

"Shut up," Ethan says.

"You better fix your personality," Maren says. "Now that you're not a rancher, you're just a community college student." She snorts. "Doubt that will impress Beth much."

"Maren Brooks," Amanda Saddler says. "Is that any way to speak to your cousin?"

Maren's eyes widen. "No, ma'am. I'm sorry."

Amanda Saddler loves that my kids, raised in the south, call every adult sir or ma'am, and now she has all the kids calling her that. It cracks me up.

Once all my citrus slices are baking, I'm free to wander around. I make a snowman out of baby socks, and then I paint a walnut to make a Rudolph later, and I finally wind up at Steve's station.

He grins when he sees me. "Well, Madame President, can I interest you in a piece of yarn? You just make a wire frame, wrap it around like so." He demonstrates. "And then dip it in wax."

"Did you forget who taught you all this?" I tilt my head.

"Right," he says. "What was I thinking?" He reaches for my hand to tug me around to his side of the table. "Maybe you could take over and I could—"

"Eww," Olivia says from two feet away. "Are you two going to be gross?"

"If you think this is gross," Steve says. "You better brace yourself for what's coming next."

"Whoa," Olivia says. "This is child abuse."

"Oh please," Whitney says. "My dad used to—" She cuts off abruptly, and looks down at her feet.

"What did he do?" Steve asks. "I'm dying to know."

Whitney raises her eyes slowly, searching for confirmation that it's okay to talk about her dad.

Steve's eyes are bright and welcoming. "Come on, now, don't make me wait forever."

"They used to smooch right in front of us," Whitney says. "And sometimes Dad would dip Mom and smooch her all sideways like that, too."

"Really?" Steve shakes his head. "I clearly need to up my game." He spins me into his arms with one tug, and then dips me in a smooth movement. And then he presses his mouth against mine.

It ought to feel *wrong*, to have Steve do the same thing Nate used to do, in front of my kids, no less. It should feel like he's trying to replace him, or like he doesn't respect the history I had with my first love.

But it doesn't.

Steve's arms around me are strong. His feelings for me are clear. His intentions are never to overshadow, to erase, or to belittle. He respects what I had with Nate, and he allows—even encourages—my kids to express how they feel, and what they remember.

He's not afraid of my past, and he's excited for our future.

That's the reason why I didn't go back home to Houston. Because my future isn't in my past. My future's right here, with Steve, with my kids, and it looks different than I ever could have imagined, and that's okay.

In the end, Steve teases me until I admit that the popcorn was actually intended for popcorn strings. "It's for a vintage look," I defend.

"And I love it," Amanda Saddler says. "Your vintage is my childhood."

"I didn't really mean to make fun of it," Stephanie says.

No one believes her, but no one argues, either. We're all too polite for that.

And after the tree's decorated, and the kitchen's picked up, we all eat dinner together. Clam chowder, to celebrate that our new home's temporarily put together, and we're all warm and snug inside. To seat everyone, Steve brought folding chairs and card tables.

"Did you ever think you'd have this many people crammed inside your house?" I ask.

Amanda Saddler shakes her head vehemently. "No, I certainly did not."

"Does it make you mad?" Gabe asks. "Or sad, that we're all making messes?"

She surreptitiously wipes a tear from her cheek. "No, honey. It doesn't."

Gabe doesn't ask anything else. He's big enough to have seen people cry when they're happy.

When it's finally time for everyone to go home and people start bundling up in coats and scarves, Amanda Saddler stops us all. "I'd like to invite everyone to come here on Christmas Eve to celebrate. My family used to be the place everyone came to have chili on Christmas Eve, and I'd love it if we could do that again."

"I'm in," Donna says.

"Me too," Eddy says.

"I may never leave," Steve jokes.

"I'm afraid I won't be able to come," Stephanie says. "Or Olivia, either."

Steve's eyes widen, and he turns toward his daughter. "Why not?"

"We were going to tell you later," Stephanie says. "But maybe this is a better way to go about it. Antonio and I have reconciled, and Olivia and I are returning to our old life." She beams.

"Excuse me?" I ask. "You're going to take her back, just like that?"

Stephanie rolls her eyes. "Antonio's the father Olivia has always known. She loves him."

"But Steve has rights now," I say. "You can't simply take those away."

"Of course not," Stephanie says. "I'm not a monster. The visitation order's still in place."

"And child support too, I'm sure," I say.

"Of course," Stephanie says. "But Olivia wants to go back to regular school with her friends. Homeschool was suffocating for her."

"We have schools here," Steve says. "You could enroll—"

"It's okay, Dad," Olivia says. "I'll still come visit over the summer and stuff."

Steve looks upset, but not frantic. It was lousy of her to spring this on him here, but I expect nothing better from Stephanie. I'm not even surprised she 'made up' with Antonio. Of course she did. Some people thrive on drama.

I couldn't possibly lie and say that I'm not delighted her car won't be parked outside of Steve's place any longer.

"We're all loaded up, too," Stephanie says. "We'll be heading back tonight."

"Tonight?" Steve asks. "Is that safe?"

Stephanie laughs. "I slept all day—you know that's how I am, a true night owl. This is the best time for me to go."

"I'll miss you," Steve says, clearly talking to Olivia.

"I'll miss you too," Stephanie says. "But our time has passed."

I suppress my laugh. She's really something.

"Call me if you need anything. Or even if you just want to talk," he says.

Olivia nods, and then her lower lip wobbles, and then she rushes over to hug him.

She's perhaps not the most angelic child, hardly a surprise given her mother, but she's warmed up a lot in the past few weeks. I'm actually sad to see her go.

"I'll be back soon," she says.

Steve presses a kiss to her forehead.

"Bye, Miss Brooks." Olivia even waves to me.

Emery and Izzy rush over and hug her without waiting to see whether she wants them to.

Whitney just waves.

Maren doesn't even do that.

Gabe's little shoulders slump. "She's not even sad to leave me."

"You should go hug her," I say. "She doesn't have siblings, so she doesn't know she should."

That's all the encouragement he needed to rush over and wrap his arms around Olivia, too. She's smiling when he finally releases her. "I'll be back, Gabe. Really, I will."

"Okay."

She pats his head and walks to her mother's car.

"We'll just go grab our stuff," Stephanie says. "We'll leave your key under the mat."

Steve, to my surprise, hugs his daughter one last time

and waves goodbye. He doesn't rush home with them. He doesn't even shed a tear as they drive off. After Donna and Eddy drive away, we linger on the porch. I love being all together at Amanda Saddler's, but privacy is at a premium.

I sit on the porch bench and blow on my hands to heat them up. Even with my jacket, the chilly wind blowing off the nearby mountains cuts through my body like a knife. "You're not upset?"

"I didn't expect them to tell me like that, but I heard Olivia talking to her mom last week. I knew it was coming." He takes my hand and tucks it into his pocket with his, lacing his fingers through mine.

"Oh."

"I figured I'd wait to tell you until they followed through. Stephanie's not known for being super reliable."

He's not wrong there.

"Are you upset?" His gaze is curious. "You seem more agitated than I thought you'd be. To be honest, I expected you'd be bouncing up and down with excitement."

"I don't hate Olivia," I say.

"Just her mother."

"You hate her too," I say. "It wasn't only me."

"Once, more than fifteen years ago, when I was still traveling for bronc riding, I picked up a little something on one of the trips." He shudders. "Bed bugs."

I yank my hand out of his pocket.

He laughs and pulls my hand back in. "It cost me an arm and a leg to get my entire house fumigated and heat treated." He shivers. "I thought about just burning it down, honestly."

"Why in the world are you bringing that up?"

"The feeling, when I went back inside my house, and the techs had certified that it was one hundred percent infestation free, that's how I feel right now."

"Because Stephanie's gone?"

He nods slowly. "I promise you, right here and right now, that while Olivia will always be welcome, I'll never be so stupid that I offer to let her mother stay at my house again."

I can't contain my smile. "Oh, good."

"I told you, I make mistakes, but I don't make them twice."

"Not like Antonio, then?"

"That man is a moron," he says. "What would possess him to invite her back?"

"I'm glad he did," I say. "Or you might never have been rid of her."

"Oh, I was working on a plan to oust her, if that hadn't gone my way. She'd have been gone by Christmas."

"Really?" I ask. "What was this plan?"

"Bedbugs," he says. "I figure even Stephanie would flee if my home had a relapse."

"Of course, then you really would have had to burn it down," I say.

"Probably so." He chuckles. "It would still have been worth it."

"Thank goodness for Antonio's stupidity."

"Amen," Steve says.

"Thanks for all the help today," I say. "I think it went pretty well."

"I'm sorry you don't have your own house," he says. "And your own tree, and all your belongings."

I lean my head against his shoulder. "You know, the first Christmas after Nate died, I thought I needed all that stuff."

"What stuff? A roof over your head? Clothing to wear?" Steve smirks. "Yeah, who needs that?"

I use my free hand to whap him, but it's across my body and it doesn't do much.

"I'm a cowboy, sweetheart. You'll have to hit harder than that to faze me."

"I wasn't trying to hurt you, just show you that you're being dumb."

"At a baseline, I assume I'm being dumb," he says.

"Good to know." I sigh and relax against him again. "The familiar decorations. The tree we've always used. The Christmas quilts and wreaths and whatnot." Now, staring at the snowy wonderland of my new front yard, crammed in with people I either didn't know or who I barely knew a year ago, I realize something. "Christmas is about new beginnings. It's about a tiny baby who changed the entire world."

"That's true," Steve says.

"And the world didn't want it, but it was better for it." A baby who changed everything. Forever. "Sometimes I resist change."

"Sometimes?" Steve laughs.

"Alright, usually I resist change. But this morning, Adam, my real estate agent called. He said the same couple who wanted my house before still want it. Their offer's still good. They hadn't found anything they liked better."

"Really?"

"I told him that I'll take it."

Steve stiffens next to me. "You're selling your house?"

I shift, pulling my hand out of his pocket and wrapping it around his back so I can hug him. "I signed the papers earlier."

"Then what—"

"I'm having trouble pinning Amanda Saddler down, but I'll do it tonight, after everyone's gone. She must have some place she can rent me, or at least she should know someone who has some place."

"Your family can have my house," Steve says. "I'll just move to the barn."

"We need a place that's *ours*," I say. "A place I can repaint or decorate. A place that we can settle into and make plans."

"You can do that at my place," Steve says.

I press my outside hand against his mouth. "Steve, I appreciate the offer. I can't live in the home of my boyfriend. I know you don't want to hear this, but if we broke up, imagine the mess. I won't do that, and I'm sorry if that hurts your feelings."

He sighs. "Fine."

"You'll be happier if you're living in your own house and not in the barn."

His suppressed laughter shakes his whole body. "You don't know me as well as you think."

"Actually, I realized that was wrong as soon as I said it. You'd move right in with the horses if you could, wouldn't you?"

"Only if you'd come with me."

"I'll come over a lot," I promise. "Leo has missed me."

"He has," Steve says. "I found him crying in his alfalfa yesterday. He just kept saying 'Abby, Abby, Abby,' over and over."

"Ha."

"Find someplace that's not too far," he says. "And don't plan on moving until January." He shifts and groans. "These old bones aren't what they used to be, and I'm still sore from moving you last week."

"Please. I hardly have anything out here, and your bones aren't sore. You'd think a doc would know, but it's your muscles that get sore." I shiver from the breeze whipping around us both.

"It's good that I have you nearby to keep me straight." He wraps his arms around me even more tightly.

"I'm the one who's happy to have you around."

He kisses me then, and the cold stops bothering me. In

fact, I don't think about much of anything at all. Until the door creaks open and Whitney shouts, "They're doing it again."

"Eww," Gabe says. "Not again."

"At least they went outside this time," Ethan says. "Shut the door."

"I should let you go inside," Steve says.

"You should."

But he doesn't, not for a few more minutes, anyway.

When he finally leaves and I do go inside, Amanda's smirking at me. "Now you're glad you decided to stay."

"I was glad before," I say. "But I'm not sad to see Stephanie leave."

"Me neither," Izzy says. "I really hate her."

"She smells like fuzzy flowers," Whitney says.

"Fuzzy flowers?" Ethan asks. "What the heck does that mean?"

"You know," Whitney says. "The kind that are fake and get all covered in dust?"

We all laugh at that one. Once the kids are finally ready for bed, I collapse on the sofa.

"That was a pretty impressive Christmas party you threw together right after moving." Amanda Saddler's holding her signature cup of tea. I never see her drinking it. I wonder whether she holds it to keep her hands warm.

"It helps that I quit my job and now have all the time in the world."

"Wait, you quit your job?" Amanda hops over the back of the sofa and plops down next to me. "Really?"

I sigh. "I was stretched too thin, and the kids were noticing it, too. Plus, it just didn't bring me joy anymore."

"Whoa, what're you going to do now?" Amanda asks.

"Well, luckily I have some friends I can sponge off of," I say. "There's this old lady whose house I've invaded."

Amanda Saddler cackles like the witch who ate Hansel

and Gretel. It's a sound I've come to love. "You can stay here as long as you want."

"I'm beginning to think you won't ever let me leave," I say. "No matter how many times I ask you about places to rent, you haven't shown me a single one."

"None of them are ready," she says. "I'm working on it."

"What exactly are you working on?" I glare. "Pouring the foundation?"

"We don't do that here," she says. "We build it—sticks and frames."

I groan. "But really, why won't you rent me a place? We can't impose on you forever."

"The holidays are busy," Amanda Saddler says. "And me and Amanda are prioritizing our locations for phase one of our new business. I promise, after Christmas, I'll show you a few places I think might work."

"On December 26th," I clarify. "Right?"

She laughs. "Yes, on the 26th, I'll show you a place that will be perfect for you."

"What about me?" Amanda asks.

"I'm not making any promises to you," Amanda Saddler says. "I like having you close by."

"Fine," Amanda says. "We can talk more about it after the holidays, too."

"You're all still awake," Ethan says. "That's good." He's holding a manila folder. He looks nervous—shifting from foot to foot, clenching and unclenching his hands around the edges of the folder.

"Are you alright?" I ask. "Is that for a class?"

"Actually, I need to speak with Mrs. Saddler, if she has a moment to spare."

"It's Miss," she says. "I never married, remember?"

Ethan blinks.

"Sit down, boy, and tell me what this is about."

"I did some poking around, and I found out that you

have almost four hundred acres."

She frowns. "That's right."

"Your family used to run this property as a ranch."

"The barn's old and ain't been used in more than fifteen years," she says. "I prefer things with engines, and something reliable that don't bite or kick or colic."

Amanda snorts. "Me too."

"But lately, it hasn't been used at all." Ethan extends the folder. "I put together a proposal, you see. Over the next few months, I could repair the fences, fix the parts of the barn that are collapsing—"

"All of it," Amanda Saddler says.

"Okay, all of it," Ethan says. "I can replace the barn, and I'd do all of that for free. And then—"

"Nope," Amanda Saddler says. "Never do things for free, my boy. Never."

"Um. Okay. But—"

"You want to run my ranch?" Her eyebrows climb. "Is that what ye're saying?"

"Well, yes, and I have some sample numbers here. We could split the profits—"

"Nope. I don't wanna take a risk with you, and you don't wanna share your wins with me, neither. If we do it, you'd pay me a flat fee."

Ethan gulps.

"I'll tell you what I told your mama. You talk to me about this on December 26th. Christmas is less than a week away, and my plate is already full."

Ethan nods, but he can't help smiling. Actually, it's less of a smile and more of a beam. "Yes ma'am. After Christmas."

When I go to bed that night, I thank God in my prayers for the many blessings He's sent our way. Even when things go wrong, there's always something good waiting around the corner.

28
DONNA

I hated the sound of Dad screaming.

Now that it's gone, a tiny part of me actually misses it. Probably because, in my mind, it was somehow tied to Mom. I was serving her by caring for him, and she felt a little bit closer to me as a result.

Going through the mountains of paperwork and rotting cloth napkins, and spoiling toiletries, I wonder why people keep all the stuff they keep. We surround ourselves with belongings in the vain hope that it will ensure our safety, I think. If we have a mountain of safety pins, when a seam splits, we'll be fine. If our drawer is full of q-tips, we'll never have waxy ears. If we buy that extra night cream, our face will never wrinkle.

But if we don't have that safety pin at school with us, we still walk around all day with our underwear hanging out. And if we don't use the q-tips, they don't help. All the night cream in the world can't stave off the wrinkles that come with age.

In spite of all our best efforts, the worst will eventually happen.

We're all going to die.

As I pack up the last box and as I close the last door, I'm actually pretty sad. My belongings and Aiden's have been reduced to three rolling suitcases and two duffel bags.

My dad's and mom's stuff has all been recycled, donated, or burned in the trash pile out back, and now the home I've been in for months is about to be gutted and repainted, retiled, and refurbished for some unknown renter. Not that I have any idea who might want to rent a home down a tiny gravel road, behind Patrick and Amelia's enormous house.

Certainly not me.

"Aiden," I say. "It's time to go."

I hate that I'm disappointed. My dad's words caused hope to swell inside me one more time.

We changed our mind.

I scoured their letters, their bills, and their tax documents, looking for a new will. Could he have been speaking the truth? Could he and Mom have actually changed their minds and left me and Aiden something after all? It's not that I need the money, not really. Between the generous child support I'm getting from Charles, and the settlement that judge gave me, Aiden and I can afford to buy our own place. I do plan to look, as soon as Christmas passes.

But with Dad gone, and with Patrick hovering, and with all the stuff cleared out, I just couldn't spend Christmas here. It was too depressing.

I'm surprised by a knock at the door. When I swing it open, it's Will Earl. He smiles at me, and the entire room brightens.

"Hey there, stranger."

"We've been pretty busy," I say. "Sorry I haven't been free much."

He's called me almost every day, and he texts when I don't pick up. Other than a few half-hearted responses, I've practically ignored him.

"Mom told me you're checking into the hotel for the holidays?"

I glance around the empty room behind me. "Dad died, and Patrick wants to rent this place. January first, if he can."

"He's such a disgusting. . ." Will swallows and his eyes shift to something behind me. "Can of soda."

I turn around and see Aiden, watching us. "Where's a can of soda? I want some."

"Mr. Earl was kidding," I say. "There's no soda."

"I panicked," he whispers.

"It's fine," I say. "He knows his uncle's a jerk."

"Uncle Patrick?" Aiden asks. "The meanie who's kicking us out at Christmas?"

Will laughs. "Alright, then. No more need to make things up."

"He's probably more disappointed to hear there's no soda than he would be to discover that you're bad-mouthing Patrick."

"Definitely," Aiden says.

"Thanks for coming to help us," I say. "It's nice to have a friend."

"Mom sent me," Will says. "She wanted me to invite you over for dinner tonight, too."

"That's so thoughtful of her," I say. "But. . ."

"We're going to play with Gabe," Aiden says.

"Gabe?" Am I imagining it? Or does Will look *jealous*?

"He has the best Legos," Aiden says.

"I like Legos too," Will says.

"You do?" I ask at the same time Aiden says, "Really?"

"I mean, I used to love them," Will says. "I still have a bunch of them in a box in the attic."

"I don't have any Legos," Aiden says. "I used to, but I had to leave them with Dad, and now—"

"You can play with mine any time you want."

"Do you have the Batman ones?" Aiden asks. "That's Gabe's favorite and he never lets me play with them first."

Will turns to me, his face full of incredulity. "What kind of guy—"

"Gabe's eight years old," I say with a smile.

"No he isn't," Aiden says. "He's still seven."

"Oh." Will shoves his hands in his pockets. "Right. I mean, of course he is."

"He's Abigail's youngest son," I say. "Abby and Amanda invited us over to their house for Christmas Eve."

"Steve said he was going over there," Will says. "That's cool."

"We don't have that many bags, either. Your mom didn't need to send you over."

"They might not all fit in your backseat," Will says.

"But between my trunk and the back and the front seat. . ."

He grabs two suitcases anyway, not even bothering to roll them, and hauls them out to his truck.

I open my mouth to ask him not to toss them into the icy back bed, but before I can, he's swinging his door open and hefting them inside. Thanks to his heavy coat, I can't see the muscles in his arms and back shifting, but I can imagine.

Which I really shouldn't be doing.

A rancher like Will? He owns his own place and his mother owns a hotel. He's good looking, single, and well off. He's way too good for me. He's just being nice to me for old-times' sake. I'm a charity case, and I need to remember that. I know exactly how much it hurts when you get your hopes up about something and then reality slaps you in the face. Which is why, in spite of Will's solicitous help and invite for dinner, I'm simply cordial and insist on handling the rest of our bags and unpacking myself.

"Thank you again," I say, as I usher him out of our newly rented room. "I'm sure I'll be seeing you around."

"And Merry Christmas," he says.

"Yeah, and same to you."

I spend half the day getting things unpacked, and then I get Aiden all dressed and ready for the party. "Why are you putting me in this shirt, Mom?" Aiden hates button down shirts. "It's not like anyone will care what I'm wearing."

"Be happy I'm not stuffing you in a reindeer sweater," I say. "I'm only skipping that because I remember how itchy they were."

Aiden rolls his eyes. "Fine."

"Let's go."

He practically races out to the car and once we arrive at Amanda Saddler's, he zips up the front steps. It's a miracle he doesn't fall and crack his head open on the patch of ice near the bottom. And once again, as if he has some kind of magical crystal ball that notifies him we're coming, Gabe whips the door open before we've even knocked.

"How did you know we were here?"

Gabe points at the red cardinal swooping over our heads. "He always makes noise and flies around when people come."

"That's so odd," I say.

"His name is Arizona," Gabe says. "And guess what else?"

"Santa Claus already came?" Aiden says.

"No," Gabe says.

"I don't think he really wanted you to guess," I say.

"No, I do," Gabe says. "Try again."

"You got new Legos for Christmas?" Aiden looks legitimately excited. I think he's going to be really disappointed in the morning, because he is most definitely not getting Legos.

"No," Gabe says. "Mom won't let us open anything

today. Just one present before bed, and it's always pajamas." He groans like he's being force fed Brussels sprouts.

"Then what?" I ask.

"Guess," Gabe says.

"Oh come on," Whitney says. "This makes everyone crazy, Gabe." She rolls her eyes. "He got a whole box of candy canes. Amanda Saddler gave them to us, so Mom can't even take them away."

"Really?" Aiden asks.

"And there's a box with your name on them, too." Gabe claps. "Come see!"

Aiden races off before I can tell him not to eat them all right away. I sigh. It's really hard to yell at the world's nicest and crotchetiest old woman, especially when she's spoiling our kids.

It's not like my parents are here to do it, and Charles' parents are luckily not getting him for Christmas until next year.

Which means, I'll probably be drinking myself into a coma this time next year.

"Donna, come in," Abigail says from the kitchen. "Sorry for the terrible manners in greeting you, yet again."

"Please," Amanda Saddler says. "You don't have to greet family."

A knot forms in my chest when she says that.

Family.

After Dad died and Patrick kicked me out, I didn't expect to hear that word, but maybe I should have. Abigail and Amanda, and now even old Ms. Saddler, have all treated me like I belong from the first day, even though I came to sabotage them.

Suddenly, tears are rolling down my face, and I can't quite stop them. The last person I expect to comfort me is the very one who does. Amanda Saddler wraps an arm around my waist and drags me into her room. "I used to hate being in here," she says. "I've had the same bedroom for more than eighty years, you know, and it felt kind of depressing. But lately I hide in here a lot, whenever I'm too happy to keep from leaking."

Leaking. The word makes me laugh. It's true—at hearing that I was family, my happiness just sort of leaked out. "Thanks."

"You stay here as long as you need, you hear? But no poking around in my drawers." She raises one eyebrow, like I might have done it if she hadn't warned me. Why would I want to peek at her underwear? The whole thought is so absurd that it has me laughing.

"Good. You look better already. Less leaky." She whizzes out and slams the door behind her.

The second she's gone, I actually have a burning desire to comb through her stuff. Which is bonkers. There's no way I'd have even considered it if she hadn't suggested it to begin with. What a crazy old woman.

But I take a look, while I'm here, at the photos on top of her dresser. The central photo must be her and Jed. They're quite young, and they look really happy. She's wearing pants that have been rolled up to her knees, and their feet are dangling off some kind of wooden structure—a dock, maybe? I bet they're on the Green River or up in the gorge. Jed's arm is slung around her shoulders, and he looks utterly at ease.

It's hard to think of the crabby old man I knew as this young boy.

Or the crotchety old woman as that carefree girl.

Life really changes us all.

When I finally duck out, it's time to eat, and Abigail doesn't disappoint. A ham, whipped sweet potatoes, those great knot rolls again, and a fluffy cranberry salad with marshmallows.

Aiden asks for three helpings before I cut him off.

Even the green beans are delicious, and I usually avoid those.

"How do you have the energy?" I ask. "Even looking at all this food wears me out."

"Mom quit her job," Izzy says. "She's unemployed."

Steve's head snaps sideways. "What?"

Abby shrugs. "I was going to tell you tomorrow."

"What are you going to do, then?" I ask. "I can't see you sitting around, whipping up culinary creations all day."

"I hear there's a cookie shop available." Maren's smile is sly.

Amanda throws a roll at her head, but Maren dodges and Roscoe snaps it up before it even hits the ground.

"Hey, don't throw perfectly good food to the dog," Abby says.

"It'll give him an upset stomach," Maren says.

"Would you really make cookies and sell them?" Emery asks. "I could help."

"I've thought of managing that," Abby says, "no lie. I do love cookies, and I think we have enough kids who might work there part time to make sense. But honestly, I've also been thinking about what Gabe said. I applied last week to be admitted to the Utah bar, and when that comes through, I might hang out a shingle in town." She shrugs. "If there's not enough work, then maybe I apply to work part time for one of the law firms in Green River or Vernal."

"That's amazing," I say. "I'll recommend you to everyone."

"I appreciate it," Abby says. "Truly."

"I couldn't love this news more," Steve says.

"I bet," Eddy says. "It's hard to get penciled in for time with these ladies."

Amanda Saddler cackles. "But you want me to rent you a place. How am I supposed to have faith you'll pay when you're unemployed?"

Abby rolls her eyes. "I have plenty of money saved, and I get Social Security—"

Amanda Saddler holds up her hand. "We can talk about it in two days, remember?"

"But you brought it up," Abby protests.

Amanda Saddler reaches toward Abby and plucks a roll off the platter. "So I did. Whoops. The foibles of old age."

Seconds later, the conversation swallows the whole issue up again, because that's how big families move. Quickly, erratically, and with love. Aiden and I both sit still and quiet amidst it all, savoring it.

Eventually, we'll have to head back home. To a hotel. Alone.

Is it irony, or something else, that the person who wanted a big family more than anyone now has just one other person to hug? It was kind of them to invite us tonight, but part of me feels like it would have been better to stay home and weep privately. All the bustle and joy of this gathering only makes my loneliness stronger. I try not to dwell on the fact that I'm semi-mourning the loss of two people who made my life awful, Charles and my dad.

Because when that's all you had and it's gone, you should still be entitled to miss it.

After dinner, and after the Brooks kids each open a pair of pajamas, we can't delay any more. It's time for us to head home so they can go to bed. "Thanks for inviting us," I say reluctantly. "But we really ought to—"

"Wait a moment," Abby says. "I have something for you."

Oh, no. It didn't occur to me that they might get us gifts, and I literally got her nothing. "Abby, I didn't realize—"

She puts a hand on my wrist. "Donna, relax. It's not like that, truly. You don't need to give me a thing."

This woman helped with my dad when Patrick was

going to just let him die. She stepped in to save me from myself, and then helped me when I testified against Charles. She found those accounts in Aiden's name that helped pay for my California divorce lawyer. And again, she donated hours and hours of her time and two days away from her kids for my divorce and custody battle.

And I didn't even get her a fruitcake.

She, however, got me something. Something she insists is nothing, which probably means it's, like, a hand-embroidered doily for my home that says Ellingson or something. Ugh.

I'm a sucky person.

"Here, come with me."

Aiden didn't need any encouragement. The second he realizes I'm not imminently leaving, he darts off, ready for his second act with Gabe, or to stuff another candy cane in his face. I follow Abigail, wracking my brain for something I could give her in return. Is there any chance she didn't notice that I've been wearing this silver bracelet all night? Could I pretend I brought it for her instead? It has an E etched on the flat, round charm, but maybe I could say that's for Ethan?

"Donna, I mean it. Don't stress."

I meet her eyes, and I can tell she's serious.

"I just had to share this. I just got it yesterday, right before close of business." She bites her lip. "I had to lie to get it. I hope you don't mind."

Abigail lied? I can't even imagine it.

"Your brother's lawyer is a real stickler, and I had to forge your signature to a representation letter." She brandishes a letter at me.

"Why?" I ask. "What is this?"

"Something he said the last time we spoke felt off to me. I wanted to see a copy of the will your parents left."

"The will?"

"One of the roles established in a will is the executor. It's important that you name someone you trust, because that person is in charge of making sure that the things delineated in the will are carried out."

"Okay."

"I didn't trust Patrick," she says. "And I worried that, like Charles, he might not have your best interest at heart."

"That's an understatement."

"I requested, as your lawyer, that he provide me with a copy of the will."

"Okay."

"If you really weren't listed as a beneficiary, he should have said he had no fiduciary duty to provide it. But he didn't say that." Abby frowns. "He questioned whether I really was representing you."

"Which you weren't," I say.

"Well, not in that, but I was for the other matters, so it's not too much of a stretch," she says. "I didn't write in the letter that I was representing you for a will contest or anything, so technically what I wrote was true."

"But it's not my signature," I point out.

"Are you going to sue me?" She grins.

I shake my head.

"For Christmas, I got you a copy of your parents' will. You can read for yourself how they changed it a year before your mother died, and how you and Patrick now take equally, in spite of you having received those payments for education expenses. They specifically say that they feel that Patrick taking all the profits from the ranch for all these years more than offsets what they paid you for the schooling."

A tightness in my chest eases with her words, but I can't quite believe them. I hold out my hand. She places a thick stack of papers in them.

"Take your time, read through it, and let me know when

you're ready to confront your brother. I'm sure he knows it's coming, because his lawyer wasn't pleased to give that to me."

"He really meant to just lie to me about it? He would have just stolen the money?"

"He gave me two copies of the will, and I think Patrick meant to probate the first one. It gives everything to him. Since you said the life insurance dumps into the estate, Patrick would have kept it all, and no one would have known it was ever changed."

The relief I feel is overshadowed by miserable disappointment. I can't decide whether it was worth it. I might have regained faith in my parents, but I lost faith in my brother, and he's the one who's still alive. Even so, none of that's Abby's fault. Once again, she's done me a tremendous favor.

She discovered something I never could have found myself. "Thank you."

"Merry Christmas," she says. "I hope it really is a good one. Feel free to come by tomorrow, any time you want. Bring Aiden and let the boys play. We really do think of you as family."

I manage to hold in my tears until I get home and get Aiden tucked into bed.

But then I release all the feelings—good and bad—from the day, the week, the year. It's funny how many things can change in such a short period of time. Who knows? Maybe this time next year, I'll look back and think the same thing.

I drop to my knees and thank God, on his birthday, for my blessings, and I pray for Patrick that he can find joy in his heart again and let go of his anger. And then I finally go to sleep, ready to celebrate Christmas tomorrow with my greatest blessing, my own little boy. I vow not to repeat all the mistakes of the people around me.

In the end, I think that's the best any of us can do.

29
AMANDA

For three hundred and sixty-four days, we wait for this day. Christmas Eve is probably the most exciting night of the entire year. Kids leap and bound and spin. Adults plan and tie and wrap. And then finally, it's all done, and it's time to sigh with relief.

Or have a glass of wine.

You know, to each their own.

But the next morning is the most anticipated day of the year. I remember when my girls insisted on waking up before the sun had even risen. I remember when *I* woke up that early, as a byproduct of all the giddy joy circulating through my system. But this year, we promised the guys that they could take care of their animals and drive over as soon as they're done. We promised not to start opening presents until Steve and Eddy are both here.

Other than little Gabe, all the kids are old enough now to want to savor the excitement as long as they possibly can. Whitney and Izzy showed Emery how they organize the gifts into piles. Maren and Abby, an unlikely pairing, make grits (blech!) and scrambled eggs and biscuits for breakfast, and just as the biscuits come out of the oven, there's a knock at the door.

"They're here!" Gabe squeals. He races over and whips the door open.

But it's only Eddy.

His tiny shoulders slump. "Come in."

"I'm happy to see you too, buddy," Eddy jokes. "Merry Christmas."

"He can't open presents until you and Steve are both here," Abby explains. "He's just a little impatient."

"We've never had to wait before," he whines. "I want to open them now."

Abby ruffles his hair. "Let's eat, and by the time—"

The door opens with a rush of wind. "I'm here!" Steve's got a red bag slung over his shoulders, like he's Santa Claus himself.

"Now I feel a little lame," Eddy says. "A little warning might've been nice."

"You brought your gifts yesterday," Steve says.

"But I could've waited," Eddy says. "Heads up, next time."

Steve salutes him and drops the sack on the ground. "Let's eat. I'm starving."

"Why did Eddy get here first?" Gabe asks.

"He has, oh, I don't know, about twenty horses fewer than I do," Steve says. "And last I checked, no chickens or cats, either."

Eddy shrugs. "True."

"I saw him pull up," Steve says. "He couldn't have been here much before I was. I had to get the bag."

"Fine," Gabe says.

Steve grins. "Breakfast smells amazing."

Abby pulls the pan of oven-baked bacon out and sets it on some potholders on the counter. "And it's ready."

We fall on the food like wild animals, the guys eating an impressive amount for old men.

"Is this homemade jam?" Eddy asks around a mouthful of biscuit.

"It sure is," Abby says. "I can't stand the store-bought stuff."

Eddy looks upward. "Thank you," he mutters. "Neither can I."

"Don't get used to it, buddy," I say. "I'm a purchase-my-stuff kind of gal."

"You had a cookie shop," he says. "I thought that meant you were home-maker-y."

I laugh. "It lasted a month."

He grimaces. "Dang."

"Besides, we can't have you getting fat."

Eddy sighs. "I guess not."

"I'm okay with getting fat." Steve grabs another biscuit.

"Hey, what about me?" Abby asks. "Shouldn't that be up to me?"

He shrugs. "Stop making jam, then."

Eventually, though, the leftovers are tossed to Roscoe, and the dishes are cleared, and just before Gabe's head actually explodes, we all sit down to open gifts.

"I just wanted to say how blessed we all are," Abby says. "And how grateful we all are to Amanda for inviting us to live with her and to celebrate Christmas with her."

Amanda Saddler jumps to her feet and dances amid various boxes to grab a flat, rectangular present. "Then, let me counter with my gratitude as well."

Abby blinks. "You, of all people, didn't need to get us a single thing."

"I beg to differ," Amanda Saddler says. "In fact, from the day Amanda brought me those letters of Jed's, I've been thinking. I loved Jed, but he and I screwed everything up royally. I figure that's probably why he was like he was, all confused and stupid."

Abby's eyebrows rise.

"Here." Amanda Saddler shoves the gift at her and she takes it.

"Well, you didn't need to do anything at all," Abby says, "but thank you."

"It's for all of you." Amanda Saddler gestures around at Gabe, at Ethan, at Izzy, and at Whitney. "The whole Abigail Brooks clan."

Abby's brow is furrowed as she opens it, clearly worried that she didn't buy an appropriate gift for Amanda in return. That kind of thing is pretty important to someone like her, someone who's unaccustomed to anyone doing anything for her.

When she finally unwraps it, it's a white men's dress shirt box. It says 'Macy's' on the top. I recognize it quickly, because I gave Paul a lot of those over the years.

But there's no shirt inside. It's a stack of papers.

"What is this?" Abby's eyes fly upward, searching Amanda Saddler's face. "This isn't—" The great Abigail Brooks chokes up and covers her mouth with her hand. She shakes her head. "We can't accept it."

Ethan snatches it out of her hands. If I'd been closer, I'd have done the same.

"What is it?" I ask.

Ethan's hands shake, and I'm worried he's going to drop the stack of paper and make a huge mess. Then he lets out a loud "*Whoop*!" And he starts racing around the room, shouting and leaping up to touch the ceiling.

"What's going on?" I ask.

"Amanda Saddler bought Birch Creek Ranch in the auction," Abigail says, "And she gifted it to us—to our whole family."

"As Jed should have done." Amanda Saddler nods.

Abigail's entire family is excited—excepting Gabe, who's desperate to start opening his fun presents—and I'm glad they're distracted.

Because I'm so consumed with anger that I doubt I hide it very well.

The rest of the present opening is a bit of a blur. Steve hands out his gifts like he really is Santa Claus, and I'm impressed by his insight on each gift. Maren got a whole set of some designer nail polish that left her absolutely tickled. Emery got a custom headstall for a standard size horse, with her name tooled on the side.

He got me an apron that says, "My cooking is so good that even the smoke alarm cheers me on." It's funny. I manage to force a laugh.

But when all the gifts are done, and all the packages have been unwrapped, I can't help but notice that Amanda Saddler gave me nothing at all.

She gave Abby a three million dollar ranch.

And I got nothing.

I'm the reason we're all friends. I'm the one she supported with a failed business. And I'm the one who asked if we could move in here with her. I'm partnering with her in remodeling all her properties and spending hours a day working with her.

Is that why? Am I such a burden that she's already giving me everything she can? Why would she say that I'm like a daughter, and then give me nothing?

I shouldn't say anything.

All I got her was a cake—that's what she said she wanted. A carrot cake, just like her mother used to make. It took me four hours to make it, and pecans are devilishly hard to find out here in Smallsville, Utah.

But obviously that's not something that deserves a reciprocal gift, and certainly not a ranch.

All the feelings of inadequacy and rage, all the feelings

that I don't belong, and that I'm not good enough, thoughts that surfaced during the lawsuit against the alien people, resurface now.

What's so unlovable about me?

Why does no one think *I* or my girls deserve a ranch, or something like that from a relative? We're still Jed's family, aren't we?

When Amanda Saddler takes a stack of plates around the corner to the pantry, I follow her. "Hey."

She smiles. "I wondered when you'd blow."

"Blow?"

Her lips are compressed but twitching, like this is all very amusing. "You've been looking like an angry volcano all morning."

"You knew!?" I ask. "You could see I was upset, and you think it's funny?"

"Not funny, per se, but I knew you well enough to know you'd be upset. I hoped you wouldn't, but I assumed you would."

"You hoped I wouldn't?" My voice is shrill. I sound a little unhinged. I try to rein it back in. "Abigail gets a *ranch*?"

"Jed would have wanted them to have his ranch," she says. "They belong there."

"And I don't?"

Amanda snorts. "To be blunt?" She sighs. "No, you don't."

I swallow. "You didn't get me anything."

"Life's not about 'getting what you deserve,' Amanda. It's time you learned that."

I blink. "This is some kind of life lesson you're teaching me?"

"Did it ever occur to you that this might be about me?" Amanda asks.

"Huh?"

"Since we met, you've needed help. Guidance, free rent, and then a new job." Her brow furrows. "I've provided it each time."

She's right. She has.

"This Christmas, I didn't give you a gift. I felt like, the things I've done, the things I'm doing, those are a gift, from me to you. They show you I love you already."

She's right. Now I feel awful. "I'm sorry," I say.

"I wanted to see if you loved me," she says. "Or if you only liked me for what I gave you."

I failed her little test.

That kind of pisses me off.

"Did it ever occur to you that testing people isn't a healthy way to live?" I ask. "Maybe that's why you and Jed wound up alone."

She flinches. "You're probably right."

"I don't appreciate people who are always testing me to see whether I'm good enough. Paul did that. His love always came with conditions, with little tests, and with terms."

Amanda sighs. "If I'd known that. . .well, I don't know. I am who I am, and it's hard to change when you're my age."

"That's an excuse," I say. "It's always hard to change."

She laughs. "You're right about that. But dear, you should know that I considered a lot of gifts for you. I thought about a big beautiful old house down the road. I thought we could fix it up together. The one with the cupolas."

I loved that place.

"Or, the cute little yellow colonial downtown."

That one was great, too.

"But in the end, I'm a selfish old woman." Amanda's eyes well with tears. "No matter what place I imagined, I couldn't bear to think of you moving away." She ducks under my arm and disappears.

I try to follow her, but Eddy grabs my arm. "We need to talk."

"Right now?" I ask. "It's not really a great time."

"I know," he says. "It's a terrible time, but they reached out last night, and I have to jump on this or turn it down by tomorrow. There's not much time."

"Time for what?"

"Can we go outside?"

I look at Amanda Saddler's closed bedroom door and falter. "I need to—"

"It'll just take a minute," Eddy says.

I sigh. "Fine." I follow him out onto the front porch. "What's wrong now?"

He smiles. "Actually, it's not that something's wrong, for a change."

"That's nice to hear."

"You know how we put up that video of my new song, in front of the holiday decor you put up?"

"Yeah."

"So, it's been busy enough that I haven't been paying much attention to it."

Me either, which is strange for me. But between the holidays, kid stuff, Abby stuff, and the work with Amanda, I have barely been checking my social. It has reaffirmed my gut—maybe it's time to give it up.

I mean, sure, I post some things now and then for a little extra cash, but I think I'm ready to earn my money doing something less fickle. "I've been thinking of telling Lololime no," I say. "I think this thing with Amanda's going to work, and I'm tired of them telling me what to do all the time."

Eddy frowns. "I've always wanted you to dump them."

"But not now?"

He shrugs. "No, I mean, yeah, go ahead. I think that's

great news." But he came to tell me something else. About his video?

"Did it go viral?"

I remember the first time one of mine went viral. It's a heady feeling, like maybe your whole life will change. Until the next big thing hits and you're back to planet Earth with a thud.

"Kind of," he says. "But that doesn't matter. As you pointed out, it's not like I have an album to point them at or anything."

"Okay." I can't figure out where he's going, which is weird. Usually Eddy broadcasts his feelings on his sleeve.

"Three labels have called me already. They're all offering deals."

I don't understand. "Deals?"

"Record deals. Apparently I'm trending, and they think it's the perfect time for me to make a comeback."

With his gorgeous face and bod? With all the notoriety created by the false accusations and his affiliation with me? Yeah, I bet it is the perfect time.

"They said comeback stories are hot right now—"

"I think they're probably always hot," I say. "I mean, everyone loves the idea that they haven't missed their shot, right?"

He pauses. "So you think it's a bad idea?"

"I didn't say that at all."

"I'd record a new album, and then go on tour." His whole face scrunches up. "There isn't really a way around that, apparently."

"I'm sure there's not," I say. "They'll want a musician to tour to promote the album."

"Plus ticket sales for the venues," he says.

"Right."

"What do you think I should do?"

I shrug. "What do you want to do?" It feels like the entire world is in some kind of strange freefall.

"I don't know," he says. "For the first time in forty years, I was happy. Truly happy. And then, out of nowhere, this crazy video surfaces, clearing me of the anvil from my past."

"It didn't surface," I say. "Abigail dug it up."

"Right." He nods. "No, I know that. I really owe her."

"Do you?" I ask. "Has it really changed that much?"

His voice is quiet. "I haven't had a nightmare about that night since I saw that video."

That really is something. "I'm glad."

"And now they want me back—the industry that chewed me up and spit me out."

"But you left for your own reasons then," I say. "You wanted to escape, right? You're a vet."

"I am, yeah." He nods. "Maybe I should turn them down?"

I shrug again. I wish I could stop, but it's either that or start talking gibberish and crying. Is he really asking if he can leave me to turn into a megastar?

First Abby gets the ranch from my mentor. Then Amanda tells me she did it because she just *loves* me so much, and now Eddy's saying I've made him so happy that he needs to leave.

"I need to talk to Amanda," I say. "We were kind of in the middle of something."

Eddy looks hurt, like I'm the one saying I'm leaving. "Do you really not have any input?"

"I thought you were a vet," I say. "I was dating a hot vet who loved animals and led a quiet life in a small town." My voice is a little too bitter.

"So I should turn them down?" His eyes are wide, and he steps closer, taking my hands in his. "The one thing I know for sure is that I need *us*. If this upsets you, I'll just turn them down."

Like I quit school for Paul.

I still resent him for that.

But if I can't convince Eddy that I'm fine with it, he'll be right where I was. He'll never be sure why he passed on this chance.

"You need to do what brings you joy," I say. "If that's singing, if that's making music, then you definitely don't need to worry about me. I'm not going anywhere."

That's true enough. Unlike Eddy, no one wants me to record an album or follow them anywhere. Even my business partner doesn't seem to want me very much. I mean, sure, she'll *not* give me a nice gift because she can't trust me not to leave, but that's not the same as caring enough about me to ask me to stay.

Come to think of it, she only wanted me to live with her if Abby would agree to move in, too. And that's who she's giving a big property to right now, ensuring they aren't going anywhere.

"I think that I could make the album, as long as my language in the agreement is alright, and I could agree to a limited tour, and if it's not working out, I can quit. Then I'll at least see whether it's a good idea."

"Sounds like you need to talk to Abby," I say.

He smiles his crooked, handsome, playboy smile. "I think I do."

"Congratulations," I lie. "I'm really happy for you."

He doesn't even notice that I don't mean it.

30

ABIGAIL

Steve has driven the same old blue pickup truck since we met. I've never seen him in anything else. So when I start looking for Gabe, and he's nowhere inside the house, and we expand the search to the exterior, I'm surprised when it's not parked outside.

There's a shiny red Ford parked next to Eddy's truck.

"Did you get a new vehicle?" I ask.

Steve scratches his head.

"Mom?" Gabe's head pops up from the pristine truck bed. "What do you think?"

"About Steve's new truck?" It occurs to me then that perhaps I've been idiotic. Steve bought me a gorgeous sapphire ring for Christmas. For a split second, when I opened it, I thought he was going to propose.

It would be stupid. I've only known him for six months.

But was that present a decoy? Did he buy me a truck? He's mentioned several times that he doesn't think a minivan is safe during the winters here.

Surely he wouldn't have picked out a car for me without any input.

"It was time," Steve says.

"Right before Christmas?" I ask. "Don't they jack up the prices?"

He shrugs. "I needed a new one."

"Well, it's lovely. Much prettier than your old blue one," I say, relieved that it's not for me. At least I'm not at all disappointed this time, like I was with that sapphire ring.

Which is stupid.

I'm the last person who wants someone to propose to me.

I'm not ready. My kids aren't ready. We're barely solid again after losing the ranch. And then regaining it.

It's been a really strange six weeks.

"I can't find it," Gabe says, "but you promised."

Ethan charges out the front door. "There you are, you rascal. Come inside and build the tower with me, like I said we could."

"Promised what?" I ask.

Steve cringes.

So does Ethan.

"My Pokemon Legos," Gabe says. "You promised, but then all you gave me was the superhero set, and I already have that one."

"But you said you were missing pieces," Steve says.

Gabe frowns. "Did you change your mind?"

"Come inside," Ethan says. "It's cold out here, and you shouldn't be climbing all over people's cars."

"It's a truck, just like yours," Gabe says.

Steve shakes his head, and Ethan jogs down the stairs. "I'm just going to carry you in there." He grabs Gabe by the back of his coat and lifts him out of the truck bed like a mother cat.

"What on earth is going on?"

"You're the worst," Ethan mutters. "You ruin everything."

"I didn't ruin anything," Gabe says. "I kept quiet, just like you said I should."

"Until New Year's, dummy," Ethan hisses.

"New Year's?" I ask. "What's going on?"

Steve sighs, digs down into his pocket, and pulls out a little box. "Lucky for you, as an ER doc, I'm always prepared."

"What on earth is that?"

Steve's kneeling in the snow.

"Your knee must be freezing," I say, my heart racing. "Stand up."

He shakes his head, a smile pushing its way through to his face. "Not a chance, Mrs. Brooks. I have something to ask you."

I swallow and look around.

Ethan's whispering in Gabe's ear. He scampers off, and a moment later, the door bangs open again. Amanda Saddler, clutching a blanket around her shoulders, comes flying outside.

Whitney, with one boot on, pulling her coat up one arm, follows right after. "This is not according to plan," she mutters.

"Wait for meeeee!" Izzy flies out the door next, hits a patch of ice on the top step and flies into the air.

In an impressive move I'm not sure he could ever duplicate, Ethan jumps two stairs and catches her before her head bangs into the steps. "Idiot."

He dumps her, rear first, on the step she nearly bloodied with her head. "Now keep quiet, you morons."

Ah, the joys of having a big brother. He'll protect you, but he'll mock you for it.

"Mrs. Brooks, I knew that in order to capture your heart, I had to show that I had the approval of your entire brood. So, to that end, I began negotiations with each of your children. They, like their mother, drive a hard bargain."

What am I hearing?

"Your youngest child, Gabe, wanted Pokémon Legos. Not just any Pokemon Legos, mind you, but Charizard, Squirtle, Pikachu and Meowth showdown, and the Pokémon Mega Construx boxset." He chuckles. "It's apparently a big deal for him to sign off on a new father, and he needs to make sure I properly value the importance of gift-giving."

Izzy glares at Gabe. "Are you kidding me?"

"What?" Gabe asks. "I've wanted them *forever.*"

"But Amazon's a little back ordered right now what with the holidays and the small town," Steve says. "They haven't yet arrived."

Gabe scowls. "Are they really coming?"

"They certainly are," Steve says, "and if you'd waited until New Years like I planned, you'd have had them in your hot little hands."

"Hmm." Gabe nods. "Alright."

"Whitney drove a hard bargain, too," Steve says. "She wants to pick a filly and she made me promise to teach her to break her herself."

"I'm not sure that's something—"

"I told her you'd let us know when we could start," Steve says.

Whitney claps. "But we're already looking, and the Earls have the cutest little grey."

Oh my word.

"Izzy was even a bit more particular," Steve says. "She wants Farrah's first baby." He grins. "She's a bright little thing. She also wants a guarantee that she—"

"Or he," Izzy says, "will get one of the deluxe stalls."

"But Ethan was the roughest one," Steve says. "He wanted me to teach him bronc riding."

Heat floods my body. “There’s absolutely no way—”

“I knew that,” Steve says. “The second I agreed to teach him that, I knew we’d be in big trouble. It was a real Catch-22. I couldn’t get his approval without losing yours.”

I glance at Ethan, realizing that he knew that I’d never agree to that. He was messing with Steve.

“So, after a bit of contemplation, I told your son no. I couldn’t train him to do something that dangerous, not in good conscience.” Steve shakes his head. “He told me I’d passed the test, and that I cared enough about you to gain his approval.”

“Wow, so all he wanted—”

“That, and he wanted my truck,” Steve says.

“Oh,” I say. “That’s what Gabe was talking about.”

Steve’s still on one knee in my front yard. He’s ordered Legos, promised to buy and breed horses, and he’s made a commitment to train them. And he’s given away his truck and bought a new one.

"You must have been pretty confident I’d say yes,” I say.

He’s *still* kneeling, and pleasantly at that. “Not at all,” he says. “I’ve been terrified you’d turn me down flat.” He drops his voice, the low timbre of it rolling through me. “But you’re worth the risk.”

And that’s the underlying point, isn’t it? Love is always a risk. But when it’s worth it, it’s worth *everything.*

“Abigail Brooks, lawyer, friend, sister, daughter, mother, I don’t just love you. I adore you. I cherish you. I want to protect you and give you everything you’ve ever wanted. I want to cheer you up and build you up and I want to make a family with you. Will you do me the very great honor of becoming my wife?”

“Yes,” I say. “I will.”

He slides a ring on my finger, but I don’t even bother looking. I pull him upward and I kiss him with everything

I've got. I'm vaguely aware the kids are cheering, but even that's not enough to distract me.

When Nate died, I thought that was the end of my love story. It never occurred to me that it might have been a new beginning as well.

I'm starting to think this new story might be pretty epic.

EPILOGUE: ABIGAIL

It's a little ridiculous for a woman my age to be thinking of planning a wedding. Signing up for bridal magazines. Scouring wedding dress websites. Looking at flower arrangements and bouquets.

But here we are.

"I can't believe you're moving out," Amanda Saddler says.

"You'll be able to sleep in again," I say, "once Gabe's gone."

She waves me off. "Please. I haven't slept in for decades. Once you get used to waking up at dawn, it's a hard habit to break."

"Speaking of things that are hard to arrange," I say. "I finally picked my colors for the wedding."

"Thank goodness," Amanda says. "And what are they?"

"Purple and silver," I say. "And now that I have colors, it's time for me to hammer out a few other details."

"Like what?" Amanda frowns.

"Amanda agreed to be one of my bridesmaids," I say. "My sister will be my maid of honor, and Donna's tried to put me off, but she's going to agree to be a bridesmaid, too, I just know it."

"That's great," Amanda says. "They'll all look lovely."

"I just have one more person to ask," I say.

Amanda Saddler frowns. "Don't you think your other daughter will be upset if you just ask Izzy?"

I can't help smiling. "It's not Izzy I'm talking about asking."

She frowns. "Who, then?"

"I was hoping you'd be one of my bridesmaids," I say.

She laughs so hard she has to wipe her eyes.

"I'm not kidding."

Her mouth dangles open and her eyes blink once, and then twice. She finally closes her mouth and shakes her head a bit. "But I'm far, far too old."

"Why?" I ask. "Donna's in her thirties, and Amanda and my sister are in their forties. Why can't you be a bridesmaid in your—" I clear my throat. "Sixties?"

She choke laughs. "My sixties? Bless you, child."

"Look, all I'm saying is that I would really like it if you'd do it, and—"

"You're thinking of the comic relief I'd bring to the wedding?" She quirks one eyebrow.

"I am not," I say, deadly serious. "I was thinking that I'd like the three women I love the most, and my sister, to stand up beside me when I marry the man I love the most."

She pauses again, and then quietly says, "I suppose this wedding already won't be like any other wedding I've ever attended."

"Absolutely it won't," I say. "But you don't seem like the kind of person who would be upset about that."

"I wasted my entire life loving a man who loved me back from afar. We were both too stubborn to say anything about it to the other person." She sighs. "I think I'm a terrible person to stand up alongside you and Steve on your happy day."

"You learned from that," I say. "And I think you have a lot of things to teach me and my kids. I'm glad you're a part of our lives." I take her hand. "And you loved Jed enough to care about his nieces and nephews and set his mistake right."

Her eyes well with tears. "That idiot. What was he thinking, leaving the ranch to those alien nuts?"

"His will is the reason I'm here," I say. "And it's what our entire family needed."

"That's true," she says. "He was always a genius who just couldn't follow through."

"If you don't want to do it," I say, "I won't pressure you. But it would make me happy to have you there. I want everyone to know you're important to us."

Amanda wipes at her cheeks again. "Alright, then. Let's give them something to stare at."

"Is that a yes?" I ask.

"Girl, that first day when I saw Amanda marching up my porch steps, I had no idea what was coming my way."

"I bet," I say.

"Isn't it funny how life can give you just what you need, exactly when you think you'll never get it? Thank you for making an old lady's day."

"You're my favorite old lady in all the world, Amanda."

She hugs me then, her grip surprising me even though I know how strong she is.

"I'm so glad we're friends," I say.

"Family, my dear," she whispers. "We're family now."

I realize that she's right. We're past friends, and that's why I wanted her to be one of my bridesmaids, so she had an official place at this ceremony.

"Jed wrote me a letter about his breakfast one day," she

says. "I'm not sure whether you read it. It was about the differences between a chicken and a pig."

I wrack my brain, but can't think of that one.

"He said his brother, who asked me to prom in high school, was the chicken because he only gave up a bit of his time. He likened himself to a pig, because he devoted his whole life to me." She cackles. "That man had no idea I'd actually have a pet pig and name it after him."

"It is sort of funny," I say. "I must've missed that letter."

"There were a lot of letters," she says. "But I've been thinking about that, and I wanted to give you a tiny piece of advice. Don't go a day where you don't share what you're thinking with that man you love. Sacrificing for the other person when it's unnecessary isn't noble. It's idiotic. Jed was too chicken to be honest, and too big of a pig to see it. Don't be a chicken or a pig."

It's some of the best advice I've ever gotten. I was too pig-headed to ask for help, and too chicken to tell Steve about what I was dealing with when his own life was hard. My refusal to ask and share almost cost me the bright future that now lies ahead. Life really does give you just what you need when you least expect it sometimes, and I'm so glad that it does.

"What color are you thinking for the bridesmaids' dresses?" Amanda asks.

"I was thinking purple," I say.

"Yellow makes me look like a sow, and so does pink," she says. "Purple might work, though."

"I've got a few ideas," I say. "I even found a few I liked online."

"Well show them to me, already," she says. "Because I can ***not*** wear orchid. It makes me look just plain sallow."

I pull up the webpage with a smile on my face. I can't imagine anything making her look sallow, but I'm sure she'll let me know if she thinks it might. "How about this one?" I point at a simple sheath dress.

"Girl, do I look like a kitchen timer to you? I moved past hourglass about thirty years ago. I need something with way more frills on it than that." She points at one a little lower down the page. "What about this one?"

Oh, my sister is going to hate everything about this wedding, this town, and especially Amanda Saddler.

So, of course, I can't wait to get her out here.

"My big sis is coming out for a visit next week," I say. "I'll order a few different styles and maybe you can all try them on."

"Your sister?" Amanda frowns. "How come I haven't heard about her until now?"

"Don't tell me you don't hide the skeletons in your closet out here in Manila."

"Oh, we do," Amanda says. "But we leave them locked up. We don't invite them to our weddings."

I laugh. "There's no way we could keep her from coming for that, unfortunately."

She pats my shoulder. "Don't worry, dear. We've got you."

***

Not DONE with the story yet? I've got you! The Retreat, book four, will be out in September 2022 at the very latest. (I usually release quite early!) You can preorder it here.

Don't want to wait for The Retreat to release? Have you tried my romances yet? They're standalone love stories with interconnected characters. The first book, Finding Faith is free on all platforms right now.

You can sign up for my newsletter at: www.BridgetEBakerWrites.com, (and get a free book!)

Or you can join my reader group on Facebook at: https://www.facebook.com/groups/750807222376182.

ACKNOWLEDGMENTS

I feel like I could almost copy and paste this part. My husband makes my writing possible, as do my children. They all cheer and support and inspire.

My friends and family and fans buoy me up. I love you all! Thanks so much for the love and support and kind words (and reviews!)

My editor Carrie and my cover artist Shaela are just the best. I love you!

And my horse Leo inspires me, as do the many trainers and vets who have helped teach me about proper care and treatment of animals. It's been really fun to write fictional stories about some of the things I love the most in my life.

ABOUT THE AUTHOR

B. E. Baker is the romance and women's fiction pen name of Bridget E. Baker.

She's a lawyer, but does as little legal work as possible. She has five kids and soooo many animals that she loses count.

Horses, dogs, cats, rabbits, and so many chickens. Animals are her great love, after the hubby, the kids, and the books.

She makes cookies waaaaay too often and believes they should be their own food group. In a (possibly misguided) attempt at balancing the scales, she kickboxes daily. So if you don't like her books, maybe don't tell her in person.

Bridget's active on social media, and has a facebook

group she comments in often. (Her husband even gets on there sometimes.) Please feel free to join her there: https://www.facebook.com/groups/750807222376182

ALSO BY B. E. BAKER

The Finding Home Series:

Finding Faith (1)

Finding Cupid (2)

Finding Spring (3)

Finding Liberty (4)

Finding Holly (5)

Finding Home (6)

Finding Balance (7)

Finding Peace (8)

The Finding Home Series Boxset Books 1-3

The Finding Home Series Boxset Books 4-6

The Birch Creek Ranch Series:

The Bequest

The Vow

The Ranch

Children's Picture Book

Yuck! What's for Dinner?

I also write contemporary fantasy and end of the world books under Bridget E. Baker.

The Birthright Series:

Displaced (1)

unForgiven (2)

Disillusioned (3)

misUnderstood (4)

Disavowed (5)

unRepentant (6)

Destroyed (7)

The Birthright Series Collection, Books 1-3

The Anchored Series:

Anchored (1)

Adrift (2)

Awoken (3)

Capsized (4)

The Sins of Our Ancestors Series:

Marked (1)

Suppressed (2)

Redeemed (3)

Renounced (4)

Reclaimed (5) a novella!

A stand alone YA romantic suspense:

Already Gone

CPSIA information can be obtained
at www.ICGtesting.com
Printed in the USA
LVHW112230300922
729674LV00003B/94